The Bard's Trail

By

Andy Regan

Copyright © 2024 Andy Regan

ISBN: 9798300518547

All rights reserved, including the right to reproduce this book, or portions thereof in any form. No part of this text may be reproduced, transmitted, downloaded, decompiled, reverse engineered, or stored, in any form or introduced into any information storage and retrieval system, in any form or by any means, whether electronic or mechanical without the express written permission of the author.

The views expressed in this work are solely those of the author and do not necessarily reflect the views of the publisher, and the publisher hereby disclaims any responsibility for them.

For my dear Mum and Dad, and your amazing influence x

About the author

Andy's career has spanned international affairs research in the House of Commons and a long stint managing high profile elections in the UK and for the United Nations. With master's degrees in both international relations and psychotherapy, he currently combines work as a solicitor with a leading sporting consultancy practice.

His first book, *The Stars Move Still*, was published in 2017.

PROLOGUE:

SPRING 1993

The bulb was temporarily blinding all in range as the bulky video camera harshly lit up the area. At first, they presumed it was an undiscovered clearing, not realising countless previous pupils had considered it their own over countless decades. It was unremarkable in many ways yet only fifteen minutes away from the principal buildings. Light brush sprawled over the twenty yard strip and, once inside, branches appeared to enclose all entrance ways. Some months before, one of their number was dared by the others to unceremoniously climb through and investigate something that appeared to sparkle from within. They couldn't be sure and were disappointed at first when the boy had returned and claimed it was a mere trick of the light, announcing that no treasure store awaited. Though the good news was that the site proved easy to access after the initial set of brambles, so could be considered their own. It appeared safe from prying eyes where they could smoke and drink with impunity.

Now, instinctively, four pairs of eyes blinked away, including those of the camera operator.

"You are one complete arsehole with that gadget," a raised voice turned towards the glare, an arm shielding his face. "The idea is to light up the scene, not to make a bloody film for Cannes. Point it away at first then swing it round. Don't you know anything?"

There was a pause. The camera operator thought of lashing out in response then decided better of it in case he damaged the expensive equipment that was carefully mounted on a metal stand. All had been liberated for the night from the sixth form store cupboard.

"One, two, three, deep breath and don't get riled," he thought. Then decided to count on to five in order to really calm down. This is not what they were here for, tonight of all nights.

A crashing sound made them all jump.

"What the hell was that?" the dominant voice boomed out. "You haven't screwed the bloody camera on properly. If it's bust you'll have to pay, my friend." The camera operator carefully shook off the scattered leaves from the machine, inspected the device cautiously then decided on an alternative cradle for it.

"It's all OK, don't panic." Deep sighs all round.

They made their way out of shot of the camera which was now precariously balanced on a tree stump. The four clasped each other's shoulders in a tight circle for reassurance one last time. All were dressed down, wearing not just casual out of school clothes but the tattiest, most expendable outfits. Levels of scruffiness consisting of mostly bedraggled sportswear that wouldn't be tolerated elsewhere in the historical precincts. These included the oldest trainers and rugby boots they could muster from lost property that approximated their shoe sizes. They may be half a mile into the woods behind the elegant chapel, with December frost that had seemed bearable on the extensive sports pitches now biting into their bodies. But the moon was all but hidden by the extensive cloud covering which seemed to signify this was no everyday outing.

One of the group shivered at the memory of being stripped in his first weeks by the older pupils, debagged as they'd referred to it, and ordered to stay in the woods all night as part of the ancestral rituals of the school. He had spent half the night in tears until sleep, at the foot of a giant oak, had afforded a short release then awakening with a shiver and the realisation that punishment would surely ensue for lateness to chapel. He consoled himself that such rituals must be the way it always was here. The requirement was to fit in or at least survive.

"Now," the first voice continued, fixing each with a hardened stare, "we've discussed this. There's to be no chickening out. The first part before the main event is a form of insurance. That's why this country is still home to the world's greatest insurance market," he grinned.

Two of the others eagerly smiled back. The fourth looked down sheepishly, seemingly lost for words. It was just easier to allow the others to take the decisions.

"First, scene one. I'll start. Are we filming?"

The clasping of arms ended with the speaker moving imperiously in the front of the camera to begin the speech he'd been planning for so long, half addressed to camera and half to those assembled. Recorded for posterity. Announcing his name then continuing, "We carry this out together, joint enterprise. Like the Musketeers just a little more…English," he smirked. "Our esteemed headmaster has taken it upon himself to act unacceptably. Are we agreed?"

Mostly enthusiastic nods all round. "If we choose to uphold the traditions of Ridgeway, establishing order amongst both juniors and the locals, playing one or two harmless pranks on the beaks, we succeed only in building men. Or fillies," he added, a slight nod of the head to one of their number.

"So now is the time for Linwood, with his godawful tedious English lessons, to receive his comeuppance. God knows he deserves it so it's time for justice. But first a word from my friends before the star of our show is summoned. I take the pledge of silence in honour of my comrades, my companions, with limitless repercussions for any who can't remain silent."

One by one the others introduced themselves to camera, before two stole their way back through the deserted woods to prepare the main event. All had been preplanned and each had delivered their name and taken the pledge on film, binding their future to the others in word and, soon to be, deed.

None of them had slept well in their rooms once it was all over. One tried to hide the tears which were spilt into their pillow. A second, gazing mournfully out of the open window in an adjacent room, puffing through a pack of twenty until the last cigarette was extinguished. A third wrote it all down, every word and deed they could recall since first discussing the plan on the coach to away venues on sports afternoons then right up to the moment of execution. It took the best part of two hours, following which, after staring at it for a considerable time, they crept down the ancient staircase to the study fire that was kept smouldering throughout every night irrespective of the season, before, without a further second's hesitation, cast it in. Pages shrivelled at the edges then, with a blaze of light, were no more.

The fourth made little movement until morning, lying with one arm behind their head trying to make sense of the whole saga.

The camaraderie, however short-lived, and now the rush of adrenaline that influencing events so significantly had provoked.

PART ONE

THE PRESENT DAY

CHAPTER ONE

FLIGHT 486

If Sam had realised he was on the verge of becoming the most famous eleven-year-old on the planet within hours, though not through choice, he just may have been better prepared. His father's bulky unkempt appearance, not doing justice to one of the sharpest legal brains on the east coast, would at least have protected his son's image rights but Richard Collins wasn't afforded the opportunity to exercise that authority. Sam's demure mother Serena could have used her fashion editor's experience to design a dynamic makeover topped by the latest trending Manhattan haircut. The Valentino clothing range would have fitted the bill perfectly.

From his window seat Sam incessantly pressed the attendant button overhead then, upon arrival of the ever-patient hostess, muttered "Coke" without averting his eyes from the headrest screen in front. Soon after, he leant back melodramatically, not caring to stifle a sizable yawn. Impatiently, he removed the latest Bang and Olufsen headphones following the third consecutive film consumed on the Airbus A380 since collapsing into his seat in London's windy Heathrow airport. The *Fast & Furious* franchise was diving at a rate of knots. The boy was bored.

Reaching absent-mindedly to the tray in front of the spare seat between him and the Brit by the aisle with the funny accent who'd tried to make conversation at first, Sam ripped open the peanuts without a second glance at precisely 13.25 Eastern time and began scoffing them at a stupendous rate, sipping the accompanying mini-Coke.

At least his parents weren't alongside, so couldn't nag him or bicker with each other in his presence, as was usually the case. As with the outbound journey for their holiday, the couple had remained resolutely in first class, affording Sam the relative solitude of premium economy. He glanced left. The weird-talking guy was snoring quietly and had been for ages. Why did the elderly look so gross as they slept? And who would purposefully wish for such a bizarre walrus-like moustache? Adults were hard to fathom at the best of times and Sam reminded himself that, under all circumstances, his destiny was to remain cool. Jay, trendiest kid in his class, had insisted on it.

Beginning at 13.55, the commotion lasted a total of ninety eight seconds. It began with a slight spluttering from his neighbour which rapidly descended into an uncontrollable coughing fit. Within moments seemingly half the plane had gathered round, expressing various levels of concern as the stranger's face appeared to mutate into an angry red balloon. His hands grasped deliriously around his neck with the appearance of trying to forcibly remove it. A strange gargling commenced soon after, being the only sound to emerge from his throat.

"Medic here. Let me through please," called a sharply dressed grey haired sixty year-old in a smart blue suit from first class, not slowing her stride. There was no time to announce her full title to the assembled throng. Patricia Beckman, Senior Clinical Professor at Massachusetts General.

"Get me an EpiPen cabin crew. Hurry," in a commanding voice and having noted the empty peanut packets alongside, then authoritatively trying to calm the frantic passenger long enough to stare into his airway for an obvious obstruction. Nothing visible. Failing to stop the desperate movements as he staggered violently into the aisle, Patricia forcefully flung him round intending to deliver the necessary blow to the back at speed. While grabbing his chest from behind and leaning his torso forward, suddenly all went limp. Patricia's fist remained in mid-air for half a second as the figure flopped onto the aircraft's floor. At that moment the breathless stewardess arrived, EpiPen in hand. Patricia hastily administered the shot, but without eliciting any reaction from the patient. No pulse either when she kneeled down to check.

Right, thought Patricia. CPR. Before she could begin, a crew member remembered they now carried a defibrillator on board. Obligatory kit only introduced in the past month.

Sam remained open mouthed and frozen at the unfolding drama, remembering only to exhale as his lungs began to hurt. Patricia rocked back on her knees eventually.

"What killed the guy? What happened?" a woman's broad Texan voice yelled from the back of the throng.

"Peanuts, it has to be the peanuts. I read about the risks just the other day," responded a man with a strong French accent.

"Yeah, I heard someone mention a guy on the plane with an allergy," a Bostonian deep pitch asserted.

"I, I never even asked for them," ventured the boy, deciding silence was no longer an option. Somewhere in Sam's subconscious, his dad's advice to hit early in any argument had clearly been entrenched.

The crowd fell silent and eyes turned to the half-finished Coke and remains of the foil packets on the centre seat's plastic tray. Then all eyes, all thirty heads gathered round, stared squarely at Sam Collins, now visibly wilting. The boy's eyes began to water.

CHAPTER TWO

FLIGHT 486

Eighty feet in front, Captain Seb Jameson cursed his luck. Since the argument last night with Samantha, his wife of twenty-two years, and specifically her complaint at having to attend bridge club alone once again due to his long haul commitments whilst everyone else would be coupled up for the hands, this trip had felt doomed. The latest unfortunate development was extreme though. No one had died on any of his flights since his earliest days with the airline a quarter of a century ago. Seb clearly recalled his superior's annoyance on that long ago voyage.

"That's a load more paperwork we're going to have to get through," Seb muttered aloud, anticipating the new delay for his arrival home. And just as the plan to surprise her with attendance at the card night had seemed a distinct possibility.

The cockpit display stated there was a mere hour and twenty until landing at Boston Logan. There was no point requesting to land in Canada on route given the proximity to the final destination. That medic on board had a string of impressive initials after her name according to traffic control; excellently qualified and even she'd been forced to throw in the towel. Seb pressed the point in his communications with the ground.

"They'll want to send a team on board pretty quick to stake out the situation," came the woman's retort from Logan. "You know the rules. Civilian deaths require an autopsy and a full review of your staff's procedures, regardless of how simple the poor guy's demise may have been."

Seb shook his head. "Nah, seems a pretty straightforward case. We couldn't have known he had an allergy unless it's flagged to the crew. Then there would be the possibility of ingesting nut oil through the air. The damn airline was about to ban peanuts from flights anyway. Why couldn't they have made the call a month ago? The dead guy was asleep just before it all went off apparently, so we're trying to work out the timing. Some kid sitting alongside opened a couple of packets. Sam Collins and his parents are going to get a hell of a grilling when we land but, for now, the boy's in shock. Seems crystal clear to me."

"Leave the questioning to the authorities," responded the calm voice from the ground. "Not, I repeat not, your jurisdiction."

Seb was now in full flow, the usual sparse communications with ground control having gone out the window. "I just don't know how it could have happened otherwise. We've checked the register and there's no mention of a nut allergy. But don't worry about any kind of interrogation up here," the Captain began to laugh. "Even if we wanted to, it's not going to happen. Sam is just a kid and his dad's a big shot lawyer so isn't allowing his boy to say a word. I suppose it doesn't really matter at this stage. This Stewart Tyler isn't going to file a complaint. His family just might though. Against the family, the airline…" his voice fell away.

"And the Captain, Seb. And the Captain. There's a precedent in suing airline captains, as well you know. Let's keep it away from the media spotlight for now though. If any passengers ask, say we think the guy had heart problems already."

The controller was right. Seb gasped. Best policy, he decided quickly, is to shoo everyone else off the flight in Boston as soon as possible, apart from those directly involved in the incident. Then report in to the twenty-four hour legal department at the Air Line Pilots Association before the shitstorm takes a major turn for the worse. If only he'd opted out of the additional flight and made up that four at the bridge club from the off.

No, better still, make that call to ALPA from the air. This absolutely couldn't wait.

Seb would have been appalled to know his day was still on a downhill trajectory. The Cockpit Voice Recorder retained these conversations. Worse, however, on the ground the recording was patched to an uninvited listener in the remote hope of hitting that jackpot. Suddenly seizing her newly upgraded iPhone whilst tapping speedily on the keyboard in front, Georgie Lansing found herself in race mode. The goal being to contact the best paying news desk in North America.

"It's dynamite," Georgie exclaimed as she broke into a huge grin as soon as the other end picked up. The second-year college student had quickly estimated the story's worth to the current affairs outlets. Enough to pay for studies and rent for an academic year here in Nova Scotia at least. Couldn't be bad for a few minutes' work. What a break.

"Take this down quick Ed," alerting her sibling in the Newsroom at Fox. "Have I got a story for you? I'll send over the recording once you've agreed my humungous fee with your bosses. Looks like we've got the youngest plane murderer in history touching down at Logan pretty damn soon. This could be the making of you, big brother, if you play your cards right."

It was later estimated just shy of two million eager followers tweeted Sam's name in the first hour of the story breaking on the ground.

CHAPTER THREE

LOGAN AIRPORT, BOSTON

After the plane landed, afternoon then evening began to drag for the investigation team at Logan.

Steve Moroney, his Airport General Manager badge polished to its usual gleam, having decided long ago that no plastic at the end of a lanyard would adorn his neck, leaned back in his swivel chair in contemplation having devoured the paperwork in front.

"It was all right for the flight crew," he said to himself. Probably something novel and exciting to break up the routine of the trans-Atlantic flight despite the macabre nature of the incident."

A corpse rider was hardly a first for him, but never a piece of cake. Troublemakers: the press, authorities, the Feds even, always looking for an angle and this one in particular couldn't fail to pique their interest.

The flight crew, a now petrified Sam, his anxious mother and bullish father, those seated uncomfortably near the incident, as well as an ever calm Patricia Beckman, were soon interviewed for initial statements on landing, then informed a follow up would be required in the next few days to drill into more detailed recollections. Steve wondered if his psychology module all those years ago at college, which covered recall, would prove of use. Take a combination of immediate recollections then a longer, drawn-out review a few days later to obtain the clearest picture. Did this approach still hold sway amongst experts?

Most of the interviewees were happy to recount the morbid event but Sam remained silent by firm order of Richard, the boy's very own counsel. Steve was already cursing Richard's name at that early stage. The lawyer had ostentatiously made clear at first the hourly rate at which he would be billing the airline; a figure that made Steve visibly wince at first. Well Richard could go to hell if he wanted to play that game, as father and son awaited

Steve's next pronouncement in the adjoining room. Make them sweat. An hour later, Steve changing his mind and concluding that he needed more from them now in case the story became a runaway horse.

Half an hour later Richard and Sam found themselves in an overly chilly interview room smelling of rotten apples. The only seating was a couple of tiny and uncomfortable grey metal chairs, and the desk in the middle looked as though it was constructed from tin and rickety to the point of collapse.

Richard noted the classic interview techniques of authority in the US as he and Sam by his side faced Steve's questioning from across the desk.

"We need to start again, I'm afraid. This just isn't adding up."

"Oh yes it does. We're off now. Tried to help but that's all we can tell you. Do I need to add that I kind of know our rights?" Richard continued, "and by the way, no comment."

"But you haven't said anything. Want to be arrested for obstruction of justice?" Steve uttered. "How much good will that do your law practice? You leave when I say so; when I've got a far clearer picture of what happened than your current story, Sam."

The lawyer stood, looming over the desk within inches of Steve's poker face.

"Really? What crime has been committed in this airport exactly? King of the skies, are you? Look, give me more time in this shithole with my boy first," loosening the $300 silk tie he'd hastily thrown round his neck before landing. They must keep the décor intentionally disgusting, he'd noted from the start, as he took in the peeling lime paint.

Once Steve had reluctantly left the room, father and son sat gloomily in silence, not having exchanged a word since the incident except Richard's strict instruction barked into his son's ear to "shut up and stay schtum." Leave the talking to him.

Richard sighed, finished the contents of the plastic cup holding tepid water from the supposed cooler, before checking his messages for the first time. Eighty-eight missed calls, the vast majority from recent hours. What the hell was happening out there?

It took seconds to realise the enormity of the family's predicament. Whatever his son had or hadn't done, Sam was obviously no murderer and they couldn't be cowered with threatened charges over the incident as long as they cooperated to the minimum at least. But the world's social media and news outlets gleefully focusing on their son already? What was that about? Then the prestigious law firm would indeed be in the spotlight. Its $65 million profit last year, only a three way share, could be next in the firing line. A particular concern given the implications for the continuing merger talks. Even Serena's stellar reputation and substantial earnings could be hit. An immediate change of strategy was required, a common order barked at all his clients amidst a losing battle. The story could only be contained if Richard could fully gauge the extent of the impending damage.

"You'd better start talking Sam. We have to give them enough. What the hell did you do to that guy?"

PART TWO

CHAPTER FOUR

SOUTH WALES

The instructor just had time to glance left at the swirling expanse of sea leading out to the Atlantic. The contrast of outdoor freedom being tinged with pain in the cool open air never ceasing to amaze. This was the harsh Pembrokeshire coast, appearing a sterner test at night. It would be hell for the others at the best of times but this mob were mostly half his age yet pathetically unathletic. They were a load of wimps herded his way to transform. It was always a pleasure, a challenge. "Bring it on," he mused.

"We run, we bloody sprint NOW," with which the largely soft featured thirty-eight-year-old with short, slightly wavy dark brown hair and intense grey eyes leapt ahead. The week-old stubble was accepted, almost encouraged for his role here, a privilege those who were deskbound seemed continually riled about.

The recruits strained to follow, desperate to impress so early in their army careers, some having pushed themselves to near bursting point in the race to achieve super fitness from a previously sedentary life of takeaways and cheap beer. One was incapacitated with a hernia a week before starting in the attempt, now awaiting notice anxiously by the phone at home as to whether his days in the military were over already. Others more casual in their approach. A kick around in the park a couple of times a week would surely suffice to master this training lark, a couple had assumed. One of those was currently vomiting at the back.

Priding himself on the intensity of the psychological and physical gauntlet he'd thrown down, one minute almost pal like in his approach and the next, their worst nightmare. Shay Mason was aware of the intensity of his running and assault course agility, all inducing respect. Many recruits may have accents from the street, sporting skull tattoos from the tough side of town and the utter, genuine, determination in most cases to better themselves. But this lot didn't bear a scar as deep and eye-catching as his. The memento from the four-inch knife wound starting behind his right ear round to the side of his throat, making him appear the toughest bastard of the lot.

He would never tell them how it originated. Never give it all away.

That final sprint was a killer for all of them. The day he couldn't lead training from the front was time to retire for a pen-pushing desk job. Gasping hungrily for breath, though priding himself on never looking worse than the others, that was the golden rule. Shay felt the emergency mobile vibrate in his breast pocket whilst the others gradually finished in dribs and drabs around, their backpacks hitting the ground with a thud as they collapsed and lunged for water bottles. He'd kept his backpack on in sheer pride until all others had removed theirs. This must be important to disturb the holy ritual that constitutes night-time training. Another six hours ahead until daylight.

"Mason," he answered.

"Lieutenant Colonel here," came Woodford's deep barking tone, a slight trace of Midlands accent. "We need you now, out of Wales. The Welsh Arms Regiment can spare you. Muller will replace you knocking that rabble into shape. Your location's tracked so he'll be with you in five minutes."

"Yes sir but…" The other end went dead. What the hell could this be about? Shay wondered if his dad had finally expired after playing roulette with his body for so long. Was Maryanne OK? Or Stephanie? That scenario would be far worse than the others. Trying to remain calm whilst his mind raced ahead. The interruption certainly wouldn't be for work though. Why extricate a fitness instructor, particularly one of the army's best in his own immodest opinion, at such short notice when this group's induction had another five days to run?

Mopping his brow, Shay attempted to appear unruffled in front of the recruits. Should he tell them? No, let's spring it on them. Anyway, how could his replacement feasibly drive out in such a short time to the sparse south Wales coastline? As far as he was aware, the nearest roads were three miles away. Three point four to be precise, having memorised the geography of the area long ago as part of his training. This was home now, the twists and turns of the landscape married with his own sense of belonging.

There was absolute silence apart from the heaving inhalations from his fellow runners which was punctuated suddenly by the thunderous whirl of rotor blades, then soon in sight the distinctive black and blue Gazelle. Shay had recognised it from afar, the French five-seater perfect for light transport. Barely half a minute later it set down gently in the adjacent field, sheep scurrying to escape just in time from its fearsome reach. Greg Muller emerged from the cabin loaded with his backpack.

"Time to swap, slowcoach," Greg started as soon as within earshot. Shay had concluded years earlier that a better soldier to have watching your back in the field would be difficult to find. He nodded a welcome to his mixed race six-foot replacement. Shay was also secretly impressed his friend could appear so sharp and ready for action at what must have been a moment's notice, despite leading his own nighttime training cadets a mere twenty-four hours earlier.

"Look, any idea what this is all about GM?"

"No idea mate, they told me twenty minutes ago to shift into costume and lead the part for the night. And there you go clocking off halfway through your stint. Lightweight." Greg clapped Shay's back.

The propellers had maintained their monotonous noise. Within 30 seconds Shay was on board staring at the rugged disappearing landscape and wondering what could possibly be so important? This was definitely a first.

Shay had certainly enjoyed the ride as it ended two hours later. Helicopters in peacetime always felt somewhat luxurious for him and almost managed to keep that nauseous omen of dread regarding his loved ones at bay.

Once the journey's sizable distance was apparent, it was clear this was a whole different ball game. The landing, on Horse Guards Parade in the heart of London, was smooth as ever. Shay's pulse had quickened slightly as the warehouses and early twentieth-century growth of suburbia on the way in, alongside near empty motorways entering the capital from the west, were replaced by Georgian mansions and central London's familiar landmarks as they snaked along parallel to the Thames. He recalled the military sites they'd passed during the journey: Salisbury Plain, Brize Norton, Benson. At each he'd assumed they'd reached their destination. He'd blinked to take in the majesty of Parliament, Buckingham Palace and Whitehall directly before landing. Of course, they'd been an attempt to engage the pilot in conversation through the headsets but his questions were met from the start with only a curt shake of the head in response.

Emotions changed, as his sense of embarrassment came to the fore. This was some colossal mistake and the order to bring home one of the training group had surely identified the wrong individual. He had been well aware that the fittest of the current group was the nephew of the Chief of the General Staff, no less. Explicit word had been passed along the chain of command only the week before, emanating from the Chief himself, not to show his relation any favours. Maybe Shay had gone in too hard and the recruit had somehow complained already? Shay shuddered at the cost of the helicopter journey. The army would surely make him pay if he was in any way at fault.

Minutes later, Shay couldn't place the building that they had crossed Whitehall to enter after landing. He had known much of the area like the back of his hand not that long ago, but this was no department he had ever encountered. Once it was realised they had plucked the wrong man, most likely he would be dumped on the pavement to hike back to base in Wales alone and in double quick time.

The building's entrance was an imposing jet black door amidst a crisp white frame, opening on to Whitehall itself and adjacent to the organ pipes-façade of Richmond House, the former Department of Health. No shining metal plates surrounded this door frame however. It must be government-owned though, being situated in the heart of political power. The pilot walked away.

Once the obligatory X ray machine at the entrance had been cleared and the opportunity to clean up provided, Shay was planted in an office devoid of people but overcrowded with oak panelling surrounded by bulging folders, hard back volumes covering centuries of military history, and stacks of yellowing newspapers from around the world. So much for the paperless office.

When finally joined in the office, Shay had the strong impression of being sized up immediately. The rotund officer took a seat behind the desk, seemingly around 60 but perhaps just worn down by the job. He was clad in an ill-fitting crumpled suit that somehow defied colour, somewhere between beige and orange. Shay concluded it wasn't deserving of a name remotely associated with the rainbow's rays. The distinctive diagonal green, red and black striped tie of the Yorkshire regiment was recognisable enough, though.

"Sit. Good evening Lieutenant Mason, or whatever time it is." An accent somehow combining Yorkshire brogue with plummy south, the officer not proffering a handshake. "Name is Major Townsend and I'm responsible for an intelligence operation you won't have come across. Despite your previous experience in Whitehall." The speaker's bushy eyebrows and thinning hair somehow added to the sense of establishment. Perhaps, Shay mused, he would have been ruling the Raj a century ago but something of a relic in today's army.

Shay was open-mouthed for a second, still none the wiser. Intelligence agencies were, in his experience, a law until themselves which probably accounted for the mix-up here. He saluted then sat.

"Sir, I'm really sorry. I think you've got the wrong man. I have no connection with military intelligence anymore."

Townsend wheezed as he leant forward to respond. "No salute, not active. This must seem a little confusing so let me explain. Unless you've changed your name from Shay Mason during the expensive little jaunt we've just laid on, you're in the right place," before pausing and staring intently. "Well to be precise I think you are but we're sort of amidst unchartered waters with this one so the recommendation of others is all I have to go on really. I don't know you from Adam if truth be told." Shay was unsure how or even whether to respond.

"What do you know about anaphylactic shock? And peanuts in particular?" Townsend continued. A pensive shrug from Shay before answering: "Only what I've read. Quite treatable in most cases, especially if an EpiPen is at hand. What has this got to do with…?"

"On a flight from Heathrow to Boston two days ago, a British traveller never arrived for his crab supper by the Bay. A gentleman with no history of allergies didn't swallow peanuts according to the first test results, eats and drinks nothing else for hours yet is witnessed by a tonne of passengers suffering shock. The boy sat next to him may have been eating the stuff apparently."

Townsend reached for his mobile, quickly found the story and slid the device over the desk. "Baby face of a murderer," the Fox website article trumpeted, with a brief description of the circumstances based overwhelmingly on supposition rather than fact and ending with a series of tweets condemning both the malice and laziness of today's younger generation.

"Except it's all utter garbage, Shay. If the dead man didn't consume them then even with an allergy the chances of peanut oil flying through the air as the cause of death are pretty much nil. Perhaps we wouldn't care if it wasn't for the dead man's identity." Shay half expected the worst, steeling himself for the photo being passed over face down by Townsend. But why would his dad be flying to Boston? Off with his old Irish cronies for one last jaunt perhaps? Surely not in his current deteriorating state. How would the reality of his old man's death hit? The unknown, like waiting for the dealer to twist.

Except the round glasses, chestnut headed man with the oversized moustache staring back at him from the four by two inch photo was neither his dad nor, indeed, anyone he recognised.

"I presume you have no idea who this is? His name is Tyler and he works for a pharmaceutical company as a lowly researcher. You know, women's fragrances, that type of product.

Or at least it's easier to keep that public image for him. The truth is a little more...exotic. Stewart Tyler is, or at least was, one of the country's sharpest research scientists at one of our lesser known microbiology labs. It's based in Cambridgeshire. The Yanks don't know about him and even if they have acquired the info, they're just waking up to the fact and haven't revealed their hand to us. We have no idea how he was killed or whether it was even murder. It could have been some unbelievably rare accident but we sure as hell mean to find out quickly."

Shay instinctively sat back in relief, just staring at the floor. The meeting felt decidedly outside his comfort zone. A quick steaming shower and change of clothing on arrival in London had been very welcome. He had recognised the blue Santoni loafers before slipping them on, despite considering himself lacking in fashion sense. Greg was always going on about luxury clothing "making it all worthwhile". Yet these people clearly had his measurements or had just guessed correctly. He sensed a few quid being spent on his attire and couldn't help speculate whose budget was footing the bill.

Shay started, not caring about causing offence. "I don't work for any intelligence department and that suits me perfectly. I'm a mere trainer, pretty lowly in your ranks I'd imagine. I make raw recruits tougher, stronger, faster. I understand some American TV hero called Steve Austin would have fitted into my training programme perfectly. That's what I do, but without the aid of microchips."

"Yes, indeed," Townsend maintained a hard stare throughout. "But we both realise that wasn't always the case. You knew military intelligence, if not inside out, then sufficiently well to carry out your job. Also, we can't risk the general intelligence community with this information. It will shoot over to the CIA's headquarters in Langley faster than Concorde ever could in the old days, and they'll be all over it. We don't keep our open investigations confidential to less than ten thousand of our own in MI5 or MI6 these days, or so it seems. That's exactly why my superiors wanted a quasi-outsider to lead this enquiry, without ruffling any feathers in public at least.

Tyler had important contacts in all sorts of unlikely spheres and I need to know if they are in jeopardy. Go as far back in his life as you need to. That is precisely what I need you to focus on and not get side-tracked." The final point was emphasised with a stubby, jabbed finger pointing in Shay's direction.

The room was too dry for Shay to return the stare so he blinked in response. Instead, he gently rose to his feet and started pacing in a clear challenge to Townsend's seniority. "You are aware why I left? Why the…outdoor life is more for me than the corridors of Whitehall? I find they have unpleasant odours." Shay couldn't recall being more disrespectful to a commanding officer.

Townsend drove on, apparently oblivious. "Yes, yes we have all that," as he wagged a pudgy forefinger. Townsend produced a two inch tattered file from alongside his laptop with Shay's name emblazoned on the front, flipping open the cover. "Oh, we have computers Mason, I'm just pretty useless with them. Also, I can separate the important info from the dross in a paper file." Townsend smiled, largely to himself, and summarised whilst flicking through the document.

"The usual in many ways. Joined up with the regulars, did Afghanistan three times, four tours to Iraq. All the chaos we walked into then, followed later by more peaceful tours abroad.

Special dispensation to impress the sporting world when you were no more than a boy. But we both know how that ended. When travelling with the army had become too wearisome for you in your early 30s, having reached the rank of lieutenant, you were recruited by MOD intelligence. Firstly desk work, first class desk work at that. Bu still, nothing too dramatic. You became a bit of a lame duck after that."

Townsend scratched at his substantial stomach absent-mindedly, Shay pretending to ignore the conversation with eyes fixed intensely on the ornate ceiling. "And then… nothing. You apparently left because of a matter of conscience. All very strange. But not an unendearing trait when we're looking for someone bright, on the periphery of all this," gesturing towards the window and surrounding Whitehall bureaucracy. "Intrigue and gossip. Some call it a viper's den whilst others call it home," delivered with an exaggerated grin.

"May I ask who put me forward?"

"No, Mason, you may not. We'll tell you what you need to know," for the first time the voice was steely, then instantly accommodating. "Very well, I suppose it's no great secret. All you need to know is that you were on the Chief of the General Staff's radar and that the order for your involvement comes from high up in our food chain. In fact, they were adamant it had to be an outsider after recent fiascos and that's not to be mentioned outside of this room." So, he noted, that well-connected nephew hadn't started telling tales after all.

Shay ceased the pacing and turned to Townsend. "There's just one problem. I'm not doing it. I love my job as passionately as I hate this square mile of London. Nothing personal and all that but this city's brought me nothing but trouble in my professional life."

Townsend's turn to rise and move towards the window, looking out towards the Thames. "We don't threaten here Lieutenant, there's no point. But we do encourage. I understand your finances are not all that they could be. The service mortgage arranged when you joined military intelligence ended abruptly when you left and it looks as if matters aren't so rosy for you financially at the moment. This will pay £50,000 for a month's work, six weeks at most. And if we deem the matter suitably resolved, there'll be another £50,000 in it for you. That rather beats a PE instructor's salary in the countryside, doesn't it?" Shay ignored the slight.

Townsend relaxed. "Look, we want you because you have a habit of acting honourably and that's what's needed here. You're lucky; it's that non-uniform investigative role you were so near to achieving but never attained. And everything's been squared with regiment command. Though of course they don't know the details of why.

There is just one aspect which I shouldn't have to remind you about, though. The Security of Information Act of course continues to apply."

Shay was afforded five minutes in the empty room to make his decision. He resisted peering at the mass of paperwork despite the temptation. The place would most likely be monitored in some way and, besides, Townsend had carried Shay's file as he walked out. He moved towards the spot that Townsend had recently occupied, taking in the sparse traffic along the Embankment and the world's most famous clock tower. Would Big Ben still chime with all that scaffolding around? A police motorboat was one of few vessels gliding along the Thames, the resulting waves lapping at the side of a dawdling all-night party vessel.

    The end of the conversation had been brief, the dominating presence of Townsend returning after five minutes exactly and responding to Shay's quick acceptance by producing a contract from his desk with a flourish, the name and signature of Terence Townsend already in place. No organisation was listed alongside his name, the major adding that a more thorough briefing would happen later in the morning by which time more information should be available about the cause of death. Townsend did add that, on balance, it was preferable for the Americans to work at their own pace on the autopsy rather than spook them with too much information.

    "Our DC diplomats will show a passing interest for now given that Tyler was a British citizen." And finally, as he waved towards the door for Shay to exit, "you know you've done the right thing."

    The rest of the night was mostly spent in the perfectly functional en suite room in the basement complex after being informed it wasn't "appropriate" to venture outside. Shay hardly slept anyway, aware that the opportunity was too good to turn down. It was notable they had made it their business to explore the desperate state of his finances. Although his monthly income was OK, he had never been a saver so there wasn't much put aside for a rainy day. He winced at the memory of Kimberley despairingly using the phrase as they'd discussed their future. Long ago.

CHAPTER FIVE

CENTRAL LONDON

Both out of restlessness and to a lesser extent to check he was in fact free to roam around and not stuck in some bizarre Whitehall trap, Shay had defied instructions at around 4.30 a.m. in order to reacquaint himself with the area he'd known so well during his desk time. Usually able to sleep at the drop of a hat, especially after manoeuvres, the offer was playing on his mind. "Why him? Why now?" The monuments he encountered alongside the Embankment, directly alongside New Scotland Yard, seemed to tempt lured like the Sirens as usual.

Korea in the 1950s, the Burmese Expedition in the 1940s, even General Gordon's nineteenth-century exploits in Khartoum, were honoured. Those were just from the old days though, he noted sorrowfully as he moved towards the statue commemorating more recent conflicts that always ended up dominating his attention.

"Up, now," as the white wooden door was thumped loudly from outside. He couldn't have got more than a couple of hours of sleep at most.

The banging on the door ceased as quickly as commencing. The effect of years of patrols, exercises and generally obeying every military command had become second nature in the vast majority of occasions. By the time he'd peeked along the corridor there was no sign of human presence. Noting it was 7 a.m., Shay bent to pick up the twice folded paper which contained a brief, typed, message, "Meet driver at reception in twenty minutes. Townsend."

Washed, shaved and dressed, they had provided all the essentials. Shay soon joined the major in the sleek black Daimler as they headed from Whitehall, continuing the tour past Westminster's grand architecture: Admiralty Arch, the Mall's wide expanse. Buckingham Palace lay beyond with just a smattering of tourists at that early hour, most of whom were aiming a phone or lens at the building. The Daimler continued heading west.

Townsend launched into a further briefing. "Seems our friends in DC were interested after all, though we're still playing a bit of a chess game with them. They haven't admitted Tyler's of any special interest, yet they rushed through the autopsy and have already given us the heads up on the results. Apparently an hour or so before all the mayhem kicked off in the air, Tyler went to use one of those infernal plane cubicles. How anyone can fit in them is beyond me." Shay avoided the inappropriate comment.

"Anyway, one of the stewardesses saw him in the queue and recalls him rubbing his upper arm. Of course, when this came to light the pathologist checked closely and a small pin prick on the rear of the shoulder was found. Clearly some kind of serum was injected. A tiny needle only 3 millimetres long would do the job these days, maybe held against the body or fired from a few inches away.

This must be a professional hit, an impressive one too, with the needle ending up within so there was nothing to see at first glance. Someone pretending to knock into him maybe; that's all it takes. We know it's murder but we don't know the whos and whys. You'll have a laptop delivered to your home, assuming you still own it, containing our files on Tyler with encryption only shared with me. And with your colleague, which explains our destination."

Shay found himself, for the second time in hours, out of guesses regarding a destination. Soon after passing along the road between the twin structures in honour of Victoria's consort, the Albert Hall and Memorial, they pulled up outside an art deco mansion block just off Kensington Church Street. This seemed an unusual choice of location for another government office. Then again it was more like a residential block. Shay was already beginning to regret his decision to leave the certainty of his career trajectory, however limited that path appeared to outsiders. His attention briefly switched to the idyllic countryside ripe to host manoeuvres and the utter determination to transform rookies into combatants adhering to the golden rule he had always instilled: "If you encounter injury in combat it won't be because of any lapse in your elite performance or that of your unit or superior officers." The subtext was clear; let the enemy earn their kill. Townsend led the way to the block's entrance, pressing the buzzer for flat eighteen. Shay's gaze drifted to the sight of the barista opening up a *Pret a Manger* at the end of the road. Oh for coffee and blueberry porridge right now, not having consumed anything since the energy bar during the night's manoeuvres. In that regard his overnight accommodation was sorely lacking.

His ears pricked up at the voice answering the buzzer and the invite to "come on in". That inflection, surely not. Was the whole saga inducing hallucination? Must be a lack of sleep too. The building may appear exclusive from outside but it was an antiquated lift, fitted with see-through metal grates, that slowly delivered them to the fourth floor. For once Townsend stood back, saying,

"I think you'd better go first."

Suddenly it was all too real with the scent hitting him first. What was that perfume called? His memory for such detail had always been poor for special occasions. They'd laughed about it. Now, knowing his face must be a picture for this near out of body experience as she stood by the door, right hand loosely resting on her chest. The healthily tanned skin, long naturally blond hair, startling blue eyes, legs that seemed to travel for ever to bare feet all on show below a silk dressing gown.

Siobhan Andersson was the last person he'd expected to encounter when the day began. On later reflection he realised Townsend must be getting weird satisfaction at the chaotic scene.

"What are we doing here sir?" he asked, turning his head sharply towards the major, not least to avoid the confusion a reunion would entail. "You really have got the wrong man."

Siobhan stepped forward, gently guiding his back towards the apartment. A luxurious high-quality home greeted him, light and airy despite being housed inside the ageing block. Walls were snow white, either recently painted or kept pristine. The carpet was striking sky blue. Various Impressionist paintings adorned three of the walls. Surely the Monet wasn't an original? So she's running art galleries now? Assorted lamps and occasional tables also seemed to bridge the stylistic gap between the mansion block and the flat. He recalled that she'd always admired 1930s designs. Her career must be stratospheric.

To feel that warm hand lightly on his body again, her scent, brought it all back in an instant. The Swedish inflection still prominently remained.

"Long time Shay. You're looking well." As if each was trying to make the best of the awkward meeting. Shay took a seat on the cream sofa alongside Townsend as Siobhan perched on the easy chair. Her face hadn't visibly aged. Possibly more subtle make up and a far more expensive Mayfair haircut? Even the lightness of her clothing somehow appeared more upmarket. Or was that just the designer surroundings?

"Yes, well you two will have a chance to reminisce soon enough I suppose but not for now. Ms Andersson here has been recruited on the same grounds, as we needed someone from the Ministry of Defence but as with you she's been seconded and her superiors know nothing about the nature of this task."

"MOD? Pleased I made the introductions all those years ago," he uttered sarcastically remembering the encouragement he provided, in happier days, to take advantage of the MOD's desperate desire for linguists all those years ago. He recalled a reference being provided by his previous commanding officer, also thoroughly smitten by her at that year's Christmas ball, which did no harm to her job prospects. The MOD's attitude towards those with a foot in different nations not least appealed due to the perceived advantage in mastering languages easily. For Siobhan UK citizenship on account of her Northern Irish mother, alongside the Swedish passport via her father, dramatically increased her attractiveness to the services.

"Why would I want to work alongside someone with whom I have quite a… colourful history? This makes no sense."

Townsend's authoritative response rang out. "Mason, you signed a document last night agreeing to our terms which includes a substantial salary. Of course we knew there may have been a passing acquaintance years ago but you're a big boy now, get over it. Andersson was handpicked too because she's bloody good at her job and your skill sets balance. She also has the contacts to liaise internally with the Defence, Science and Technology boffins. So be a good chap and stop throwing your toys out of the pram. This is the last thing I expected from you and I'm starting to question whether I made the right call in your case."

Shay sat back on the sofa truculently.

"Good, let's crack on," continued Townsend without pause. "A further little surprise cropped up on that flight. We know Stewart Tyler was being watched and we know he was killed. As I've repeated to you both, you've signed the OSA so no one is to know what I'm about to tell you. Tyler was also watched by us. He'd been under suspicion for some time, as his actions seemed odd. Just routine surveillance anyway, but with limited success. We actually encountered a stroke of luck when the body was identified with the help of our consulate in Boston. Apparently it's pretty routine for the Americans to hand back all items found with a British corpse and they did so immediately. Either the yanks really don't know anything about him or some department out there is now livid it's all been treated so routinely to date. Anyway, he had an onward flight ticket from America to Cairo in his luggage, as well as a reservation for a room at the Four Seasons there. Then back to the UK. All foreign travel has to be cleared by his seniors at work first. Guess what? The US trip was, but they know nothing about Egypt.

I gave you clear instructions yesterday, Mason. Keep your eyes on the prize. I'll ask for your items to be brought up. The quicker you get started the better."

Townsend whispered commands into his mobile whilst he shuffled towards the window. Once the driver had deposited the two purple cases containing Stealth MacBook Pros, as well as a bag containing Shay's freshly laundered manoeuvres kit from the previous night, Townsend explained the security procedures. Access to the machines could only be gained by logging on to the security clearance section set up for them with seven-digit codes they were required to memorise. The codes would also act as their call-in number; all trace would be deleted from their phone after finishing a call or their MacBook once they'd logged off. "Who knows what the Russians are capable of?" he added with a smile.

Travel and indeed any assistance would be provided only via Sally in the Ministry; a healthy budget was available.

"Get moving. We're paying top dollar to you two for bloody quick and accurate results so you'd better not let me down." Townsend paused. "Although this seems a mile away from your day jobs, there would of course be consequences if the ministry is not happy with your performances."

That wasn't in the contract, Shay recoiled, or had he missed it? That useless excuse of a contract could hardly be relied on anyway if this all went wrong. There was no logical place in which Townsend fitted, if Shay's limited knowledge of the current structures of the defence apparatus in Whitehall was anything to go by.

Shay and Siobhan stared at each other without a word for several seconds, as if taking each other in afresh, as Townsend and his driver moved towards the lift. How long had it been exactly? And together again in these circumstances with such bizarre planning. The distant sound of the creaky lift as well as the block's entrance door banging shut four floors below, could be heard.

Immediately, silence was shattered by the screech of motorbike brakes and a sound all too familiar. Two thuds followed by the throttle of the bike as it sped away.

"Oh my God." Siobhan flung her hands to her mouth.

"What the heck?" Shay sprinted to the window alongside, witnessing the powerful green and black Kawasaki Ninja disappearing round the corner. There was no trace of a number plate at the rear so presumably the rider would plate up nearby. Terence clutched his stomach in the near-deserted street, doubled over yet still just about standing, before being sharply pushed into the back seat of his Daimler with the door slammed shut by the driver. Within seconds they were speeding down the street, hurriedly out of sight.

Siobhan hurtled towards the front door as Shay lurched forward to place an arm in front, barring her way.

"There's no point. There won't be anything to see and we'll only attract attention to ourselves. Particularly with you dressed like that. Dressing gowns chasing shooters aren't a usual sight in London. Even in Kensington. Surely the world and his wife noticed anyway, or do shootings take place in front of you on a daily basis?"

Shay sighed. "Anyway, it looked like Townsend was alive when chucked into the back at least. I'd suggest our best move is to get away from here given we can only presume it's linked to our operation. Pack a bag quickly. They must have been tailing the official car but surely don't know about my flat. That had better be the case, anyway." After a pause, visibly shaken, Siobhan nodded before heading next door. Wandering out to the immaculate hallway, Shay randomly picked up what must be a ten-inch bronze figurine. Faceless and feeling rough in his hands, there were swirls of metal where the arms and legs would ordinarily be. He'd give a quid in a market for this but somehow doubted he'd got the value right. As Shay replaced it carefully he noticed for the first time a couple of smaller coats and pairs of shoes by the front door. Siobhan's voice rang out from the bedroom seemingly reading his thoughts.

"Those are Tommy's, my boy. Thank god he's away at school at the moment." A pause. "You know, Shay, you've always been trouble and somehow I doubt that will ever change." Siobhan's face appeared briefly from behind the door.

"But before you ask, I'm fuming about them fitting us together as much as you evidently are. They just dropped it on me, but the terms are good. Now let's get out of here just in case they work out more targets are in the vicinity. In fact, let's take the service stairs at the back when I'm packed." She had changed into expensive designer light blue jeans, suede Deyissa ankle boots and a white silk blouse within minutes.

The pair took the stairs down the back at a rate of knots a light drizzle starting to fall before they managed to hail a taxi on Kensington High Street. Local residents seemed to compete for personalised transport into London's centre at the start of the working day.

"North London, Crouch End," Shay directed to the driver as they swung into the traffic.

Siobhan's hands were shaking slightly before she sat back hard against the seat, staring out of the window for a second then nodding towards the driver. She turned to Shay, her voice no more than a whisper. "I'd better not call in to check on recent developments yet. Let's just hope he's OK. That incident really got to me not surprisingly. I'm not used to the frontline. This is not what I signed up for.

Take my mind off it. Please. What water's flown under the bridge after all this time? And before you start, we have to keep this relationship professional despite our past. We both have bills to pay and careers to chase so I, at least, need to make this work. What happened to you at military intelligence? It sounds like it's not part of your life anymore if you've been recruited from outside?"

Shay inhaled deeply. "Counterterrorism had a list, in fact they probably have a significantly longer one today. In effect it's a suspicious person's roster. I'd assumed, of course, that they had to follow suspects, tap phones, all the necessary surveillance. No problem with that if they tail the right people. But anyone on the list, and I mean anyone, then gets placed on the civilian barring database without even knowing they had been under surveillance. To get on the list just one person can phone in with a name and the briefest of excuses for doubting them. That could include your neighbour if you've fallen out over the colour of the roses on your shared drive. Once you're on though, you can't get any job in the public sector. If you're a doctor with ten years' experience or a teacher with twenty, that's it. Your career working for the state is finished and the poor sod probably doesn't know why. They even sacked a fifty-five year old lollipop woman who'd been supposedly outed locally just because her son, an Afghan native, may have held anti-western views out there. It's wholly in line with what the Stasi were perpetrating in East Germany until the end of the 80s, being condemned without trial. And all to ensure, in the remotest of likelihoods that the suspect carries out something, the Government can state it didn't put the public in harm's way."

Siobhan appeared annoyed. "And you just walked away on a promising career when you could have climbed high enough up the ladder to have changed the rules one day? I bet you didn't think of that."

Shay laughed throatily. "You never get high enough to change the rules. In case you haven't noticed, leaders climb down from protecting the human rights of the innocent when it suits. It may have been an implementation issue and not legally binding, but that's how they chose to apply it. There was no mechanism to question, let alone reverse, the process apparently, not least as those on the list were oblivious to it. Catch-22. It was made clear to me that I carry out those procedures or choose the exit."

By now they were arriving just off Crouch End Hill with Siobhan first out of the taxi, punching in her mobile's call-in her code which she had already memorised.

"How's Townsend? We saw he'd been hit." After a brief conversation she turned to Shay, standing alongside. "He's being operated on now but the doctors expect minimal damage. If they fix a trace on the shooter it'll be reported on the system. They even reprimanded me for dialling in to check. Shay, we seem to be on pretty uncertain ground without Townsend at the helm. He'd better be back soon." She paused. "I'm really not up to the world of cloaks and daggers."

"And I'd rather not be," Shay agreed instinctively.

They soon entered the ground floor flat of the Edwardian three storey block, cobwebs blocking up a corner of the shared entranceway and a rusty bike on top of a leaking oil patch taking up another significant portion. Once in the flat, Siobhan peered through to the back garden twenty-five feet away. "Cosy," she commented, taking in the sparsely furnished hallway and living room, a cheap Afghan rug thrown over what appeared a dated royal blue carpet underneath, rose coloured fading wallpaper all around. The TV was at least ten years' old and a few paperbacks were stacked in the corner, nothing highbrow still, she noted. She glanced outside the room noting the double bed through the doorway. No sign of a girlfriend, the only sign of companionship being an empty cat bowl in the living room corner.

She was taking in the room still, appearing apprehensive as he returned from the kitchen with two coffees. "A neighbour's cat comes to visit on occasion. No way I could keep an animal full time. I know it's all pretty minimalist, maybe not quite as arty as your place, but it works for me."

Siobhan shrugged, "Let's get to work and start digging." Opening their MacBooks, sat alongside the worn surface masquerading as a coffee table, the pair split sections of files. Soon they were sharing information, both engrossed in uncovering the complicated life of Stewart Henry Tyler, who'd hit the high point of his public career when winning the Nobel Prize for Chemistry at the strikingly young age of twenty-eight. Pre-loaded files were well organised in the system with his life story broken down into sections. The first batch ended with his First at Cambridge; another covering his commercial stint for a company named Porterfield Labs when he made his discovery to such public acclaim, the prestigious international award attained for analysing the molecular structure of anti-leukaemia treatments. A third summarised his work for the Government.

Siobhan tried to explain the science behind Tyler's commercial and governmental work in layman's terms, unsure he was grasping the scientific importance. The final section included the results of surveillance from the past two years. Yet, as far as they pair could make out, there appeared no grounds for suspicion apart from Stewart showing vague signs of stress. He had become more preoccupied at work, snappier with colleagues and less involved with the workplace socially over time. Not that evenings spent at greyhound races or ten pin bowling were particularly encouraged at the MOD, Shay added. The oddest aspect, which didn't fit, was two sightings at the House of Commons. Everyone was fully aware that contact between politicians and government servants of whatever hue were, at best, frowned on outside official channels without very good reason. Members of Parliament had their own researchers or the House of Commons Library team to commission; it was a no-no to contact government employees outside of those strict parameters, particularly after the Iraq dossier fiasco two decades ago.

"It says here," he started, "Tyler always used the name of his local MP when signing for admission to the Palace of Westminster and just last month the MP in question was approached by the security services. She claimed to know nothing about the visits. The matter was referred back to Palace security, one of whom on duty at the time vaguely remembered Tyler presenting a mobile number to call, supposedly for the MP. No further details were available. It was deemed inappropriate for surveillance services to carry out any further investigation and risk the wrath of politicians as to why they were being watched.

Bank accounts had been checked, a few friends surreptitiously tapped to ask if there were any known problems, but nothing important had materialised. It may just be that the individual in Parliament whom Stewart was meeting wanted their anonymity preserved for some quite innocent reason. Or Tyler was overly friendly with someone without wanting questions asked."

Siobhan raised her eyebrows and smiled. "So, how do we break this down? We can hardly cover every avenue. Each report seems to have stacks of photos from student days onwards, biogs of his wife, close friends, relatives."

Shay responded by trying to mimic Townsend. "Friends in jeopardy dear boy, friends in jeopardy," then adding, "hardly helps in knowing who, when or where."

She sat back with a laugh. Shay recalled that, under the surface, barely hidden from sight, was the opposite of the quintessential Scandinavian ice maiden. All that time ago, seemingly exaggerating her emotions at will to tease him almost as a counterpoint to his natural introversion. They'd made quite a couple but he also remembered the sense of doom about it all ending that he'd harboured from early on.

If they started on that now they'd be here all day. "Let's break down the checks and start with the most obvious. It says here he's been married to… Where is it?" flipping through the file.

"Harriet, that's right," she jumped in. "Why don't you go and interview her? The latest message update section says she's been informed already. Although in any other profession it's only polite to allow space for grieving, we haven't exactly got time for that."

"That's fine," he replied. "Why don't you head to the Cambridgeshire lab to speak to his colleagues? I guess we both have to walk the fine line to extract intel about anything out of the ordinary, but diplomatically. The lab boffins will probably close ranks to an outsider, irrespective of how strongly they've been advised to cooperate. Now, how do we sort the admin stuff? Must say I was usually desk bound in Whitehall."

The instructions section of the programme provided a source of amusement, including every relevant requirement in the index they could possibly need. Booking airline tickets and hotels, ordering cars, what to do in the event of a fatality – broken down into accidental or intentional deaths – right down to the mundane topic of reclaiming expenses. Best of all they smiled at the health and safety section which included the law regarding wearing seat belts in vehicles, set out clearly for two hundred countries in a further index. Also, a contacts section for many of the individuals and associates named in the reports. Sally, or whatever her real name was, appeared impressively thorough to date.

Shay reached for the mobile to arrange his meeting just as hers sounded alongside. *Beethoven's Ninth.* So, she'd moved on from the excerpt of *Dancing Queen,* presumably no longer appreciating the irony, when a student, of announcing she was Swedish to all and sundry.

After arranging their impending appointments, Shay requested transport for both via Sally. He'd originally started to check train times, local buses, maybe a taxi if Uber wouldn't operate that far. Siobhan tapped him on the wrist. "I presume you're joking. Didn't you hear Townsend? Time of the essence and a great big expense account. Use it boy," with a smile. Sally's response had appeared in seconds anyway. "Your vehicles are outside. Drive yourselves. Enjoy. Keys are under your window box." They also received confirmation their appointment targets would be notified as they travelled.

"What's the commotion outside?" he started, jumping to his feet and rushing to the flat's front door, soon laughing instead. A red VW Polo sat outside. "Our budget obviously doesn't stretch that far after all. I just hope they have engines under those bonnets."

CHAPTER SIX

LOGAN AIRPORT, BOSTON

Steve Moroney recalled his college days as the bombardment started. After a heavy night's drinking they'd all decided to go paintballing. It was certainly doubtful that even he, as the driver, was under the limit by the time they set off. Once kitted up, Steve had tried to dodge the balls fired at him later but found it impossible given his slow, lager-induced, reactions and the unexpected speed of the projectiles anyway. Fast forward to the present day and, though the missiles were only verbal assaults, there seemed no escape from the southern female voice currently yelling at him down the phone.

"You let them what? All the passengers just waltz away from the terminal without a thorough check on the system? And I mean thorough, not just some five second OK on the database. No prints, photos, eye scans even? Do you even care if some half-crazed lunatic is roaming free on American soil?" The tirade was five minutes in.

This felt unfair and completely unreasonable but not the time to answer back. He just had to suck it up or it may just be his final day in the job. Remaining silent also afforded more time to think of an excuse for when she finally finished.

CHAPTER SEVEN

NORTH LONDON

Siobhan tossed him the keys of the Polo and marched towards the Audi TT alongside yet still managed to sound disappointed.

"Oh well, an R8 would have been preferable but I guess the Ministry couldn't be expected to fork out for a hundred grand car for me. This will have to do I suppose. Enjoy your ride Shay," she added before speeding off before he'd locked up the flat.

The R8 was soon heading north-east towards the M11 and Cambridge, whilst the Polo worked his way through heavy traffic blocking up north London near Finchley. For the first time since the overnight stay in Whitehall, Shey felt he could draw breath and try and take stock. Manoeuvres were all very well and he loved the challenge of leading troops full on towards elite performance but, maybe whoever had plucked him for the role knew him too well. This investigative work was exactly the type he'd originally aspired to before his moralistic outburst had got the better of him. Had he ever regretted speaking out? The uncomfortable fact was that he'd lost a great opportunity. Later, self-questioning what positive results his complaints had yielded resulted in near depression, having wrecked the potential trajectory within intelligence. This was a second bite at the cherry, albeit in typically bizarre Whitehall fashion. There was no choice but to give it full focus and time wasn't on their side in uncovering the reasons for Stewart Tyler's demise before the Americans shook themselves into action.

Now there was another spanner in the works. What idiot had thrown him together with Siobhan after she'd thrown their relationship away? She had moved on with a family, certainly a son. Most confusingly, what was the bizarre charade played out right in front of them earlier in the day? The MOD and security services could never resist laying down endless trails from his recollection. The prospect of being a spectator in their machinations was, for some incomprehensible reason, a gauntlet carefully thrown down in his direction.

CHAPTER EIGHT

CAMBRIDGESHIRE

Shay tried to stick to vaguely stick to the speed limit as he drove towards Huntingdon on the A1 before arriving at a picturesque two-storey cottage with refurbished oak beams on parade. A small but immaculate lawn and various types of rose bushes surrounded the building providing a contented and homely impression. Pristine, that was the word, the flowers orderly and managed.

Three words appeared in Shay's mind to describe Harriet Tyler as she opened the front door before he'd started on the twenty-foot path. Poised, attractive, sombre. How do you interview such a recent widow, he mused? Instinctively shaking hands, perhaps the gesture would bring home to Harriet that she wasn't dealing with the police today. He needed her off duty, off guard somehow.

"Shay Mason. I trust you received my text, Mrs Tyler. I'm so sorry for your loss." A perfunctory nod in return, as she immediately turned and led inside offering tea. Now they sat opposite each other on petite but comfortable flower-patterned sofas. Maybe a traditional cottage like this only housed tea drinkers, Shay reflected. Despite feeling awkward for some reason, he'd dared to spoil the environment by requesting coffee. Harriet was slim, mid-height and a couple of inches shorter than Shay, dressed in a plain sleeveless blue dress with light brown shoulder length hair. Her movements were the epitome of gracefulness.

Shay offered an abridged version of his responsibility and rank, explaining that due to Stewart's significant role an investigation was necessary at the MOD as a matter of standard procedure.

She sighed. "I know my husband was involved in important scientific work for his country but don't quite see why you'd want to visit me."

"Sorry Mrs Tyler, what exactly have you been told about Stewart's plane flight?"

"That he had some choking accident, unlikely as it sounds. I suppose they do happen on rare occasions though. I've seen the story in the news about that boy, Sam, was it? But the press appear to have completely overshot the mark. Let's just say I won't be suing a child even if my husband had some previously unknown allergy." A pause. "What are you suggesting happened?" All delivered calmly, Shay acknowledging the prickly sensation that she was trying to throw him off guard. For the first time her face travelled from lonely gentleness to eager interest. He recalled her background; occasional theatre work at the National prior to early retirement from the stage at 33 and, what appeared, a quiet, settled marriage thereafter.

"We're not quite sure what transpired but have to look at all the possibilities." It felt comforting to trot out the formal response for now though she'd soon see right through it.

"Did Stewart ever talk about his occupation? What he thought of working at the Cambridge lab?" The questions didn't elicit more information as he then casually tried to throw in Stewart's dedication to his research. Harriet's impression was that he'd had no regrets in walking away from the relative glamour and pay rates of the commercial sector for a career of service to his country. Even though most travelled in the opposite direction within the field during their working lives.

The conversation was succinct. Harriet clearly had no intention of reminiscing with a stranger in the wake of such emotional shock. The comfortable future envisaged with her husband had been shredded without warning.

As Harriet prepared a refill in the kitchen, he checked out the room, or at least the features on display. On the mantelpiece were photos of the couple at various locations around the world: alongside an attractive younger woman overlooking a bay; outside the Taj Mahal; Rome's Colosseum. Alongside almost incongruously was a toy snowmobile design that he recognised, with a date scrawled in white marker pen.

It was time to up the pace. "Mrs Tyler…"

"Call me Harriet, please."

"I have other aspects requiring your help but I'll keep questions brief for now. Could you tell me how you met and, please excuse my bluntness, the state of your relationship?"

Another sigh. "I suppose you may as well. It was years ago. He was working on research not that far from here and some mutual friends invited him to a production. At that time I was desperate to further my career, or at least thought I was, as the years ticked away after drama school. Everyone knows that you have a receding chance of fame, or at least of a good stage career, the longer it takes to be spotted after leaving. To be honest, there was disillusionment by then. Not least after the pathetic expressions of a couple of producers actually looking askance when I turned down their fabulous offers to share the casting couch.

Stewart was a breath of fresh air really, because he wasn't part of that arty set, not always talking himself up. I could tell from the little I knew and understood of his work that he was genuinely talented and he didn't need to constantly remind the world of his brilliance. That was reassuring in contrast to the self-obsession of the acting community. His Nobel Prize a couple of years later said it all, as in 'There, stick that on your mantelpiece.'"

"And more recently?"

Harriet reached for a cigarette and her gold lighter. "I presume you don't mind?" Shay couldn't remember when he was last around someone smoking indoors. Given it was Harriet's home, objection hardly possible even with the cultural shift away from smoking over recent years. He hated the habit.

"Shay, isn't it? You're very direct, clearly not out of the Government's customer service section. But the truth is we were very content. At least I was and didn't notice any dissatisfaction from Stewart. We were exceedingly close."

"And what exactly were your husband's travel plans on this trip?"

"Well I know it was mostly work-based. My husband wasn't having an affair if that's what you're suggesting. He couldn't have lied if he'd tried. Some mention of popping in to see Bryony along the way."

"Sorry, Bryony is___?"

"My younger sister, well half-sister if you like. Dad remarried an American and all but faded from my life when I was young. Just me and mum left over here. Bryony and I met properly at dad's funeral and just hit it off. We used to joke that we'd each found the sister for whom we'd longed. My only regret is not having her with me throughout all my childhood."

"Stewart was coming home straight after?"

"Yes of course. Why do you ask?"

"Apparently an onward ticket for Egypt was found in his luggage as well as a reservation at the Four Seasons in Cairo. You don't know why he might have wanted to go there?"

"Egypt? The plan had been, very loosely, for me to join him in America in a few days, that is if I could arrange time off from my job at a local charity. I'm co-manager there. My colleague and I do half the week each usually but we're short-staffed and all have to muck in sometimes. So it literally would have been a last-minute decision. We'd always promised ourselves a short break after the conservatory was built and other bits of work round the house were completed. We could have spent next weekend together in Boston with Bryony. You see, Boston was home to his real favourite of the two Cambridges, despite his university days down the road from here. So no, he'd never expressed any interest in going to Egypt at any point and was coming straight home with or without me after the States. There must be some mix-up with plane and hotel bookings. We've travelled a lot in recent years anyway, as I could see you've been checking," as her hand pointed to the mantelpiece.

That curve ball hadn't worked. Time to try another. "Any idea who your husband may have been seeing during visits to Parliament? I presume they were work-related?"

The same calm response, though with eyebrows raised in slight surprise. "I didn't even know he was there. You'd expect that bunch were queuing up to find out what his team at the lab were up to but he wasn't a talker, he was a doer. He would have run a mile from getting involved in any political disputes about his work. Even had exemption from appearing before select committees due to the OSA."

Shay scratched his head, no further forward but conscious of not taking up too much time given that Harriet surely had further arrangements to occupy her. As he rose to leave, Shay could only conclude that her façade must have covered how beleaguered, all at sea, she was underneath.

"Just one last point for now," he started as they approached the front door. "Do you have any photos, mementoes, diaries even, of his that I could look through please? Some people have them scattered all over the place but I know some___"

"___ have them neatly contained in a single location," she completed. "Well that was Stewart. I'll just find them but would like them back in time for the funeral please, whenever that is. All sorts of relatives may be over who'll want a memento."

Soon after driving away, he tried Siobhan on the hands-free but reached voicemail. Having left a message as to his next movements, he wound his way along deserted country lanes to one of his favourite pubs outside the capital. Radio news didn't reveal any more about the murder, although authorities on both sides of the Atlantic were desperately trying to take the heat out of the situation by stating that no charges would be pressed against Sam as the death was attributable to natural courses. This could only mean the Americans were trying to mount their own investigation away from the three sets of prying eyes: media, the public and the UK. Mulling over the case and hardly absorbing the rest of the news: riots in Turkey, stringent clampdowns in Russia, yet another football bribery scandal.

Half an hour later Shay was ensconced in the restful, spacious garden of the Eight Bells pub, just outside Hitchin. The old ale house had been taken over and renamed years before by a retired boxer. With a pint of Young's bitter alongside, he steadily worked his way through the large cardboard box provided by Harriet. It all felt impossible once he started on notebooks, keepsakes, pocketbooks; the haystack too high and the needle camouflaged. How could he know where to begin?

It would be an easy drive over for Siobhan. After half an hour the Audi swung into the car park and soon Siobhan sat opposite helping sift through the box's contents with a glass of Chablis alongside. She'd bunched her hair in response to the light breeze and was nodding knowingly towards his drink.

"That still not got the better of you, I hope, after your dad's fantastic example? How is he? Relationship any better?"

Shay sat back abruptly, his arms instinctively crossed. Changing the subject was automatic.

"Do you still snore?"

"Still grinding your teeth at night?"

"Okay, OK. No, he's better than in those days when mum died and he hit the bottle rather than remember he had a son to bring up. Whichever idiot OKed him to take over a tied pub needs shooting unless the intention was some tax dodge where the publican is guaranteed to drink the profits. I had little contact with the old man for years, truth to tell, and I can't say I have any regrets. I'm pretty sure he doesn't either."

"And Maryanne?"

"A lot worse than when you knew her. She started mimicking dad with the bottle in recent years and we hardly speak. She feels honour bound to keep up with him I guess. Vodka's her weapon of choice, apparently. You know, she once told me in a moment of unrequested candour there's a 75% chance of keeping it from her boss when drinking before work." A pause. "But they're not my problem. It took me a long time to work that one out."

She continued delving into the box, stacked high with Stewart's reminiscences. They soldiered through numerous newspaper cuttings that, presumably, Tyler's parents and, later Harriet, proudly stored for him. These covered his degree, the gradual increase in publicity focusing principally on his growing celebrity in the scientific world rather than the intricacies of his research projects, a few diaries from evenly spaced years in his life. Eighth, sixteen and twenty-four only. How better to ration mementoes than by keeping three from regular intervals? Was this a clear indication the scientist was in exactly the right profession for someone with such extreme OCD? None of it was helpful though.

Shay inadvertently started rubbing his neck. Had he even stretched since all that activity in Wales? It was unbelievable, the battalion physio at the Welsh Arms would haul him over the coals for forgetting that one at his age, whatever the circumstances. And rightly so.

Siobhan glanced up and started giggling. "You still do it. When you're deep in concentration you automatically scratch near the scar. I told you once it's your comfort blanket, your reminder of the scars of war. Well, maybe a kind of war."

He looked up sharply, the words pouring out before he could control them. "And you? Your comfort blanket? Ditto."

Instinctively she shifted one, then both, hands to the top of her neck, an automatic shield. The mood hostile all at once. Both arms were now huddled high on her body. "That's a low blow. Really low, Shay. Not everyone finds life a bed of roses by the time they arrive at adulthood. And to answer your question, no I don't self-harm anymore."

"Sorry Siobhan, I know that was uncalled for. Truce. Please. Look, we have enough to deal with here. Also, Terence's escapade yesterday? None of it makes sense."

Still glaring at him, Siobhan rose and took both glasses for a refill in one swift motion. "It's diet lemonade this time. Beer clearly makes you cranky. And you're driving."

The rule clearly applied solely for Shay. Ten minutes later that she carried back a soft drink for him and another Chablis for herself.

"I needed time at the bar. This has all brought a lot back for both of us, not least that temper of yours." She paused. "Remember we always were joined at the hip. Your dad insisting on Shay for your name, my Irish mum won with Siobhan. I certainly didn't encounter any others with the same name when as a child in Gothenburg, pre-London. I just don't think we can avoid talking about the past. It's there with us whether we like it or not. Just like the remnants of my scars.

Anyway, there was nothing of note at the lab and everything seemed to be run by the book. I guess a bunch of autistic scientists are hardly going to go easy on the OSA just because a blonde turns up to dig into their research. Though when I was speaking to the director and a couple of Tyler's colleagues they opened up a bit more about Stewart as a person. He was hardly the life and soul of their parties but he was largely easy-going or used to be anyway. It was the same scenario we've heard before. He was distracted in recent years. His boss speculated Stewart wanted out because of the money and opportunities elsewhere.

Maybe a research fellowship, or a professorship at Stanford or Harvard? Who wouldn't turn that down in his position? In fact, speculation about the appeal of the US really arose from a couple of trips in which he'd addressed small groups of researchers at Harvard. He was building up both a reputation and contacts over there. We don't have anything else to go on relating to his work."

"Okay," Shay responded. "Let's check back with Sally and start making arrangements for the next destination."

There were no others nearby, theirs being the only occupied table in the garden before the evening's regular clientele would appear. Any risks involved in making the call seemed worthwhile, given they couldn't be overheard.

"How's Townsend doing? Is he OK?" asked Siobhan on speaker.

Sally's Essex accent in response fast becoming familiar. "He's in surgery but demanded before going under that he still wants regular updates as soon as he comes around. He even had a message for you: 'When are you going to step up to the plate?' He's somewhat demanding, in case you haven't noticed.

An update came in though and I can't imagine the boss wants me to keep it back from you. The CIA think they've uncovered a possible Iranian extremist who may have been on the flight, named Zarek Behzadi. Of course he was using fake ID, posing as a postgrad student at an Ivy League university, so escaped any kind of interrogation when he boarded the plane. His documents all seemed perfectly in order. When they disembarked, he started kicking up a fuss about a master's degree specialising in human rights law so Homeland Security were wary about detaining him any longer than they absolutely had to. It was only after most passengers had cleared off that Tyler's cause of death came under suspicion. Now, not surprisingly, Behzadi has vanished into thin air. There's a picture coming over now."

They peered at the picture. Tall, neat beard, thin, sharp suit and tie. Behzadi could have been mistaken for an aspiring head teacher or bank manager.

"And, get this, the woman sitting behind Sam Collins' seat remembers a 'foreign looking man' starting the peanut allergy rumour. Not a particularly helpful description but I guess in this instance she means Middle Eastern. Either the American authorities are on to him and playing a waiting game or they've really lost Behzadi in the US. Whichever way, this won't hit the news bulletins any time soon."

"They came out and told you this?" he asked.

Sally laughed. "No way. We just have our sources within intelligence there. Nothing compromising their security, no theft involved, just sharing info sometimes. That's our problem, and yours is to get ahead on all this before the old man wakes up."

There was no need for a reminder that the situation was gathering momentum without them. The drive afforded space to think this through, home in on the leads. The pair headed back in convoy down the adjacent A1 towards London with Shay in front.

Unfortunately, Shay only landed on grime and Coldplay easily to hand on the radio, feeling too long in the tooth for the former and too young for the latter. He soon gave up and opted for the news, not bothering to set up Bluetooth.

Soon after, he noticed a sleek bright green 4 by 4 Land Rover behind her Audi, sticking with her as she'd changed lanes but not overtaking. Were they being tailed? Presumably she'd spotted it too, it was difficult to miss. Turning off at the next junction then onto a sparse country lane and slowing, he notified Siobhan on the mobile to follow his lead before both stopped. After, the 4 by 4 nowhere to be seen so their convoy resumed, sticking to back lanes until snaking their way on to the North Circular. He weighed it up. Being tailed by anyone incompetent enough to stay hidden was preferable to someone desperate enough to pose a threat, particularly after the shooting. Being adjacent to a deserted field would have been the perfect opportunity. Or was he just imagining the threat. Decent sleep, he concluded, was a necessity soon.

As they entered London she was out of sight, presumably stuck in traffic. Just after parking at the flat, his phone rang. The lab's director said he hadn't been able to reach Siobhan so had called Shay after she'd left both their numbers earlier. He was mildly apologetic about withholding information earlier but concluded there was something else they should know about Tyler. From Siobhan's earlier description, Shay wondered if the director was just more trusting of another man.

"OSA and all that strictly applies of course?"

"Naturally."

"How's your chemistry? $C_4H_{10}FO_2P$ mean anything to you?"

This was certainly out of Shay's depth. He'd hardly understood CO_2 in school exams, any more than the first few symbols of the periodic table defeating him all those years ago.

"Doesn't ring a bell."

The director continued. "Our labs have to replicate harmful products quite simply for research purposes, so we can stay one step ahead of the game in learning how to protect the population. If we don't know the worst we can face, how can we prepare our defences?"

"So what's the agent?"

"Sarin is its most common title. Over twenty-five times more lethal than conventional mustard gas and five hundred times more so than chlorine. Stewart was working on a breakthrough for a more advanced formula than the scientific community had thought feasible, which reduces the volume needed for catastrophic damage to a whole new level."

Back at the flat, Siobhan shrugged off the failure of the scientist to fully confide in her earlier. "Happens all the time in our line of work. Whatever. At least Tyler's work explains the angle for all this."

"Does it? It's a possible strand but why want him dead? Surely there are many who'd want him on their side instead?"

They delved through more records during the evening, including checks on bank accounts, savings plans and investments. Again, nothing out of the ordinary for a high level civil servant.

"Townsend's right, we have to push deeper. We just need a break to get this moving," he prompted. They worked for hours, breaking only to consume a Chinese take away. At eleven the decision was made to call it a day and restart the next morning. She needed little convincing to have the bed as he contemplated how, if at all, comfortable his sofa would prove.

"Are you still, you know, suffering in bed?" she started casually as she rose. Having kicked off her shoes on arrival this almost seemed like old times, her presence strangely reassuring.

He laughed. "You make it sound like impotence. But yes, it's still there. Looks like my lifetime companion. Hardly the worst hardship in the world, though."

Siobhan smiled. "I guess everyone has phobias of some sort. Mine was always a weakness for soldiers. That's a joke Shay, definitely not a come on."

Shay reciprocated with an expression of mock disappointment.

After washing, she idly waved goodnight from the door clad in knickers and T-shirt. Her swan tattoo visible on her thigh, reminding him also of the angel on her back. This was the most he'd ever seen her wearing when going to bed. It really was a different era.

An hour later and sleep still at bay, the living room's table lamp casting its brightness alongside the sofa. Maybe late night telly would do the trick, though the remote control wasn't in sight and he couldn't be bothered to hunt for it. Instead, Shay's eyes alighted on Tyler's box dumped nearby. He may as well keep going. Next out was a torn magazine page showing what appeared to be a high end celebration, black tie for the men, stunning gowns adorning women. The occasion was the impending presentation of the Nobel Prize. Noting the publication, it seemed even *Hello* wanted to include the in-vogue scientist of the moment albeit a couple of decades ago. To one side, in a sleek strapless creation was Harriet, on the other a recognisable front bench politician. Presumably he was barely an MP at that point, probably just starting out on the lowest rungs. How would there be any benefit in gate-crashing Tyler's big night? Shay guessed he must have made it to the science committee, one of the All-Party groups, in Parliament by then.

On removing the next item, another photo but this time showing school days, he grinned and jolted to life. Quickly carrying out a few checks online Shay bounded towards the bedroom door and entered without knocking.

"I was just starting to fall asleep," the mumbled response.

"Siobhan I've found a lead. If there's nothing in it, it's a hell of a coincidence." He reached forward, taking her hand to encourage sitting up all the faster. Positively tame in comparison to waking recruits so she couldn't complain. Sat side by side on the sofa a minute later, he recounted the steps.

"Okay, I've found a couple of items that seem irrelevant at first. Here's a picture from ages ago of some celebration, maybe even the prize day itself," he tapped on the image of the politician.

She stared hard. "Bill Atkinson, interesting. And they don't look like casual acquaintances. Arms around each other with broad grins. Presumably Atkinson was chasing every publication to get his mugshot into at the time. What a typical politician."

He pointed to the figures in turn grinning at the camera in the next item. "Okay, look at this photo though. Four schoolmates together. I've checked and they were all at Ridgeway Hall in Oxfordshire. It's remained under the radar compared to Eton, Harrow and the other big name schools but it's for the children of high rollers all right. Cabinet ministers, Saudi princes, the richest baseball club owner in the States; they all send their children off to board for years. They probably come back stuffed with ambition spilling out of every pore. Next to him in this one is, well you can see."

She answered, "Atkinson again. So what? They went to school together." His finger moved to the next figure as Siobhan peered closer. "That looks like a young Rory Nicholls; the press still claim he looks boyish and he really was then. Same healthy, year round tan. The same mop of hair. And a leading member of the Government was good mates with the Leader of the Opposition once upon a time. Funny, but hardly career ending."

He nodded, "Yup, Nicholls apparently has the best people's touch amongst politicians for years; no one does estuary English like the product of a fee paying school. I guess all those drama classes have to count for something. All lost on me though; they're all salesmen. But that's not the greatest significance. Who's this?" he asked tapping the picture of the fourth individual.

"No idea," she sat back. "Maybe one of them had a sister or girlfriend at the time."

"She's wearing a girl's version of the same uniform. It's Linda Maddison, possibly the highest profile of the lot these days. Ridgeway had admitted girls a few years before apparently.

One of the gang by the look of it. You see, footy knowledge does have some benefits. She's in the news at the moment, trying to steer clear of the latest slush fund scandal to hit football's top cronies and, if she does stay above the pack, in a matter of hours she could be the first female President of FIFA. You do know where their congress is being held in the next few days? It was on the radio this afternoon."

"Egypt," she leant over, running through the news story on his screen. "That's a coincidence and a half."

"I've got an idea." He rummaged through the box flicking through one of the diaries, then reached for his mobile. "Harriet, I'm so sorry to call you at this time but I wondered if you could shed light on something new? Did Stewart talk about his school days much? You wouldn't know if he stayed friendly with Linda Maddison by any chance?"

He tried to ignore Siobhan's withering glance and whispered admonishment that "You don't call someone in the middle of the night unless it's an emergency."

"I bloody do," he mouthed back.

Siobhan turned away, hearing a sizable exhalation on the other end of the line. She could make out Harriet's response though. "You didn't ask so I didn't think it was relevant. They were schoolmates apparently and he started mentioning them at times, eventually saying it was all "coming home to roost." I didn't know what he was referring to and he wouldn't expand on that. Some bet, some dare, I didn't know what he'd done but a couple of times he broke down. Definitely not like Stewart, very out of character from the man I fell in love with. You don't achieve all he did without being determined and even bloody-minded."

"You don't happen to know who he was closest to from that group?"

"I can't really say. He seldom mentioned specific names. Nicholls, Atkinson. But there was a piece on the TV news the other day about Linda and the football world that he seemed particularly fixated on, but again without commenting. It was a bit out of character that. Following sport was never his bag."

"One more question if I may. Does the Bard mean anything to you?"

51

"No, he wouldn't elaborate. Sorry, I don't know any more than that."

After the call, Siobhan looked at him quizzically. "What's the Bard when it's at home?"

"I wish I knew. But look at 4th December from his diary at the time he was sixteen, his age in the photo according to the date on the back of it." He passed over the open diary. "Those words are capitalised on the page for some reason whereas every other piece of information, including school exams, rugby matches, dates, the occasional party location in London, are crossed out. With the initials of his best mates next to them: LA, WA, RN. All underlined. It's as if it's the reminder he most wanted but, by the sound of it, most feared from schooldays for some reason."

"So, what next?"

He glanced at his watch. "I've looked into timing and Sally can organise seats for the 7am flight. We can get a couple of hours kip first. It looks like a trip to Cairo is in order to see the UK's esteemed FIFA candidate as soon as possible. We should be in the hall just after lunch."

CHAPTER NINE

CAIRO

Siobhan took in the crowded urban sprawl from the air. At first the city appeared akin to a Lego set of tiny sandcastle structures, many seemingly half built, in the more impoverished parts of town particularly. As the aircraft lowered, the division between prosperous luxury hotels and conditions for the vast majority were visibly more pronounced, all interspersed with minarets in huge numbers. He pointed out Tahrir Square.

"Focal point of the 2011 Revolution, now back to its everyday use as a giant transport hub by the look of it. The promise of the golden dawn just a distant memory," she added.

Siobhan had driven them to Heathrow in the Audi, the sun starting to brighten the capital, or at least the North Circular, during the journey. Their plan for a couple of hours' sleep was ruined by an irate Townsend in shouting mode just as both had dropped off. Apparently, he bellowed, the media were about to break the Tyler story despite the best efforts of Whitehall to pull rank due to the story's national security implications. Tyler's job and the manner of death were subjects of intense speculation but, fortunately, with few genuine facts circulating. Eventually Townsend calmed, reminding them to steer completely clear of media attention. There was no opportunity to ask about his health; the bungled shooting and subsequent operation obviously hadn't impaired his hands-on management style so he must be in decent shape.

The pair used the opportunity to catch up on sleep during the flight despite the business class facilities laid on for them. It also afforded the chance to wade through uploaded reams of material on the upcoming FIFA event and Linda Maddison's stellar career, as well as articles on Stewart's professional life they'd skated over earlier. Sally's fast moving organisational skills had delivered them diplomatic waiver forms as well. If forced to explain on arrival, the FIFA conference was of particular interest in the UK given its high-flying candidate and the UK authorities had requested official observer status. As the flight circled Cairo International Airport for landing, the city loomed large below. He'd enough experience of the Middle East to last a lifetime, albeit in more dangerous circumstances.

Now, the temperature hit them immediately walking across the tarmac, Siobhan wiping her brow and reaching for her shades quickly. Sally had laid on a chauffeur-driven limo with diplomatic plates; she, and presumably her back up team, were something else. After dropping their luggage off at the Four Seasons, they continued to the International Convention Centre across town. A garish banner welcoming the FIFA Congress dominated the outside of the building. FIFA didn't appear to do modest or humble, from his limited observations of them in the media.

"Welcome to our little meeting," an exceptionally tall dapper man with slicked-back hair and an accent Shay couldn't place turned to them, completed with a lime green handkerchief jutting out from his top pocket. Looking across the registration area, what seemed acres of white linen covered tables offering champagne and canapes. Shay couldn't help linking the guy's hairstyle to Kraftwerk in their heyday. He must be German. They offered their accreditation.

"Apologies my name is Christian Kruger, please ask for any way we may be of assistance," providing their badges and leading through two sets of double doors to the roped off area at the side of the vast, largely packed, double tiered blue seated auditorium.

"The session is about to begin. To what do we owe the pleasure of representatives of His Majesty's Government?" Shay revised his opinion; more of a modern-day Bond villain than a 70's electronic music pioneer.

"Oh, the usual. Trade," Siobhan replied with a smile. "We are of course optimistic for a British leader being elected to your esteemed organisation and that can only help our reputation in the world. Especially during such uncertain times politically in the UK."

Kruger hastily whispered a reply as the lights came down on all but the central stage. "I wish your candidate luck," as he took his leave. Both noticed half the room cordoned off for the world's media; presumably the golden chance to redeem the association's tarnished reputation after the endless series of scandals surrounding their actions over recent decades.

Confidently taking to the stage, the Secretary General declared the Congress open, anticipating its "supremely important decisions to be taken for the future of the world's most prized sport – loved and cherished by an estimated population of three and a half billion." Shay wondered how many PR experts it had taken to polish the rest of the speech to the point of tedium. As administrative details for the sessions were covered laboriously, Siobhan gently dug Shay's ribs and nodded across the room. An elegantly dressed woman emerged from the side of the stage to fill the last remaining place amongst the FIFA Council's mostly male line up on the podium, whilst casting broad smiles all round.

"She certainly knows how to make an entrance," Siobhan whispered as both noted the expensive cream suit which perfectly offset the shoulder length auburn hair. Shay kept his eyes on the representative; it could have been Julia Roberts on that stage. The fact she still apparently worked out for two hours a day despite retiring from the professional game years before contrasted sharply with the mostly chubby colleagues around; evidently too many canapes for some. The council was complete now. He counted 38 in total of the game's supposedly great and good.

Business dragged on with reports from each of the six international confederations in minute detail until late in the afternoon. "Do we need to be here? Really?" complained Siobhan. "Surely they'll get on with it soon," he sympathised.

"And now," the Secretary General could have read their thoughts, "it's time to meet the candidates for leadership of our esteemed body. As you know we have three Council members in the room who have offered to fulfil the position: Xue Zhou from the Chinese Association, Cesar Moya from Mexico and Linda Maddison of the English Football Association. Each will present a short film as to how they envisage the role, with your chance to speak to them this evening at our reception before voting is conducted tomorrow morning."

The twenty minute films were a combination of vain autobiography, confidently taking credit for the transformation not just of the game in their own country but also for their entire confederation, in addition to plans for an ever greater international reach in tandem with increased commercial exposure.

Absenting himself for much of the first two speeches, Shay checked for messages outside, then rushing back to his seat to the annoyance of those concentrating nearby. "Tyler's story hasn't just broken. The Middle East connection appears to be front and centre for the media. They're trying to delve into Behzadi's involvement, speculating exactly who he's working for. Thank God they don't know about Linda Maddison's connection or all the media in here may as well train their cameras on us. Staying ahead of the press is almost the one advantage we've got at the moment."

Linda began her pitch with a supremely well-polished presentation containing a series of short interviews, sound bites and overdubbed comments set amidst a glossy production about her ambitious goals for the next era for the game. Notably, she claimed credit for bringing the congress to Egypt and for expanding the game in both the Middle East and Africa. So that was her plan. Roll up the votes from those delegations to see her over the line tomorrow.

"Absolutely no point just being here, we have to find a way to speak to her," he whispered as proceedings for the day came to an end and all rose to leave. Creaking joints all around for those moving after two and a half hours. The candidates were whisked away first followed by delegates and, finally, the press.

"Do I look stupid?" Siobhan turned to him. "I kind of figured that out."

Later, after most had changed for the black tie reception, the great throng reconvened in the convention centre's giant reception area prior to the lavish banquet for the heads of national associations only. There was no expense spared; women sporting tiaras may or may not have been genuine princesses; Rolex watches aplenty adorning the arms of the men. Shay found it surprising they'd want to be seen with such adornments at all, given the controversies regarding similar items as under the table gifts a few years before. Silver trays were carried round laden with champagne, quails' eggs and caviar by immaculately turned-out staff.

"Forgot my tux," he whispered, "silly me." His dark blue suit would have to suffice.

"She's quite the centrepiece," Siobhan glanced towards the candidates dominating the middle of the room. Patience would be the key in getting anywhere near Linda, as an eager throng of delegates and media commentators, appeared to gravitate to her side, rather than towards the other candidates. Voters amongst appeared desperate for her to learn of their reassuring pledge, in return for potential patronage if elected.

After some time, realising that numbers around Linda were only slightly thinning, he managed to move near enough for a few words. Siobhan was no longer at his side. Some vague level of honesty may well prove the best option.

"Ms Maddison, we're here on behalf of the British Government. There are some urgent matters we really need to discuss with you." With the broadest campaign smile, an impeccable game face, the answer was firm. "I'm so sorry but I have rather a number of delegates I'm looking forward to meeting tonight so it will have to wait." With that, she'd moved on to the next delegate, who didn't need an invite to start his pitch.

"So, what? We kidnap her?" His irritation was apparent once he'd located Siobhan.

"What did you expect? Possibly the most famous candidate in the world for the next twenty-four hours and you want to steal voter time?" Turning to him half-mockingly, she suddenly pushed ahead towards the ground that Shay had just ceded. Reaching the front, her few whispered words didn't elicit a reply from Linda, a wry smile apart. Siobhan turned back abruptly.

"What's that all about? I hardly saw a probing interview," he muttered disconsolately a few seconds later.

Siobhan smiled. "Sometimes the male ego has to be put to one side. In fact, sometimes women have no time for anything a man can offer. You clearly haven't done your online research about

Maddison. You won't see any mention of it in interviews but in the UK, when off duty, she loves nothing more than clubbing with younger blonde women. I slipped her my room number as they're all staying in the Four Seasons, which may just entice her to take a break from campaigning at some stage tonight."

"Clever. Not a trick I could have pulled, I guess. Shameful though," with a grin.

"She has to keep it quiet. Some of the national associations probably have enough reservations about voting for a woman in the ballot. Some delegations have insinuated in public that leadership of this mob should remain a male preserve. The fact she's gay would certainly be beyond the pale. I'm going back to spruce up in case she arrives at any time. It may not even work out but it's our best chance of securing an audience."

Shay nodded, opting to hover around the reception on the off chance of further information about Maddison's ambitions coming to light. Whilst standing to one side with a glass of Dom Perignon loosely in his left hand, a Mancunian accent addressed him.

"She's good, isn't she," pointing in Linda's direction. "But then it's taken years of dedication for her to get to the verge of the summit. Who are you exactly?"

Shay took in the man's appearance, slightly plump and of apparent Asian descent. This guy stood out like a sore thumb as one of the few men not wearing a tux or at least a smart suit, instead sporting a crumpled cheap two-piece that appeared older than his approaching middle age, with matching brown polyester tie askew. The lack of formality was completed by the oversized thick, black-rimmed glasses, probably the only non-designer pair in the room. The look was completed with a sizable inch-long earring in his left ear.

"Hmm, government back home. I'm just here to accompany our delegation," Shay hesitated, regretting immediately not having an instant back story in place. The accreditation round his neck made it pointless to lie about his name, even if tempted. "And you?" he felt impelled to enquire.

"Rahman Siddique from the *Daily Investigator* website," the journalist thrust out his hand to shake. Now Shay could place the man. One of the country's leading journalists for uncovering financial scandals in both the City of London's square mile and in major sports administration. He recalled the reporter scarcely being out of the news a couple of years ago when uncovering the largest corruption story in tennis. It had resulted in six of the world's leading male and female players receiving lifetime bans. Shay fleetingly wondered if the guy was even safe to be around given the number of enemies presumably dedicated to placing this man's head on a spike. Anyway, this would be a battle for quick information. Pick up what he could then get out.

"What's the *Investigator* doing at FIFA's Congress? I know the meeting is big time but, for the first occasion in ages, the football world seems dirt free."

"Really? The rumours about Iran spreading the cash around to garner votes for Maddison haven't appeared on your radar? That's what I'm here to find out but as usual someone high up would need to have real guts to leak the story from inside, if there is any substance to it." Rahman appeared to ponder. "Who knows? May just be rubbish spread around by her rivals. It would hardly be the first time in an election."

"That's sad to hear," responded Shay. "She seems a positive role model for the top job. The first female president and, from purely selfish national interests, a strong chance to deliver hosting a World Cup in England for however many centuries. What actual evidence is there?"

Rahman smiled, "Nothing hard and fast as yet but please take my card in case the Government hears anything. It would be of more embarrassment for all concerned if she has to step down once in office rather than coming up with some fictitious reason to pull out of the election beforehand. Ill health is always a good one, if you need it."

Rahman gradually turned away before, turning one hundred and eighty degrees, he grabbed and peered at Shay's accreditation lanyard round his neck. "That name. Now that is an interesting detour for my spheres of interest. It must be twenty years ago but I don't forget a face. Not really Shay Mason, is it?"

Shay mumbled a barely audible response. "It is now," before beating a swift retreat. How absolutely stupid to engage in conversation with someone boasting that level of sporting knowledge.

There was little fresh air outside, the sunset heat a contrast to the cool of evenings on the Welsh coast. As he climbed into the orange taxi that had swung round hastily, Shay tried to control his breathing, lost in memory of broken dreams. It seldom got to him anymore but that journalist had succeeded. He was seldom approached so directly these days. Now he was wondering whether he'd completely compromised any semblance of professionalism and should pull out of the case immediately with a swift call to Townsend. It could all be over so quickly.

Shay's mind crept back. On joining the army, the first period of leave found him in the company of fellow recruits wandering along Blackpool beach, a cloudy day for the tourists. They'd convinced him to visit a fortune teller on the pier who'd spotted it straight away, delivering the announcement about his future in high-pitched, French staccato breaths. Something about everyone having a vice that they choose and the path he was currently taking. The initial reaction had been laughter from the group when recounting the conversation. After the rest of the drunken night in a succession of the city's clubs, his hangover the next morning left him unsure there had been an encounter with Madame Vichery at all. It seemed a weird and not so wonderful dream. But the encounter stuck in his memory, once earnestly deliberating with Siobhan what it all meant.

He'd lost track of the present, noting that the Cairo taxi was heading through a maze of mosques and churches packed tightly together. Colourful bazaars were still trading, busy and noisy even at that late hour.

"What route are you—?" he started as they swung at pace into a narrow alley, screeched to a halt and the back door was flung open. A giant hand appeared to reach in and lift him from the vehicle, the area seemingly deserted apart from a collection of kittens oblivious to the scene barely twenty feet away.

The driver sped off which at least increased his odds when faced by the two-person welcoming committee, extreme in height and weight, one clean shaven the other with full beard and moustache but otherwise bald. Their appearances were the least of Shay's problems; presumably a night club had lost its bouncers for the evening. Stealth over strength, the thought flashed through Shay's mind too late for a punch from the first to rain down on his shoulder. He'd had enough boxing training to keep his head out of range for initial blows at least. Winded for a second, Shay registered a kick in the groin of the first whilst the bald assailant also landed a punch, connecting with Shay's shoulder forcefully enough to bundle him to the ground. The first stumbled back to his feet as the two loomed towards Shay. The only chance was a quick roll to the side on to the injured shoulder.

Shay's speed of movement was too great even with the injury. If his job wasn't of benefit now, it never would be, as he completed the manoeuvre and jumped up in a single movement, ignoring the sharp pain. The assailants appeared for a second to share a single brain cell, caught unawares as they shifted their gaze from his previous location. If they weren't armed, he'd be fine now as he raced along the alleyway towards the apparent safety of bazaar lights at one end. He awaited the noise of following footsteps knowing these guys would hardly tread lightly, or alternatively a car swinging round. Any sign of pursuit, though none materialised. Gingerly reaching for his mobile to track his way back to the hotel once on the main road, he concluded it was too risky to hire another taxi as he couldn't be sure of avoiding a similar trap. The shoulder was in agony but the safest choice was to walk.

The sound of perfume being sprayed was apparent during his call with Siobhan. Confirmation that he was safe seemed pointless given her lack of acknowledgement he'd been in any danger so Shay chose not to regale her with the entire series of events, merely a tall story about getting lost in the walk between the Conference Centre and Four Seasons. He'd been the recipient of a warning not to tamper. But by whom and why? If they'd wanted to kill him, an attempted snap of the neck without warning, or some use of weaponry, would have afforded no chance of escape.

An hour later, after suffering Christian Kruger's smarmy frown at Shay's dishevelled state on arrival at the Four Seasons lobby, he instinctively peered round for the goons in case they were lying in wait. The coast seemed clear. Following a quick shower and concluding that no serious damage had been suffered, this time Shay provided a full update to Siobhan in her room, including reference to the journalist's disclosure. Her look of shock at the most recent events was followed by an automatic embrace before his wince suggested the gesture was not ideal.

Muffled footsteps down the corridor alerted both to the impending knock on the door.

"I guess campaigning has finished for the night," venture Shay. There was no time to leave the room so Siobhan bundled him into the ornate walk-in wardrobe containing a velvet-seated stool in front of an eight foot-wide mirror. The temptation to fall asleep was immense, particularly as lighting within was at a low setting, given the rocky ride over the past twenty-four hours. Somehow the urge was resisted. It was also strange to think events on the other side of the door constituted part of their assignment. How far was Siobhan prepared to go, exactly?

It was easy to imagine the scene. If her hunch had been right, why would Linda turn up otherwise? Their guest would be taking in the sight of his ex looking a million dollars in corset and suspenders covered only by a silk, rose coloured, thigh length kimono. He'd tried not to glance when she'd opened the door earlier. Surely Linda would never fall for something so obvious.

There was little conversation filtering from the bedroom and Shay couldn't resist risking a peak through the open few centimetres. Perched on the corner of the bed, the pair were sipping a bottle of Moet Siobhan had ordered from room service. Linda was already aggressively kissing Siobhan, her left hand climbing unsubtly under the kimono. Memory of Siobhan's long-limbed body fleetingly passed through his mind. Would it be so bad for the couple to have sex before the intended conversation? Not exactly the plan but Shay couldn't help fleetingly wondering.

"Linda," Siobhan's voice suddenly clear and assertive. "I really want to sort out my client's vote then we can…resume," standing suddenly. "Our chairman is really impressed by you, as of course am I. But he needs to know you have the South African Federation's interests at heart. And I am responsible for their PR after all."

Linda shrugged disconsolately. "You invited me up here to canvass votes? Really? I presumed we were most definitely off duty," she sighed.

"I can't believe someone as powerful as you is ever off duty." Siobhan's comment sounded too scornful and mocking or was that just Shay's reading of it given the plan. Most certainly not sycophantic.

"Okay, it's business first," Linda sounded authoritative again. "How much is your client interested in procuring for its development programmes? South Africa, you said?"

"Actually, we're also concerned about rumours regarding Iranian sponsorship of your campaign. It's still such an unstable country. What would make the Iranians pay a fortune just to see you obtain the presidency? We don't want to support a candidate who...falls away under a scandal in no time at all." It was worth the gamble from Siddique's info although Siobhan immediately regretted the threatening tone as Linda jumped up with a start, suddenly resolute, fearsome even.

"Now you listen here, as there's plainly another agenda on your mind. And your badge didn't mention South Africa, come to think of it. I've heard those rumours since I started my campaign and, do you know the truth? They're crap. FIFA is and always has been a male domain and those vested interests will do all they can to keep it that way. They preach about equality, an inclusive game for all and similar lip service, but as soon as their cosy men's club is threatened, the knives come out."

Linda reached for her Saint Laurent clutch bag. This was their best opportunity and it was slipping away fast. With a creek, the wardrobe door fell open a few inches, his presence startling Linda for a second.

"I'm not hanging round for some honeytrap, whoever you are. Forgot your bloody camera, did you?" The latter comment aimed at Shay.

It was now or never. "Okay, let's calm this down. We're sorry we had to entice you like this but it really is a matter of national security. British national security, that is. What does the Bard mean to you? I really think you should talk to us rather than the press," he asserted forcefully.

Linda's face instantly confused, then in control again. "You've got five minutes to ask what you like. British Government?" She accepted Shay's nod and continued. "Okay, let's take that at face value. We all know it's in Westminster's interest to get me the presidency. Then we may just get the big trophy of hosting the competition chucked our way one day." She perched back on the edge of the bed. "I really don't know anything about the Iranians. Why, what do you know about it?"

Shay responded first. "Well you appeared to hang out with some interesting characters who've all hit the headlines for various reasons. And one of them died only days ago at the hands of a suspected Iranian hitman."

"Stewart?" Linda's voice mellowed. "Yes I heard, but the media seemed to be speculating on his death without any facts. And what could that possibly have to do with me? We haven't been in contact for years and I hardly knew him at school. We are in rather different fields of business, if you hadn't noticed."

It was pointless asking about Tyler's travel plans given her comments; she'd only deny knowledge of that as well. Her answers made clear she was testing their knowledge. Shay suspected she'd happily hide the truth whenever it suited, so the only hope was to rattle that calm exterior. "Perhaps you shouldn't be so sure of the Government's support. We'll host the World Cup if hundreds of delegates fancy trips to Harrods and Selfridges in the years building up to it, not whether you ask them politely." Almost indiscernibly, Linda shifted position. "Perfect CV for the presidency though. Captain of England's football team for a decade, started on the political ladder at our Football Association then a minor blip paying for a girlfriend's dinner on expenses."

Linda sounded genuinely offended. "She was in the national squad and it was her birthday. That's not fair, it was a legitimate expense."

Shay ploughed on. "A masseur at best that you'd picked up perhaps, certainly not one with any talent on a football pitch. You swore you were intending to give her a job but that sounds like bullshit. But none of this prevented you from ascending to the prestigious role of FA chair at 38. Then you had a clear path to the hire echelons of FIFA. 'A breath of fresh air,' you'd been called in the press and so that incident was all hushed up, but a well-placed media scandal now could bring the whole edifice crashing down by breakfast. As well as a leak about this little rendezvous. I'll ask again. What do you know about the Bard? And can we stop playing games this time, please?"

A hefty sigh from Linda. "Performing live on camera never floated my boat if that's what you're thinking." Shay and Siobhan looked questioningly at each other, unsure as to what she was referring. They hadn't threatened a recording of the bedroom visit.

Linda continued. "I don't even remember a video being made. Stewart, the others…it was a long time ago. Probably all of us completely pissed on vodka at a party. Embarrassing but no more than that. Rory, Bill…we were all young, for god's sake. Now, enough of these fond reminiscences but if I'm not getting some light relief, I may as well grab a few hours' sleep to look my best. Despite your empty threats, tomorrow – or later today rather – no one gets in the way. Sleep tight lovebirds," as she slammed the door behind her.

Silence for a second, broken by Shay. "Sorry you didn't get your leg over."

"I'll live, though she's a fantastic kisser," Siobhan responded. "Highflyers know what they want, after all."

"I guess," he nodded. "But we never told her precisely who was in that video and she appeared to know anyway. Maybe Ms Maddison recollects exactly what the Bard is all about."

CHAPTER TEN

CAIRO

Half an hour later. At the heart of the encounter, at the heart of the sting, had been Siobhan on a bed dressed to thrill. Nursing a whiskey in the lobby, Shay toyed with the ethics of their intended sting but his mind kept floating back for a different reason. It was mere weakness and folly. That genie should be stuffed back in the bottle at the earliest opportunity. He'd lost his room key and slumped into a comfy armchair on the way to the reception desk, calling over the waiter and ordering a Talisker for a much needed nightcap.

They'd met at Lee Valley Athletics Club just north of London over a decade ago, during a rare holiday for him. Old habits dying hard, even during time away from the physical graft of the army. He must have been a picture, bent double on the ground after completing the final sprints on the running track, gradually sitting up and straightening to notice her emerging from the main building alongside a couple of his former female training buddies. Not wanting to appear overeager, he'd completed his warm down at the side, utilising a full half hour despite the pain, before slowly making his way to the changing rooms. Feeling compelled to engineer an opening somehow so, nursing a coffee, he had hung around at the building's entrance, counting on the trio returning from training together. His luck was in, so striking up a conversation with the other two as they sauntered towards the changing rooms was as natural as he could make it sound. The silent blonde hung behind slightly. None were in a rush so, after changing, they all stopped for lunch in the canteen.

The other memory from that meeting formed quite a contrast. The pain had been genuine enough but wasn't a result of an injury from sprinting. His appendix was removed early the next day following a speedy diagnosis.

A twenty-three-year old language student from Sweden, Siobhan Andersson soon proved chatty, friendly and absolutely clear from the outset that she had a "significant other," in her words, to whom she'd return home after studies at King's College in Aldwych were completed. All elicited during a phone conversation a few days later as he was convalescing. That's fine, he tried to sound casual, the friendship would be purely platonic if they met for dinner. That was the agreement and those were the terms, which lasted approximately three hours from meeting in Covent Garden. Within a week she solemnly informed Shay that she'd split from her long-term boyfriend, who was left heartbroken with only an ongoing doctoral thesis in engineering for consolation in Malmo.

Idyllic sunlight virtually blinded during their walk in Green Park one cloudless summer day, though any hope for peaceful surroundings was shattered by overexcited groups of schoolchildren weighed down with backpacks, ostensibly coached into London to experience the sights but already feasting early on their picnics out of boredom. Some were more active, chasing the otherwise laid back pigeons. That had been the first occasion on which a semblance of their joint future was mapped out. They'd move in together. Conveniently, Ade Matthews, Shay's best friend since school who'd signed up for the forces on the same day but later chose such a different direction, was renting out his flat in east London. Siobhan could stay there alone during the week whilst, recently promoted, he'd join her whenever leave or postings in London allowed. Somehow, they would make it work.

Despite the couple's time camped in the cramped bed in the East End, he later speculated if there'd been too much to occupy his time elsewhere. Promotion entailed leadership of his own platoon including a marked increase in paperwork that sometimes challenged his morale, checking facilities, approving deployment details. It seemed at times to be an admin role all day long. At the same time, his dad was taking a distinct nosedive at the pub. Shay still considered himself sufficiently duty bound to actively support reshaping the business, even the occasional shift behind the bar and delving through yet more paperwork, though the attempt to keep it afloat proved ultimately futile. Dad's drink problem was turning nasty, with Maryanne opting to keep him company in some twisted gesture of family loyalty. As if his mother's absence, so many years after her death, was the only glue uniting their unspoken sorrow.

Siobhan had completed her studies with first class honours and yearned to work for at governmental level, either back in Sweden or here at the MOD. Ultimately one rainy Sunday, two years and a day since that initial Covent Garden date, the couple lay intertwined on the bedraggled sofa. Shay recalled there was yet another Beatles album playing on Spotify, her love of English having been accelerated by memorising the group's lyrics as a child. All felt as comfortable as ever. She looked up suddenly, staring into Shay's eyes with tears soon forming in her own. His principal memory of the afternoon wasn't her speech but rather Yesterday's wistful refrain a few minutes later. He'd hated that song ever since.

She'd tried to speak, to explain; her reasoning seemed non-sensical. He'd been living the life of a singleton on leave; out half the night painting the town. So what? It wasn't out of malice and he wasn't cheating so what was the problem in a little harmless fun around the cheaper casinos of the West End? After the explosion of anger and acrimony in her direction had subsided over the coming weeks, moving on appealed. Any half-decent squaddie, let alone an officer, could bag another lay, so what did it matter? Soon concluding the relationship had been going nowhere. Even then deep down aware he was fooling himself.

Kimberly arrived later in his life. He'd come very close to quitting the forces to try his luck as a professional poker player but acknowledged the in-built recklessness that would have blown away any limited ability with cards. A few hands at semi-professional tournaments during leave convinced him of his unsuitability.

Only a year ago, during a heavily drunken night out, he'd confessed to Ade that losing the "golden haired Swede" from his life was his biggest regret. Now, having dozed in the comfy oversized armchair near the closed bar. What time was it? Early daylight crept through the immaculate windows. As he headed for his room, certain that a few hours' snatched sleep would welcome him in the oversized bed, a familiar figure was staring from the entrance.

"Sir, to what does the seating in our foyer owe the pleasure? Have you not booked a room for your stay?" Kruger's sarcasm all the more galling given his earnest expression. If Shay had found the man's supercilious attitude annoying before, that was nothing compared to the disdain growing now.

"Just testing the furniture Christian," without breaking stride before adding, on a hunch, "and you wouldn't have arranged a special welcoming committee for me in the backstreets of Cairo by any chance?" Kruger's naturally haughty bearing unravelled for a second before regaining control. "I don't know what you're suggesting Mr Mason. My role is simply to carry out the commands of the elected leadership within this esteemed institution." Beautifully non-committal, Shay noted.

But the further into the saga he was drawn, the less likely to walk away, despite the bruising. A sarin attack in London or any major city was worth the acquisition of a few light bruises, though the pain in his shoulder wasn't easing at all. A few ibuprofens had helped but this was no time to check in for X-rays. He may as well stay awake now but waited until 6.30 to make the call.

"I've been thinking Siobhan. Surely Maddison is at least bound up with Tyler due to the air tickets and hotel booking. And this damn film keeps turning up at every avenue even though we don't know the content. The other lead we had from Tyler has got to be worth pursuing though."

An eminently sleepy response. "Good morning usually works wonders at this time of day."

"Yes, yes. Whatever."

"Charmer. I told you, I've been stonewalled at every turn regarding his research but maybe we don't need anything more concrete from there. We know the gist of his work and therefore why it may be attractive to every psychotic ruler and half-baked terrorist group in the world, if not to carry out attacks then to threaten, cajole, hold to ransom. Anything the crazies want to achieve."

Crazies. She'd always thrown that word around randomly for anyone who fell within the spectrum of mildly disagreeing with her, right through to brutal dictators. The subtleties of how the term may prove offensive to some held no interest to her.

Shay interjected. "This journalist poking around the election, Siddique, delving into corruption rumours. As time is precious, I suggest you stay at the congress until it's conclusion. How about pressing Siddique to give you more information? Maybe imply in return that the government may indeed pull the rug from under Maddison without warning if it's all too damaging. Most journalists would never compromise a potential scoop against a powerful name but this guy may be attracted to influencing events for what he considers the good of the sport. His track record is kind of impressive. After all, Xue Zhou made his name as a prosecutor in Beijing exposing the worst excesses of bribery amongst the Chinese political elite and genuinely does have a stellar reputation to offer FIFA. I've done my homework."

She weighed it up. "It's a plan, I suppose. Who are you going to see in Cairo?"

"Cairo? Oh, one of us remaining here is more than enough in this city on election day. Besides, I won't hang around to give anyone the opportunity for another swipe at me. I'm heading to the US to follow up another lead. A quick message to Sally and I'll be off before breakfast. See you on some continent in the next few days."

For no particular reason, he'd pictured Sally being in her early 50s, tortoiseshell glasses and no social life. Definitely a spinster, married to the job. On this occasion, sounding impossibly efficient and alert as ever despite the early hour there, she was unable to come up with a quicker route than a short stopover in Rome in order to arrive on the east coast as speedily as possible.

Later, his mobile buzzed insistently with messages as he sipped a coffee at Leonardo da Vinci International in the transit area, settling into the plush royal blue upholstered seats. Townsend or Siobhan to call first? The latter didn't answer but within seconds messaged back "Can't speak now."

Townsend, however, answered at the first ring. "I thought you'd like to know that I've just touched down for the stopover in Rome."

"I know where you bloody well are. The Ministry does have other issues to deal with, you know. Problem is the politicos here are getting increasingly nervous. All that seems to be happening is louder speculation in the press about chemical weapons falling into the wrong hands and potential attacks on our shores. They're a load of panic merchants if you ask me. We have tabs on thousands of suspects who can't move an inch as we're on top of them. They fart and we're on top of them, excuse my language. Their psychopathic mates in IS received a drubbing and dissuaded a lot of potential converts because of their barbarism. It's a war being won every day here. Keep the lid on this and give us something positive regarding Stewart's old contacts. Siobhan knows the ropes, even if you're rusty."

What did that mean, exactly? Look to her for guidance? The line went dead just as the Air France flight to Boston was called. There was barely time to try Cairo again. Siobhan answered this time, sounding reticent, in response to his "What's up?"

"I got a bollocking from Townsend as you English call it, presume you have too. He told me about the terror threat in the UK apparently being of little concern to him."

Shay sighed. "Yup, the same. Is there anything new there?"

"Well, Linda has made the runoff for the presidency. Moya came a distant third so drops out so she and Zhou go forward to the final ballot. Linda's got a lot of ground to make up on Zhou according to the none too subtle delegates who'll freely gossip away if you corner them over coffee, but there are rumours both North and South America may rally behind her to stop Pacific Rim domination of the game. That's how they perceive it anyway, with all the money the Far East could pour into televised events." The line went quiet.

Shay dived in. "I only have a minute. I could look all this up on the net. What are you not telling me?"

"I ran into that journalist, Rahman. He must be the only attendee whose attire costs less than a grand and the only man sporting an earring. To call this place conservative is an understatement. He's easy to spot at least, so I tried to push him on the Iranian link. Apparently, he received a tip off months ago which suggested funding for Linda's campaign was arriving from unexpected sources. He started delving into it. How you get this stuff out of FIFA's headquarters in Zurich I have no idea but he's virtually accessed her schedule, which is meant to be kept completely confidential. And get this, he suspects Linda's had twelve to fourteen meetings with Iranian delegations in the past six months which is more than she's had with the US and the rest of the Asian federations put together. It stands out like a sore thumb. He's trying to find records of the meetings but most weren't minuted."

"Siobhan, top journalists don't share their stories with anyone without a reciprocal deal. What's in it for him?"

Her hesitation was palpable. "Well he said he didn't have enough to publish and bring her down without evidence. If he rushed the story out now, she could be forced to pull out and drop the biggest lawsuit in history on the *Investigator* for hinting at corruption, so he's not running it before the vote. And he also wanted the low-down on you. He's desperate for an exclusive interview; how come you're working for the state now? Reflections all these years later, you can imagine. Shay, I know you did something foolish when you were young but not that it was front page news. Do you expect a journalist investigating the sports world to leave you alone?" Then a gentler tone, "I promised to ask."

"No way am I revisiting all that," he instinctively felt his heart rate escalate. "It took years to overcome the rumours and the crap that surrounded it all; I've rebuilt my life now. You can tell him to stick his questions where the sun doesn't shine," ending the call brusquely.

As the final call for his flight was announced Shay approached the ticket check, still irate from reference to the distant past. The media leeches could shove it. He had more urgent concerns to address in America.

There was time for a quick follow-up as he boarded the aircraft. "I'm sorry, you're only doing your job. I'd chase up any lead I could as well at this stage."

Silence from Cairo, broken by Siobhan. "I know it hurts." He switched his phone to airplane mode and faced the welcome from the gleaming stewarding team on board.

CHAPTER ELEVEN

BOSTON

Jetlag was definitely starting to creep in despite catching a couple of hours on the plane. Short bursts of largely restless sleep over several nights was more than acceptable breaking in new recruits or sharpening up the more experienced ranks through the cold nights of South Wales or in the challenging openness of the Yorkshire moors. SAS physical training was a whole different ball game. You couldn't outwork the elite but, through sheer bloody-mindedness, it was possible to just hang in there. At times he'd pondered for how many more years his body could cope with such a battering just to keep pace. In addition to the exhausting accomplishment of the forty mile endurance hike with sixty pounds of weight on his back, the attitude – his attitude – had to be commanding and confident non-stop, in addition to evaluating his charges incessantly. This was a young man's game and the years were ticking by, or so his muscles screamed at times. Retirement from the role would feel like such a retreat though.

Eight hours later Shay quickly disembarked. After being whisked through diplomatic arrivals for his passport check, he waited by the luggage carousel. Adjacent to the crowd in the area, the bank of TVs above displayed NBC News, set at excessively loud volume.

"This is Conrad Mackenzie reporting live from Cairo where the results of FIFA's presidential election have just been announced. Just to recap, the vote was delayed at the request of the final two candidates for some unannounced reason at first, and soon rumours of lawsuits were the subject of whispers in all directions. It all seems to relate to this story," at which Conrad raised his iPad to view. "There are concerns about a possible sex scandal relating to Chinese candidate Xue Zhou. Remember Mr Zhou was the clear front runner after the first round of voting but he is alleged – and we can say no more than that – to be a participant an encounter with a prostitute during a canvassing trip to Rome last month. The female in question is revealed to have been an underage migrant trafficked from Kazakhstan. This story would have been problematic enough for any candidate seeking to lead such a high profile organisation but for one who consistently champions its anti-slavery campaign at the forefront of FIFA's billion pound social inclusion programme, it may well sound the death knell for Mr Zhou's political aspirations here."

CHAPTER TWELVE

CAIRO

Over 5,000 miles away, Siobhan was gripped by the race. It had been a very long slog but ultimately FIFA's Council, and in particular the Secretary General, was determined the embarrassment of the crisis should be replaced by a good news story – and fast. The familiar face of Christian Kruger was visible in handing the Secretary General the result envelope at the side of the stage before the latter bounded on and, milking the moment, made his announcement to the world.

"We now have the final votes cast in our leadership race. As you know FIFA has suffered some turbulent years due to the improper actions of former leadership; long gone former leadership. This is a new dawn for the world's football management and we are delighted that the winning candidate to lead us into an even greater, brighter future will be, by one hundred and twenty-six votes to one hundred and twenty-four, from the English football association, Ms Linda Maddison. Our first female president. A new era."

Siobhan was instantly self-conscious as many in the throng of delegates erupted in applause. Turning round, she returned Rahman's raised eyebrows with a shrug. So his bosses hadn't used the story that could have derailed Maddison's candidacy and, given the swirling rumours about Zhou, called into question the whole election. Instead, only Zhou's scandal had fallen into the lap of the world's press.

It was time for a rapid exit anyway, beating the mass of attendees to the taxis to secure a flight out tonight if possible. The beaming successful candidate was still milking applause from the now unified Congress. All of course would claim to have voted for Linda, with her smile lighting up the series of massive screens in and around the main auditorium.

So she had ridden out the potential storm after all. Siobhan felt a slight sense of pride, despite no interest in the sport, that a woman had arrived at the summit. Who knows, maybe the fighter in Linda had utilised the difficult encounter last night for the final jolt to canvass for the narrowest of wins. That and the help of the rumours from Rome.

CHAPTER THIRTEEN

BOSTON

Shay stretched out in the back of the white Lincoln Sedan as it crawled away from Logan. He could have saved Whitehall a few dollars by jumping on the T public system, but concluded they could afford it. Additionally, it allowed time to confirm the information he'd discovered with increasing incredulity on the plane about his next meeting. There'd only been a few minutes to download articles about Bryony Simmons online prior to take off. The MacBook security archive now confirmed the facts.

After forty-five minutes the bottleneck of traffic started to clear; they'd moved half a mile, tops. It was always best to decide tactics before an interview, intelligence training had dictated. What's to extract? How long would obtaining it take? Townsend's insistence on quick results wouldn't go down well in the forthcoming meeting if he rushed it. Acquisition by stealth was needed here.

The Oceanaire Bay by the harbour was unquestionably popular. It appeared the place to be seen which in itself made Shay instantly uncomfortable amidst the cream and beige mock baroque surroundings. Maybe Bryony had decided to get her money's worth in suggesting the location. She couldn't be blamed for that.

Arriving promptly at seven, she was easy to spot even before she'd cast her piercing dark brown eyes around the crowded room which housed smart Bostonian stock, mostly in couples; well-groomed men enjoying the company of expensively bedecked women.

Shay raised a hand in recognition. The photos did her justice, returning a broad smile in his direction as the maître d' led her over. Impeccably brushed long dark hair framed an angelic face with wide forehead and perfect teeth. Whatever professional hours her work required, she unmistakably had sufficient time and money to maintain a perfectly sculpted appearance was shoehorned into her schedule too. A white silk blouse and mid-length patterned turquoise skirt completed the look. Sensing he was underdressed in chinos and blue cotton shirt, in fact he must have been on the verge of breaching the dress code.

Bryony's accent, as she sat, was noticeably more California than clipped New England in comparison to those around. A speedily fired cocktail order to the Hispanic waiter, "Cape Cod," was followed by a nod towards Shay. "You should try it if vodka's your thing." After pleasantries and her description of the restaurant as being "only for the rich and famous; I'm neither," he led the conversation round to Harriet, who'd arranged the introduction at his request.

"She's cool. We met seven years ago at the funeral when my – our – dad died. Both Harriet and I always were desperate for siblings when we were growing up on different continents. I guess it wasn't helped by dad being so remote all the time so it was just me and mom for long periods when he was travelling for work." Her openness hopefully wouldn't make for a wasted journey, the waiter carefully setting down the drinks.

"That's a West Coast accent though?"

"Oh, I guess it was all part of dad's lifetime travelling and getting away from something. As you probably know, he was English then went to some conference in California when he was already married and met my mom. They became an item and he left his English family behind. Kind of cruel but romantic at the same time. Of course, I knew none of this when I was growing up. LA became home for him by the time I appeared and that's where I was raised. In my early teens they split up and dad moved on. Whether he had another woman squirrelled away at the time, I don't know, but we kind of lost touch—."

"You must have missed him. I don't exactly have the greatest relationship with my dad either."

Her cheerfulness subdued slightly. "At least yours is still alive, right? At least he didn't disappear just when you're trying to figure out how to be a teenager and need your dad more than ever for stability. And for showing you that all boys aren't…well, you know," her voice trailed off.

"Yeah, all our faults. We should eat. What's good here?" The waiter had returned, flourishing a pad and pen.

"It's called Oceanaire for a reason. The clue's in the title," she raised her eyebrows with a smile.

"Sorry, long flights recently." After they'd ordered Lump Crab and stuffed lobster with a large Chardonnay for Bryony and his beer, Shay resumed. "Are you close to Harriet now? And were you to Stewart as well?"

"Despite, maybe because of, sharing only one parent, one dead parent, we just get on like a house on fire. As for Stewart, well he's such an English gent. Always caring and protective. It's strange. I've been told that after a couple of drinks I'm the life and soul of the party and I guess I'm not exactly reserved. Yet we clicked so much. I felt like I could talk to him about anything, even dumbass boyfriends." Her eyes moist, Bryony waved a hand as if keeping tears at bay, excusing herself then heading towards the washroom to avoid creating a scene.

Pathetic, he reminded himself. We have to uncover exactly how sarin is being dumped into the western world and she's got me hooked. The seconds became minutes. Had she done a runner? But it wasn't a date. On those grounds he was safe.

"Sorry, I don't usually melt down so fast," as she resumed her seat. "Do you even know how he died? Harriet said you were leading some kind of inquest or putting to bed all the stupid rumours about his work life. That snot-nosed kid who was accused of being a murderer, then accusations Stewart was a spy of some sort…I didn't even know what he did precisely."

He continued after they'd started eating. "No idea what Stewart did for a living? That's interesting, considering you were so close. Where were you planning to go on this trip?"

"To go? I…we were just going to take in some of the sights of Boston, wander around Harvard, bookshops in Cambridge. Deep down maybe they both planned to move here on the pretext of work but really just to get his hands on good quality research funding. I wouldn't blame him for an instant. So…why was he killed?"

"Why was he really coming to America, that's the question?" responded Shay. "When his work was seemingly so interconnected with yours? It looks like Bircham is investigating the same areas and not to any great public ovation."

Bryony appeared annoyed, the trace of a scowl appearing. "Just because we're one of the largest researchers in our field in harnessing priority pesticides around the world – for the benefit of developing countries, not to wreak havoc - the press doesn't give you an inch. Dimethyl methylphosphonate and phosphorous trichloride are the basis of vital products for humanity. You should learn your facts."

Shay raised his hands. "I'm just repeating what I've read. I'm certainly no scientist and maybe my colleague should be here chatting chemistry with you instead. You're talking to a complete no hoper when it comes to the subject. Don't shoot the messenger, please."

"Shooting you was definitely not on my mind." Was that extended eye contact? The merest brush of her leg against his? Maybe he was imagining the interest, drawn in by the bubbly personality.

She continued. "Well we're on the same wavelength as I'm not a scientist either. I started work in DC working for a congresswoman, seems another lifetime ago, fresh out of college and thrown in at the deep end. My career progressed from there. After a couple of years, I joined Bircham's DC team coordinating liaison with congress."

"And now?"

"Now I head Bircham's public development fund. You do know that we've contributed $35 million to community projects in the past five years alone? Not only do our products cultivate land where otherwise whole communities would starve? We also resource education programmes, healthcare planning, build communal facilities."

"Have you ever talked business with Stewart? You make it sound like a huge coincidence," he ventured, sensing he was still being scrutinised.

"Well, considering I joined Bircham long before I met my sister, let alone her husband, and considering Stewart won a Nobel prize on the chemical side about a zillion years ago, I don't quite see how that would fit. As well as my lack of detailed knowledge of his area, the British Government of course gagged

Stewart from discussing his work. I'd also have my arse sued to the point of living on the streets if I leak anything, so absolutely not. When we spoke face to face or by phone, 'How's your day been?' was about the start and end of that particular avenue."

His attention was briefly caught by an elderly lady seemingly weighed down by a tonne of inch thick pearls round her scraggy neck pointing at their table from ten feet away and embarking on a hissy fit, aimed primarily at her overwhelmed husband clad in country club jacket and tie, as well as the maître d.

"But that's the table we always have Bernardo, you know that. Why can't the waiter grab it for us? I'm known for having my own table here."

Bryony shrugged and leaned in. "Maybe we're a bit too young for this place." Shay turned the conversation to his work, not revealing his recruitment specifically for this operation but admitting to his usual work in the army. Also their private lives; she had a "couple of friends with benefits…and don't ever intend to get hitched again." The best Shay could muster in self-description was "absolutely single."

He broke the spell momentarily. "Well the seafood's been exceptional – let's leave the table for the good citizens of Boston, probably been dining here since the day the Mayflower docked along the coast. It's the first time I've sat down to enjoy any such luxury for ages. Excuse me though, I just have to call into the office."

During the last five minutes the vibrations from the mobile had been increasingly frequent. The best option for privacy outside appeared to be along from the assorted gang of smokers hanging round near the service entrance. "Siobhan, what's up?" The view over Boston Bay was only momentarily able to maintain his recent mood of relaxation.

"The shit's really hit the fan here."

"Don't tell me Linda's blown the Presidency already. That would be a record own goal, even for FIFA."

"Funny, no not problems in Cairo. I'm to report back to the MOD for a belated briefing. The others are having theirs while I'll be in the air, despite it being the start of the weekend. Some big shakeups apparently; I checked with Townsend and he wants me in, not least as business at FIFA seemed all wrapped up.

Before I left the Congress though, I almost crawled back to Siddique and promised you'd sign up for an interview soon. For a reason though, as I prised out the *Investigator*'s research into Tyler while I was at it. Perfect timing as Siddique is being assigned that gig now he's decided to back off from Linda, for now anyway. The guy's proving a useful contact across the board. Almost as if he's tailing us."

The last comment almost passed him by, mulling over the restaurant conversation. Sounds like Stewart and his wife were very much an item still, so no traction there.

"Good stuff. You know, we may have missed a trick as we haven't looked into Harriet's finances? What if money's been heading her way? It's worth a check at least."

"I'll set the ball rolling with Sally."

"She's hyper efficient. Do you know her at Defence?"

She laughed, breaking the tension. "You're not the brightest, sometimes. There is no Sally, not one individual anyway. A whole administrative support team uses the same voice box when you call them, to maintain absolute anonymity."

"What's Sally about then?"

"Stands for Surveillance and Liaison Logistics. They stuck Yard at the end as a joke… like Scotland Yard I guess. I've gotta go."

A different voice, initially ten feet away but gradually advancing, brought him back to his present surroundings. "Must be a very exciting life you lead hanging about the smoking service doors. But you don't smoke Mr Englishman and you don't seem a big drinker. What's your recreation?"

He inclined his head for a kiss presuming he'd read the signs correctly, before Bryony sharply pulled back. Oh Christ.

"I don't sleep with someone on a first date. You should know that. Our dad was very strict teaching us morality in principle, despite his own unimpressive history, and stressed that you could never trust a guy with a scar. Let's walk.," Her expression impassive, leading him by the arm away from the restaurant.

"What about the bill?"

"Taken care of. Daddy also said if a woman doesn't pay, men just expect their wicked way."

"Was he full of fantastic advice or a string of clichés? I'm not quite sure which."

"Oh, he had his faults but it was his way of showing he cared. A bit of a chancer, our pa, loved nothing more than one-upmanship in business. In the end he took on one too many cagey deals. Some goons turned up at our home claiming he owed them his life savings. Big man, he left us to take the rap before running off."

"Did they catch him? Put pressure on your mum?"

By now, still arms linked, they had walked a fair chunk of Commercial Street; the harbour water glinted back at them from one hundred metres.

"I doubt the former but definitely the latter." Bryony took a deep breath, then sounded tentative. "They hounded us a few times so we downsized. Then left us alone, so we got on with our lives. You know, the wheeler dealer side appealed to me, hence Washington I guess," she shrugged. After a pause, "Are you sure you don't have someone waiting for you in the UK?"

Intensity was broken by a huge shaggy-haired old English sheepdog bounding towards them, its lead flailing helplessly in tow and without a walker in sight. Noticeably taking a shine to Shay, it playfully ran up for attention, Bryony laughing at the sight. A teenage boy jogged towards them, floppy hair spilling out of reversed pale blue cap, Nirvana T-shirt not enhanced by perspiration and, noted Shay, exceedingly expensive Reeboks.

"Hey, good job sir," the boy arrived out of breath, reclaiming the lead. "I'm new to dog walking and figured as Doggone knows the area so well, I could allow him some freedom down the street."

"Well, who would have thought?" Bryony started. "A city dog, used to a lead to save him from life-threatening cars and psychopathic drivers, would freak when some dumb-assed kid set him free?" The boy's eyes by now lowered, muttered sorry as he sauntered away before a "Fuck you," shouted at them from what he considered safety distance as he turned a corner.

Bryony sensed Shay's brief quandary as to whether to chase after the boy. They were inches apart now, this time no mistaking the incline of her head. The warm breath lightly tickled his ear as their lips drew close, no expert in perfume but that was Miracle by Lancôme on her neck, a reminder of Kimberly. And the scent had always driven him wild. Work could surely wait a while.

CHAPTER FOURTEEN

BOSTON

Sally had certainly not matched the grandeur of a Four Seasons this time, Shay's reservation in a cheap motel on the edge of the city being explained as all she good find at short notice. No chance, Bryony whispered in the cab, if it's on expenses we can do better. The drive to the Liberty Hotel had them entwined on the back seat. On arrival she'd insisted on making the most of the luxurious high-tech suite, adding, "Surely the British Government can afford a little champagne." Besides she'd added, it was Friday night so they had a Saturday morning to fill too.

Long after clothes were shed, Bryony was draped alongside in the king size bed, running her arm along the side of his torso, maintaining his excitement even now.

"Bryony?"

"Hmm?"

"English traditions when you're in the sack for the first time. A question each. Anything goes."

"Anything? Interesting, well ladies first. How many women have you slept with?"

"Oh, that's easy. A gentleman never tells."

"But I didn't ask for their names. Okay, the real question, second time lucky. How did you acquire this fine scar on your neck? It's incredibly sexy for some strange reason," following the mark with her tongue from top to bottom with featherlike tenderness. He inhaled sharply.

Shay hesitated. "Serving in Iraq years ago, real backs to the wall stuff. I had to rescue a whole platoon by taking on Saddam's last loyal troops – about fifty of them – single handed. You should have seen the mess I caused to their faces though."

"Stop teasing Shay," she kicked out.

"Ouch. You're like a mule, has anyone told you that before?" Another blow to his leg. "Okay, OK; the truth is perhaps slightly less dramatic. Ade and I used to bunk off school a fair bit if it got in the way of anything more fun."

"Bunk? Define 'bunk'."

"Play hooky basically. You get the gist. One day, I was fourteen or fifteen, we went up to the Marquee Club in London to see a new band starting to break through. There were all of one hundred and fifty there, late afternoon as they were small time. Someone threw a bottle which started it. Dad was livid the next day…"

"I'm not surprised, a school kid getting involved in fights at that age. I'd be terrified if my child started a fight with adults."

"Yes…except we didn't. Ade was just in the wrong place at the wrong time and the guy who got hit thought my mate had chucked it. Soon a couple of blokes turned on him so I helped get him out. I punched one of them as we ran. I was pretty fast in those days and knew they couldn't catch me but it gave Ade a chance to run the other way. Except I tripped. Unfortunately they were out of it on something and looking for trouble. Fourteen stitches, not a pretty sight at the time."

"I don't know. Imperfections aren't so bad." Again, stroking his neck tantalisingly then caressing his stubble. "And the band turned a blind eye?"

"No idea, never heard of Oasis again." One last kick before she rolled on top of him.

Afterwards, Bryony reaching to switch the lamp off, then a sharp movement as he quickly grabbed her wrist.

"What the heck?" she started.

"Sorry, I need light." He honestly couldn't recall when he had last explained it. Despite their nakedness, it seemed too vulnerable an intrusion. Only a handful had ever been trusted with the facts. Siobhan, a couple of girlfriends over the years. Ade was the only man he'd ever let into his secret. Well, not counting that therapist who'd tried to induce a sense of calmness, painstakingly rationalising the condition and even attempting to hypnotise the problem away. Eventually the man had shaken his head after their military-funded six sessions, giving up on his client as a lost cause.

Thank god she hadn't asked why. Instead, "How do you manage in the army? Surely you're in pitch blackness when you're in the field?"

"Never quite full darkness, though when the moon can't be seen I go a bit loopy. Like a werewolf."

She smiled. "What about in a trench or under a rock…I don't know. Don't you have to do lizard impressions at times when you're serving?"

"I use the torch on my watch. It remains under my sleeve so others can't see it even if I'm in a group. When sleeping, I just tuck my arm round so it's visible only to me."

A pause. "Hmm, I'll remember that if I ever want you to jump up to attention again."

Sleep for only a few hours, the light in the suite's adjacent lounge kept on, with door ajar, as a compromise. Two-thirty a.m.. Bryony lay awake with a half-smile, studying his face. Her hand lightly moving to his chest.

Shay took a deep breath knowing he had to go for it sometime. "Now my turn for question time," he ventured softly. "Whatever happened to that well-intentioned advice from your dad regarding a scar face?"

"Oh that? He was English too, remember. I assumed his advice applied only to my fellow countrymen and not his chivalrous nationality. Is that your real question?"

He dived in, changing the tone. "There were problems in Washington, all those years ago. I've read about them."

"Honey, there are always problems in DC. But you've been checking up? On me?" A deep sigh as Bryony removed her arm. "I suppose it's there in the public arena. I was set up by a couple of senators when lobbying; should have been a lot sharper to the fact not everyone views the world the same way I do. A political sting you'd call it. They suggested we chuck some money their way to oil the wheels and secure their support for Bircham over some significant legislation we were championing. Not knowing how to respond, I said nothing and intended to report it all to my boss. Before I could do so, the press got hold of it and concluded Bircham hands out bribes like confetti. But Bircham stood by me, saw I had potential and just withdrew me from the front line. My name was largely, not entirely, kept out of the media."

"You haven't mentioned the other half of the sting? The allegation that you were pushing those bribes to fund Israeli counterintelligence operating in America, so money didn't have to be accounted for in and out of the country. You also could have sued Bircham's arses off if they'd tried to fire you."

Bryony considered this. "I guess so, but fortunately that never arose. The rest was all in the imagination of some over excited journalists just out of media school, dreaming of the next Iran-Contra affair."

"Yet for all that, Bryony, you've got an incredibly low profile for a corporate publicist. It's as if Bircham is desperate to protect you and won't risk letting you out of its sight. Now why would that be? Bircham is also one of the largest funders of congressional campaigns and maybe you're too risky to have running wild."

A scowl was clearly etched. Bryony swiftly moved to the side and wrapped the hotel's complimentary gown around her. She was in the bathroom in seconds, all tenderness removed. He felt stupid. Was it worth acting like an idiot? After all, Bryony wasn't a suspect in any way. Shay slumped back on the pillows disconsolately.

CHAPTER FIFTEEN

ESSEX

Drizzle under threatening skies was falling on the edge of the Thames estuary as the small Russian trawler glided towards the centre of London. Only eleven onboard, the delivery of caviar had started its journey in the Caspian Sea before re-joining water to cross the Mediterranean. Top restaurants in the city of London were prepared to stump up payment not only for the produce itself, but also to speed paperwork in order to acquire the luxury quickly. It was best not to dwell on the fact their payments also contributed towards a senior member of customs staff, in desperate need of cash to keep an expensive mistress happy, turned a blind eye if the quantities strayed way above the amount recorded in documents.

Under cover of darkness, another part of the cargo decided it was time to disembark. As the trawler slowed, it drifted towards the bank at Shoeburyness and a short plump Iranian climbed awkwardly down the trawler's rope ladder into the moored rowing boat that was already in position for the final section of his journey. All was conducted silently, and with a brief hand raised in acknowledgement, the Russian captain bade farewell to the departing figure. He hadn't wanted to know more about the passenger and certainly hadn't asked. The additional fee couldn't do any harm.

The vessel continued towards London's bright lights with the rest of its cargo.

CHAPTER SIXTEEN

BOSTON

The shower ran loudly for ten minutes, steam crawling under the door, before Bryony returned draped in a giant black towel, wet hair immaculately combed. Shay looked across from the bed acknowledging she was still stunning without last night's make up. Once dressed, carefully keeping her back to him, Bryony stepped to the door, her hand pressed lightly against the door handle. Then, after a moment of clear hesitation, she returned to the bed, sitting next to him.

"When you contacted me, you implied this was a security matter I could help with. That it was all to do with Stewart's death. I deserve to know more."

Shay reluctantly agreed, explaining the sarin concerns regarding Tyler and adding they were completely in the dark about his motives. They may have been financial but they were drawing a blank. Official channels had stalled and were no help, not least as the Pentagon and the rest of American intelligence had yet to admit they even knew of his importance. He threw in the fact that Stewart and Bryony planning to meet could be relevant in some way.

Would she take the bait? It was worth the chance of moving the investigation on. Bryony hesitated. "Maybe I knew a little about his research but any sarin developments–. There is no way Bircham would be second best to anything Stewart's lab was producing. I just have a hunch though. Meet me at my place at six and I'll see what I can uncover." She slapped his hand in response to the grin. "Yes, maybe that too."

He'd already hypothesised Bryony's role in discussions with Siobhan. There was no way Bircham weren't coupled to Homeland Security or one of the various monitoring agencies run from DC. Not least, the new grandly titled deputy president for global expansion at Bircham was the former head of the CIA's

Middle East bureau. That was subtle. Other connections at many levels were too numerous to be coincidental. Word would get back to Bircham, hopefully via Bryony, that there needed to be some cooperation here. She texted her address in Jamaica Plain, not far from the city centre, and following a quick kiss to his cheek she was gone.

An unsettled pall hung over him. Was it despite, or because of, the intensity of the encounter? Maybe the Americans were involved, maybe they were on to Tyler too and ready to pounce, though their initial response suggested they were clueless. It was worth feeding Bryony information for a number of reasons. After all, if there was genuine affection between her and the Tylers, she'd try her best on those grounds alone.

The phone shone again. He'd ignored it for too long as he noticed Siobhan had messaged him hours ago. Also, an email from Whitehall had arrived. Only mildly feeling guilty at his unprofessionalism in failing to respond though. Sally's communications were efficient as ever with account extracts accompanied by a summary:

"Account discovered at Zento Bank in the Cayman Islands in the name of Ms Harriet Tyler. Access requirements: External fingerprint recognition activation for both deposits and withdrawals from either Stewart Tyler or Harriet Tyler.

Current funds held in account: $2,473,629.

Recent activity: Regular deposits and withdrawals of up to $150,000 since initial deposit four months ago"

Shay called in, ignoring the time difference. Ever alert, Sally seemed fine to run through it despite it being night-time there. She explained that somehow a device from or via the UK was allowing access and fund movement. London had already initiated a tail on Harriet. The opportunity would arise at some point to search the Tylers' property at Huntingdon and, in fact, Siobhan was working on a pretext to lure Harriet out of the house for a sufficient period. Equally, the race was on to uncover the source of the funds.

Siobhan picked up quickly too, sounding decidedly groggy. A quick catch up about the Tyler account first though she couldn't add much to Sally's explanation.

Shay pressed on. "So, what was that important in dragging you straight to the MOD?"

"It's a major overhaul. Atkinson has been promoted to Defence, specifically to oversee greater anti-terrorist measures after all his experience in the Home Office. He's taken on responsibilities including monitoring, surveillance…the lot. It's the new Department for Homeland Security and Defence, swallowing the former Ministry of Defence in one giant shark-sized bite. He's still officially a Secretary of State but the press is already dubbing him Britain's 'Security Tsar'. I half expected a shake-up, given how much scaremongering exists in the UK media about possible attacks.

All staff had to stand through a great rallying cry from him apparently, going on about the security of the nation being at stake in the greatest threat to freedom since the Second World War. More importantly staff were pissed that all leave is cancelled. It also shows how little we're all trusted here. Not only is everyone covered by the OSA but stemming leaks is an increased priority. MOD securing ordered all personal phones to be banned in the offices going forwards; also, no recordings of meetings anymore, though official minutes are fine if sanctioned by a minister. And, surprise surprise, it took only quarter of an hour for both the announcements, and staff reaction to the new kindergarten rules, to light up the media."

"The Prime Minister had better watch her back in that case," he mused. "She came into power claiming that the country could stay calm and prosperous, which is why cuts in national security spending appeared so benign. It appears Atkinson is throwing down the gauntlet in accusing the PM of not protecting the country."

Siobhan sighed. "Yup, the greasy pole and all that; we're expendable in comparison. Anyway, I have to get Harriet to London on some half-arsed excuse, to borrow your language. But I need some rest first. Stop calling me in the middle of the night."

Shay pondered how to spend the rest of the day. Maybe work on that Cayman connection? Lying back, he considered other angles that the authorities couldn't or wouldn't be wise to. Could it work? It was a long shot but Ade worked at International Banking Security, a little known quango to which all major banks eagerly contributed in order to assist law enforcers in tackling money laundering and worldwide banking scams. Eagerly, as in most banks wanted to be seen to be on the right side of the law. It was also the best way of avoiding scrutiny for them too, he presumed.

After showering, he noticed another text awaiting, this time a surprising message from Bryony changing the location of the meeting. He laughed aloud. The new rendezvous was no skin off his back. Had he mentioned a desire to go there? Another tick on the bucket list with a few hours to kill before trekking across town.

Despite years in the army working with some of the most genuine and big hearted colleagues, outside the forces no one came close to Ade Matthews. Throughout schooldays his friend had been fearless despite the utter certainty that, by diving into the opposing forwards' sharp boots on the rugby pitch, or standing up to smirking bullies regardless of number, size and, at times, weaponry, each encounter would not end well. Where they differed was over the principles of their actions. Soon after his fourteenth birthday, Ade began his tireless references to philosophers, whom Shay couldn't spell let alone had any inclination to read, as justification for his actions. With Ade's shock of spikey ginger hair, endless spots and frequently torn T-shirts for their weekend trips when escaping the clutch of the Sussex Downs for the lights of London, Shay understood from an early age that his friend considered he was inviting trouble to prove a point. It was often hard to fathom what that point was, exactly.

It was 7am UK time now. He thought better of reaching for his mobile and, taking the stairs for exercise, strolled to the public call boxes five yards beyond reception. It was worth a go, with the pleasant surprise that the phones were operational despite surely one hundred per cent of Americans and tourists having mobiles. This call had to be strictly off limits though.

"Hi Shay, what's up?" answered Ade. "Julie's been awake all night with Bradley so I'm trying to help her out. Being a good dad and all that."

Shay hesitated. Technically he was breaching the OSA even discussing the operation with an unauthorised individual and, unlike Bryony, not a potential lead either. Briefly setting out the request, he held back on emphasising the urgency or explaining the context.

His friend had once explained the set up at the organisation. If Ade went into the IBS offices today, or even checked any information online, the research would most likely be flagged up on the security reports of his boss. Despite the unwanted time lag, Shay would have to wait until Monday, at least, for any results.

Jogging back up the eight flights, Shay turned the corner into the corridor just in time to witness a large, dark-suited figure walking away from his suite at speed, now approaching the other end. Presuming at first it was a coincidence, this was dispelled by noticing the man's sweat by the suite door, and again inside. Shay couldn't have been downstairs for more than a few minutes. A quick check established that nothing had been taken, but the risk of having information copied was a concern despite the safety features on the MacBook asserting that decryption was impossible. Fortunately, his mobile had remained in his pocket throughout.

It was definitely time to move on, whoever these guys were. The only certainty was that someone else knew of his presence in the city. Hastily packing, checking for obvious bugs planted in his possessions, he presumed the visitor didn't have enough time for anything more elaborate. Through a combination of subway, two cabs and a swift walk across Boston Common – not overly complex but enough to throw off the undetermined follower – he arrived at the ticket machine at South Station. Purchase for a specific Amtrak destination wasn't required so he plumped for Albany near the top of the alphabetical options. The $3 ticket for his small overnight luggage seemed a small price to pay; they'd ask to see his Amtrak ticket as proof of travel but couldn't care about the destination. After quick deliberation, he opted to leave the MacBook too on the basis he'd look really bizarre lugging it to their meeting.

Shay crisscrossed streets whilst heading east at a rapid pace, then sauntered in and out of boutiques along Newbury and Boylston back near the hotel. He immediately wore a quick purchase from a small boutique, a dark jacket, over his polo shirt. However assiduous there'd proven to be in tracking him to the hotel, enlarged crowds now in the vicinity, plus the half-hearted costume change, would make it all the harder.

A Mexican sporting dyed black hair with matching moustache huddled in a doorway initially drove a hard bargain. The vendor promoted his wares by the distinctive Red Sox T-shirt stretched taut around his belly and raised an eyebrow as Shay insisted his seat must be in block 92 and ideally in row 7. A stack of tickets was soon whipped out from the man's back pocket and the ticket transaction concluded. The seat was near row 7 at least.

Swarming towards Fenway Park, the throng made for last-minute food and drink stands outside the stadium, as if there was any likelihood of lack of sustenance inside. Soon, Shay was within the confines of the stadium. The seat view was perfect to view most of the entirety of the stadium bowl. Towards the end of the second innings, Boston were two down to the Cubs but showing signs of life, before the stadium erupted as the pitcher slammed the ball out of the park. Shay tried hard to remain disinterested in the game and focus on his neighbours.

The crowd was a strange mix of Americans and tourists, local youngsters around him in particular knowledgeable about the team, the batting stats, the form of the pitchers.

"Martinez, hit it you bum," from a child no more than 8, standing to berate the batter down on his luck throughout, similar shouts from around the ground made in despair rather than anger. The embarrassed father next to him, tugging at the boy's sleeve to sit and quieten down with the promise of a coke.

Shay checked the time, five forty-five. He inched along to the empty seat specified in the text and waited patiently. A six p.m. rendezvous so a few minutes to take in more of the game, as another massive roar heralded the tied score. Yet six o'clock came and went, as did a further fifteen then thirty minutes. No Bryony and no messages received. No pickup on her number either.

By the action's end, he rubbed his neck, confused. Another thought occurred but a hurried call confirmed no word had been left at the hotel either apparently, so there was no alternative. As the crowd dispersed from the immediate area, with the exception of those heading for local bars and clubs, Shay chose speed over subtlety as he leapt down the stairs and almost bulldozed an irate

Red Sox fan out of his path to grab the one free cab in sight. During the ride he checked in again with Siobhan. Whatever developments this side of the Atlantic, their best leads still appeared to be European-based. Plus, the FIFA shenanigans.

Siobhan wide awake now. "We haven't managed to lure Harriet away. To be honest, she'd be very suspicious of any attempt to do so given the fingers she has in that lucrative bank account. A much better approach instead. One of Stewart's best friends from the lab should call together a few friends to remember him tomorrow and press Harriet into joining them. An early wake if you like, as his body won't be released for a very long time in all likelihood."

"Good plan," he responded. "But we need to push on all fronts. I know he's your boss now but somehow you must get in front of Atkinson, however informally, to discuss the school gang, their contact after, even what they know about each other now. And how the hell the Bard tallies with events, whatever it is. Atkinson must be aware of our activities anyway."

A pause at first, "I am quite capable of managing my own schedule, Shay. It's been that way without you for a very long time."

"Sorry. Used to taking charge of my recruits."

"Am I your recruit?" Silence before she moved on. "I've already spoken to Townsend given the chain of command; permission has been denied to approach Atkinson at all. The clear instructions were not to worry politicians about our investigation or our team as they have more than enough on their plates." The impersonation following elicited a smile from Shay, the Swede attempting a gruff English upper crust accent. "You can't let the cat out of the bag, don't you know."

He turned serious. "Not to alert politicians? But this was instigated from high up, according to Townsend's original briefing. Though come to think of it he didn't say who handed down the orders. How exactly do we take this forward without getting in front of the right people?"

"Beats me," Shay imagined her shrug. But I won't be sitting down with my boss for a cosy chat any time soon if I want to keep my job...and earn this massive bonus."

"I'm off, Siobhan," as the cab drew up at the smart apartment block in McBride Street, past picturesque Jamaica Plain along the way, pushing a $50 note into the driver's hand and racing up. That feeling of something amiss. He tried a few buzzers to gain entrance, a frail sounding pensioner by the name of Eloise Pickering in an adjacent apartment presuming he was the mailman and obliging. Climbing the stairs two at a time up three storeys, he was soon outside Bryony's apartment, the brilliant yellow front door slightly ajar. Half-acknowledging that someone may lurk within, Shay eased it open carefully with his foot.

From the little he knew of Bryony, it was no surprise the home was tastefully decorated in simple, expensive dark blue and white swirls on the walls throughout. Furniture would usually have been tastefully set out in what were good sized rooms for a sole tenant. Now the site displayed chaos; clothes and possessions strewn across the floor. Books intermingled with running clothes, saucepans with underwear. There was no need to explore the place with a fine toothcomb; 'cleaners' had been nothing but thorough in exploring every nook and cranny of the apartment. Most disconcertingly there was no sign of Bryony. Concluding it was best not to encounter the ransackers, a quick rummage through the piles was enough for Shay. There was clearly no point delaying there for long.

Pacing to the front door to mull over his next move, there was no point calling the authorities and he'd avoided leaving fingerprints on surfaces. A ginger cat meandered towards him from the staircase. He tried to ignore the muffled sound of a phone ringing in the bedroom. Who has a landline these days? Then again, any clue could be helpful, as he discovered the device on the floor under a pile of clothes. A female voice without introduction. "Shay, we'd very much appreciate you having a chat with us. If that isn't too much of an inconvenience."

"Who is—?" Sensing a presence Shay swung round to be confronted by a hefty guy sporting a red goatee, whose tap on the chest of his suit jacket made out the clear outline of the weapon underneath. The caller's voice continued, "Hope this fits your schedule. And we may be able to assist each other."

With a shrug, Shay decided he had nothing to lose, particularly on foreign soil. Not that a real choice existed. Unquestionably, what he did elicit as he was led to the stairs, was the distinctive stale smell from the hotel corridor and suite that he'd noted only hours before.

CHAPTER SEVENTEEN

BOSTON

It was apparent his courier was under strict instructions, placing Shay carefully on the back seat after blindfolding him. Just about managing to take in the small amount of natural light seeping through during the journey, Shay sensed sweat forming on his brow already. Fortunately enough the car soon pulled up and the engine was switched off. He was guided carefully with the blindfold in place, before his arm instinctively reached towards his unfocusing eyes as the cover was removed once inside. Why had he walked into this damn stupid assignment in the first place? The instinctive thought in trying to take in his surroundings. Kitted out like a big time corporation's head office, the reception area was all Kandinsky, Picasso and even a sizable Dali. They must be copies, surely, he concluded.

He was suddenly left alone to ponder and explore once they'd entered a minimally but tastefully decorated cream conference room. As had been the case in the lobby, there was no sign of the outside world through the windows; no clues as to location. A chair had been politely indicated for him around the eight-person table, before his minder left. He soon concluded there couldn't be much else to discover in the room or they wouldn't have left him alone but he couldn't resist nosing around. The small wooden cupboard to the side proved less than exciting, reams of paper and pens only.

After a couple of minutes, the door opened and, with a languid entrance, a short black woman with shoulder length cornrows, around mid-40s, clad in a smart crimson woollen suit, entered with a smile and the offer of a handshake as she took her seat alongside. The same accent as the phone invitation was pure southern. "May Archibald, thanks for joining me. You may have wondered how you came to arrive at our little guest house."

"Getting here was the easy bit."

"Okay, more precisely, who we are and why you're here."

"Again, I could hazard a guess. A professional bump could have been applied designed to induce concussion for a relatively short time, nothing permanent. That's if I'd said no. And you don't act like ruthless terrorists. You're CIA or one of its many offshoots, unless I'm mistaken."

"Very good Shay," she grinned and leant forward to pat his leg. He felt like an obedient puppy. "Let's just leave it at that."

"Talking of identities, you picked yourself a suitably English false name on my account, I presume. I feel honoured. Ms Archibald."

The friendliness on her face didn't fade but the voice became business-like. "We need to talk. What were you doing at Bryony Simmons' apartment and why have you spent so much time cultivating her? As such a close friend, that is."

"Simple, she's a friend of a friend and I wanted a few days' holiday in the States so we hooked up. It's what grown-ups do these days."

May feigned a yawn. "Would you like to get over yourself? We know who you are and presumably why you're here."

He shrugged. "Okay, you tell me. If that's the case, why are you asking me? Seems we're running in circles."

"This is no laughing matter. The United States is incredibly concerned that civil weaponry, as we now term non-military capability, could be used on both our citizens and yours. It seems pretty obvious that we're obligated to work together to pool information and ensure any high-level leaks are dealt with at source. Just as Stewart Tyler was dealt with by someone perceiving him as a problem." Suddenly holding her hands up in mock surrender. "Not us, not our style, in case you were wondering."

"The problem, May, is that I don't know who the hell you are and I'm not authorised to give you any classified information. Not that I have anything of interest anyway. Okay, so you know my name; you know I was trying to uncover connections between Tyler and Bryony and you probably have a far better picture of where she is than I do. In fact, she's probably in the next cell along so why don't you ask her."

May stared, then leaning in and enunciating slowly no more than six inches from his face, "These are not cells and, I can reassure you, you're not being held against your will. Just to get this right, you have no idea of her location?"

"We only met recently. She's great fun but I guess you didn't want to know that and, no, I haven't uncovered her life story. If you don't have her locked away, who changed our meet up venue to Fenway? Surely you can use Bircham to get to the bottom of all this and flush out any undue overseas pressure, if there is any? Not least from Iranians on planes."

"Shay, I'm levelling with you here. We may have had a sneak at her apartment, but without success and we have no idea where she is. We also weren't behind any location change. The chance of an afternoon pitch side at Fenway would be a fine distraction; it doesn't feel like I've had a vacation in a very long time. And as for the Iranians, let's just say some of the Republican hawks linked to Bircham are chomping at the bit to tell the world the Iranians are the bad guys again and should be nuked to kingdom come. You may just have noticed the President likes to throw in a few curveballs to keep the right-wing of his party sated with raw meat.

It took us a while to work out what happened on the plane and, well, between you and me one service wasn't communicating with another, so by the time we'd uncovered who Tyler is and that he wasn't promoting peace conferences over here, we were playing catch up. Even though Homeland Security should have been trying to pull it all together."

Shay had enough experience of inter-departmental rivalry getting in the way. Memories of many pub conversations, Ade had always been adamant the cock-up theory of organisations applies 99% of the time, rather than conspiracies between government and big business. Maybe he was right after all.

"You mean you let your one sure fire lead – an Iranian hitman – out of your hands and now you're scrapping around in the dark? You'd better find Bryony and protect her, she's—"

"Special? Keep it in your pants – or trousers as I believe you call them in England, Shay. You've been precisely no help to us and we won't embarrass you by making you collect your possessions as you leave the country. Also, don't worry, we haven't attempted to tamper with any electronic device. We know better than to try and open technology belonging to our friends in the UK. My guess is that one incorrect attempt at decryption and half of Whitehall's alarms start shrieking. So go – you'll be on a plane from Logan in two hours." He started to rise. "Just one question first. Any idea what we may have found that was unusual in Stewart Tyler's autopsy? The little matter of being poisoned apart?"

He shrugged, "Are you going to tell me more?"

"Not if you don't already know Shay, not if you don't know. Now, apologies for the blindfold that you'll have to endure leaving our building as well. Of course, this conversation never happened, I don't exist and consider yourself banned from the United States for a very lengthy spell, just to be on the safe side. It's all right, your government won't be told."

With that, May left abruptly, almost slamming the door after and leaving him to contemplate that the whole episode was spiralling out of control. The nebulous genie was proving impossible to bring into focus, let alone shove back into the bottle. Just go easy with the blindfold, he prayed.

CHAPTER EIGHTEEN

SURREY

Orange House on the outskirts of Horsham lacked the colour of its title externally; in fact, it lacked any hint of brightness to offset the dull grey peeling paint which, combined with various presents deposited on the walls from passing birds over the years, gave the appearance of a very unloved building. Even the windows no longer shone, uncleaned, seemingly, since the current use for the premises began under new ownership.

Nevertheless, a grin appeared at the corner of Shay's mouth as the taxi pulled up outside the spacious three storey building. He'd asked the warden about the name once; perhaps an orangery attempted by some local lord on his estate in previous centuries? The warden had laughed, though not as much as Shay once he'd received the explanation: a tribute to William of Orange over three centuries before. Best not to tell Dad.

His flight had landed soon after 7am at Gatwick, an hour and a half prior to the start of visiting time. One of the few kiosks open at the airport's arrival gate at that time afforded an opportunity to purchase the appropriate gift.

"This time, you have to come. Do your bit, M." Maryanne's text one of countless sent over many months since Dad had taken up residence in his local council-run nursing home. He well recalled the day she'd phoned with the news, nine months ago, that the diagnosis was clear. It would be terminal but not necessarily quick. It had been utterly predictable that their father would opt to leave his dank, one-bedroom, pad just off the town's high street in preference for round the clock care at the earliest opportunity. Hanging around at home for one moment more than needed wasn't in his nature. Cancer would finish him off so he may as well be cooked and cleaned for, long before it was impossible to take care of himself. For a short time, Shay had questioned his feeling of resentment, acknowledging that not much about the old man could be viewed positively, given the state of their relationship.

There was also the strictly selfish, though valid, question. Was the family predisposed to some form of the disease, given its frequency amongst relatives? Still, there wasn't much option if the illness was intent on invading his body too.

"Donal O'Doherty free for a visit?" he'd enquired on arrival, noting a new receptionist on the front desk. It would be a bit of a wasted journey if not. Led along the narrow corridors, the pungent whiffs of detergent and overboiled vegetables assailed his senses.

"Dad, how are you keeping?" Shay entered, folding his arms then remaining motionless at the far side of the room, taking in the sight. The patient remained still; his dad's time-honoured habit of pretending to be asleep until he's prepared a response.

"Honoured you've found time son. You've come to see your old dad, that's big of you. When were you last here? Have you even visited me stuck in this run down shack before?" The Galway accent remained entrenched despite all these years exposed so directly to pronunciation by the Brits.

"Not that long, really." Maybe months rather than weeks since the last visit, with both pretending not to recall the argument that resulted in the trip's abrupt end. "And it's not so bad here; you could have stayed at home for now but opted to rent out your place for better food, a better room, more attention. It suits you down to the ground. Orange House."

His dad winced at the name; maybe he knew. His probable final port of call for a staunch Republican. "Yes, well one day I'll need all the care they can provide, morphine and all, so at least I'm in the right place. This isn't the end of me yet," as he wagged a finger towards his son. Then, "Maryanne was here again yesterday."

"Good for her. I've been travelling. In Boston actually." The famous Irish links with the city may have elicited further questioning from his father but it didn't arise.

Silence filled the room as Shay noted dust bouncing off all surfaces in the airless space.

"Have you brought me a present? A little gift to get me through my days?"

"Clean forgot," Shay slapped his knees before reaching into his bag to produce the half litre of vintage Glenmorangie. "Good stuff these days. I may even be on a bonus this month."

"Better than the usual crap you bring, though I must say I'm grateful this time. You'll not be taking a drop yourself?"

Shay's lips pursed. He couldn't resist rising to the bait every time and, ignoring the whining tone he knew to be present in his own voice, responded, "What do you think Dad? Implying I could follow your path, drink myself into a stupor and waste away my life? When have you ever see me take a—"?

His flow was abruptly stopped by rapid footsteps outside before the flaking door was flung open with a loud bang. Within seconds his ill will was transformed into a wide beam, arms outstretched, lowering to the height of the embrace.

"Grandad. Uncle Shay." the small figure changed direction from heading to the bed and rushed at him. Behind the child, Maryanne appeared, chubby, bleached blonde hair in what was recently a perm, a face Ade had once uncharitably described as 'lived in', reeking of Marlboro.

"Look who's here Mum. You didn't tell me he was coming."

He'd unthinkingly swept Stephanie into the air with a grand gesture and was now holding the bright eyed girl suspended in front of him. Five years old, missing a front tooth already, dark hair after her father presumably. Growing so fast, even toddlerhood seemed an eternity ago. The next minutes, with Stephanie chattering incessantly, garnered his full attention. He could appreciate his niece, in stark contrast to the cool and stilted atmosphere conversing with the adults in the room.

Maryanne clucked, shaking her head. Had she always been dad's favourite? Certainly as far as he could recall. She and their father were birds of a feather after all, and with each stage of separation from the age of eighteen, he'd known instinctively he was escaping a cul de sac: The pub, home, family and relatives. All thanks to taking the leap to run far away after studying for A levels. Anything seemed preferable to the pair in front of him, sharing the oppressive environment. An intolerant father and myopic sister.

"Someone came round asking about you recently," Maryanne threw in casually, patently proud of betraying a secret and annoying her brother. Double points. "Told me to keep quiet and it was official business so I suppose you're in trouble. Off to your old haunts, is it? Or shooting up too many foreigners for the Government? Though they'd probably just hand you another medal for that," she smirked.

Stephanie, oblivious to the sarcasm, was now at the window pointing out the sights of the garden to her stuffed zebra. Shay nodded sharply towards her whilst addressing his sister. "Some phrases are best left alone. Even you should know that." It was impossible that his niece could inhabit a world of positive role models with Maryanne as her mum. Phil, her occasional boyfriend, having disappeared at the first mention of pregnancy. Still, Shay had somehow managed to escape home life, so maybe there was a route out one day.

His annoyance had almost made him forget to ask. "When? Recently?"

"How the hell am I supposed to remember? Just know I sent them packing. Don't you remember all that about not being my brother's keeper? Or did Sunday School not stick in your mind?"

Shay kept his voice to a low growl. "If you remember rightly, we would have killed for that kind of structure from him." Dad glowered from the bed in response.

Maryanne and their dad looked as if they'd sucked lemons, as he made his excuses soon after and not just in desperation to return to work. A deep breath as he hung around outside for a taxi, reflecting that whoever 'they' were, approaching Maryanne for a character reference was a pretty pointless exercise. Less of an intention to evaluate his qualities and more a sure-fire way of underlining they could get to his family too, presumably.

Soon, he was basking in the sunshine. The taxi was ten minutes late as he begun to flick through The *Investigator* he'd picked up at the airport and stowed away in his hand luggage. The Government was clearly undergoing a massive power struggle, an in-depth piece highlighting Atkinson as the coming leader, apparently prepared to embrace the battle with terrorism that the Prime Minister so visibly intended to play down. Maybe Atkinson would prove their golden boy? Little of the media appeared to back the PM when elected to the party leadership and even that narrow band had since dwindled, according to the article. During an immediate interview post-promotion, Atkinson had emphasised his uncompromising stance over what he claimed to "passionately believe, the country would welcome". Measures under consideration included a further restriction on "individuals of interest" arriving in the country and an independent external review of anti-terrorism policy, possibly led by the leading management consultancy in the US, with input from both UK and overseas public and private intelligence resources. Notably he hadn't discounted "individuals of interest" being widely interpreted to include all those from specific countries. There was additionally a threat to break off all diplomatic relations with Iran over its terrorist links, though stopping short of confirming Tyler's death was in any way connected to that country.

The additional threat to "enhance covert measures" against suspects in this country was particularly concerning. Shay had seen at first-hand what this meant on the ground. What now? Round up all teachers and nurses who attend a mosque visited by any extremist in the past twenty years and throw away the key? The rule of law invariably an early casualty of panic.

Focusing on more immediate matters, there seemed no chance of Siobhan, let alone him, getting near Atkinson at the moment. The man was too occupied lauding his own gung-ho image. On the airport newsstand, Shay's attention had caught a tabloid headline screaming "Bash Em Bill" above a superimposed image of him in combat gear rushing at the enemy, pistol in one hand and Stanley knife clutched in the other. Reminiscent of Rambo posters from decades ago; Atkinson only needed to sport a headband to enhance the image.

Another familiar face appearing in the *Investigator*'s magazine section was a four page profile of Rory Nicholls. Shay was surprised to see Rahman's name as one of the co-authors. The accompanying photo of Rory next to a political colleague was carefully stage-managed to avoid Rory appearing short for a political leader; patently the ability not to let his limited height threaten his growing popularity. Noting the politician's upright bearing and those perfect, polished teeth would instead draw the eye of voters. Shay couldn't help admiring Nicholls' highly polished Oxford shoes, which would even pass muster for a forces inspection.

The stellar career was mapped out in sections, starting with university days. Precociously obsessed with current affairs from an early age, Rory was, in effect, a political player throughout his adult life. From winning the Presidency of the Cambridge Union, through his MBA at Harvard with the help of a party scholarship then arriving firmly in the public consciousness, or at least the awareness of parliamentarians, as the Chancellor of the Exchequer's Head of Political Affairs at the unprecedented age of twenty-six. The reward was a safe seat at the following election and it was apparent to all interested observers that front bench recognition would swiftly follow.

Both politician and the political media seemed to realise simultaneously that his opportunity to grab the party's leadership had arrived following its return to opposition after the last election. The upside for him was the ability to shape direction as he saw fit, whilst impatiently waiting once again for government.

The final paragraph had particularly caught Shay's interest and provided the perfect opening. A couple of phone calls later, made from the back of the taxi, the appointment was set. He'd noted Nicholls' appearance scheduled for the following day at a special Chatham House conference on international relations convened at Westminster's Methodist Hall, over the road to Parliament. It was the perfect opportunity and, with Rahman's name on the largely glowing article, doors may just open. Rahman rang back in minutes. The opportunity of joining him for a ten minute pre-speech chat in the guise of an assistant, was confirmed for 5.30.

Rahman had even sounded enthusiastic. "You and Siobhan must have some kind of inside track for the Tyler debacle. What's the scene with the two of you anyway?" Shay managed to sound non-committal on that one.

Siobhan agreed to meet the following lunchtime before the speech for a full update. His choice, a back street greasy spoon that he'd passed regularly near Westminster during his Whitehall days. It was both out of the way and conveniently located. Staring at the fry up photo displayed on the laminated, peeling menu atop the dulled Formica table, Shay began to wonder what the hell had tempted him. For once, he was spruced up after a stopover in his north London flat for the night, Siobhan trusting her own home again at least. After all the manic pace of recent days, he'd slept like a log. Now, his concentration was focused on avoiding runny egg spilling on to his carefully ironed shirt so he passed on the fry up. Siobhan ordered what was described dubiously as a mixed cheese sandwich and, one hesitant nibble later, pushed it away, nursing only her bottle of Evian. Chicken bagel for Shay, which was just about edible.

Despite the mobile, despite the MacBook's secure messaging system, he'd been tailed in the States and any technology utilised may just be compromised. He hoped any snooping authorities would accept this meeting as a simple catch up.

Siobhan's face was a picture of incredulity by the time he'd finished relating the encounter with the Agency – or whoever the hell they were, he'd added. The only corner he'd cut in relating events was any reference to his overnight companion. There was no need for her to know though Shay would be hard pressed to explain why. He was only phoning Bryony regularly out of concern, he explained, as her number remained unresponsive.

It was time to up the search and approach Harriet possibly, they pondered, though there would be downsides too. After the trauma of dealing with her husband's death, she'd now have to confront the fact of her sister's disappearance. Besides, she probably wasn't close enough to Bryony's day to day life anyway to have a clue who'd be aware of her whereabouts across the Atlantic.

Siobhan sounded sceptical. "The grieving widow is not exactly on speaking terms with me, or probably you, at the moment."

"Because of the wake?" taking a bite.

Siobhan shook her head. "Harriet was basically badgered into attending yesterday. The poor woman said she wanted to be left alone but at least she made the effort to drive over. I arrived to check on progress of the house search about an hour after she'd left. Unfortunately—".

"Let me guess," he interrupted. "She couldn't face a crowd and headed back?"

"Oh no, she was away for much of the day all right but the message hadn't got through for a covert check only, so instead major ransacking appeared to be top priority. Clothes and possessions were strewn everywhere. Even the contents of a soup can and tuna tin were prised open; Sofas and mattresses were ripped apart. It was a bloody fiasco. According to the commander of the search team, the Department formally changed its procedure manual at Atkinson's instigation on Saturday night so new rules automatically applied. Subtlety in any terrorist-related investigation is now completely out of the window, even for a virtual non-suspect such as Harriet. They don't care who knows they've been snooping," she sighed. "It kills off any potential to gain trust, that's for sure."

"And as much as soup can be rinsed away, a lot of damage presumably remained on show," added Shay. "Let me guess – convincing the Government to accept legal liability for replacements, let alone compensation, involves completing five hundred forms in triplicate. Probably followed by deafening silence from the Department."

Siobhan took a sip, nodding, "I tried to clear up but had no chance. In fact, there was only time to take photos of the scene and even that was close run. I'll send you a set. Harriet was on the phone to Stewart's old boss within seconds of arriving back home, giving him an earful and telling him to pass on a message to the security services to get stuffed. They didn't find anything of use anyway after all that, so we have to try a different avenue."

"That reminds me—" Shay reached for his mobile and speed dialled Ade.

His friend answered quickly. "I've just completed the checks on the access points for the account in the lab. Of course, this is all unofficial and can't be attributed to me or the business."

"Ade, your secrets are safe with me. I love the way you still refer to it as a lab even though it's just another faceless tonne of computers tucked away in a vault. You know I wouldn't have asked, or begged to be precise, if this wasn't vital."

"Okay, OK, stop crawling. The prints don't match. They're a brilliant imitation but I can say with, oh, 99% accuracy, that neither Harriet nor Stewart used their own fingerprints to access funds into that account. Though the impressions of Harriet's must have been close enough to circumvent the bank's, what do you call it? Failsafe," the word delivered sarcastically, "restrictions enabling access for it all. I've got a meeting in Finsbury Park later. I'll drop the print outs through the letter box.

After thanking Ade and promising a meet up soon for a curry, Shay turned to Siobhan with a self-satisfied grin. "My hunch, our hunches, were right. Someone's trying to set Tyler and Harriet up. So, who and why?"

Siobhan shook her head. "We're missing something. Let's see what Nicholls comes up with for you tonight, though being a politician, the answer presumably is whatever he wants to give away and no more. Maybe roping in Rahman was the only way."

Shay stood to pay at the counter, soon noticing his companion remained seated and suddenly appeared glum with her arms crossed. That look, as if a fight were just around the corner once. He headed back to the table gingerly.

"If you had slept with Bryony, I wouldn't have minded," she started, eyes scanning his face keenly. Were his half-truths that transparent? "You and I, we haven't had a chance to discuss—. Maybe it's all too long ago anyway."

It seemed an appropriate time to leave, Shay not containing the slight indignation in his voice. "You're right, it's none of your business, in fact it was a different lifetime. Whatever was going on, we're different people now so let's keep it professional. At least we seem to manage that well enough." Seconds later, Siobhan stared after his hurrying form as he departed towards the impatient traffic jam starting to clog up Victoria Street.

There was just time for Shay to make another call before the next meeting, as he continued past the crowd who displayed varying levels of enthusiasm as they milled around the entrance to Westminster Cathedral, many searching for tour guides with umbrellas of different hues held aloft. He couldn't help speculating whether McDonalds next door, or the religious edifice, received more daily visitors. At regular intervals he'd attempted to call Bryony, but after the first few occasions he went straight to voicemail. It was as if all trace of her existence had been removed. Even if the Americans were right and it was best to leave the matter to their experts for investigation, there was still one obvious route left. He huddled in one corner of the cathedral square, out of earshot, for the next call.

"Harriet, I have bad news for you. Bryony seems to have disappeared." Deciding once again that certain facts were irrelevant, he recounted their dinner together, the promise to meet up the next evening, the change of venue and the ransacked apartment. He failed to relay the encounter with May. Wondering how she'd handle the call, having been thrown a second piece of bad news, Harriet surprised him with the note of steel in her voice.

After a brief pause, she started. "So far you lot failed to foresee any threat to my husband despite the high sensitivity of his research. The security services let a killer stroll off the plane and might as well have handed him a bunch of roses at the same time. And now my sister has gone missing on your watch. Excuse me for losing all faith in the fucking lot of you to keep the nation safe, but with that track record we may as well give up the ghost now," the call ending tersely. A couple of minutes later her number flashed up on the screen.

"I'm sorry Shay. I know you're not personally responsible for all this—. I just want to bury my husband and now the rest of my family are at risk. The answer to the question you presumably were about to ask is no, I have no idea of her possible whereabouts, her social life or work routine. We went to her apartment a couple of times to meet before dinner but that's it, really. She played tennis to keep fit, had a few boyfriends on the go and no intention of settling down any time soon as far as I could gather. Typical successful youngster, I guess. I wish I'd had the gumption to develop my career throughout my time with Stewart, but he insisted on having a homemaker for a wife. You probably view that as very old fashioned, I suppose."

"No hunch at all of her whereabouts?"

Her voice was pensive. "There was a lovely little old lady next door who used to feed her cat if she stayed out on the town for a night or two, or away on business. Bryony probably wouldn't have even mentioned her but the woman was returning laden with shopping bags as we arrived once, so my sister introduced us and we helped her in. Elaine, possibly?"

"Eloise? Eloise Pickering by any chance?" his ears pricking up.

"Yes, that was it. You know her? Eloise must be 85 at least, so I don't foresee a *Misery* style scenario."

Promising to keep her updated with any news, Shay added what he hardly believed. There was probably an innocent reason and she'd turn up soon, completely unaware of the fuss. That sounded more reassuring than the security services not having a clue.

Victoria Street was still bustling with office workers and visitors, interspersed with a highly visible enhanced policing operation. He hadn't remembered seeing machine guns carried by any but elite special forces in his youth but London's population was evidently getting twitchy now. During training on terror warning levels in his brief stint with intelligence, his instructor, Ms Hansen, who never offered a first name, with a clipped accent perfected at Roedean or Cheltenham College by the sound of it, explained that visibility of officers on the streets, whether armed or not, is ninety-nine per cent a response to 'public demand' for enhanced security from the media, and one per cent a tactical assessment of how best to maintain safety. All the real work, she'd added, was clandestine and sometimes veered so close to illegality as to peer over that particular wall. But not cross it. "Down and dirty," as Ms Hansen had summarised, incongruously.

A familiar figure in the distance walked towards him on approaching Parliament a few minutes later.

"Tell me what you want from the meeting and I'll lead the conversation when we're in. You know what I'm looking for in return?" Rahman patted Shay's arm in welcome outside St Stephen's entrance at the Palace of Westminster. "I'm getting you in to see Bobby, feeding you morsels about Linda's dodgy connections and I want payback for this." All delivered with a warm smile.

"Bobby?"

"You really don't know your stuff. He loves the nickname. When studying at Harvard, Teddy Kennedy gave a lecture and spotted Nicholls in the front row. "Wow," he apparently said admiringly, "you look the spitting image of Bobby." What crusading reformist politician wouldn't love the Kennedy connection?"

Shay raised his eyebrows in acknowledgement. "I'm just surprised that Nicholls doesn't choose an expansive bright modern office in Portcullis House over the road, or one of the equally shiny bureaucrat dens. He'd actually rather be based in Parliament?"

"Gone are the days when most MPs shared poky broom cupboards for offices amongst the rat-infested nineteenth-century brickwork in the Palace itself. It's all perception. He's desperate to be on hand to run into the chamber of the House of Commons at a moment's notice to hog the headlines with another barb, irrespective of the subject being debated. He's all the nearer to the action here. Rory's leadership acceptance speech was based around holding the Government to account every second of every day until he pushes them to the country for a general election. 'Never more than 60 seconds from the chamber' was a key slogan, though I'm not sure how he handles toilet breaks let alone constituency visits," grinned Rahman.

By then they were queuing. Security checks were far more comprehensive since Shay had last had cause to visit Parliament and now made airport security appear woefully understaffed in comparison. Photos and iris scans were captured. Once the pair were fully patted down and had all additional items carefully searched and scanned, in addition to the standard shoe check procedure, ten minutes had elapsed. Then, striding across Westminster Hall, footsteps clattering on the stone floor as, not for the first time, Shay admired the huge hammer beam roof.

"William Wallace, Guy Fawkes, Chares I, Sir Thomas More—," he started.

"Yup, one unlucky location for your trial. Those guys were lucky if the sentence was mere beheading. Frightening."

"Weren't we a fine example for justice through the ages?" Best not to mention that the human rights brigade would have had a field day at the heart of operations he'd encountered in battle. Stopping halfway, he explained what he was after from the meeting, Rahman appearing nonplussed.

"In return I want two thank yous. An in on whatever muck turns up from this. I know you had Linda in your sights and now a politician who, what a surprise, was best mates with her and a recently deceased scientist. I want the scoop, or at least cross checking facts with you when it can all be revealed."

"Fair enough, it'll be off the record of course. And secondly?"

"You've got a history; everyone's got a history. We sit down in a pub after the interview and you reveal your little secret from all those years ago. Again, only to be used when your real identity doesn't have to be locked away. After all, not everyone dominates the news for a day. You were famous."

Shay paused, looking into the distance, muttering "I'm honoured." Drawing a deep breath he continued. "Okay, but let's grill Nicholls first."

"Deal," replied Rahman instantly. The corridors, as with all the Palace rebuilt substantially in the nineteenth-century, was a sandy shade of limestone. Shay was impressed his companion had no trouble navigating the labyrinth of corridors, staircases and turns to arrive, a few minutes later, at the top of a tall flight of stairs away from the mass of civil servants, researchers, politicians and constituents they'd passed. Apart from a security officer, with a brief nod of recognition at Rahman, the spacious corridor with green carpet was empty. A double tap from Rahman on the one oversized wooden door in the vicinity led to rapid footsteps within, before it was opened by the familiar face.

"Everyone's favourite puppy," his party's most loyal tabloid dubbed him during the leadership contest. The description was apt. Foppish almost blond hair and an eager grin, suited but tieless, presenting an aura of boundless energy. The desk was packed with scribbled paper; presumably polishing tonight's speech prior to the switch to autocue. At the end of the process his assistants would probably have only minutes to type away before curtain up. Tonight was a significant opportunity for Nicholls to prove he'd mastered his international brief, so it was no surprise he'd be slaving over the wording.

"Good to see you again Rahman. And Shay, welcome. I'm Rory Nicholls. Rahman mentioned he'd be bringing a colleague." Warm handshakes all round.

After Rory poured from the cafetiere, Rahman and Shay were seated opposite the politician, divided by a gleaming near empty coffee table, in contrast to the chaos of the desk. A raised eyebrow from Rahman as he held up his phone elicited a curt nod from Rory and the journalist started recording.

Rory addressed Shay first with a twinkle in his eye. "Rahman, here, is in my good books after his latest piece. Not every journalist can be trusted to relate facts as they are. I've lost count of the number of times I've been stitched up by the media so it makes a pleasant change. So, how can I help?"

Rahman started assuredly. "We're thinking about a follow-up piece. So far, the content has been quite general – your aspirations for the party and country. What it doesn't include is your specialist area and how you really made your name in Westminster. Marlands, in particular, and why it's still relevant."

Rory scratched his head, his smile if anything stretching even broader. "Marlands, now that's a story and a half. You've probably become the expert by now, Siddique."

Shay had carried out his research. Marlands Construction and Development Limited. The name, abbreviated to a single word by the media, had become shorthand for public service contract fraud. Apparently, at Rory's insistence, his party wouldn't bow down to the largest construction firm in the country, even though it was backed by the two richest men in Thailand who were also distant cousins of the king. In his stint as Business Secretary, Nicholls had been tenacious in chasing the pair through the courts for one hundred and fifty million dollars in damages to compensate victims and the affected city after the horrific events, in addition to the pair having to stump up their unpaid tax bill. Millions were paid in bribes and there was clear evidence of shoddy workmanship by the company.

Poor quality steel resulted in a crumbling building that killed a family of eight in Leeds. The award-winning block, housing 900, had to be entirely rebuilt. Just as the media stopped congratulating Rory and began to panic that 90,000 direct and indirect construction jobs could be wiped out in an instant should Marlands collapse under the weight of the pay-outs, the two billionaires grudgingly agreed to repay the sums in full personally. They added a personal guarantee for the company to continue trading for at least the next decade. Even the other side's media supporters had to grudgingly admit they were impressed. Whether the very real threat of extradition home convinced the pair to pay up was never confirmed, but a bilateral arrangement could have resulted in each serving fifty years in Thailand's most notorious jail. Whatever pressure behind the scenes, it clearly worked.

Shay decided to pitch in. "Mr Nicholls, could I ask you about Bill Atkinson. Not only does he appear on the other side of the despatch box, but I understand the two of you were close school friends. Does the name 'Bard' ring a bell?"

Rory shrugged, maintaining his relaxed demeanour. "We were in the same year at Ridgeway, but I'd hardly say we were friends."

"I'm sorry, I thought you were particularly close to him?"

"And I'm sorry, but I can't shed any more light on non-existent friendships, so I don't know who's spreading inaccurate rumours." Rory looked away, appearing to stare at the black ornate railings surrounding one of the Palace's multitude of tiny courtyards, before returning his gaze far less amicably. "This is off the record. Right? I won't be quoted?" Rahman reached forward, switching off the mobile.

"William Atkinson, or rather William St John Atkinson," the politician started, exaggerating the middle name. "St John doesn't play well with the Great British public anymore. In fact, his great uncle, Lord St John Grangeforth, was an ageing turncoat and helped the Nazis with propaganda during the war. Bill's kept that under wraps well.

We were in the same year, so I knew him from a distance. Born to money instead of us scholarship boys, but that's no sin. I can't say we socialised together. We all mucked in at Ridgeway and I won't pretend I didn't enjoy my time there. Despite the cliché, I learnt a lot about self-sufficiency, standing up for yourself to avoid being pushed around. But also teamwork. Relying on others to share the burden when you're really up against it. In effect, knowing who you can depend on."

Nicholls paused before continuing. "Let's start with what you know about him. His financial track record, for instance? Right up your street, Siddique."

Rahman reeled off the known facts, "Earned substantial money in the city working for Saunders & Forth's investment bank whilst spending his spare time doing charitable good works.

Soup kitchens at weekends, Crisis on Christmas Day, holidays spent in refugee camps feeding the poor. 'Capitalism with a heart,' he almost invented the phrase after the approach gripped his party's conference a few years ago. 'A generally good egg,' as they'd probably say in the House of Lords. A social conscience at least."

"Is that it?" Rory stared at Rahman, leaning forward eagerly with arms spread on the table in front. "You think that's the whole story?"

Rahman scratched his ear and shrugged. "Well also that he gave away his last dividend, a cool five million pounds, to charity. He has a reputation as an all-rounder, strong on law and order. In fact, he could take his pick of any top job now he's got the PM by the balls. So to speak." All smiled.

"Well, politically you're spot on. His latest not so subtle cry from the front bench this afternoon shows he has the dagger poised, by implying completely insufficient resources went into homeland security. A predicament which will take months to overhaul. Any attack now, god forbid, will play right into his hands as far as the leadership is concerned."

"That's politics, I guess. It doesn't make him a bad man," ventured Shay.

Rory's eyes appeared to bore into Shay. "There's no more to Bill's business reputation at Saunders? He has kept a lid on it well. I thought you were more thorough than that, Siddique. Around a decade ago when he was on the verge of grabbing that cosy family Cheshire parliamentary seat, poor Bill and whichever girlfriend he was screwing – Theresa was away with the kids – received an unexpected visitor. There are gates around his compound, sorry, house in Hampstead so it was probably kept from the neighbours, but nevertheless the Serious Fraud Office conducted a bust in the very early hours. He was grilled for days; told he was free to walk out at any time but if so they'd arrest him on suspicion of planning a runner overseas."

"Go on," a quiet voice, Rahman's interest was aroused. Shay speculated on a hint of professional embarrassment from the journalist at not having picked up the story from other sources.

Nicholls continued, "All to do with a dodgy deal involving insider dealing. South African diamonds spattered blood all the way back down the chain," Rory walked his fingers across the table. Rahman smiled in recognition at Nicholls' well-known love of excessive gesticulation during speeches.

"Of course, he chose to stay and talk despite his lawyer trying to play hardball in insisting they'd never have the guts to charge him. However, the lawyer didn't have his master's political instincts. After a few weeks of haggling, and Bill squirming when the SFO leaked who else was in the house at the time to Theresa, a shabby deal was struck. To no one's credit. The organisation had overspent by ten million that financial year and its chief exec knew his job was on the line if they went cap in hand to the exchequer. So a payment of ten million came from Bill, as if by magic." Again, the accompanying hand gestures.

"Apparently the truce was called a 'voluntary submission,' but you won't find any reference in legislation. Everyone benefits except law-abiding citizens. And the beauty is, the PM has refused to let the matter see the light of day on grounds of national security, would you believe it? Permanent confidentiality apparently, which can't be overturned by any future administration. How's that for open government and trustworthiness?"

Rahman was, for once, open-mouthed, "Thank you seems an understatement. It's just a shame I can't use it." Silence all round broken by Nicholls, "Maybe everything will change one day."

"Mr Nicholls, there appears to be a link from you to Stewart Tyler from schooldays as well?" Shay gambled.

"Stewart? Really upsetting to hear what happened, if indeed the authorities have got to the bottom of it. The seeds of his downfall were written in the stars all those years ago. Despite the calm exterior and scientific rigour, he always had a reckless streak. It may even explain his desperation."

"Sorry?" responded Shay. "I don't quite under—?"

"His...problem. I'd heard about it on the grapevine. Secrets he managed to keep hidden from the authorities whilst working for the government in recent years, if my sources are correct. Or more likely no one wanted to look too closely given the invaluable work the media's hinting about since his death."

Nicholls removed the cups as he continued. "Hardly a social deviant, our Mr Tyler. I hear it got out of hand, just grew drastically and Bill may have been recommending unscrupulous doctors to help him out. Stewart would have been left without a pot to piss in without his job. Harriet, the house, their future; it could all go down the pan if he didn't get a grip."

"What problem exactly?" Rahman asked as his mobile's vibrations began. It was probably his boss, desperate to get advance copy of Nicholls' speech.

"I've probably said too much. I just prayed he'd come through his difficult times with the help and love of his friends. Now gentlemen, you'll have to excuse me but I have to tidy up the speech for tonight."

Rahman's big chance to keep the office happy. "Any advance notice?"

"Well of course, I'll be making clear why the government's anti-terror policies can't possibly keep the country safe after their intense frugality. I'll save the details for later. And Rahman, you know what I'm going to say to you?" a grin spreading.

"I know. Your constant advice to lose the earring." Both smiled.

A minute later, Shay and Rahman retraced their steps in silence along the well-trodden corridors, until emerging into the relative cool of evening alongside Parliament Square with Westminster Abbey opposite.

"I'll be off, thanks for setting it up," Shay started quickly, offering a handshake.

Rahman stared at the outstretched hand, vigorously shaking his head. "No, you bloody don't. We have a deal by the way. Come on, two halves of orange juice at the Red Lion, home of all local Westminster gossip."

Substantial traffic signalled they were still in the midst of rush hour's grip, vehicles crawling around at a few miles an hour, as if the machinery was absorbing the architectural grandeur of the area. They passed visitors to the area of all looks, ages and sizes clicking away on phones, a fair proportion of selfie sticks held at arm's length to the detriment of civil servants trying to rush by unobtrusively. Shay couldn't resist a smile at the sight of the portly male MP tucked on the inside of the pavement, red-faced and seemingly shouting at his mobile, as he recalled one of Westminster's more salacious stories of recent years.

Shay shrugged as they walked off, returning his attention to his companion. "What's with the earring comment?"

"Nicholls always says it looks unprofessional. That's the intention, which I'm sure he knows. Certainly, on the way up to working on big scoops I absolutely didn't want to be taken seriously by the higher echelons. It proved a successful tactic. And by the way, what's this Bard reference? Shakespearean quote or something?"

Shay had noted that Nicholls never attempted to answer that question. "Yes probably," he responded. "I'll check it out later." For some reason it felt right to keep that aspect hidden away from the journalist. The meaning was opaque anyway.

An angry car horn sounded as traffic kept inching around Parliament Square, followed by another. The pair glanced up as the traffic came to a standstill.

"What a place to break down." Rahman nodded his head at the black cab that others were starting to navigate around. Rahman just about caught the bag his companion instantly threw at him before Shay bolted into the middle of the four-lane thoroughfare towards the vehicle as a figure sprang from the driver's seat gesticulating frantically at the cars around but seemingly tongue-tied. Soon arriving at the taxi, one glance into the back seat from Shay was enough to take in the black briefcase. Procedure from deployments was kicking in with a rush of adrenaline. He shouted at full volume to the drivers behind, both voice and body language as authoritative as possible, "Evacuate the area now."

Instantly orders were obeyed, as vehicles were left abandoned, some with shrieks of terror from motorists and their passengers. Attacks in the past few years around the area remained high in the public consciousness. By contrast, others were responding firmly and calmly. From the Porsche behind, a well-dressed woman in her 30s calmly hoisted a toddler into her arms from the back seat and, leading a stunned small boy alongside by the hand with soothing words, moved away. A couple of armed police in body armour rushed towards the scene from the opposite side of Whitehall. Shooters would fire first and ask questions later, if in any doubt, so Shay was fully aware his next words had to be perfect, every syllable clear. Importantly, he'd have to beat them to the first utterance. Raising his hands in the air, he recognised the Sig 516s trained on him. "Intelligence, twelve-ten. Vehicle under suspicion, evacuate the area."

Shay had no idea if the phraseology, let alone the code, was entirely up to date. He could only pray he'd made it apparent that he was from a security background. One of the good guys. Sensing his body clamming up now, holding his breath, the thought flashing through his head, not for the first time, whether a fatal bullet would hurt or all be over in the blink of an eye.

He exhaled deeply as that threat to his life was curtailed, one of the policemen joining him in shouting to clear the area, whilst the other radioed in an instruction that, within seconds, led to loudspeakers out of sight at ear splitting volume ordering all to evacuate the vicinity in an automatic message. This drowned out the similar exhortations from both Shay and the first policeman, now joined by other colleagues, for the few drivers and pedestrians still around to get their skates on. There was no point staying near the abandoned taxi if it was going to blow so he ran towards the comparative safety of Westminster tube station. Memories of wartime footage with stations used as bomb shelters all those years ago. This must be the safest place for now. The Prime Minister would not be sharing her bunker with the likes of him.

All at once, there was some kind of commotion on the pavement as Rahman appeared to be remonstrating with a small crowd. Shay rushed towards the scene concerned about a further prong to the attack but quickly realising the problem wasn't a second wave, but rather tourists and bystanders intent on filming the scene to replay to transfixed folks back home or, better still, flog to the media for a packet. Arriving next to the journalist, he roughly pushed an elderly man who had kept his mobile trained on the scene. As the pensioner started to fall, other bystanders in the immediate vicinity clearly got the message and scattered. Lurching forward, Shay tried to grab the collapsing figure, but not in time to stop the man's fall.

"Police. Lie on the ground now or we shoot." This was clearly aimed at Shay. There was no time to explain, as, within an instant he lay prostrate with a Sig pointed at his head. He could make out three stretching over him now, his head then wrenched sharply to the left. Yanked to his feet then aggressively patted down, handcuffs were clamped tightly, binding his wrists despite his protestations. The pavements around were eerily quiet now, apart from the repeated tannoy warnings and occasional shouts from the forces. Shay started to explain.

"Shut it," the command loud and clear in his ear. They wouldn't shoot now so he may as well obey. At least he wasn't fighting for his life.

"Area evacuated, bomb squad can enter. Suspect is detained," the tallest of the trio confirmed to his radio. Pulled sharply to his feet, Shay was bundled forcefully into a waiting van fifty yards away by the Embankment, which sped off at breakneck speed across Westminster Bridge. The back of the van was dark enough anyway but immediately a hood was pulled roughly over his head for pitch blackness to engulf him. His legs were kicked from underneath and however many others were riding in the back made clear he remain face down and not utter a word. He counted four voices in all. Their orders were urgent, no nonsense, and certainly not inviting dissent. He couldn't have trained his conscripts better.

"I'm going to—," he started out loud before a sharp kick to his ribs. Then, trying to control his breathing, Shay desperately dived into the mental techniques imprinted all those years ago. The methods hadn't worked then. He had no choice but to keep the panic at bay by any means. Focusing on clearing his mind, not sucking up the limited oxygen. He'd been advised to picture a relaxing desert island once. No chance of it working now either.

Maybe there was another way, namely mapping out his journey. The encyclopaedic knowledge of central London's layout could just work for a short time. They'd headed over Westminster Bridge presumably to avoid the mayhem around, circling then heading east along the south side of the Embankment, crossing back to the north of the Thames at, he calculated, Vauxhall Bridge, before they began a near four mile journey north-west through the capital at breakneck speed. Surely it couldn't be Paddington? Terrorists since time immemorial were brought to Paddington Green but hadn't it closed?

Despite his best intentions, the relaxation method wasn't working as he fought the urge to scream through the hood, sweat pouring down his brow. Why would they do this to him? His immediate, non-sensical thought had been why they hadn't checked his medical record before the ride?

Shay was on the verge of passing out.

CHAPTER NINETEEN

WEST LONDON

Manhandled unceremoniously, Shay landed on another hard floor, his hands still bound. Thank god they were removing the hood at least, into a room with minimal light. He took in a great lungful of air. No furniture in the room. Was this some kind of very basic holding cell? For a long time, all was uneasily quiet; at least another hour he'd guess. Why were they not peppering him with questions? Or ensuring a few subtle kicks and punches to the appropriate regions, without inducing bruising, if they were so sure of his involvement? By now, it was proving relatively easy to slow his breathing and calm his thoughts. On safe ground, literally. As he had nothing to hide, overanalysing the situation wouldn't benefit. The aim was to remain patient.

Time stretched uncomfortably, hours must have passed and he'd drifted off. Eventually the iron door was flung open, footsteps and furniture scraping on the stone flooring. His body was hoisted, raised to a cold metal seat after the cuffs were removed. The room was now bathed in light as the brightness of the solitary bulb threw his vision at first. Two figures left the room.

Terence Townsend was sitting opposite, glancing at him, tapping incessantly on the plastic table between them that wouldn't last a gust of wind.

"Mason. What have you done, you idiot?" the words suddenly pouring out.

"You know as well as I do what's happened. Some kind of bomb in the back of a taxi and I helped clear the area. And I resent…" Townsend paused for him to continue. "You don't think I was involved in some way?"

"In what? Terrifying the entire bloody population? We're starting to piece the whole episode together and it looks as if you've overreacted, old boy. Old trick that the Provos used in

Northern Ireland in the 70s but unreported largely in those days thanks to more obedient and helpful media then. A terrorist or sympathiser, or even just a hoaxer, gets in the back of a taxi, tells the cabbie they're leaving a bomb primed to explode if the terrified driver doesn't end up at some specific high-profile location. Driver's been told the cab's wired up and will be taken down with it if the destination isn't reached, or if the cabbie chooses to do a runner before arriving.

Well in this case the driver was told it was sarin and you played the fall guy. Terrified the whole city instead of letting security in the area deal with it a bit more surreptitiously, on top of fracturing the skull of an OAP tourist who just happens to be the brother of the Pakistani Ambassador to London. Now, Lieutenant, would you call that a good day's work?"

Remaining silent whilst trying to process events, Shay began working out how, if at all, he could have reacted differently.

"So," continued Townsend haughtily. "Has the cat got your tongue? At least the initial clips on YouTube by Joe Public don't appear to include your ugly mug so maybe we can spin our way out of it. A false alarm and all that. What I do want, though, is the full story of what you've uncovered regarding Tyler and where you go from here, if indeed we decide to keep you. And that's a very big if at present."

He felt himself rise to the bait. "Well, the biggest operation you should be running is where to find Bryony Simmons. Siobhan knows all about her so I assumed you'd be on the case too but it seems your contacts across the pond have completely failed to locate her. I know Tyler's important but it seems obvious she's linked in some way too."

"What, to the four amigos from schooldays. Really? Or has it all got a bit personal for you, Mason?"

"That's not the point," he responded snappily before continuing with as full an explanation as he could muster. It was becoming a habit not to include all details. Townsend nodded sagely as Shay spoke, before the pair were interrupted by a double knock on the door.

Siobhan appeared in a light grey business suit, slightly breathless. "I just followed procedure. Accompanied the briefcase to the Home Office toxicology lab where it's safely quarantined and, as suspected, initial reports suggest it isn't dangerous. I was able to concentrate on the documentation within it, in Farsi—"

Townsend couldn't help interrupting, "I told you those language skills are never wasted."

She ignored the compliment. "As instructed, no one else has access to them for now. The container may have been harmless but the contents reveal what appear to be credible threats about possible attacks. It's virtually official propaganda, stating that the Iranian Government is tired of being pushed around by the west and having its every action since Barjam questioned."

"Barjam?" Shay queried.

"It's the Farsi acronym for the Iranian nuclear deal," continued Siobhan. "The Iranians consider they bent over backwards to accede to the concerns of the west and now they're being royally shafted, even though guaranteeing behind the scenes they won't be developing any nuclear weapon capability. It looks like some dissident group within the regime want to stick it to the west after backtracking from Barjam, or at least regain the west's respect. Names mentioned in the document fit with Foreign Office analysis of the key players of the Tehran regime. The documents threaten release of sarin on our transport systems, just like the Tokyo mayhem over twenty years ago.

It also makes clear they have the precise formula and lab facilities to make the product in vast quantities. This is all initial analysis and supposition from the sources I could access, but even so—".

Townsend stroked his chin. "Well, you see, we're correct. There's no immediate sarin risk to the public and we can play the whole episode down in public. Anyone could post vague threats but if they haven't backed it up with large quantities of their chosen weapon, then there's no threat to the public worth spooking them. We'll just up security in public places as watchdogs. Extra surveillance on the hardliners over here."

Shay shook his head slowly, staring at Siobhan. "Surely you can't go along with this? It's complete madness to play down such a danger. Transport network users should know exactly what threat they're facing when it's so direct and detailed."

Townsend rose to his feet, looking uncomfortable in his attempted formality. "Mason you're a subordinate and so far, not a particularly obedient or successful one. I wouldn't have known you've had to take orders for so many years. In fact, not only have you failed to deliver chapter and verse on Tyler's motives, but you seriously suggest the public should be terrified solely due to your panic attack when faced with a startled taxi driver."

Still standing, Siobhan interjected, "By the way, the passenger's been identified as an Abdul Hamouni. We're still waiting for full details on him."

Townsend paused. "Hmm, the name rings a bell. Decidedly a lowlife character who wreaked havoc against the moderate Iranian community abroad with Behzadi a few years ago, but firmly staying under the radar recently. Hamouni's shifty, squat and overweight, couldn't outrun a donkey." Shay resisted making the obvious comparison, still unsure if he was still under fire or back in the fold.

"Sir, if I may," Siobhan ventured quietly. "There's another factor that may be relevant, apart from the fact I trust Shay with my life." Good timing for the reference. "There were other items in the case," lifting the six by four-inch photos gingerly which showed senior political figures from the two major parties. Wording was scrawled at the top of each in a white marker pen, also in Farsi, saying 'Traitors to international peace'.

The Major's booming voice in response. "I made your operational goal quite clear originally and all this shouldn't sidetrack you," before approaching the door then sharply turning. "You seem very mixed up in this Mason, and for the wrong reasons. You'd better prove trustworthy, however much she vouches for you," a nod towards Siobhan. "Otherwise, you're out and not just foregoing the benefits we discussed but I shall personally ensure you never work in any military role again," before stomping out and slamming the door.

Shay, at least relieved the encounter was over, couldn't resist the question. "Do you think I'm free to go?"

"Only one way to find out," as she held open the door for him.

The few station staff on duty remained preoccupied as they left with hardly a glance in their direction, let alone any official release to sign. They stepped into an alleyway, then towards the evening surrounds of Paddington.

"I thought Paddington nick had been closed?" he queried.

"Officially it was, but unofficially a section is kept open for interviews the government wants to keep strictly off record."

Siobhan sensed he needed a friendly face after the drama of recent hours, accompanying him towards Hyde Park. Walking in silence for a while, the mood was broken by the latest bundle of the Standard thrown from a van towards a vendor.

The pair hardly had to wait, as the seasoned distributor opened the package and passed the newspaper to the couple. Shay's face sagged as the headline screamed out: 'Mass murder attempt on Parliament.' They scanned the lead story together, as Siobhan read aloud.

"'According to sources, London today faced attack at the hands of terrorists linked to the Middle East. A suspected strike on the capital was only averted when security forces intercepted a vehicle aimed to strike at the heart of Parliament. Armed police were quickly at the scene and investigations are proceeding at full speed.

There is a fear Iranian extremists linked to the regime in Tehran are behind the incident. The Prime Minister will issue a statement tonight to clarify the threat that London is currently facing. The Iranian Government is being monitored at every turn by the United States regarding its finances, military capability and diplomatic relations with the west, to find any hint of intentions to disrupt our democracies.' Wow that's quick," she added.

Already, less than three hours after the event and the press were filing the story, if not in full then with selected snippets surrounded by a tonne of speculation. The editorial was no less vague in calling on the Government to toughen up its act on all suspected threats to the capital's safety with heavy hints about Arab countries and their neighbours.

"Right place to be having this conversation," he looked up, noting their surroundings. Edgware Road was still the heart of Middle Eastern shoppers and residents in London, their restaurants lining both sides of the wide thoroughfare.

"We seem to be scratching the surface," Siobhan continued. "There is one way the Iranians could get anything through they wanted. Money, chemicals, instructions to sleepers, all well away from diplomatic channels. A route that's likely to be absolutely confidential if those involved want to keep it that way. And linked directly to Tyler."

His eyes lit up. "FIFA. Linda Maddison to be exact. Now head of one of the world's largest and richest NGOs with a more enviable corruption record than the mob. And I've got an idea how we can get to the bottom of this." Then, blushing, as if the thought had just occurred, "I just wanted to say that…before at the café—".

"No, leave it. It really wasn't my place to say that, was it?" Hard to work out if she was genuine or just practical; certainly, no sign of resentment in her eyes.

Shay nodded slowly before they continued their stroll, working out how best to uncover if Linda Maddison was embroiled in – as the Standard's editorial had melodramatically described it – the immense threat to the free world. Just to cover all the bases, the newspaper had a centre section summarising various methods terrorists had used to sow destruction around the world since 1945. Maybe they had a similar pull-out prepared for insertion regardless of the identity of assailants. An 'insert enemy here' special.

"Listen, we have to tap sources all the harder," he continued. "Give Maddison one more go, now her role appears to be coming into focus. Somehow, we need to make certain she agrees to a meeting, even if you threaten pushing ahead with blackmail and she wants to gain the upper hand by planning some kind of counter-sting. Her motive for meeting really doesn't matter. We need to make clear in private that she's suspected of far worse than handing out a few quid to greedy sport administrators. That should make her sit up and take notice."

Siobhan nodded, "Well I'm the one who's supposed to undertake most of the desk work but I'm sure Townsend will go with that. What are you concentrating on? Boss," the last syllable stretched dramatically.

Shay didn't rise to the bait. "Well, you haven't exactly had success getting to Atkinson, so I'll use my contacts to see if I have any joy."

"Good luck with that, Shay," Siobhan stopped and laughed. "Talking of bosses, ultimately Atkinson is yours given he's

Secretary of State, if you haven't already noticed. Either he knows that and will tell you where to go if you get near him—".

He stepped in, "Or Townsend's operating so far out of control that Atkinson will be livid and probably send us both to the gallows. By the way, you have no idea how envious I'll be of your jet setting trip to visit Maddison. I'm taking one for the team here."

"Why's that? A stuffy hotel room followed by a meeting in the gilt-edged headquarters of FIFA in Zurich is hardly the trip of a lifetime for someone who hates football."

"You really don't follow the sports world, do you? Linda Maddison is probably on a plane as we speak for a short hop across Europe. One of the few guarantees is that she'll attend the Champions League final in Milan. The FIFA President certainly has to be on parade, despite the storm of abuse she's received on social media following the allegations in securing the top job. Besides there's talk of some high-level meeting there first for the FIFA bigwigs. Ask Sally to sort you a ticket – she'll probably arrange a VIP pass for you in seconds."

"You're missing out on a football match of that importance?"

He shrugged before continuing. "And by the way, the more I think about it, I'm convinced Christian Kruger was behind the beating I received in the Cairo alleyways. Give him one back for me if you get a shot, or better still, catch him with his hand in the till and let Rahman eat him alive in the media," he smirked. Later, Shay was crossing London alone by tube to Finsbury Park before embarking on the twenty minute walk to his flat. Siobhan headed for the tube as well, resisting the walk back to her flat. Staying in a friend's spare room on the other side of town tonight, she'd maintained.

Shay started from the north London station, the route winding past pizza restaurants being locked by exhausted, dishevelled staff; Turkish grocers still trading and Cypriot cafes with pastry aromas emanating from within. Then, in the familiar surroundings of the flat, puzzling how to get to Atkinson without giving the game away. Desperately needed a breakthrough.

CHAPTER TWENTY

NORTH LONDON

The doorbell was pressed impatiently the next morning, to his extreme annoyance. He must have taken more of a hit being tossed around the pavement, van and station by the heavy hand of the law than he'd realised at the time, in particular as if the shoulder injured in Cairo was once again the target. The strongest painkillers he'd laid his hands on in the flat afforded some respite at least.

Rahman was leaning on the door frame. "Mason I've tried to call all night and early morning. Already performed Fajr – first prayers – and crossed London whilst you put your feet up." Holding up a paper bag, Rahman continued. "Pastries to wake you up. You fix the coffee."

Shay rubbed his eyes as he stood aside for his guest. What time was it anyway? It certainly seemed early.

"Sorry Rahman. Let's just say I've been otherwise occupied. Anyway, I didn't have you down as a practising believer."

"Think you can tell by how I look? Interesting concept.

Besides, you think trying to save Parliament from another Guy Fawkes, then being hauled away by the authorities, can stay under the radar? I was there you know, just had no clue what was happening or what you were thinking. This may astound you Shay, but being caught up in counterterrorism operations is not why I chose my profession. Give me a FTSE top ten company director with a fetish for high class hookers any time. The whole story please, if we're in this together."

Shay averted his gaze. The journalist had proven incredibly helpful with the tip off at FIFA, then again with the Nicholls interview. It was clear they needed his input more than ever. Siobhan must have been persuasive in tempting Rahman that their leads had substance in the first place.

Recounting the events from Whitehall to being hauled away to Paddington Green, Shay added only that he'd been questioned about his actions briefly. There were other omissions too, not least details of the taxi's contents and Townsend's irritating involvement. Passing through to the kitchen, Shay flicked on the kettle as Rahman stretched on the sofa and started on the pastries.

"Tell me," Shay called through, "is there any chance of getting to Bill Atkinson? Nicholls gave up so much dirt on him."

The sound of munching from the living room punctuated the reply. "How did I know it would come to that? Even if I wanted to help out, there are three potential problems. What are you going to do? Launch a series of random allegations against him? Firstly, we were told that information in confidence and you never betray a source unless they give the green light. Also, it won't stick. We have no proof and you, in particular, should be aware that those in the public eye have mud thrown at them constantly. It's the nature of the PR game, particularly politics. If I chuck that at Atkinson, I'm a dead man walking as far as press relations are concerned with the government – even informal channels. You may just have noticed my trade depends on access and information. His city lawyers will tear me to shreds to guard a reputation.

Shay returned with two steaming coffees. "Go on, why else?"

"Because I can't even get near him at the moment. Strictly no interviews for anyone apart from a couple of sycophantic believers in the media who are desperate for him to bring down the PM. Not so much for political reasons but because they pick their horses years back in the hope of riding a winner all the way to 10 Downing Street."

The journalist continued as Shay sat. "Sorry, that's not going to work. Why exactly do you need Atkinson? What are you not telling me?"

"Rahman, we promised to keep you in the loop and give you the scoop at the end. Just go with me on this."

"Okay, I'll give it some thought," came the reply. "For now, let's focus on my other angle. Shay Mason and the corruption scandal of the year. Some two decades ago. Not really your name though, was it? Don't worry, we won't spill the beans about your identity, but I will want to know why." Rahman raised his right palm in Shay's direction. "And no staged terrorist stunts as an excuse to run off and hide from my questions. Anything to avoid the Red Lion."

Shay felt played, a flash of annoyance, then relented. "Alright. It's all ancient history, of no interest to any of your readers, but a deal's a deal. Fire away, though don't be surprised if I hate every second of this."

Rahman reached for his mobile, presumably recording, before casually throwing his hand in the air. "The build-up, your running success, how you got selected, all the background stuff. You go through it."

A deep breath before Shay launched in. "Like any kid, like the kids I hung out with anyway, I loved sport. Anything – kicking a football, smashing a cricket ball, whatever. We played a lot of rugby at school and I guess my sports career, as you seem to think of it, really started on the wing for the school team at thirteen mostly because of my speed. I was small back then, didn't mind the hits but my body couldn't take it. I picked up a lower back injury so was out for a while. The rugby coach at school ran an athletics camp in the summer and the timing coincided so towards the end of my recovery, I spent all summer there in the lead up to chucking a rugby ball again. I couldn't wait to get back really. Then the local borough coach spotted me. The county, nationals at under sixteen. It came naturally and by then I was hooked."

"National four hundred metres champion at eighteen, fastest in Europe a year later. Impressive," Rahman interjected.

"Guess I'd had a growth spurt beyond the average, so it all came together. I was just thrown from one competition to another. At that age you just go where you're told. Shoes on. Run."

Rahman shook his head profusely. "Sorry, no one just gets thrown into the Olympics without it being a big deal."

Shay shrugged, "You watch it all on the telly as a kid but when I was selected at such a young age. It doesn't mean as much when you're a teenager. Maybe I was a bit oblivious to the hype. 'This is the first of four, at least.' That's stuck in my mind from the telly build up, for sure. Not that I was dedicating everything to it – my diet, drinking at parties – not the stuff that top champions are made of. I certainly didn't have tunnel vision but loved being on the track. It came easy in a way.

By then I'd signed up for the army. Maybe the reason I still appreciate working there today is having been given time off for training, meets, travel."

"Wait." In no time Rahman reached for his laptop, sharing the screen. A close up photo of fresh-faced Shay followed, a few clicks later, by a clip showing him sprinting full pelt on the track with captions underneath: "Join the army; run the Olympics; live your dream." Both smiled.

"Then it went wrong. What happened?" Rahman continued. "Same qualifying heat as Michael Johnson's successor, the current world champion. You were expected to push him and definitely qualify for the semis in the top two; even your times weren't far off his in the build-up. Did the pressure get to you?"

Rahman could have been subtle, gentle, compromising in extracting the memories. This was a blessing, Shay acknowledged fleetingly. He'd rather Rahman didn't lay on any pretence.

"Yeah, pressure. The whole world had an opinion after I ran one rubbish race, which just happened to be at the Olympics. I was young and had no tactical nous, bit of a rabbit in headlights with the size of the crowd too. It happens."

Silence, daring Rahman to break it.

"Finishing way down in your heat? It wasn't the marathon, Shay. How much bloody tactical expertise does it take? I'm giving you a chance to set out your stall here."

"Rahman, the fact is you can train all you like but until you're up against the best, who are genuinely going to be faster, you can't know—".

Shay's mobile started ringing; he dived to escape the conversation. He could make out the drone of flights taking off in the distance and moved into the hallway. Whichever airport Siobhan had made it to, the tone of excitement in her voice was unmistakable.

"I gave it a stab arranging to meet up with Linda via FIFA's offices, rather than sneaking around after her. Ended up speaking to her guard dog Kruger, asking him to pass on a message. Much to my amazement, five minutes later she called. Well, she's intrigued – or worried – about what we've got our hands on. Not surprisingly, I didn't want to go into detail but she started alluding to information on 'our mutual friends' as she termed them. I asked if she meant British friends and she said yes. It could just be concrete evidence that Atkinson, Nicholls and Tyler were all tighter than we thought. We're taking off in half an hour so I just wanted to update you. She'd better not lose her nerve before I get there or be bullshitting me."

Shay sensed a hesitancy. Siobhan paused to hear a tannoy announcement before continuing. "She sounded different, almost relieved to hear from me or scared of something. Not the high-flying confidence of Cairo."

"That's great news. Keep me posted."

"Anything I should know about?" Rahman asked as the call ended. "We are on the same team after all."

Shay was tempted to give him something, anything, to avoid dredging up the past. "Maddison may be about to spill information to Siobhan about a possible corruption chain. Iran, FIFA, Tyler, we just don't know yet. And Bryony's disappearance." Shay spelt out the family and professional connections between Bryony and Stewart, attempting to sound unfazed.

A couple of crumbs from another almond croissant began to scatter on the dusty carpet after Rahman reached into the paper bag. Maybe a change of tack was needed. Shay turned abruptly.

"Come on Siddique, we're leaving. You should check out any financial links, especially if they centre around the new czar, or whatever Atkinson's self-styled title is these days."

Rahman hastily returned the pastry to the bag. "What about you? We haven't finished our conversation—."

"I'm off to the countryside and as for your recce on me, you've got your answers now," as he ushered his guest out of the front door. Checking ahead to arrange his visit, Shay was soon driving north-east out of the capital again. Harriet reluctantly agreed to the visit, but still understandably sounded as if she was fuming that her home was trashed.

The landscape was warming up for summer as wheat fields surrounding the motorway shimmered. The surrounds of the country roads nearer Huntingdon were spreading their array of colour as Shay, annoyed it had slipped his mind, started on another call. Hopefully cameras weren't picking up his call on the hands free.

Sally agreed to assist straight away as the Polo, having gunned along the A roads, pulled up at the Tylers' cottage. Her text popped up with the requisite information at that moment. Checking the time, he thought better of calling America now and, besides, the alibi had to be watertight. It made sense to consider it thoroughly first.

Shay smiled at the sight of Harriet stooping to tend roses outside the cottage. Homely, reassuring. Perhaps her way of dealing with the drama befalling her – grief for her husband of decades mixed with apprehension for her missing sibling. He almost felt guilty approaching. Despite the calm outward front from a distance, close up it was apparent how distraught she remained, her face a picture of worry.

There was also something intangible nagging about her looks. It must have been ads that she's appeared in all those years ago, the same small TV roles they all go through when starting in acting, before she'd jacked it all in.

"Sorry Harriet, there's still no news about Bryony. I'm hopeful she just wanted to steer clear of any gossip about links to Stewart's work. The science correspondent on the CNN website alluded to connections but probably doesn't have a clue as to the exact nature of their work. And there may be nothing in that link anyway."

"You've come all this way to tell me nothing new?" Frustration was etched in her voice. "And I can't believe I'm being treated like a suspect in all this. I've told your colleagues a million times. Stewart didn't keep any work papers at home. He would have breached every official rule under the sun if he had. So why turn my house upside down when I'm clearly cooperating? After all, I've got nothing to hide. I'm just desperate to find out why this stupid administration placed him in danger in the first place. Is that so bad? Really?"

He raised his hand slightly in an act of appeasement. "We have to explore every avenue, Harriet. Believe me, I want to get to the bottom of this as well and return her home safely. I—". He cut himself short.

Nodding slowly, Harried led the way to the living room, in sight of the memento he'd remembered from his last visit before continuing. "There's more. This may prove a long shot but I've brought evidence about money transfers and wanted your take on them."

Removing the print outs from his bag, Shay passed over several sheets detailing the account and its sizable movements. From Harriet's expression, he didn't need to wait for an answer. It was immediately apparent she either had no knowledge of the fund or alternatively was revisiting those acting skills again. Then appearing pensive as she reached for a cigarette and lit up.

"The dates," Harriet looked up suddenly, exhaling. "Let me take another look." Gradually a broad smile emerged, the first time innate sadness seemed at bay today. She walked to the mahogany desk in the corner and pulled out two items – a large blue diary and a passport. Flicking through each, she proudly presented them to Shay without a word, by now seated.

Shay read carefully. "I thought I recognised the toy snowmobile. They sold them after rides on the snow mobiles," he nodded at the item on the mantelpiece. "I went to the Arctic too last year. Wangled a stay with a British deployment even though it was mostly a holiday for me. We spent time larking on those bikes. And I certainly didn't have any internet access for a week," he started, comparing the dates on the account. "Neither would you. All reception is dead as a dodo round there, so you'd hardly be transferring vast sums across the world," he smiled at Harriet. "Thanks, this is just what I need."

"Stewart and I were desperate for a break. He'd been very down due to what I presumed was his workload."

"Did he have any specific issues you were aware of?"

"What do you mean by issues? How vague. We all have issues. My suntan can be an issue."

Shay ignored the sarcasm. "Major concerns. Money? Drink? Health generally?"

"That's quite a list. Financially fine. I suppose he was a drinker when young – a bit of a tearaway alongside his studies in his teens by all accounts. I get the impression it became a bit of a problem at one stage, before he was given a stern talking to by his tutor when he wasn't attending tutorials. He was even threatened with being sent down from Cambridge so that must have been a major crossroads. Stewart hardly drank since...well, a very long time".

Shay had a creeping thought that he was being fobbed off. Harriet stared, arms crossed. "And more recently. What happened exactly? I've heard rumours—."

After a deep inhalation of her cigarette, Harriet appeared to weigh up her words before anger appeared in her voice. "That bloody snowmobile. Our lives changed in an instant, or at least some parts of it did. Surely you've done your homework? The machine was faulty and toppled over. I was thrown clear but it landed on Stewart's leg. Four operations and a lot of pain later, agony to be precise, well that was it for ski trips and climbing holidays. That was for sure. Did you know?"

He avoided answering the question directly. "He must have been in a lot of pain. Is that when the painkillers started? Opioids, even?"

"Yes, oxymorphone at first. Stewart started increasing doses at a hell of a rate. Pure self-medication. Our GP was worried about the risk of dependence and stopped prescribing."

"It was too late, wasn't it? By that stage?"

"Does this have to go on his record? I guess it won't make any difference. He was in too deep, if that's what you mean. Addicted, getting what he could under the counter in larger and large doses. I was terrified and begged him to go for some kind of detox, rehab, whatever you want to call it. But he was stubborn and insisted he'd come off it in his own time."

"In time to evade the stringent drug and alcohol testing they were about to introduce in the lab?"

She sighed. "It would have been the end of him, after all he'd achieved. Stewart would have been thrown out on the gutter. He was starting to panic, not helped by whatever those disgusting drugs, legal or otherwise, were doing to his mental faculties."

"Easy for it to happen," Shay sympathised. "You should know the Americans found significant traces in his bloodstream during the autopsy. I can see why everything was starting to tumble down for him. Is that why it's the only item on the mantelpiece with a date written on? To differentiate before and after?"

Harriet stared at the distant landscape for a moment. Then her tone was suddenly calm and almost mocking.

"We all have secrets, don't we? It's strange you of all people should be asking about this, isn't it? You don't seem to remember me but we were in the same athletics club all those decades ago. You may have been a few years younger, but you stood out even at that age. Fastest runner in the club by a country mile, whereas I was strictly club level and had to stay in shape for my career. That was my incentive. I must say, I admired you from afar but we were probably only training at the same time on a handful of occasions.

So, Shay Mason," the syllables elongated. "You tell me. What really happened at the Olympics?

Shay felt the familiar tension in his muscles on the few occasions the subject was mentioned these days. The fleeting thought also appeared that it was bizarre Harriet appeared to be continuing an interview started over 50 miles away by someone with whom she'd had no contact, presumably.

Is that where he'd recognised her from? "Okay, the athletics club. What two buildings were alongside the entrance?"

Harriet smiled. "McDonalds and the cinema. Are you testing me out?"

He nodded playfully in response. "I just loved poker at school. It was also a sizable element of our social life when locked away in my early army days. There was no danger of it spiralling out of control before the big event. I just owed a bit to clubs who would let me in despite my age."

"Hah," she leaned forward, reaching for the ashtray to forcefully stub out the last of her cigarette. "And you're having a go at my husband over his addiction."

"I wasn't addicted, Harriet. Just screwed up that heat in the Olympics. Coincidentally, within days some syndicate was exposed for bribing loads of athletes at the Games. Even a couple of my mates on the British team, Dougie and Helen, were sent home to face criminal prosecution. It was scary stuff for them and, well, the rest is history. Very old history."

She patently relished seeing him on the back foot, a hint of sharpness. "Not quite the whole story though, is it?"

She had got to him. "The press had more front-page hacks following the Games out there than there were sports journalists. If you remember, lottery funding was kicking in and they seemed determined to trumpet that we didn't deserve the money in preference to nurses and teachers. That pack of hyenas looked at every angle then dived in without any evidence or care about reputations. My poker losses came out in the wash and, to cap it all, I responded like a rabbit stuck in headlights.

What are kids like us going to do? Sue the lot of them? On fifteen grand a year?

The Great British public love nothing more than building up a new kid on the block then kicking them in the balls. You know, the first occasion I realised I was famous was when hundreds of journos and photographers were gathered by the arrivals gate at Heathrow when I touched down, not counting the arsehole who ran on to the plane as soon as the steps were in place pretending to be airport security in order to catch the first snap of the condemned man. But, do you know what? I ran badly, it's as simple as that. No one tried it on with me but you get tarred by this crap."

Self-conscious suddenly, annoyed at having to defend himself at all in the midst of an investigation he was supposed to control. He pictured Townsend furious and Siobhan embarrassed.

He hadn't added the fact that his career in the army was in the balance for months afterwards. The realisation that the regiment's head who, it later transpired, had to be cajoled by higher ranks to allow sufficient training pre-Games in the first place, was now itching to throw him overboard via a court martial. Whilst fellow soldiers encouraged Shay not to pack it all in, eventually he was allowed to continue. He'd never forget the unwarranted name of the Colonel at the time. Gracious. He was just envious of all Shay's attention, his friends had advised.

"I never saw you run again, even on telly," Harriet added calmly.

"Of course, you didn't. Four months later I snapped my cruciate on manoeuvres, which suited everyone down to the ground. Even though I was desperate to prove the doubters wrong and rebuild my career, the injury ended any chance of that. The army's medical corps were laughably amateurish, or so I discovered later. The doctor who operated on mine wasn't even a trained surgeon. And that spelt no more running career. It also meant the army could shield me from the outside world, so within a year I doubted anyone would remember my name."

"If you hadn't changed your surname, Shay."

"Okay, if I hadn't changed it. But I understand injury and rehab and, if it's any consolation, I can see how Stewart ended up in his mess."

"How kind," her sarcasm shone through once again.

It was as if Harriet needed the exchange for breathing space, however biting at his expense it had proven. Her despondency appeared to be creeping back by the time he left. In a game of happy families, all had not been as it had seemed from the outside for the Tylers. At least there was clear evidence she was no criminal mastermind. The truth appeared to be that a government civil servant, albeit one with a brilliant scientific mind, had shown no inclination to amass a fortune and was being framed to look like the wronged party.

Afterwards, a wide rainbow framed the windscreen as the wipers swayed gently, Shay speeding along the winding country road heading home. He mulled over the exchange about his running career, just as he thought he'd escaped Siddique's questioning about the Olympics.

A thought occurred for the more immediate problems at hand. The time difference should be fine now, Shay decided, as a traffic jam on the A1 ground all vehicles to a halt. He dialled the landline Sally had provided, for some reason expecting to wait ages for the phone to pick up, but within seconds was endeavouring to gain a friend.

"Eloise Pickering? Hello, my name is Shay Mason." No response. "I'm a friend of Bryony's." Each expressed shock and concern at their mutual friend's disappearance. Suddenly, bullseye. He established that Eloise still possessed Bryony's front door key and regularly took care of the cat.

He maintained the patter. "I could really do with help in finding her, as the authorities haven't managed to track her down." It was difficult trying not to sound as if he were firing questions. Bryony's career, friends, social life; he tried to tease it all out from her without knowing the direction of the conversation. On a whim he thought of the mailboxes downstairs and established that a common key gained access to everyone's post in the hallway downstairs. Eloise was eating out of his hand in no time, agreeing to collect post on a daily basis and keep him abreast of any significant developments, in the unlikely chance of something emerging. She drew the line at opening other people's mail though, so Shay attempted to sound shocked that he'd ever contemplate making such a request.

His thoughts switched back after the call. Having carefully guided Harriet into dispelling any notion of her or Stewart accepting bribes, in return he'd been on the end of a verbal attack that felt like an ambush. Maybe she'd clocked his identity from the outset and bided her time in lobbing the missile that was his running career. Occasionally younger cadets in the mess heard rumours and Googled the sparse internet coverage from the time. They were kids though, and he would probably have done the same in their position. Yet Harriet took obvious pleasure in his discomfort. She'd got to him.

Traffic picked up apace. The phone rang and suddenly it was all over. Townsend's two-minute call was brutal, as orders were relayed to head straight home where his 'company car' would be collected imminently. He could even leave the key in the ignition. Townsend explained that, after the previous day's shenanigans, his superiors now ordered a complete scaling down. Continuation would only be for a limited operation with fewer personnel. Atkinson, as Secretary of State, was apparently livid on reading Townsend's file on the 'Parliament Square Fiasco,' as it was titled in the media. Shay would receive ten per cent of his fee and was ordered, in no uncertain terms, to return to base tomorrow under his own steam.

Desperately trying to contact Siobhan immediately but guessing that her mobile must be tucked away on board the Milan flight. There was nothing to do but follow orders and reluctantly give up on the case, despite its importance. Absolutely no benefit in trying to argue against what felt like failure. And it was failure.

Could he have acted differently yesterday? "No bloody way," his words bellowed in the otherwise empty vehicle.

CHAPTER TWENTY-ONE

NORTH LONDON

There was urgency in his actions as Shay arrived back in Crouch End, beginning with moving the car keys to the requested position. Straight after, packing had begun. It had not been a lengthy process given he'd returned with so little. Then a quick shave and off to re-join the base in rural Wales.

Of course, that's what orders had stated. But it was not happening. There was never a perfect plan, but his decision was worth a shot, particularly if his commanding officers had failed to be provided with full details of the timescale for his absence.

It was impossible to recall the moment when the rigid formality of the army first appealed, promising a contrast to the mundanity of schoolwork and, of course, the promise of leaving home. The precision of rules, albeit some being ridiculously arcane such as boot polishing for those more senior with ample time to shine their own. Now, Woodford rated him when not all would afford Shay the time of day after returning from his Whitehall stint with his tail between his legs all those years ago. Some had made their disdain clear to his face. Now, the minimum of deception would produce the minimum of guilt.

The Polo was already out of sight as he emerged into the terraced street, builders he'd chatted to on and off during their six-month basement conversion two doors down were clearly finding the sight amusing. "Looks like your HP credit just ran out mate," from one. "They've nicked your supercharged Merc back" from another.

Shay raised his eyes to the heavens with a smile in reply, before walking briskly towards Finsbury Park station. He was aware that this speed was akin to the jogging pace of most civilians, passing alongside north London rush hour's snail pace of movement, with no hint of a bus in sight heading the right way anyway.

An hour later, the 18.20 stuttered away from Paddington Station towards Pembrokeshire. On board, Shay tallied up the resources that remained at his disposal. Fortunately, it appeared that disparate departments were responsible for the loan of items so, to his surprise, the MacBook was still accessible for confidential information. There was no point risking any contact with Sally though. He also remembered to turn off location devices on his phone for the trip.

Having called ahead, Woodford was still in his office near midnight as he finally returned to base. It had felt like a type of homecoming, the welcome sight of the Welsh Arms insignia shining in moonlight at the gates. No one was quite sure how long the title had been the nickname at the regiment base, but everyone referred to it in that way.

A typical request for advance leave would go through the usual channels but permission for immediate vacation was highly unusual. Sticking to the facts as much as possible after saluting, Shay could only try his best. Yes, he was still seconded in London for confidential business but there was a lull. Anyway, as training duties were allocated to colleagues for the following week, this would be the opportune moment to use up annual leave he'd accrued throughout the year. One of the lessons he'd learnt from early days of army life was to make life easy for your bosses and he was offering minimum disruption for the regiment. To think that, so recently, he'd had no idea how to spend his leave given his physical exhaustion from the job. Mountain walking almost appealed less than a beach in recent months. Almost, but not quite.

The signature was a formality but it had been far from a wasted journey. The Lieutenant Colonel clearly appreciated his request being made in person.

There was no point heading straight off in the middle of the night, so it was after catching five hours sleep that he started out for the English south-east coast and, as far as his superior was aware, the Budapest marathon via training runs around Lake Como. Airports and sea crossings would be the easiest method to track passport movement across a continent. Choosing the latter as his preferred option for the first leg, Shay withdrew one thousand pounds in cash from a branch at Folkestone shortly before lunchtime, then quickly changed it to Euros at another. Hopefully, once travelling across the continent, his movements would be harder to trace should Townsend or his minions attempt to do so. Woodford must be in the dark regarding Shay's orders, regardless of whether he'd been tipped off about the embarrassing events in London. Fortunately, Woodford was a stickler for not prying into other's missions, so it was unsurprising his commanding officer knew better than to ask.

The rest of the journey afforded the chance to switch off, utilising a combination of buses, local trains and hitch-hiking to cross France during the next day and overnight in the optimistic attempt to camouflage his movements. It could all prove to be of no avail. Although anyone attempting to follow would struggle, tracking him down electronically would probably prove successful given the plethora of monitoring means. He'd decided to keep hold of the phone for now, along with the MacBook. When the time was right, he'd use other devices. Besides, all those games apps would help pass the time on his travels.

Opting to travel via Lyon and Turin avoided crossing the Alps, much as he had fond memories of a climbing trip there with Greg. This route was the most sure-fire guarantee of getting there speedily by land.

Unfortunately, there was a fair chance Siobhan had already wrapped up any significant meeting with Linda and was already scooting smartly back to the UK. That concern was promptly dispelled thanks to free internet use in the lounge of Turin's five star Principe di Piemonte Hotel, having determined that the MacBook was maybe too risky, after all, to access sensitive information in the search for the Iranians. By now Terence Townsend may well be suspicious and not consider him such a spent force.

On entering the building, he recalled the sage advice by a colleague years before, when they'd emerged in sweat from a Bavarian forest after three nights of reconnaissance training to find the incongruous site of a luxury hotel in front. Saunter inside as if you own the place and the doormen and women will doff their caps, not daring to question your right to be there. Regardless of your look – and smell. Soon the pair had spruced up in the washroom and were tucking into the restaurant's prestigious menu.

The lead story on the *BBC* website was Linda being locked in talks at FIFA headquarters in Zurich. He briefly considered heading there, but admission to football's worldwide administrative offices, let alone to the President's presumably palatial high security private residence, would be nigh on impossible. No, he'd hedge what must be a safer bet. The head of world football had to be seen at Europe's centrepiece, all of an hour's flight away for her.

He wondered about Siobhan, deciding it best not to alert her about his impending arrival. What had she been told as the reason he was, in effect grounded? For insubordination? Unacceptable performance? Lack of results? Maybe Townsend hadn't provided any reasoning. She must know he was off the trail officially though and wondered if she'd even care.

It would certainly be worthwhile making contact with Rahman though, and hopefully the journalist was not on the grid as far as Townsend's team were aware. Shay reached for his phone. Successful hacks pride themselves on access, as he'd seen first-hand in Parliament. It was therefore no surprise that Rahman confirmed immediately that, yes, the top brass of FIFA was expected to be on display in Milan.

Another hunch was worth pursuing. "Any chance of meeting up there, Rahman? I presume their meeting beforehand is to try and sweep the Iranian connection under the carpet before it gets out of hand?"

"Yup, certainly regarding Iran," came the reply. "Organisations like that protect their own so, somewhere along the line, I must have probed too deep in Cairo. I'm banned from FIFA for all high-profile events now, including the annual jewel in the crown of the Champions League Final. Bastards. So as for your other request, there's no point in me coming over, which is particularly a shame considering Guiseppe Fermini, a mate at *La Gazetta dello Sport*, had a ticket waiting for me. And he gets reservations in the best eateries in town, no matter how packed the city is."

A pause before Shay launched in. "There wouldn't be any chance of swinging that for me, by any chance? I plan to be in

Milan tomorrow night. I wouldn't ask for the favour, but I don't have many pals there at present."

"I'll see what I can do, assuming you're still on to finish that interview? The scandal engulfing your teammates may be long ago but that was child's play at the time for gangs who rigged events. It could still be useful for any clues as to how they got their claws into your fellow athletes." Then, "I swear, I'm not out to get you."

Shay shrugged. "There's not much I'd be able to tell you apart from hearsay, but sure, it's a deal."

Rahman promised to call back soon and, within minutes, Shay's mobile rang. The journalist provided the address of the *Gazetta* office in Milan – Via Cosimo del Fante, before adding, "It looks like you're going to the ball. If you bump into La Presidenta, tell her I'd love to sit down for a chat when she's free. But I've got enough to wade through here first."

Like a politician, Shay mused, Rahman was adept at allowing the impression of being easy-going and enthusiastic in exchanging information. As he moved away from the lounge's PC, it occurred to Shay not for the first time that Rahman may have some wider agenda that was just out of sight. Or maybe he was just so desperate for Shay's take on the Olympics from what seemed a lifetime ago.

Trains through Italy appeared less organised than the equivalent transport in France, a sense of chaos seemingly shared by the passengers who appeared en masse at the next station. Small children were soon clambering over the seats alongside, with food wrappers discarded randomly in a morass of noise and movement. The journey was speedy and efficient enough, though he passed on the buffet trolley offerings given the volume of dust on sandwich and confectionary packaging. Excellent coffee fuelled the rest of his ride instead.

There was no need to rush the journey. Indeed, any element of surprise should take precedence given there was little overt investigation he could undertake from a train carriage. It was preferable to keep a low profile with a day to fill before the match, not least given his shopping spree in adopting the current appearance. Soon after the conversations with Rahman, he'd sauntered at tourist pace around Turin's cheaper boutiques,

Vespas shooting past at regular intervals with their whining snarl. Peering at a shop window and catching sight of his reflection, the idea came instantly. His dark chinos and sky-blue stone wash Levi shirt were all well and good, but it was time to assimilate. After all, there was no Sally or diplomatic corps on whom to rely.

It didn't take long to assemble his new uniform. His new jeans and trainers were somehow more down at heel, whilst his chest now boasted the dark blue and red centre stripe of the Paris St Germain shirt. A light jacket and PSG baseball cap completed the look. For good measure, he picked up smarter clothes as well in case a change was called for later. The unshaven guise was maintained, he even contemplated shearing off his hair but decided against it at the last-minute. It was a good enough disguise. How better to fit into the crowds pouring towards Milan for European football's showpiece event, than to show support for a finalist? His French had been passable at school, not a disaster anyway. There was no way he'd risk more than a few offhand words in the language though, if challenged.

Bring on the final.

CHAPTER TWENTY-TWO

MILAN

It was soon after five when Shay arrived at the host city, in two minds as to whether he should alert Siobhan of his presence. On balance he decided to keep his distance. Either Townsend had been given prior knowledge of where she was heading or, if not, Shay presumed she'd be easier to track. No, he'd adopted the French supporter uniform, so he may as well maintain his anonymity to the maximum.

At first, Milan Central Station gave Shay the impression of passengers roaming in a human version of a giant ant farm, before concluding that ants were more organised in their movement. Black concourses shone with expensive stone or excess cleaning. It was hard to discern which given the number of fans being disgorged on to the platforms from around Europe, France and Germany in particular.

He'd soon opted for leaving the MacBook in a left luggage locker, the key safely stowed in his pocket. Twenty Euros well spent.

Shay hazarded a guess that FIFA appreciated continuity in their choice of accommodation. The Four Seasons would afford a consistent level of privacy and, after consulting the station's information desk, he set out on the three kilometre hike to the hotel. He hit the bullseye. On arrival, noting his outfit blended with the crowd of supporters surrounding the entrance to the hotel. He should avoid standing out. There was no sign of Siobhan, as a limousine swept into the street, Via Gesu, towards the slightly low key and unremarkable entrance for such a prestigious landmark. The security detail was already opening the rear door as the Mercedes slowed to a halt, Linda confidently emerging with Kruger alongside. Shay remembered his instinctive dislike of the man, who appeared to reek of arrogance without opening his mouth. A small grouping alongside Shay had patently shown up just to barrack FIFA personnel, whilst the majority of those in the vicinity had just strayed down random streets in search of the next pre-match bar, whiling away the hours until kick off and sauntering over to see what all the fuss was about.

In an instant, dignitaries disappeared into the confines of the Four Seasons. There was no point in trying to secure an audience via the front entrance, so he edged slowly towards a group of Paris fans belting out *La Marseillaise* in a variety of keys. Suddenly, there she was, Siobhan only twenty yards away, striding along the street then presenting some form of paper credentials that didn't appear to pass muster. Instead, the two security officers, one male and one female, both donning black, shook their heads in unison like some eccentric new dance move. The female security guard sighed and took a note of Siobhan's details before going inside for five minutes, whilst her colleague ostentatiously blocked Siobhan's path. The first re-emerged, shrugging and shaking her head, making clear access was denied. He backed away swiftly down the street in case she turned and spotted him. Would there even be an expression of surprise? There was no way of knowing.

The relaxed journey across the continent had been useful, in many respects. Not least in questioning his own motives. Was he just being chivalrous in supposing that she needed watching as much as Linda, albeit for different reasons? Townsend had clearly understood the complexity of emotion that Siobhan's presence alongside him would spark. Was he a puppet, a pawn, in all this? Perhaps, but only if he chose to play that role. There was no chance of walking away now though. Bryony's disappearance and the threat of attacks in the UK, despite Townsend's half-brained dismissal of the risk, saw to that.

He had secured another route into the proceedings at least, all the more useful if Siobhan wasn't making progress. "Dove si trova?" he asked for directions to a well-groomed businessman whilst handing over a scribbled address. Fortunately, the man explained the route in perfect English with only a slight Italian accent. Even the PSG top hadn't hidden Shay's English roots.

Taking in the city on the way to Via Cosimo Del Fante, Shay's walk blended in with the international gaggle of shoppers alongside who appeared to move with no sense of urgency. Shay noted the eye-catching displays of sharp suits, perfectly matching shirts and ties, dresses revealing more skin than fabric, as he approached Galleria Vittoria Emanuele ii, Italy's oldest shopping gallery. All were sparingly set out on display and enveloped under the massive stately roof. Classy, definitely beats Swansea, he concluded.

A figure barged into him just as he emerged in front of the religious gothic riches of the Duomo di Milano, the city's stunning cathedral. Immediately sensing the reduced weight of his jacket, Shay took up the sprint challenge across the Piazza towards the pickpocket now running at full pelt from the scene. Both were oblivious to the tourists jumping out of their path, who hurled screams and angry shouts towards them in a number of languages. The bastard had stolen his phone. Some kind of targeted theft? Security must be on to him to disrupt his plans, surely.

The thief was no slouch. Determination kicked in. By the far side of the square, with a rugby dive, the youth was sent sprawling, landing jaw first on concrete. That would serve the bastard right. Two policewomen had started to give chase at the same time. Catching up, they roughly shoved the pair to their feet. The dishevelled would-be robber launched into his explanation at rocket speed in Italian that Shay had no chance of understanding, only for two American tourists to sidle over and disprove whatever desperate excuse was being uttered. Handing the mobile back, one of the policewomen displayed evident relief when he declined to press charges. After all, the city had a strict maximum limit for logging criminal incidents on the day of the final in order to talk up Milan's bravura performance in handling the international event. All had been decided in advance.

The pair shrugged at Shay as they roughly frogmarched the culprit away for a talking to. Shay wondered if he'd overreacted, the guy probably having no agenda save a quick buck. It wouldn't do any harm to remain vigilant though. A lesson well learnt.

Nonplussed glances from the Milanese who were now all but ignoring the scene. Twenty minutes after a further stroll south through the city around smaller churches and courtyards, passing couples nonchalantly touching hands who were sat basking outside half empty cafes, crowds dwindled dramatically in this decidedly less commercial area. He emerged outside the underwhelming newspaper office by the near empty botanical gardens. Here, seemingly, the swipe card entry protocol of shiny modern offices, didn't hold sway. The building's old-fashioned air suggested *Gazetta* had been housed there long, long before the twenty-first century.

Just as Shay was about to press the buzzer he caught a faint murmur inside, expanding to voices at talking pitch, then shouting. The commotion within instinctively made him pause. Suddenly the front door sprang open as a woman clad in a burgundy coat, early 30s, burst past, shouting what appeared to be dog's abuse at the trailing, out of breath figure approaching from the stairs. Within seconds the woman was yards down the street. Shay found himself face to face with a stocky figure staring back from the doorway. The reincarnation of Pavarotti, complete with facial hair.

"Guiseppe Fermini. You must be Shay Mason. Excuse her—," a general wave in the woman's direction initially.

They shook hands. "Your girlfriend? Sorry if the timing—."

"Girlfriend?" Guiseppe's lungs opened like bellows as his laugh reverberated around the echoing entranceway. "My editor, Eleni. That's my editor. She was telling me to enjoy the match." He led the way inside.

"Sorry, the lift is out of order," raising his hands and shrugging. "Please come this way," and with a deep breath started upstairs with Shay apace behind. "Rahman said you are a special friend. This must be the first Champions League final he and I haven't attended together for years. But then, you understand he is no friend of the authorities."

"You mean he's really banned from the match?"

Guiseppe's deep breaths intensified. He smiled whilst continuing to puff his way up the staircase. "Officially no, he is not on the hooligan list. But, in practice, if an official on the gate recognised him they would probably find an excuse not to allow him entry. I trust you're not on any list of banned spectators? If you are, Eleni would have my, how do you say it, balls for garters."

"Something like that, Guiseppe. Something like that."

They reached the fifth-floor office. If a digital blogger had caught sight of Guiseppe's overcrowded, poky, office, they'd conclude the stone age was alive and well. No surface was left uncovered with old editions of the *Gazetta*, the nation's most famous sports paper, in addition to newspapers and international magazines in a myriad of languages, piled high.

Noting Shay's wry expression, Guiseppe explained. "The archivists won't take any more paper. So, I ignored their digital fetish and commenced my own archive here. Otherwise, the traditions of the past die out, never to be reclaimed." Then sitting them down with espressos made by the receptionist from a noisy silver machine in the corner.

"Guiseppe, presumably you have good contacts at FIFA. I'm trying to arrange a few minutes with Linda Maddison. Actually, my colleague was, but I get the impression she hasn't been successful."

That hearty laugh repeated by Guiseppe. "Mr Mason, you are a funny one. Even if I had those contacts, Linda Maddison isn't someone with an empty diary ready for a chat night and day." No more nighttime visits, certainly, Shay resolved.

"And you may have noticed there is an important game on, so the whole of UEFA will be fawning around FIFA like bees in a hive. It's like a royal court. A wave here, a bow of the head there," Guiseppe gestured along. "And favours dispensed from on high."

"But in your home city, surely *Gazetta* can arrange a quick meeting with her? That's all I ask."

Guiseppe's face grew visibly red. "We are not some tool of government or private business or whoever you represent. Frankly, I'm a little disappointed that you want to use our paper for some grubby approach." Reaching into a drawer he extracted a DL size white envelope. "Here is your ticket for the match and I suggest we don't meet beforehand. Now I must escort you out, not least as I have a press conference to attend for one of the managers."

The pace was more of a frogmarch than Shay had considered capable from Guiseppe as, without a handshake, he was perfunctorily marched out of the front door.

Outside, loitering down the road, Shay decided how best to spend the coming hours. He was in luck. Three minutes later, Guiseppe left the building, glancing in both directions presumably for a cab, yet missing Shay who quickly stepped into a doorway out of sight. The journalist headed towards the busier streets to improve his likelihood of transport. The quicker Guiseppe left the area, the better.

After returning to the building, Shay pressed the office's buzzer. Fingers crossed. Fortunately, the receptionist answered. "I'm really sorry, I appear to have dropped my pen in Guiseppe's office when he was showing me an old article. Could I come and retrieve it please? You'd never find the right pile," with a laugh. If she didn't speak English, he'd be in trouble.

"Oh Guiseppe, the day can't come soon enough for him to throw out that old tat. He'll join the twenty-first century eventually," came the response.

The front door buzzed open. As he arrived upstairs, she was completely engrossed in a heated phone discussion that completely bypassed his rudimentary knowledge of Italian. Fortunately, she just waved him through to Guiseppe's chaotic office. With press conferences for teams, managers and directors taking place around the city alongside final public training sessions, presumably the majority of staff were also out covering the build-up.

He'd already selected his target. As one of the biggest names in Italian football journalism, Guiseppe must have contacts galore at all levels of the game. The higher, the better. He'd earlier noticed a bulging rolodex on the desk, as outdated as a museum exhibit, and, quickly flicking through, soon hit the jackpot. Cards were in surname order and the one for 'Maddison, Linda' contained both an email address and mobile number. He could only hope the information was up to date. After noting them down on an adjacent scrap, he prepared to leave before turning back. The press rooms did indeed appear deserted. If he dialled now, hopefully the respected name of the newspaper would flash up on the recipient's screen.

The call was answered within three rings, the voice on the other end a disappointment though. It was too much to hope for the boss herself. The gatekeeper answered. "Linda Maddison's phone," announced the crisp accent of Christian Kruger.

Shay hesitated for a moment before deciding it was best to plough on with some degree of honesty. Had he possessed any ability with languages, an attempt at deception may have helped, but there was no point trying. Particularly if Guiseppe's direct number had flashed up.

He took a deep breath. "Christian, it's Shay Mason. My colleague was invited to set up a meeting as soon as possible with Ms Maddison regarding a matter of mutual importance. When would be a convenient moment?"

Only two words, "Hold please," were uttered in response. Raised voices indicated an argument, unmistakably with Linda's growing increasingly assertive and ending with her taking the call.

"Look, I said to your colleague that I may be able to assist, no guarantees. I certainly haven't any time before the final, given the huge number of functions and meetings. And no, before you ask, I have no intention of a late-night rendezvous with your colleague, Mr Mason. Christian advises me to meet you and get whatever you want out of the way. But please be under no illusions that any attempt at blackmail will rebound in your face so that incident is not, I repeat not, to be mentioned ever again."

"That's a deal. We really didn't want—."

Linda continued without pause. "The match should be finished by eleven. Come to the FIFA suite at the stadium half an hour later. We'll be less conspicuous than meeting at the hotel."

There was no opportunity to reply as the call abruptly ended. He'd swung a ticket for the big occasion so at least he would be in the stadium. He hoped Siobhan wouldn't be able to break through the tight cordon around the Four Seasons, or at the match, so he'd have a massive head start even if she somehow found out about the meeting. He could only make a wild stab at the story she'd tried to concoct to interest Linda earlier. But this was too important for Townsend to unilaterally decide that Shay's services weren't needed and, after all, he'd broken no laws.

For good measure, he threw a Euro in to Guiseppe's top drawer to cover the call and was soon whistling along the street, heading to the nearby canal restaurants for a well-earned break and merging with supporters. And speculating just how much influence Kruger apparently held over the top echelon.

CHAPTER TWENTY-THREE

MILAN

To the disappointment of city officials, match day hadn't begun with the bright May sunshine envisaged for the prestigious occasion, rain clouds soon filling the skies. He may as well kill time, idly glancing at a copy of the *Gazetta* over a double macchiato, sat amidst the shadow of the Duomo. His eye drawn to Guiseppe's apparent in-depth piece on the game, though he couldn't understand much. Where better to stay anonymous for the day and still in match shirt? Various nationalities were already mixing together in the official city centre fan zone, with a bizarre hybrid set of tunes blaring over the speakers. National songs from each country interspersed with dizzy Europop. Quite a cacophony.

The background noise fitted perfectly to *Gazetta*'s inside scoop for the day. Shay asked the reluctant waiter about the paper's headline, who explained that the polite agreement for Eurovision and the Champions League Final to avoid a clash on the same day came unstuck some months ago. Both had laid claim to the same Saturday, so, after a toss of a coin following an intervention by the EU President, the result was a Eurovision victory. Hence today's fine being relegated to a midweek evening match. There was a long wait for kick-off.

A lazy morning, taking minimal risks with his location, was interrupted at lunchtime when the mobile rang. Noting the number, but reluctant to pick up in case he was being monitored, Shay made his way from the main square. Night had been spent back at the station, sleeping alongside hundreds of fans who had no inclination to spend vast Euros on an overpriced room, or simply couldn't find a vacancy. The spot suited him fine; the risk was too great to approach a hotel, where a passport would surely be demanded. Bed was where you closed your eyes, a mantra drummed into him initially as a cadet. The concrete bench, with a half-filled bag as a makeshift pillow, seemed luxurious in comparison to some overnight stays he'd endured.

A seedy looking pension a fair distance away from the expensive streets would be ideal as his next hangout. '*Buono Turisti,*' hung the tired sign in neon, with all tourists who paid presumably deemed to be good. No point in lying, he persuaded the acne-ridden teenager to accept a bunch of Euros in exchange for use of the reception phone for a quick call to America. Judging by the boy's nervous glances and hasty pocketing of the cash, this would go unaccounted for to his boss.

"Eloise, sorry I missed your call. Sorry, it's Shay here. Is Bryony back?"

Eloise Pickering's response was disappointing, but she soon perked up in providing detailed descriptions of the various postal items recovered from her neighbour's mailbox. "Tickets from the ballet, magazine for the mall, a couple of dreary rental updates from the apartment owners here. And her tennis club renewal, very important. None of this looks unexpected, don't you think, dear?"

Despite their previous conversation, Eloise abundantly relished the task to which they'd agreed to the extent of opening every item. The list went on. Maybe his presence on the other end of the line constituted some kind of justification for the lonely pensioner. It was just as well no lawyers were listening in. Hopefully.

"That's everything concerning her financial affairs. I presume in this day and age everyone younger than me receives their bank statements online. But I appreciate the comfort of a paper statement myself."

Trying to hide his disappointment, Shay was about to ring off before Eloise started again. "Then I had an Edison light bulb moment and remembered on the off chance that there's an empty apartment next door on our floor. We have three per level, as you might remember. Every now and then a stand-in mailman accidentally puts our mail in the box for the empty flat. You do call them flats in England, don't you? But as the key is common for everyone, I thought it would do no harm.

Very strange, but inside was a card addressed to that property. That's bizarre considering it's remained empty for so long, in fact since Bryony moved in about two years ago to be precise. I wonder if it's a friend of hers who just took down the address incorrectly? The picture on the front is a lovely panoramic view of Jerusalem and whoever it is must be having a wonderful time. Who knows, another rival for her affections maybe?"

Shay let the comment hang, surprising Eloise for the exact wording on the reverse. "Well, if you like Shay. 'The sights are wonderful. Tel Aviv night life as magical as ever and our float in the Dead Sea miraculous'. And it's dated two days after she went missing. It doesn't sound very helpful to me but then, what would I know?"

He thanked her profusely, suggesting she send a photo of both sides to his private email account. If the sender or the message contained any relevance to Bryony's predicament, then it was clear as mud. But there was precious little else to go on, given his role firmly on the outside.

Surely it had nothing to do with the rumours of Bryony's political connections abroad all those years ago? Yet Israel was a strange coincidence. Having a few hours to kill prior to the big event, Shay peeled off more bills in return for continued internet use. He noticed porn on the screen as he hastily moved round to use the receptionist's laptop. The image quickly vanished with a flick of the youth's finger and an angry look in Shay's direction. Accessing his email account to double check the postcard's wording, even changing the order of the words, all yielded nothing. One luxury he had at present was time, picking out the first letters of each word, then the second, and so on; highlighting the capitals only. Then on to the internet. Free sites assisting with anagrams and other letter rearrangements. After an hour and a half, he had nothing to show for his time. It probably wasn't of any relevance anyway and, besides, it may not have been intended for Bryony after all. Anyone in the block could be the intended recipient.

Not for the first time, Shay felt a pang of guilt that Bryony was missing. For her, for Harriet, for himself. Was his presence in some way the tipping point for her vanishing? Why did the CIA, or who the hell they are, not come up with any results? Is it possible she was working for them all along and in some way was testing him, seeing if he came up to scratch?

Sitting back with a sigh, Shay took in the few residents sat near reception in the dive. The overnight bench seemed significantly more hygienic than this place with, certainly, a lower chance of bed bugs and head lice. A small pile of stamped postcards sat alongside the PC, presumably awaiting the receptionist to take them for posting. Then something clicked.

Reaching across for the reception phone again, on this occasion Shay concluded he'd contributed enough to the receptionist's black market operation so didn't bother to offer up further compensation. The receptionist briefly looked angry before Shay pointed to the screen and opened up his hands in questioning. It was unlikely the boy's employer would approve of the choice of viewing. The receptionist sulkily stood back.

Fortunately, Eloise was still in and Shay set out his suggestion. "Under the stamp?" she exclaimed in surprise. I'll try and tear it off if you want."

"No, please don't Eloise. You'll need to steam it slowly. I'm sure it's not relevant but we need to know we've done everything to find her. Right?"

Soon after, Eloise called back on the reception number provided. "Well, you were right young man. Who would have thought a boyfriend was sending such messages? Maybe they're a bit too racy to include in the main text. Not many letters though."

"Great. Could you read it to me please?"

"I'm afraid not. You see, it's not my language, the fine lettering is in Hebrew. The good news is that I'm seeing a young chap myself who lives on the second floor. I say young, eighty-seven this month, but who's counting? He's taken advanced studies in the subject and should be able to help. I'll call you on this line right after."

"You do realise I'm in Italy?"

"It's OK, my calls cover there as my granddaughter's studying in Florence. Anything to help find Bryony. Besides, it's an adventure."

The teenager on reception was now mumbling obscenities in Shay's direction. What proportion of the call had the youth understood? Little, hopefully, if he was as lazy with schoolwork. As the phone rang ten minutes later, the dance continued. The pair were seemingly playing a version of musical chairs, as both lunged for the phone simultaneously. Shay's faster reflexes carried the day.

"Good call Shay. Harry translated it as two simple words: 'Leave now.' Is that why she's disappeared?"

"Presumably she never saw that warning," he responded. The bigger question, unspoken. What is she mixed up in?

The next few hours were spent trying to fit the pieces together logically, including a further conversation with Rahman from a different hotel querying any Israeli links relating to the corruption rumours. Just a hunch, but there was no joy from his journalistic source. After further internet research, this time at an internet café, he still couldn't link Bryony with Israel in any way. The day was feeling like a dead waste, one step forward and a couple backwards, yet again. At last, it was time for the night's grand occasion.

CHAPTER TWENTY-FOUR

MILAN

Checking the match ticket, it appeared the seat was adjacent to the sizable press areas set aside within the ground, and on the same tier as the dignitaries. This was no area for scruffy jeans, and the strict instructions on the back made clear that dress code was less casual. A noticeably better class of journalist was evidently required for attendance at the Champions League Final, so during the afternoon Shay retrieved his bag and located the nearest luxury hotel. Within minutes the change of clothes gave way to fine Italian dark grey trousers, a light pink shirt and burgundy silk tie, his less formal clothing now disposed of in a skip down the road.

The excitement on the walk to the ground was palpable amongst fans. On the approach to the stadium, brass bands welcomed the city's guests. The San Siro, the shared home to Milan's leading teams, was certainly an unusual design. Giant spiral staircases on the outside appeared to prop up a bowl the size and design of an almighty spaceship. With intense floodlighting spilling out of the stadium's roof, the sight was massively impressive.

As Shay walked the final section of concourse outside, it was clear security was tight, including for corporate and press areas. Even so, he was surprised to have to follow a queue through an airport style security scanner and undergo a thorough frisk. Suddenly Siobhan strolled into his eye line ten yards in front, dressed more for a night at the opera in bright silk ballgown than for a football match, yet not out of place alongside female VIP and corporate attendees. If she managed to get past Kruger to question Linda prior to him, so be it. But getting the information out of FIFA's President would be quite a coup and he relished the opportunity of proving his worth to Townsend. That may be enough to place him back on the team. Besides, he hated to admit, there was something tantalisingly competitive in their relationship currently and he was well aware she wouldn't have given an inch too. Either way, there was nothing to lose and, for the first time in ages, the prospect of heading back to the Pembrokeshire coast to lead training held less appeal.

Celebrations had started early with a giant party in full swing behind the scenes. At least, that's what was observable across the ropes in the VIP area, the media staircase alas cordoned off to the side. Moet was being consumed at a phenomenal rate with waiters struggling to swap empty bottles for refills at the required pace. The spread didn't look bad either. A life size football team sculpted in ice took centre stage, with former superstars of the sport dotted around the room as well. This really must have cost a tidy sum.

Somehow, he would have to navigate this barrier to secure the meeting with Maddison later. For now, a tap on the shoulder and Guiseppe nodded towards the stairs for his companion to follow. He felt a pang of relief at not being entirely cold-shouldered by his Italian host despite their earlier interaction.

"Not for us, the mere fourth estate," Guiseppe exhaled between stairs to the middle tier. "And at least you're dressed suitably. Even the press can't wear team shirts for such a major occasion here." He added, referring to the local teams, "it's just as well Inter or Milan aren't in the final or they'd be a riot amongst the media if forbidden to show their favours."

At the top of the stairs, Shay sought the words for an apology. "Look Guiseppe, I know we got off on the wrong foot. I'm sorry if I put you in a difficult position. It was presumptuous—."

Guiseppe again produced that throaty laugh, jabbing a podgy finger in Shay's chest. "Presumptuous. Yes, presumptuous." walking off slowly with Shay in tow. Apology accepted by the sound of it.

The stadium appeared to grow before them as they approached the inner bowl, soon taking their places as Guiseppe pulled out a laptop. There was no way of circumventing technology in sending match reports, even for old school reporters. Supporters of Dortmund to the right and PSG to the left were in good voice and had presumably filled the ground, for the most part, hours before. Flares started to appear in the air, presumably security not very successful in confiscating the objects. Or maybe they just plain weren't bothered about such items being brought in. Shay shuddered, recalling the rumours in the UK of the unpleasant lengths fans were prepared to suffer in sneaking the objects into grounds.

All was set as kick-off approached, Shay having difficult reminding himself this was work, not play. A marching band and drum majorettes crossed the pitch, all but drowned out by the crescendo of pre-match support from the ends of the grounds.

Linda was waiting pitch-side to greet the approaching teams. Italy's President was alongside, a wizened elderly man relying on a stick to shuffle along the lines of players, which made shaking hands with each, something of a trial. He appeared to dive back to the safety of his stick to stay upright after each greeting.

Soon the match kicked off, with Linda, by now up in the VIP area on the same tier, only some thirty feet away. At one point, as she whispered to the President sat next to her, her eyes met Shay's. He couldn't be sure but, after inclining his head slightly with a quizzical glance in her direction, she appeared to respond with a clear nod. The meeting was on.

A roar emerged from the right of the stadium as the Germans took the lead from a free kick, soon cancelled out by a close-range header from PSG. At the rear of the VIP section, a familiar figure could be seen arguing with Kruger, he deduced from the body language. Siobhan was in heated discussion for some minutes, oblivious to the action, before taking her place disconsolately some ten rows behind Linda. Had she been given the brush off again? Maybe Kruger had let the cat out of the bag about Shay's presence? She didn't glance around searching for him, so perhaps his name hadn't come up at all.

Guiseppe exchanged loud observations with the rest of the press box throughout, seemingly on good terms with them all. Shay was being left alone to watch both the VIP area and the match, which suited him just fine.

Half time saw livelier entertainment, with Europe's latest pop sensation, Jonah, looking barely out of junior school, appearing for a medley of his greatest hits. All three to be precise. Dortmund took the lead to an explosion of joy from their fans at the restart, Paris spent the next forty-five minutes all but camped in their opponent's half. Five minutes of injury time was announced on the assistant's board. The tension was palpable for fans of the finalists. Towards the end of the five additional minutes, many Dortmund fans had their heads in their hands as Paris were awarded a penalty, which they duly contrived to miss. The match was over.

In normal circumstances, Shay would have welcomed the drama of extra time and possibly a penalty shoot-out but, on this occasion, any reason for Linda sticking to their schedule was welcome.

There was some movement nearby. The presentation party were leaving their seats, comprising of Linda, Federico Anastasi – the Italian President, and Stefan Persson who was President of UEFA, whose famous bald dome was shining from a distance. They edged towards the exit for the short journey to pitch side as Dortmund's fans, officials and players were ecstatic in celebration. Shay noticed that Siobhan was now moving along her row as well. Etiquette usually demanded that no one in the dignitaries' section left before the presentation. Such traditions didn't apply to the losing team, though, as Parisian fans quickly emptied their end of the San Siro, heading disconsolately for Milan's bars.

Who knows? Maybe Kruger had said no to her for the meeting, so he was left with a clear run.

Carpet had already been hastily laid down on the pitch for the ceremony, hoardings proclaiming "Champions League Winners" being in place as the presentation group was visible at pitch level. They hovered at the edge of the tunnel under the VIP area, different to the one used by the teams and down which the PSG manager was stomping. The Italian President slipped and two policemen moved forward to help re-establish his footing. Techno music reverberated around the ground as players, some dancing along and others in tears, were swept up in the emotion.

Anastasi, followed by Persson and Linda, moved from the tunnel's entrance and started walking towards the pitch, at a pace dictated by the elderly leader. Despite the UEFA Anthem which then kicked in and Dortmund's fans in full voice, a cracker could be heard loud and clear on the top gantry the far side of the stadium, accompanied by a slight puff of smoke emerging. More fun mayhem. An extra cheer arose from some fans, celebrations continuing in full swing for a moment. Shay glanced at the source of the noise before, as if in slow motion, Linda's legs appeared to collapse as she slumped to the ground, the clear sight of blood emerging from her head.

This couldn't be happening. Shay was unable to process events for a split second before reactions set in. Apart from the continuing Anthem, the stadium paused as one before screams filled the air. Immediately, security guards around were pointing to the gantry as supporters hurriedly clambered towards the exits. Shay moved quickly along to the VIP area. Fearing for Siobhan, he couldn't spot her. Was she safe? Had she left already? Suddenly the familiar shock of blond hair came into view at the back of the tier. Her startled expression was instantly obvious, presumably one of the few who hadn't been in the bowl at the time. They almost collided.

"What are you—?" she started, picking up on the panic all around as he grabbed her shoulder all but ordering her to leave the stadium as quickly as possible, pushing her along with those heading for the concourse exits. He'd move faster without her and anything he could glean now could prove vital.

The vast majority didn't need to be told to head for the main exit staircase and certainly there was no one in charge now. To the side, a far smaller staircase which Shay headed for, jumping over the rope for the cordoned off route downstairs. Shay guessed this headed towards the tunnel so he began to sprint, ignoring the lift alongside, and emerged quickly at pitch side with the small crowd near Linda. Medics were surrounding the victim but he'd have to take a risk and join them. After all, no one had prevented him so far. A bodyguard in a pristine suit and, despite it being evening, sporting dark glasses, had tried to drag her back to the tunnel initially in case of further shots. Although the right response, it couldn't have helped her chances for any wound already inflicted. The scene was generally frantic, security personnel in the immediate area constituted a mixture of police unsure where to point their machine guns and at least five dark suited personnel with handguns drawn. It almost looked like a Mexican standoff. Most gesticulated towards the top of the opposite stand. Carabinieri, with weapons drawn, were visible in the distance, clambering towards the origin of the initial smoke, climbing over a few rows of seats at speed then pausing, crouched low momentarily, in fear of further shots before repeating the sequence.

    Anastasi was already out of sight. Shay hadn't noticed any sign of injury to the elderly leader at the time, but his security brief evidently didn't want him trundling out of harm's way at snail pace. Within seconds he'd been hoisted back down the tunnel. To one side of the throng surrounding Linda, Persson stood trembling, checking his arms for injury. Probably just the bruises of diving to the ground. Shay assessed that the giant of European football, once renowned for staying cool on the pitch in Real Madrid's defence, was suffering from shock and not a bullet wound. He presumed Persson's English was excellent. The Swede would presume Shay was part of official security. No better opportunity to interview a close eyewitness.

    "Sir, what happened?"

    "Everyone is chasing there," signalling the stand opposite, his heavily accented English clear enough. "But they're wrong. I feel a bullet whistle past me from behind. It came from here," he shakily pointed to the tunnel, like Macbeth witnessing Banquo's ghost. "Someone told me hours ago that the Italian President gets claustrophobic so no one can be in or around the tunnel once we have taken the lift down. So, we three wait alone briefly before walking on. And now—," Persson's voice tailed away.

    You couldn't condemn the man for his state of shock. Shay recalled trembling, not immediately, but later all night, following his first encounter with gunfire. A quick pat on the official's shoulder before Shay moved away swiftly to check the tunnel. Surely anyone following the official party down from their VIP seats would be noticed? He took a closer look at the area he'd rushed through, the ornate carpet still pristine, devoid of players and staff accessing their changing rooms via the opposite corner of the ground, so no muddy boots and shouting competitors.

    How did—? There only seemed to be the lift and a door still ajar within, the latter leading to the stairs he'd bound down. On closer inspection though, a smaller door alongside it containing a cupboard with basic pitch maintenance equipment including rakes, brooms and brushes. But also just large enough to fit a person inside. Returning to the larger adjacent door, Shay followed the narrow flight of stairs back up to the VIP area, noting a fire escape on the floor in between. There was something else he hadn't picked up moments ago, not surprisingly, in his haste. A strong smell of cigar smoke wafted through. What was that about? Presumably one of the three dignitaries had puffed away during the journey down. But they would all have taken the lift and, anyway, surely a cigar was hardly a one-minute treat?

If Persson was right and the bullet had been fired from the area, most likely either someone was waiting in the cupboard to discharge the bullet from behind, or they'd used the stairs to follow their prey down. The lift would be too visible, even before the presentation party. Either way, the cupboard would have been the perfect hiding place afterwards as, presumably, the tunnel was soon full of frenzied activity. The gunman could pick their moment to emerge so as not to appear suspicious.

By now he'd returned upstairs. The Italian authorities had, not surprisingly, nervously held back on announcements for the last few minutes, and with good cause. Only a few years before, such an incident within a stadium would trigger an automatic message to clear a site immediately, but now no such comparative certainty existed. The possibility of a trap, with weaponry trained on the crowd outside or other potential forms of attack, couldn't be discounted. Realising there was no safe option to advise on anymore, the stadium's authorities were under strict instructions to stay quiet. Indeed, their insurers stressed on pain of invalidating their policy that no advice to the crowd trumped the wrong advice. It all reduced the possibility of mass litigation against them later.

There was no point trying to retrace his steps to the scene of the shooting. With every passing second, the area was more likely to be sealed off. Anyone asking suspicious questions would most likely be shoved into a police van and taken for questioning. He could make out the carabinieri high above in the opposite stand, having reached the gantry then suddenly slowing, all tension having exacerbated. What if this wasn't a turkey shoot from various vantage points, after all? Mass panic in a football stadium with officials at heightened sensitivity. It occurred to

Shay that a simulated rifle sound effect and simple smoke device from the far side would be perfect for diverting attention. It was certainly easier to plan than smuggling a telescopic rifle into the stands. Not only would some 80,000 fans fear for their lives but the identity of the would-be assassin could be hidden more easily.

He started to leave. Shay tried to remember the positioning of all he could recognise prior to the incident, instinctively starting with that slimeball Kruger who could never be trusted. Strangely, for once, he hadn't been at his mistress' side at the time of the hit, but so many were huddled round her quickly that Shay could have been mistaken.

A familiar voice at his side began. "I—" Siobhan started.

"Just keep walking," he instructed. Police with machine guns were now pushing fans down the outside steps to street level. The order had arrived on their radios to evacuate and they weren't standing on ceremony, whatever the risks awaiting outside. The couple followed orders.

A small number of officials alongside black vehicles stood in line outside the stand, uncertainty etched on the faces of the chauffeured drivers. Their car radios were blaring commentary from the scene, adding to their indecision as to whether to leave the vicinity without their passengers. Strangest of all whilst pedestrians rushed and shouted in seemingly random directions, alone on the other side of the street was the unexpected sight of a British army captain in uniform beckoning the pair over. How the hell did they know he was here? It could only be because of Siobhan. She pulled his hand towards the attendant vehicle, like a mother guiding a reluctant child. He'd been in charge upstairs and, now, she was assuming the lead.

As they clambered into the back seats, she started to explain.

"I tried to tell you. I told Townsend I'd seen you and he ordered me to get you out straight after the match. Not during it, as he was concerned you'd cause a scene even before all this bloodshed at the end."

"You knew I was here?"

"Of course, I'd noticed you beforehand. Not a face I'm likely to forget. Let's just say Townsend's not best pleased. What made you come out to Italy anyway? I could handle all this, or at least I thought I could."

"Okay," Shay tried to sound calm. "You mean you got past Kruger to set up a meeting?"

"Well, sort of. It was all arranged then when I turned up at the hotel yesterday, he said they'd been delays and that all interviews, of any variety, were suspended until after the final. Then some madman with a telescopic goes and attacks the presentation party. I presume Anastasi was the target, or maybe it was just to take out any dignitary."

"No" shaking his head. "I've got a hunch it was all more subtle. I'm betting they'll draw a blank from the apparent direction of the shot."

"How could you—?"

"Later, let's leave it all until then. If I'm right, they won't be catching the shooter at the scene. And a marksman half a stadium away has no certainty of a hit."

Suddenly, there was a series of garbled messages from the drivers' position on hands free. Shay had paid little attention to their getaway source.

"Captain Ray Leonard," the driver turned to introduce himself at a red light. "My orders are to escort you to the airport, post haste. And whatever happened back there, it sounds like you're right. I'm afraid Linda Maddison has just been confirmed dead at the scene. Either someone couldn't shoot straight or Anastasi wasn't the target."

Shay thought of escape. He'd evaded the authorities once, he thought, and needed to investigate further in Italy somehow. Instinctively sidling up to the car door as the vehicle slid to a gradual halt at another traffic light. An old woman covered from head to toe in black attire, clutching rosary beads in her right hand and a bible in her left, inched across the road despite the light reverting to green.

Shay let his true thoughts pour out. "The authorities obviously had no idea of the true sequence of events. They're pissing in the dark." Despite gently squeezing the metal handle, the door didn't budge at all. The doors were centrally locked and Shay's creeping sense of suspicion between him and Leonard must be mutual. Any official escort out of the country at this time could only be bad news.

Immediately a red light flashed on the dashboard, indicating Shay's attempt to escape. His reactions proved too slow, Leonard abruptly swinging round with a spray which flashed before Shay's eyes. His last sight before unconsciousness took hold was Siobhan's hands instinctively covering her mouth at the sudden violence meted out, or to protect herself from inhalation. He couldn't be sure. And then, blackness.

CHAPTER TWENTY-FIVE

CENTRAL LONDON

At first, uncertainty whether he had bridged the divide between sleep and wakefulness, so unfamiliar were the surrounds. Shay was decidedly groggy. However, various aspects within a space of seconds dispelled any notion that his unconscious was dictating events. The first was any sharp resistance to movement, limited by the metal chains on each leg and arm. They weren't painful if he remained still but were clearly designed to prevent him moving from the hard surface on which he laid prostrate. It was soon apparent that no attempt at force would loosen their grip. Additionally, there was the distinct scuttling on the floor in the corners. Mice or rats presumably.

His mind flashed to the memory of rodents at school. Thank god they weren't a phobia too. The science teacher had casually announced at the end of term that a ballot would be held by means of lots being drawn to acquire each of the four tiny field mice. Shay's name was called second, his response to which was a manic shake of the head. Yet years of differentiating between dangerous animals and harmless wildlife had gradually dispelled any over concern from a rodent. That is, as long as they stuck to their corners, peace could be maintained. Not that he was in any position to dictate terms here. And not that the room was any larger than a cell, that much was visible as a dim light overhead cast its few rays across the room. "No darkness, no problem," Shay reminded himself, unsure if he'd said that aloud.

Retching constituted the final sign. There was no time to call out, but at least sufficient manoeuvrability to lean his head away and release the contents of his stomach on the floor. It took a minute for the acidic aftertaste to lessen.

The bulbs were cranked up as, suddenly, a piercing light crammed the room. The intensity of the glare took a further minute to take in, by which time two figures stood next to the makeshift bed, both in army uniform. The younger, a corporal, was already busily unlocking the chains. Neither of the pair spoke despite Shay's near constant flow of questions and demands to be released. Instead, the door was soon locked behind them on exiting. In the corner was a basic toilet and dirty enamel basin with a wash kit alongside. He may as well clean himself up, noting he was still dressed in his clothes from the match.

Nine a.m. showed on his watch display. He was locked away in some army base around the Italian lakes presumably, clear of any fuss. But now different noises intruded, his first assumptions contradicted by the swish of traffic outside. Despite the lack of natural light, there was patently a great deal of vehicle movement around. And then, the unmistakable sound of Big Ben. Eight chimes. Some kind of weird mind games were succeeding in inducing disorientation.

After freshening up, he began shouting, with the door quickly reopening and the corporal uttering a curt "Follow me, Sir" as they made their way along a basic stone corridor. No further response was provided, despite Shay repeating his constant questioning, as they soon arrived outside a lift big enough only for three.

He'd almost forgotten to check. After hunting around in his pockets, the left luggage key was no longer there. No more MacBook presumably. Relief that his mobile, keys and wallet were still intact though.

His questions ceased as the soldier plainly had no orders to impart information. Four floors up, the corporal led the way, this time along a series of deep blue carpeted corridors with walnut panels to the sides. What a contrast. A knock on the door from the soldier eliciting an "Enter" from within. The door was held open by the soldier, and Shay found himself in a room with just one companion.

The figure with his back to the fireplace was engrossed in documents but instantly recognisable. Over six foot tall, slightly chubby, effortlessly smooth. Shay recalled the rather grand description of "…an easy charm that pervades all his mannerisms," from a recent article. Mauve tie, no jacket accompanying the formal trousers. Black, probably dyed, receding hair. And oily according to his political opponents, very oily.

"Come in, sit down. I suspect now is the best time for a chat." A nod from Bill Atkinson towards the ornate Queen Anne chair opposite his sumptuous walnut desk, which aimed to complement the grandeur of the walls pervading most of that floor presumably. The desk must have occupied at least a quarter of the massive, resplendently decorated room. Atkinson continued his paperwork for a minute, head down, affording the opportunity for Shay to take in the Holbein and two Turners, originals presumably, and the monarch's head and shoulders in a bust behind the desk. This was not only designed to impress generally, but more significantly to stress the eternal power and wealth of the state.

Shay felt restless, still groggy from whatever had been shoved from that spray, presumably hours ago now. The politician tossed aside the gold ink pen which clattered on to the desk. Scratching his head briefly, Atkinson peered at him as if establishing focus.

"Firstly, apologies Lieutenant Mason. This is not the usual way I meet British military personnel. The question I have to ask though, is why?" The voice was clipped, decidedly upper class, used to commanding.

"I don't follow, sir. Unless the question is what's wrong with politely asking for my cooperation rather than all manner of pulling me in for questioning. It looks like everyone wants to pick my brains." Shay took in the room again. "I don't even know where I am."

Atkinson looked puzzled. Shay regretted his comments immediately, as it was best not to expand on the Americans having already pumped him for information. Definitely preferable that his own government were unaware of that aspect.

"Officially this conversation isn't happening," continued Atkinson. "You'll be returned to Paddington Green in a few minutes, a location I understand you're fast becoming familiar with. The formalities are being finalised with the Italian Embassy then we'll have to invite them in to carry out the investigation alongside our staff, I'm afraid. Our official line is that we only realised you may be a bad apple after you'd landed in the UK, so we'd hardly turn the plane around to parachute you out over the

San Siro. It'll take a few days for i's to be dotted and t's crossed on the paperwork, then we may just have to extradite you to our Italian friends. So, it's really important there are no misunderstandings here," the politician attempting to sound reasonable alongside his threats.

"What made some rogue British officer, highly decorated at that," Atkinson tapped a file, "murder a prominent personality in front of the eyes of the world?" The supposed 'easy charm' was decidedly grating now. Shay had a flashback to his attempt at escape from Leonard and the car. What exactly had run through his mind there? All still seemed foggy. Was it to get away from them because there was more to investigate. or because, deep down, the vehicle's timely presence smacked of a set up?

"Sir, there's been some mistake. I was authorised by Townsend to investigate the links between—."

He hastily stopped in order to avert the car crash of a sentence. There was no way of diplomatically setting out the links between the former school colleagues, given that the most powerful of the lot, and one of only two left alive, was perched in front of him.

"Go on, man."

"Between Stewart Tyler's death and potential links with dubious overseas regimes, Iran in particular."

A slight shake of the head. "I'm sure you weren't. And anyway, who may Townsend be exactly? My knowledge of the geopolitical threats to the state may be excellent but remember I've only taken operational control recently. I can hardly be expected to know the full roster of intelligence personnel in days."

"I understood that you intervened in his project and tried to close it down Sir?"

Standing, the Secretary of State obscuring the monarch's expressionless image. "Let me see if I understand you, Mason. You consider that I stepped in to close an operation by some maverick I've never heard of, who's working somewhere in intelligence. Even if I had given such an order, that doesn't explain your presence in Milan at the site of an old school friend's assassination. You do see that, don't you? I can't believe that was your remit."

Shay grasped the conversation was fraught with danger and, in a sense, it was too late to hold back. "That's what I was told about Townsend, sir. That he had a direct link to the higher echelons of government. And I concluded that it was a mistake to halt the mission whilst the Iranians were causing havoc on our streets in London. I had a meeting arranged with Maddison to take place after the match so I happened to be on the scene, nothing more than that. It appeared for all the world to be a long range hit but, somehow, she was taken out by someone able to get within feet."

Atkinson turned and approached the slightly ajar window, Shay aware of the weight of traffic outside as a bus and taxi were involved in an unmistakable war of words and horns in Whitehall.

"You concluded that you'd run some…covert business?" the last two words elongated. "In your own time and travelling with a backpack around Europe? Which placed you at the scene of Linda's murder as the prime suspect. Then you try and escape when military intelligence attempted to reel you in." Atkinson turned abruptly. "You have a fair amount of explaining to do before there's even a one per cent chance of evading extradition. If what you say is true and some rogue operation is playing out within Whitehall, which I strongly doubt, it strikes me that you keep showing up at the wrong place at the wrong time. Having single-handedly tried to frighten our capital's residents, you now show up at the most public assassination for years."

Since Atkinson first uttered the allegations, Shay had tried to narrow down the multitude of possible reasons for the meeting. But the shift in conversation was now apparent, as he suddenly grasped why he'd been summoned. And in particular why the second most important politician in the country was meeting a supposed assassin alone, with not a hint of security or restraining equipment in sight. He was being probed for information that Atkinson couldn't acquire elsewhere.

There was no way Atkinson would climb down in denying any knowledge of Townsend, whatever the facts. If Shay were handed over to the Italian authorities, he could kiss goodbye to his career, though surely he could prove his innocence for the shooting in Milan? It could take many years and a huge legal bill to do so however, particularly if his own government was disowning him. What a price to pay. He may as well push the boat out.

"Sir, if I may. I presume your people have poured over my file and won't have come up with any reason for me to act against my country, let alone why I'd be involved in a conspiracy to murder. Also, it's suited your agenda perfectly well to terrify the population at every turn. I've not been the one stoking up charges of cowardice in number ten. In fact, this supersized Department wouldn't have emerged if the public weren't shaken up at every turn."

Atkinson paused at the aggressive tone, before his puffed-up retort would have perfectly suited a public information broadcast. "Alarm is never in the interests of the state but we have a duty to protect our citizens to the utmost of our ability."

Then, less pompously, "Anyway, you don't quite get it. It's one thing for the public to be worried about a couple of rogue assassins who'll soon be locked away. Quite another to be terrified of Iran, which may well be armed with nuclear weapons by now. I genuinely want Barjam to succeed—," his voice trailed away. "Is there anything else you want to inform me about? We may be able to look at the charges in more detail before we involve the Italians formally."

"Is there any connection with the Bard Sir?"

At last, it was out in the open. Shay presumed the question was fully expected as Atkinson visibly relaxed, despite the latter responding, "What's that, exactly?"

"Something to do with your school days perhaps?"

Atkinson stared indignantly, his hand straightening a non-existent crease on his silk tie for some seconds, as if weighing up his response. "Yes, well that was Rory's scam. All just a schoolboy prank. It was nothing to do with me and it's not likely to raise its ugly head now. Unless, you know differently? Now is the time to reveal all."

Shay shook his head adamantly at which Atkinson reached for a buzzer, the door being opened without delay by the young corporal.

"You'll make a full disclosure of what you saw in the stadium to my staff, without any hypothesis of your own added. Then you'll remember that the Security of Information Act prohibits release of any classified information including names, locations, units, operations. The lot. Any breach of that, irrespective of whether the Italians charge you, and your life will be one hellish struggle. Then when we're satisfied your version of events doesn't present more problems, we'll pass the account to the Italians."

Atkinson nodded, dismissing him. Crossing the deep carpet, Shay made to leave.

"Oh, and one more point Mason. When you're sent an obvious warning not to interfere, it's best to be heeded. Get back to your day job and stop causing us all headaches. Crisis days are over. There's no imminent threat to the country, whatever the warning levels suggest."

What had Shay missed from the meeting that bothered him so much? As he was led down by lift to the police van in the underground car park for the short journey to Paddington Green, confusion still held sway. His head was pushed roughly to avoid the vehicle's roof as he entered.

His hatred of Whitehall double speak only sharpened. The sooner he could return to the field, whether in training or combat, the better. For the first time, he really wished he'd foregone the financial incentive dangled in front of him to take the mission. At least reliance on each other was a given in the ranks. But here, amidst self-serving machinations, the order appeared to be to shut up in the hope the allegations may, just may, all go away.

It suddenly dawned, as the vehicle entered daylight. How come Atkinson had denied knowledge of Townsend, yet seemed pretty certain of the limits of the mission's instructions?

CHAPTER TWENTY-SIX

WEST LONDON

Unloved. Unwanted. Familiar station names, the train hurtling on the well-trodden tracks back to Wales. The modern glass façades of west London at first, making way to nineteenth-century housing on the route out of the capital. The arrival at Slough Station raised a smile as Shay's first sight was a teenager, most likely local, with mobile seemingly glued to his ear. Did the boy even know the first telegraphed message in the world was sent from Slough to Paddington to catch a murderer over one hundred and seventy years ago? Did he care?

Then the start of rolling countryside, sporadically at least. Reading Station's nearby ski run with sloping roofs. And on. Whilst some considered it a downward step from London, Shay was decidedly at home outside the city. Tracts of land beyond Reading now more spacious, soon vast areas of farmland between the cities. Bristol, Cardiff and, beyond, via Swansea. Finally, a jeep in place to collect him for the final seven-mile route over the hills. Only three hours from Paddington, Greg's was the first face welcoming him on arrival back at base after the checks. Was security even tighter now? A procedure he must have passed through a thousand times entering or leaving without a cursory glance from the guard, who now insisted on carefully checking his ID papers. Had his break been that long? Equally, was his name the object of questioning or a source of disgrace at the barracks? With self-doubt mounting, Shay uneasily recalled both Milan and the incident in Parliament Square.

The stark fortified entrance, with electronic bollards added years before, gave way to a central courtyard of five, equally sized, sand-coloured three storey buildings. One for HQ, two for sleeping quarters in each of which half shared dormitories for sixteen, one for the mess and recreation, plus the fifth comprising classrooms and training pods.

All familiar, all home. He'd tried to track down Siobhan. Inscrutable Siobhan, deciding she was the only possibility of helping to fill in the gaps. She'd appeared stunned in the stadium and surely no one had given her a hard time afterwards as well. Like some love lost kid, he'd tried turning up at her apartment, sending a number of unanswered messages and making calls which all landed on voicemail. All in vain.

"Any fine whiskeys for a snifter stashed in your case? And why are you in uniform? Thought that was holiday," Greg's outstretched hand in greeting. No quick wittedness in response, the prospect of admitting Shay had been anywhere near Milan for the dramatic events seemed abhorrent. Why hadn't he worked out his story for the benefit of colleagues? Simple, he had no idea what they knew of his whereabouts. Hopefully his mug hadn't appeared in TV reports, after all he'd only been on the scene after the shooting. He'd have to take the plunge, though, and trust that, if Greg didn't know, none of them did.

"Just some health and safety bollocks in London which our new supersized Department panicked about introducing." Shay warmed to his line. "Unbelievably, they wanted to run it by someone in the field rather than publish the bloody thing and watch it crumble in front of them when a Freddie needs a sticking plaster and sues their arses off for a million." Greg smiled. Neither was sure who'd come up with the epithet of 'Freddie' to describe the fresh-faced newbies, mostly keen to impress and ready to be moulded. "Then they gave me time off, because Dad may be on his way out."

"But I thought—?" started Greg, hands on hips.

"Leave it GM," Shay waved a hand and started towards the officers' mess. Kill it now.

The prospect of a lack of stress contrasted beautifully with the events of recent weeks. It appeared a blessing and, even with the forecast of summer's soaring temperatures, entailing racking up the miles with the next intake in full fatigues as if burning up in a sauna, all felt like a homecoming. Two days after arriving back, a new batch would be passed his way for brutal introduction to the army. He acknowledged the crueller side, not just the challenge of knocking them into shape for a career of extreme physical achievement. There was also, as Greg described it, the near sadistic pleasure of picking from the Freddies, on first sight, those who would thrive and those for whom a rapid return to civilian life, or a desk job, would emerge all too soon. Many a bet changed hands amongst the trainers before the first challenging run ensued.

A fortnight later the first overnighter with the Freddies was being completed.

"Ayesha, Tim, buck up your ideas now or you've got hours left in the army," Greg provided the dressing down as he walked past. He and Shay were jointly responsible for overseeing this trek through marshes, three hours of crouching behind trees with no movement allowed, followed by a five mile backpack run to be completed within forty minutes. The penalty for failure was thirty push ups, all with backpack still in place.

Every one of the twelve-person unit appeared exhausted. It was no surprise that a couple of the recruits were being given a dressing down so early. As training officers, there was a mountain of reports to complete on each recruit. Weariness, tension, anger, collapsing in front of their trainers; all happened regularly. There were many acceptable responses to the sessions over the years. But tears, as Ayesha and Tim, though only eighteen, had fallen prey to at the end, were deemed unacceptable in the field. For this neither Shay nor Greg felt any remorse. Both had witnessed such a collapse by colleagues in the midst of combat in the Middle East and Central Asian battlefields. Greg had even lost his brother in combat due to a colleague's tearful breakdown at a crucial moment, according to the report from Basra years before. He was least sympathetic of all.

An hour's lie down now would be heaven-sent, Shay mused as he approached the mess for the full English breakfast before starting on the reports. To his surprise, Woodford awaited him at the entrance to the canteen. A quick salute.

"You have a surprise visitor, Mason. Accompany me now please," marching off at pace towards his office, with the slight imbalance as ever in his gait. Maybe he'd never got used to the artificial leg supporting him for thirty-five years since the roadside explosion outside Belfast. Removing his distinctive red and gold cap as he held the office door open for Shay, Woodford nodded and walked off, adding, "I'll leave you two to catch up."

A familiar figure occupied the chair behind the Lieutenant Colonel's desk.

"Good man, you've stayed away and let the experts re-establish control of the situation." Townsend didn't offer a seat.

"I was told—"

"Yes, you've decided to follow instructions at last, which is what I'd expect of someone of your rank. But I thought you deserved to know the latest. The Department has received information that it's all blown over. To be precise, both Behzadi and Hamouni appear to have made a dash for Syria where, presumably, the Iranian Government will find a way of protecting them. They were chased over land by Interpol, who somehow lost them by seconds. At least the sarin threat, if any existed in the first place, has ended with their quite welcome departure from Europe."

"Sir, I appreciate you coming all this way to tell me. But there are still loose ends, surely."

"There may be Mason, but those are for the combined might of British and American intelligence to unravel, not for the likes of you." Having already resigned himself to leaving the whole turmoil in London behind anyway, there was no point arguing. Siobhan, who was still fully out of contact, Townsend, the bloody politicians. It was no contest, especially with the weariness of the night's escapades now being fully felt. It just seemed he'd been set up to fail, though why and by whom, he didn't know. The jigsaw wouldn't fall into place, which left only nagging doubts.

After Townsend had left the room, Woodford caught up with Shay as they started towards the mess. Clearly, his commanding officer was no fan of Townsend according to the rare moment of candour, despite being patently uncomfortable in criticising a colleague.

"Former regimental colleague in Yorkshire. A sneaky sort whom I never particularly took to. I encountered him at one of our dinners and he was all bravado. He banged on about his social life consisting of a four handicap on the golf course and his uber-successful local Sunday night quiz team. A four handicap? In his dreams. Still, ours is not to question why."

As Shay settled down to a substantial bowl of spaghetti bolognese that evening, it was as if Townsend's visit had stirred his emotions again. It didn't seem possible to dip into the convoluted lives of those suffering, Harriet's and Bryony's in particular, then walk away without remorse.

Remaining in the mess after, Shay was the sole occupant apart from the catering staff clearing up around him amidst a soundtrack of quiet conversations, clattering plates and the rattling of cutlery. The halfway house to continue untangling events was to follow up on every avenue electronically, try and piece it all together, at least until Bryony was safe again. Surely she'd run off, been mixed up in something too big and spotted the warning signs. Now the Iranian threat had lessened, she'd reappear, perhaps have to undergo a dressing down from the Agency across the Atlantic whether she was their stooge or not, but at least re-emerge unharmed. There'd been a connection in Boston. He smiled. Or maybe it had just been too long since he'd slept with anyone.

Over the coming weeks, he became used to being shunted around training bases where needed. The Highlands of Scotland, East Anglia, Cumbria; he seriously wondered if this was all intended to keep him firmly occupied, not least as he was afforded no days off.

The standard patten was a couple of weeks' training at each base in order to get under the skins of his team, be they Freddies, elite forces or the vast bulk of soldiers somewhere in-between. His itinerary was supplemented by three days in Gibraltar and only four days on-ship for an elite corps stationed off the Libyan coast. It felt like being inside a child's kaleidoscope that was frantically being shaken to keep him busy. Orders from above?

At last, he perceived a chink of light in the timetable. There was little respite for his anxiety, despite trying to put the events earlier in the year firmly in the past. Bryony and Harriet occupied his thoughts, more than uncovering Tyler's past, and no one was offering an update of any kind. Due a long weekend off, Shay arrived back at the Crouch End flat on a muggy Thursday evening, opting to spend the night in north London prior to taking the train down to Horsham.

The message had been clear enough from Townsend and the Department. He'd been saved by a thread from having to acquit himself, trussed up like a Christmas turkey, from facing the

Italian authorities. No one wanted to hear his take on events but, feeling a new lease of life, he started on further research anyway.

If the Iranians were behind the assassination in Milan, well, they were on the run by now. Absorbing a number of follow-up articles about events in the San Siro had only proved frustrating. Yet all led back to the closed ranks of the official investigation, the main hypothesis of a lone gunman evaporating behind a puff of smoke on the stadium's far side. An Iranian man was "still awaiting identification" apparently. How long could it take? It was notable there was already an official line on events, given that the investigation was supposedly still underway. Italian authorities tried to be draconian about seizing and claiming ownership of all recordings from the stadium in order that the "truth not be tainted", if his Google translation was accurate enough. Apart from brief footage that found its way onto the internet straight after the event, which the authorities succeeded in removing quickly, they'd largely been successful through the threat of legal action. And given that most fans had panicked rather than filmed at the time, there wasn't a huge amount of footage to confiscate or silence.

The visit south via a heaving crowd at Victoria Station did nothing for his spirits. Dad was taciturn by temperament rather than due to his illness and, he suspected, neither relished his visits. There was no sign of Maryanne this time. What you never had you never miss, wasn't that the phrase? He managed to block the pair out of his mind quite successfully between visits.

The pavement outside the nursing home was sun-baked and, not wanting to face the stuffy train journey to the capital immediately, the opportunity to stroll to the town centre and utilise facilities opposite the Sussex station was too good to turn down. Horsham Library was officially part of a "business and innovation regeneration centre" apparently, according to the laminated blue and red sign outside. Cheap plastic chairs were dotted alongside the few, sparsely covered, shelves within; the local council probably investing in technology instead. There was no shortage of PCs to sit and use without presenting identification though.

With the weekend to while away, Ade in Tenerife with the family for a week round a pool, he started to delve into further updates. Firstly, anything about the sisters? He drew a bland. Nothing, no reappearance from the younger in America. The sarin scare was still prominent news but, without any suspects in custody in the UK and the Government adamantly denying any knowledge of events in Milan, the general media angle implied a receding terrorist threat here. Unofficial sources stressed there was no terrorist cell of concern operating in the UK.

Now the search he'd staved off so far. Taking a deep breath, he slowly pressed the keys. Fortunately, there were no recent references to himself online, save the old reports about the Olympics embarrassment all those years before. His fists unclenched and breathing slowed once again. Presumably Rahman had considered the brief chat didn't warrant a further splash.

But Bryony was still lost. Standing up to leave, he grabbed a macchiato from the coffee shop next door. Siobhan's refusal to speak, or even to make contact, couldn't remain an obstacle. They had no choice other than to work as a team, even if the prospect seemed unappealing to her.

PART THREE

CHAPTER TWENTY-SEVEN

CENTRAL LONDON

Arriving near the Kensington address on the Saturday morning, Shay held back, having ensured the trade bell would prove sufficient for entry. He'd have to bide his time, though it surely wouldn't take long for such a sizable mansion block. In the end his waiting time was around twenty minutes, as he pretended to be preoccupied with his mobile just along the street before a Harrods delivery van pulled up directly outside, part blocking the road with hazard lights flashing. The driver didn't bother removing his headphones, whilst grabbing a foot-long package from the adjacent seat and heading towards the flats. Shay timed his intervention to perfection, pressing the tradesman bell just ahead of the other's arrival. Fortunately, the door buzzed open.

"After you mate," Shay started. "Where are you delivering to?"

"Thanks, err—, Mrs Sainsbury apparently. Flat 13." Both moved towards the lift.

"Not the first time that's happened," Shay added chattily. "She's dyslexic and mistakes a 13 for an 18, awful typing skills. It's on the fourth floor." The delivery man, named Brad according to his badge, shrugged, following him into the lift.

Rap continued to seep out of Brad's headphones. His likely pay was at the rate of a few quid per delivery, with a deduction for costs, which was insufficient to warrant full concentration presumably. On arrival, Shay pretended to fumble for keys outside the adjacent flat. Out of eyeline, Shay heard her door opening.

"Mrs Sainsbury?" Brad began to hand over the package with one hand, thrusting the proof of delivery device forward with the other.

"I'm afraid not" Shay recognised the familiar voice, having quickly moved round the corner to avoid Brad's confused glance in his direction. With a shrug, the delivery man headed towards the lift to descend to number 13.

Shay returned to 18 and pressed.

"Look I've just told you," Siobhan's voice was sharp now, as the door swiftly reopened. Taking her by surprise, Shay pushed past her quickly before turning, raising both hands in mock surrender. Closing the door, she leant back against it with arms firmly crossed. "And if I don't want you here? Will you please leave?"

"I don't want an argument. I've absolutely no intention to bother you but the one gift I can't give is to walk out of this flat without answers."

"Right, well if you're not going, then I am," she retorted, face reddening in annoyance. "I'll grab my coat. I'm NEVER talking to you again, either inside or outside this flat."

Incredulous at first, Shay stood back as she grabbed her black jacket and door keys then swiftly passed him, heading out of the front door and towards the stairway at a swift rate. Shaking his head, he started following. Hopefully the neighbours wouldn't hear her raised voice and call the police. That was just what he didn't need in his life.

Shay could just make out her strides in the distance heading round the corner towards Kensington High Street. He broke into a slow jog to catch up but she showed no acknowledgement to his presence when only ten feet behind.

A hand reached out from an Arabic café as he passed, almost jerking him inside.

"Well that was clever Shay. Turn up at my flat to pump me for information. What type of idiot are you?"

"I tried to contact you so many times. Phone, doorbell. Sorry about the subterfuge. I just had to see you and try to get this all sorted. It's just as well I've got a good memory. You pulled that stunt a couple of times when we were together." He mimicked her voice badly: "I'm never talking to you either inside or outside." Then off you'd trot down the street waiting for me to catch up. Usually with some sadistic grin as a I desperately chased after you for forgiveness."

Her shoulders visibly relaxed. "Yes, well, forgiveness was sometimes called for. The one no-no is talking in that flat. I don't trust the bastards and neither should you." After a friendly dig in the ribs aimed in his direction, the two began to walk through the busying retail area, crowds building, retail outlets and eateries competing for attention despite eleven a.m. having only just passed.

"In fact, they told me to avoid contact with you at all costs. Ever. Especially after the caper you pulled in Milan."

"Caper? You can't really believe I had anything to do with Linda's murder. Seriously? I'd be behind bars if that was the case. They just made me sign some crappy little statement admitting to the Italian authorities that I was acting in contravention to the UK Government when delving around but had no involvement in the actual events in the San Siro. In fact, I wouldn't be surprised if that statement was never handed over to the Carabinieri so I probably didn't appear on their radar at all. Now, does that sound to you like someone who Interpol are hunting in connection with the highest profile political assassination of the century?"

Stopping, she turned and smiled. "I know that, of course you didn't. Not only wouldn't you have carried out such a seemingly pointless act. Also, if the authorities tried to frame you for it, there's no way you'd go down quietly. But you are trouble, yet again."

They had to step around sauntering shoppers as they strolled in companionable silence, firstly arriving in Kensington Gardens, then onto Hyde Park. Passing well-turned out youngsters with parents who, presumably, were heading for the Diana Memorial Playground.

She spoke first. "You never wanted children at all, did you?" He coughed.

"I thought you hadn't wanted that for us, to be honest? But I'm sure you're a great mum. Where is he now?"

"Boarding school. Young, I know, but it suits us. I can hardly be there for him all the time given the hours my job takes up. And then, when you and I trekked around Europe at a moment's notice...well, it confirms it was the right decision."

"And if he'd been in the flat when I came calling today? You wouldn't have left without so much as a goodbye to him." Her blue eyes took on a steely edge as she stopped and stared at him. "Let's just say that any man who places my boy in danger would have the opportunity to father his own children removed."

Another playful dig in the ribs from her and they moved on, turning over the events they'd worked on together from every angle. The American connection, Bryony's secret postcards, former schoolfriends turned power-mad, the Westminster connection, Iranian terror attacks. Shay felt little room to manoeuvre, as trusting her was itself risky given he couldn't be sure how far Townsend's control was exerted. Maybe the whole conversation would be reported back, his whole military career dissolving before his eyes. And if he had the forces removed from his life now? Personal training instruction in a back-street gym at a tenner an hour, if he was lucky, would be no comparison to helping shape the young guns coming through, and not just for financial reasons.

It was a difficult balance, but he had no one else to turn to who'd shared their experience. Her capacity for listening, really taking on board his feelings, at least held strong. Long ago he'd felt they could kick around any topic at the right time.

"Siobhan, all this," he swept his arm. "You should know there's one aspect I can't leave to the authorities. It feels personal."

"Embarrassment in Whitehall? Yes, I can imagine the ribbing in the barracks was pretty harsh after."

"No, that I can deal with. I've not been picked up by the press. It's America, Bryony. After all, she was digging around for information on my behalf. And she's been missing since. We got close—"

The accepting nod before her voice gradually rose. "I knew it. Twenty-four hours overseas and you can't resist a leg over with a witness, a suspect, a—, I don't even know how to describe her? How professional, Shay. How bloody professional."

"It just happened, I didn't plan it," trying to explain. "Two consenting adults, Siobhan. What's the big deal?" No words emerged as her lips moved to respond, before shaking her head and walking off. "What's the big deal? Why does it concern you?" catching her up.

"Because," she stopped, "if this mission gets tainted by emotion, none of us have a hope." He could only stare in response.

The two fell into step. It was absolutely not the time to go down that route, he prayed. Now in uncomfortable silence, they returned to the facts of the disappearance, bringing her up to speed with the Israeli connection from Bryony's postcard. Unexpectedly, Siobhan reassured him on those grounds, speculating that the US Government would bend over backwards to ensure no harm came to her if working for Israel.

They tried to work out the way forward. Narrowing choices appeared stark. A return to the two big cats from schooldays, stalking each other? They could hardly arrange another interview on spurious grounds with Nicholls. Siobhan pointed out she was in no position to burst into her boss' office accusing him of…what exactly? She could hardly interrogate him to determine whether there was any truth in his throwaway allegations about Nicholls and the Bard, or if dissembling was just second nature to him.

There was another way, Shay concluded, as he followed up the conversation with a quick request to Rahman by mobile, as they stood in the long afternoon's park rays. He was getting tired of the subterfuge of secretive phone calls. Maybe the politicians shouldn't be under any illusions that they were determined to follow this through. Rahman's response was disappointing though. It was one thing to have Shay tag along to meetings provided he played the part quietly, the journalist admonished. And quite another to set up some kind of dialogue on spurious grounds with Nicholls, not least as he could well be the next PM.

"You may as well ask me out for a non-Halal burger. Not my cup of tea. Besides, I've heard you pissed off my friend in Milan by pushing too hard. Not a good idea Shay, definitely not a bright move."

"Siddique isn't playing ball," Shay pursed his lips after finishing the call. "I can't say I blame him. He's hardly our nanny. And Atkinson is almost Teflon-proof at present, so I don't see how we can get to him."

"Okay," tentatively from her. "Me and Nicholls though?"

Shay nodded slowly. "Yup, you may as well go for it. We're really running out of options and no one's talking. At least with anything useful."

CHAPTER TWENTY-EIGHT

CENTRAL LONDON

The whole conversation was relayed crystal clear to him, listening in from his living room and recorded digitally at his end. They'd decided it was best to keep away from phones and only later it occurred to Shay that he couldn't be sure of privacy in his own home anyway. But by then it was too late to alter plans.

Monday morning, soon after 9 a.m.. On her return to work at the Department after the weekend, Siobhan had arranged lunch with Joe, a colleague with a sympathetic ear from the tech section. Her expression of fear regarding a former violent boyfriend had hit the right tone; she'd made clear there seemed no way out. Joe took the bait and suggested trying to entrap him. What a great idea. Her face lit up, but she added that her mobile would be the first item the boyfriend would demand to see for texts and messages as, in his warped imagination if not actually true, she'd found someone else. Joe's quick response was again on the button. How about a two way bugging device from their department that could be monitored by an outsider at the same time? The conversation could be recorded and law enforcement brought it.

"Why hadn't I thought of that?" Siobhan pronounced with relief. Was there any chance of borrowing the equipment for twenty-four hours?

As early as the next day, the lure had proved successful to entice a meeting. Shay felt self-satisfied in finding the way in. He'd read up about Margot Guillard's reputation – the press pack apparently joked she was part guard dog and part hunting dog, prepared to rip up anyone in the path to power of her boss, Rory Nicholls. More Alsatian than Retriever by the sound of it, though. Many years after she'd left Toronto after cutting her teeth in Canadian politics.

Siobhan found herself strolling by Lambeth Palace, just south of Parliament, with the Leader of the Opposition. Guillard's deputy, Graham McMahon, known for his more approachable manner, had been holding the fort as Guillard was in hospital.

"At least that's one day we won't get any calls from the Canadian ripping into us," a loose-tongued radio news presenter had announced on air recently, before being forced by her editor to make a swift apology minutes later. Not so much for the fact that Guillard hadn't lived in her home country for so long, but rather that McMahon had put word out that her health had further deteriorated. Nicholls seemed only to benefit from the sad news, his popularity going up a further percentage point with the update on his famous press secretary.

Siobhan had tempted McMahon to agree to the meeting without specifying how she'd stumbled across "concerning information about the Government's role in the crisis," hinting only that her job allowed prime access to Whitehall confidential material. No, she added, she'd only inform Nicholls directly about this. That, in turn, incentivised McMahon to carry out research on her and she evidently passed their vetting process. Within minutes, she'd received an eager call back from McMahon to set up the outdoor meeting with Nicholls. There was no way they could resist.

Nicholls had proposed a walk around the adjacent bridges.

He started at something of a march, presumably affording her five minutes and turning back if the conversation had proven useless. Groups of tourists, sprinkled along Westminster Bridge, ignored them, training their cameras on Big Ben's clock tower. There was only the occasional glance from a Westminster aide or eagle-eyed voters acknowledging the politician. Preliminary chat was brief, not surprisingly, though Nicholls sounded attentive.

"So, Siobhan. Can I call you that? I understand you've come across something of concern in your role. We all have to be vigilant about those in authority. I absolutely understand your concerns."

She'd discussed with Shay how to dress up any allegations to grab Nicholls' interest from the start, knowing the positive impression had to start quickly. She explained that her position at Defence gave clearance to view high level minutes. One set had proven Atkinson's desire to ramp up the fear factor nationally far in excess of the advice he was receiving from his officials. Did she retain a copy? No. Did she recall exactly who attended the meeting? No. When did the meeting take place? She guessed at an approximate, convincing date. All vague.

The questioning grew more intense. Could she get hold of it? Yes, there was a good chance, if she put her mind to it, but it might take time. She would require some pretext to access the information on the classified system. Yet, to her surprise, Nicholls appeared hooked, desperate for the smoking gun. In particular, a golden opportunity of shaming his rival. The King may push for a general election, he mused aloud, ignoring the unlikelihood of a royal intervention.

They batted it back and forth, all hypothetically. The distance they walked must be a positive sign, she noted. They'd continued to the end of the Bridge and turned right south of the river until the junction with Lambeth Bridge, before recrossing the river and heading back. Just before arriving at St Stephen's entrance, Nicholls paused briefly in the adjacent leafy space of Victoria Tower Gardens. He'd walked speedily but given her fifteen minutes of precious time. She sensed all was proceeding well, reeling in her prey.

"Mr Nicholls, I'm happy to help out the country only because it's a complete abuse of power and not because it's clearly personal between you two. And I take no sides in the bigger political picture. But it seems to be a crusade, your dislike of Atkinson. Beyond politics, I mean. May I ask why?"

Nicholls paused, sweeping his hair from his face. He stared into the distance, looking out over the Thames towards Waterloo Bridge, deciding how much to reveal.

"Yes, it's personal. Atkinson was vicious at school, a sadist. He was cool to know as his family had so much influence. Certainly, the parties he held were something else, when we were teenagers, if you were on the right side of him. But he would turn on someone at random and it didn't matter if you were his closest friend. Then the knives were out, you'd be shunned, held out as bait for the rest of the group to prove their loyalty to Bill."

"And you were sacrificed by the group as a kid? Is that what you're saying? We all get teased at some point in life—"

"Not one word of any of this appearing on government files, Siobhan."

"I'm in Defence, Mr Nicholls. We don't exactly specialise in hunting down teasing classmates. Especially when we're talking about my boss."

"Would it make any difference to add he had more than a sharp tongue? Let me put it bluntly, your Department is being led by a psychopath. The level of violence he'd meet out, even at that age, resulted in all sorts of punishments at school which included two suspensions and a near expulsion. Sanctions I'm sure the family's money helped to expunge from any records."

Trying to maintain eye contact wasn't working now. Ultimately it was only worthwhile being here if she could break through with a real lead.

"Mr Nicholls, there will be huge risks involved in me trying to access documents for which I'm not authorised. You know all about the relevant legislation, in your position. Are you telling me I'd be risking my current job, my potential for future employment, possibly even my freedom, to stop some angry bully from schooldays rising to the position of PM? I could probably find far worse amongst current politicians and even past Prime Ministers from a quick trawl on the internet. Even drug-fuelled university parties haven't got in the way of some getting to the top. Please level with me. Rory. Why am I doing this exactly? I know you had a colourful array of characters at your school, it's all over the press."

He leant against the railing and stared intently at her face, as if searching for weakness.

"Okay. I didn't stay friends with Bill of course, but the others did. I have my way of knowing who pals up with whom, even today. He must have hatched a plan to use either the reality or the threat of terrorism to secure power. Tyler could access the chemical information whilst Linda was unmistakably playing games with dubious acquaintances in the Middle East, maybe offering a reward if she pushed international tournaments their way. The World Cup even? Who knows. Is there a bigger statement in making clear your country has arrived at the top table of respected nation status? And they'd be nothing the Americans could do to stop them."

"Boycott the World Cup?"

"Boycott? Who cares. Soccer is one market the Yanks don't own yet. Any drop in advertising revenue would be more than compensated for by driving up the price elsewhere."

"But the Iranians are suspected of murdering Tyler?"

"Wake up Siobhan, you work for the MoD. Or however the hell it's rebranded by Atkinson now. There is no single Iranian state acting in any kind of unified way. The ideal of Iran impressing the world diplomatically isn't shared throughout their government and its bureaucracy. If ever a country was composed of factions amongst factions...the only certainty is that the direction targeted by one influential grouping there will be countered by another gang."

"Based on internal religious battles?"

"Based on power. It makes the world go round. If you're ever tempted to question whether it's more significant than money as the priority, just look at Putin. A penniless youth, doing OK on the rise up, but then the Presidency comes into view. And, hey presto. Worth what now? A hundred, two hundred million dollars, or more? With a whole network, a whole state, in place to protect him.

Now, I need to prep for Prime Minister's Questions, so please excuse me. It sounds as if we're on the same page with this… mutual interest. Who knows where it may lead? I'm not asking you to break the law. But the authorities will probably reward you handsomely if you prove Atkinson's actions are ultra vires. And, of course, I'll argue for immunity if I ever take power, should your role come to light in doing the right thing."

Nicholls turned to leave after a pat on her shoulder and flashing that eye-catching smile. Evidently used to ordering his team around. Siobhan sensed there was something undeniably attractive in it.

As he strode away, she continued talking, the microphone hopefully still rolling.

"Got it?" she ventured to Shay as Nicholls returned to Parliament.

"Got it," he returned, sounding smug.

With the substantive meeting clearly over, the pair had no hesitation where to take this now. Shay took over communications, calling Rahman from the café in Crouch End where he'd monitored and recorded the conversation.

"Fancy a burger and walk in the centre of town? Halal of course, my treat. Where suits to meet?"

"The king's fictional author lying under a car park in Leicester. You work it out Mr award winning journalist."

Hours later, Shay spotted Rahman approaching from some distance, whilst waiting patiently amidst neon boards advertising the latest movie blockbusters, musicals, pizzas – the lot. He couldn't contain a smile at Rahman's appearance. Sunglasses worn in defiance of the cloudy weather, still looking like a dishevelled Hollywood star without the budget.

The journalist nodded to the statue of Shakespeare alongside them in Leicester Square. "Hope the pigeons treat him well."

As they ambled along, Shay launched into hints about having obtained more FIFA information. Crowds were milling around that part of central London, a film premiere scheduled for later in the day, by the look of it.

Rahman sighed. "It had better be good this time. You can't just string a hack along each time you want a digger for hire. We do have our own work as well, you know. Even if you have picked a convenient place where we can't be overheard."

"The problem I have with this…the difficulty I've had throughout, is who to trust. Even those who've entrusted me with supposed secrets."

Siddique shrugged. "It's not uncommon to be led along the garden path in this line of work."

"More chucked headlong down a bowling lane actually. I'm sure you're ambitious, but how do I know you won't stitch me up?"

"Feeling a bit unloved, are we?" Rahman scoffed. Then, moving to an adjacent bench, he started to strip off his coat, shirt, shoes and socks. As he reached for his trouser belt, Shay couldn't resist giggling.

"I didn't mean to imply…"

The striptease came to a halt, the voice annoyed. "I'm not coming on to you. Just proving I don't have any recording crap on me." The irony of how Siobhan had obtained new information wasn't lost on Shay.

Rahman continued. "Look, I said before I had no gripe with you. No disrespect, but your 'poor me tale' may pick me up another twenty Twitter followers. I'm out to hit the big targets, always have been."

Clothing now reassembled, the pair continued strolling, Rahman's coat hanging loosely over his arm.

"Maybe you should know how I got into this game. It might help. My family started their British odyssey in Manchester. Dad was a builder and could hardly speak a word of English, let alone read it at first. Mum even less so. I was just a kid, one of five, trying to have some fun at school. But at that age you pick up whatever language is around you quickly, I suppose.

Anyway, a letter arrived one day, casually chucked to the side of the kitchen table when I came back from school. I only thought about the delay later, suppose my parents ignored it in the hope it didn't matter. A couple of days later some council staff arrived in bright yellow bibs and booted us all out of the flat. Talk about unceremonious, we hardly had time to collect any possessions. My parents tried to explain they were up to date with rent, that there was no justification for this. The following Monday, I bunked off school and accompanied them to social services, trying to explain their position in English. I didn't really understand what it was about but did my best. The appeals committee didn't seem to care. They'd received some story from the neighbours complaining about us kids making a racket. It was all bullshit. I'd overheard them months before boasting they had a plan for their pregnant daughter and her boyfriend to take over our flat.

There were some savings left over and we had no choice but to go private. The council said we were too much trouble. This time, it was an unscrupulous landlord who rented my parents some insect-infested dump with no heating, despite my parents being adamant they were told rent covered all bills. They'd even paid a year ahead. So, when my dad tried to complain, we were all kicked out. We were almost penniless as there was no return of the advance payment.

At thirteen, I just knew my life would involve rooting out corruption, just no idea how and I probably couldn't have articulated it anyway. Eventually, fell into sports and political journalism. And you can see the battles I've been prepared to fight since."

Shay was silent for a while then nodded slowly in acknowledgement. They continued to an outdoor table at a café situated behind the National Portrait Gallery and, once sitting, he handed over the digital recording and earpiece.

"Okay, this is only for you to hear, for now anyway. There's just one condition. These links – Iran, FIFA, the chemical aspect – remain completely hushed up until I give the word. If not, both I and those involved will completely disown the story. I have no doubt Nicholls will anyway."

"Well if those are your terms, what choice do I have?" Rahman began to listen to the recording, eyebrows rising and a half smile appearing as the conversation developed. He paused at the end.

"It's good, but deniable. Let me go through it thoroughly later."

Shay had pondered his next words since arranging the meeting. Maybe the story of Rahman's background had mellowed him. He raised a hand.

"There's more you should know. I'm liable to be thrown in the Tower for saying this, but events in Milan just didn't seem right. Here's what I saw, and it's decidedly not the official line." Sometime later, after a series of interruptions from Rahman clarifying facts along the way, they finished their drinks and started to leave in opposite directions.

"What about my burger?" Rahman called after him.

"It'll have to wait until next time. You're far too busy for that now. Get working – that device needs returning to the owner soon," as he pointed to the bugging device. "Or the Government will add it to your tax bill."

CHAPTER TWENTY-NINE

NORTH LONDON

What had been missed? The journalist had run after him requesting a written account of everything he remembered from Italy and the FIFA conference, anything that could possibly be relevant but that Shay had omitted in their previous discussions. It should be sent by post only to avoid electronic interception. Rahman had scribbled down an address.

By severely downplaying his role regarding security contacts and responsibilities, that wouldn't present a problem for Shay. After setting down what he'd been asked about and no more once back in his flat, he hesitated before sealing the envelope, chewing over the fact no one had uncovered Bryony's whereabouts. An extra section about her disappearance and its possible importance from the Bircham angle could only help locate her. He wanted her found, not outed. There was no mention of the postcard discovery therefore.

After a run to Hampstead Heath to clear his mind, he opted for another scour through the paperwork they'd painstakingly checked previously. The box was barely hidden, just pushed to the back of his half empty wardrobe in a half-hearted measure. Rahman could hardly go poking around Stewart's workplace and, besides, he'd have his hands full with the FIFA links to Iran. But why hadn't the authorities taken back the items provided by Harriet? Presumably because they didn't know or had thought them unimportant. Siobhan certainly wouldn't have reminded them.

Breathing deeply, he arrived back at the flat, going straight to the wardrobe but suspecting, somehow, it wouldn't be there. To his surprise, it was.

After a shower, he started pouring through the items. Three hours down the line, with a play mix of chilled music - in the background, he sat back disconsolately, his hand lightly brushing by his scar. It all seemed overwhelming being left to check these leads alone. What about the account Harriet and Stewart were supposed to have control of? Others were far better placed to follow that chain. There was the option of contacting the Americans again to see if there was progress with Bryony. He pictured the conversation. "Excuse me, Ms Archibald, I'm that Brit you interrogated so politely and perhaps we could work together?" That was sure to go down a storm.

He grabbed a sandwich before restarting. The next batch seemed unfamiliar at first before he recalled the pictures fired off at the Tylers' home before Harriet had returned, after the ill-fated unofficial ransack. A set had arrived in the post, hardly meriting a glance at the time before being discarded to the box.

His attention was definitely waning as he went through them one by one. The cottage's inside was left a complete mess, not surprising that Harriet had moaned away to the authorities. He'd have stuck their heads down a toilet if they'd tried that with his possessions. A shot of the living room wall, with those holiday reminders at one side. Another section of the room displaying photos from younger days. Had she started as an actress then? Off in the corner, the impressive garden was visible. And the conservatory –

what was Harriet's comment? Something about just having built it alongside other work. He continued scanning through the multitude of photos from the search, including one of the entrances to the house before the start of the fiasco within.

And then he spotted it, all in plain sight. It was probably nothing but he may as well follow this up whilst the experts were investigating the high-level trails. Even if all of it was meant to be none of his business, by order of the Government.

Fortunately, Tariq, a former colleague from Afghanistan, was still working in his Islington garage despite the late hour. The guy seemed to labour round the clock these days. Yes, he could provide a vehicle tomorrow morning at short notice but it wouldn't be big. Anything, preferably with four wheels, Shay had replied.

Setting off early the next day for what was becoming the familiar trek to Cambridgeshire, Shay was undecided if it was preferable for her to be in or not. If the former, how rude exactly was it to just arrive unannounced? Shay decided on a seemingly casual call to Harriet when half an hour away, asking if it was OK for him to drop by. Of course, she'd responded, anything to help Bryony.

This was the height of summer so it was particularly unfortunate that the windows didn't open and the semblance of air con was decidedly not chilled. Parking the Fiat, pleased to escape the mini oven, his hopes arose when glancing at the cottage's façade. The front door was already ajar, as Harriet called from the kitchen to say his coffee was on the way adding "I remembered, no tea." Like an old family friend already. Shay joined her, trying to contain his thoughts. She was unmistakably trying to cheer herself up for company but, soon asking for an update on Bryony, her smile melted away once he'd shaken his head.

"I'm afraid not. You know, I'm not officially involved but if I hear anything, of course, I'll tell you immediately." Was she privy to the fact he was off the operation altogether? If so, there was no trace in her demeanour.

He paused. "No, this is another angle altogether. Just a hunch," he added, "but worth checking." As he led the way to the front, Shay pointed to the small patch of new brickwork, only two feet up, that had just been visible behind the roses in the photo. It was rare to have modern brickwork added to the feel of a nineteenth-century cottage. He pointed to the newly added cement, explained his plan and was hardly surprised that Harriet immediately took against it. But, he attempted to reassure her, the Government would pick up the bill in repairing the brickwork if he was wrong. The truth would be slightly different, as the police would, most likely, clap him in irons for his efforts instead.

Harriet relented after a while, indicating the small wooden shed with a corrugated roof by the side of the house in explaining where the toolkit usually lived. A rusting chisel and hammer did the trick; soon he'd loosened and removed the two new bricks. At first, he couldn't make out what was within. Some kind of black, shiny object encased in a thick plastic wallet. His sense of optimism increased as he reached through, extracting the video and lifting it high to show Harriet, who'd waited to one side with arms folded. A video cassette seemed a relic from a bygone age.

He genuinely had no idea how she'd react and her expression remained impassive. Had she known? Or suspected? Shay recalled her former profession and remembered there was, at times, no way of reading her.

"You wouldn't happen to have—?" he started.

Harriet sighed and led the way into the house. "Somewhere in the attic. God knows why Stewart thought we'd ever watch a VHS again but he insisted on keeping it."

Returning ten minutes later with the machine, complete with remote control and wires amassed on top, the box seemed decades old. It took time to set up the facility in the living room before, glancing at each other as they sat, Harriet nodded for him to press play.

The filming was amateurish, the picture grainy. He could feel his mouth remaining open like some amateur ventriloquist's dummy, as they endured the entire minutes of film. Not even daring to glance at his companion. A young Stewart was palpably recognisable, shivering more than the rest for whatever reason. Linda seemingly relaxed, a ruse? Perhaps desperate to fit into the boys' world regardless of the actions, of the consequences.

How could he know their motives? They were irrelevant anyway. On one level, their reactions were irrelevant. The only certainty was that a dog referred to as the Bard was walked into view on a lead and had its front right paw stuck into some kind of iron clamp so it couldn't escape, howling wildly by this stage, and was then beaten to death with solid, metal looking implements. Small rocks, too.

All four could distinctly be seen wielding weapons at different points, each varying their levels of aggression over time. Stewart, Linda, Atkinson and Nicholls. The camera was static so probably no one else present, just a fixed view chosen.

The scene ended and the grey blankness of the tape kicked in. Neither could move for minutes. Glancing over, Harriet was crying steadily, and Shay was aware of the dampness in his own eyes. That was as low an incident of aggression as he'd encountered against any living creature. As barbaric as the excesses he'd encountered in military campaigns, there was something particularly horrific in those actions.

"So," she broke the silence, her voice rising in anger. "I was married to a nasty little sadist who wanted to be in with the crowd, so acted like that?"

"We don't know—"

"We do know, Shay. Stewart had mentioned something about an incident he'd regret forever. I can't believe what I've just watched."

Pausing, his mind filled with questions about the discovery, mostly regarding his companion's role. To what extent had Harriet helped hide the tape in the first place? Was she aware of the contents? Are the tears, was the anger all genuine or pretence?

There was no point asking now. The video appeared verifiable and the individuals definitely comprised three whom he'd encountered in person in recent months, whilst the fourth was a face he'd come to know through endless photos and footage. The facts didn't lie.

Harriet appeared to hunt around for an explanation, a softer voice now. If she had loved her husband, the man she was still presumably mourning, somehow she had to marry that affection with the events she'd just witnessed.

"He mentioned something about a cruel piece of revenge some of his schoolmates had carried out against the headmaster, but I can't believe they were capable of this. Stewart always maintained he was picked on there. And I bet you're wondering if I knew. That there may be evidence of some misdemeanour? Yes. That it was this? Not at all. I do remember something unusual though. Late on the penultimate day of building work, he expressed concern to the workmen about a tiny patch of damp seeping in from outside and asked them to remove a little brickwork. Then a call to them that evening saying that he'd inspected the hole himself and was confident it wasn't the source of the damp so had replaced the bricks himself. I overheard the conversation but thought little of it.

Only the next day, we were walking in the woods five miles away. He was nervous, uptight. The pressure of work and...other issues you know about. Then lapsing into sobs, referring to the past catching up with him and how his future could be haunted too. We had money worries—"

"Really, you said you had no financial concerns?" Shay knew his tone was stern, not fully discounting the possibility of her greater involvement in the cover up.

Harriet turned to stare at him, sounding disconcerted. "Well, that was understandable. You have to excuse me for that. My husband was dead. God knows how or why, and he had an impressive array of friends. His work was in extremely sensitive national security areas. You can understand my reluctance to add to that list by admitting that, let's say, income and expenditure were in danger of appearing misproportioned."

"You were broke, Harriet. I'm called in to try and get to the bottom of another 'misdemeanour', your husband's death, in case you'd forgotten. And you lie about your finances? And lie about hiding evidence that links Stewart to the others for ever? Period. That video is gold dust for anyone trying to get to your husband or the others, all high profile in their careers with glittering reputations to lose. In addition to potential criminal charges for animal abuse I'd imagine, for which, frankly, I'd still throw the book at the remaining two if it were my decision. And I don't care that they're two of the country's top law makers."

Now self-conscious of the rising volume in his voice. All the deceit, false trails, the physical threat aimed at him at times, all massed together in a rage. It had all started here amidst the seemingly blissful countryside in the first days of the investigation. It seemed fine for politicians to lie, but not here amidst this tranquility for some reason. Not her. Her look of concern next to him on the sofa was soft, welcoming and confusing. She leaned over slowly, her hand moving to his lap, lips inches away.

He stood suddenly, shaking his head angrily. Harriet's voice businesslike. "I'll get rid of it. It's only caused heartache since it was made and did nothing to protect my husband. If only I'd known—"

Without a word, he returned to the car. Maybe the tape's destruction would be for the best, he couldn't think straight at the moment. Neither did he have any interest in speaking to Harriet again.

The arrival of a message pinged on his phone, catching it was from Siobhan. He'd check it later. Then another. It must be important for her to text on their usual numbers. Noting he was near the turn for the Eight Bells, Shay emitted a sigh. He may as well stop for a breather to check messages before the airless return journey. Also acknowledging the need for a quiet drink after the degradation witnessed on magnetic tape.

"*Daily Investigator*" stated the first. "What HAVE you done?" the second. He clicked through immediately to the website which still bore its masthead in red and black. The old colours of Fleet Street print.

There it was, the lead story. "Is Atkinson fit to stay in government? Allegations of a reckless past, an unreliable and callous personality." The story appeared to be built on snippets of the conversation between Nicholls and Siobhan. No direct quotes and no suggestions as to who was behind the information, just a "senior political source with longstanding connections to Atkinson." The claims appeared credible if they came from a colleague or, even, the PM's office.

His first call wasn't to Siobhan, as Siddique picked up immediately. "I thought I could trust you Rahman. We had a deal and now you spread all that information in the *Investigator*. You've let me down badly here."

To Shay's surprise, the response was confident and measured. Certainly far from apologetic.

"We agreed I wouldn't reveal any conspiracies that Atkinson may have been hatching. Iran, the terror threat. That could take ages to uncover fully and I wouldn't have released any of that without your go-ahead. But this…character stuff, that's surely all fair game. It was a trade-off and I almost had to beg the editor to allow me time to investigate the big ticket stuff. In return he wanted something to lead with now. That's the game, Shay. That's how it works."

Lost for words. Had he been clear enough? Was political speculation fair game for any news site anyway? Shay wondered if he'd overreacted and also knew he was in no mood for another fight so soon, the video and aftermath playing on his mind.

He was unsuccessful in attempting to contact Siobhan to discuss the story. Maybe she rued working with him now. But he had no choice. Rahman had the contacts and sources, the means of delving into connections he could never realistically access alone. After the welcome pint, Shay headed back home. The quicker Siddique came up with hard facts, the faster they could all return to their normal lives. Not a day too soon either. For now, he'd have to trust that the journalist wouldn't spread more selective information on a personal whim.

CHAPTER THIRTY

SOUTH WALES

Woodford had placed the phone on his desk cautiously the previous Sunday evening. That was the second Mason-related call in one day, which was strange enough. The first was from Shay informing him of knee damage from a climbing accident over the weekend, adding that a friend had highly recommended a particular armed forces approved physio in north London. Self-diagnosis suggested it could be bursitis and he could just about hobble at present. As he had already booked an appointment for early in the week, he suggested there was no point hanging around base with an injury like that. A proper diagnosis with a return to work in days would be the ideal outcome.

Woodford couldn't recall the trainer relying on any kind of excuse before. Reaching into his filing cabinet confirmed this. Mason had never taken so much as a day's sick leave. Best to trust Shay's instincts and approve the extended stay in London.

The second call was from Whitehall, Townsend asking after Mason. Woodford was asked what appeared strange questions, the caller seeming anxious about his Lieutenant and didn't relate at all to the recent injury. Had Shay been behaving unusually? Was he settling back into army life at the base? Later, the Lieutenant Colonel struggled to put his finger on why he'd withheld reference to the leave request. Townsend's desperation had been unsettling, that was probably the truth of it. The protection and morale of troops here as ever was Woodford's only consideration, after all. Or was he getting soft-hearted after so many years in the army, maybe overprotective? Still, retirement was not far away. And travel, lots of it, would take up his time.

Checking in again with Woodford at four p.m. on Wednesday, Shay reported that the physio had, unfortunately, recommended complete rest for his injury until the weekend. Couldn't he return to base at least?

Apparently not, responded Shay. He shouldn't even place light weight on it for a while, then all would be fine to resume training. He added, for good measure, that a mountain of paperwork awaited completion regarding all the recent recruits, then there were programmes for the next three months to update and schedule. In other words, he had more than enough to occupy himself from a distance.

Woodford tried to sound displeased, sensing his reprimand appeared hollow. Shay had better be ready for training by next week, otherwise a medical certificate would be required on his desk at eight a.m. on Monday with no excuses.

Rain knocked hard against Shay's north London bedroom window, on the soaking wet Thursday morning that week. He instinctively reached for the TV remote. A quick Love Island rerun to start the day before checking his mobile. He'd slept soundly, to the extent that although calls were on silent, texts must have sounded though he hadn't stirred. Three missed ones, hours ago, from Rahman, insisting "call me now," the next "...please," then "it's OK, will check with Siobhan."

No further clues and the messages didn't seem urgent by the end. Presumably some follow up to their uncomfortable exchange, an apology even? He could call Siobhan now but she'll be rushing to work.

He flicked through the news channels first for the seven thirty headlines, doubting that recent media criticism of Atkinson was likely to carry into today's news for all but hardened political hacks. Just as he was about to dial Rahman, the newsreader, looking impossibly pristine for such an early start, began.

"Today's main story, Homeland Security and Defence Secretary William Atkinson is alleged by the *Daily Investigator* to be having an affair with a Mossad agent by the name of Bryony Simmons. Ms Simmons is the sister-in-law of UK scientist Stewart Tyler, whose suspicious death earlier in the year has continued to be the subject of much speculation. Mr Atkinson was a prominent advocate for increasing the UK's readiness to tackle international threats, prior to his recent appointment. This is obviously a significant development and we now talk to..."

Simple journalism was his first thought. Report what others have stated to be a crisis without embellishment and you can't be sued. His next reaction was not so charitable, aimed at Rahman in his absence.

"I can't believe—" he got Rahman on the first ring.

"Let me stop you right there. It was a courtesy call to you both before we released the story, not least as you were so touchy, when we met up, about anything linked to Tyler. We kept researching and uncovered the Simmons connection late last night. Of course this comes out straightaway to avoid being gazumped.

If it's any consolation, it hadn't come from you anyway."

"Yes, but the fact is you didn't reach me Rahman. I shouldn't be finding out like this. How did you even uncover what Bryony is up to? And why release it all now?"

"You sound like she's a friend, Shay. Anything I should know?" Silence. "Her phone records suggested the Atkinson affair, and then texts making clear what had gone on between them. And we were told via other channels about the Mossad connection." Shay was confused. Jealousy or anger? Only a one-night stand, yet he resented her former lovers? Ridiculous, everyone has a history.

The journalist continued. "Given that she vanished, we had to inform the authorities in America immediately or may be violating US law, given it's significant information on a national security level there. That's what the lawyers advised, still leaving the 'legal crack'."

"What's that when it's at home?"

"Simple, there's often a small window between authorities receiving information and them obtaining an injunction from preventing publication. Literally a matter of hours, or minutes sometimes. There was no way we could miss the chance to run this. My promise to avoid publishing anything to implicate who Siobhan talked to still holds, but it didn't come from there anyway. I can tell you're angry but, actually, Siobhan was fine about it. Not that we could have held back." The call ended abruptly.

This had to be face to face. Calculating she would surely be behind her desk by the time he reached central London, Shay made straight for Whitehall in the rented vehicle, enjoying the change in travel options and accepting the additional cost added by the congestion charge. Besides, the extra time alone would come in useful to try and rationalise it all. How could he keep ending up as piggy in the middle?

Parking in the underground car park near Leicester Square, Shay strode through the rain to the Department in Whitehall. Camera crews were packed outside with a number of journalists, mikes in hand, jostling for space as he approached the building. All smelt blood from the latest revelations. But what they hoped to achieve out here, god only knows, he reflected. A curt nod and quick wave from the security guard ensured access through to reception after whispering he wasn't a 'bloody journalist'; showing army credentials did the trick.

There had been no response from her mobile as he'd walked towards the building, and now there appeared to be further silence as reception tried to call up in vain and reached only her voicemail. Soon, reluctantly turning to leave, he headed back towards Trafalgar Square. Slowly, just in case.

He felt her breath in his ear. "Seems we're well-practised in following each other around." Facing her, Shay shook his head in disappointment. They fell into step alongside each other.

"Sorry," she added. "It was best that I didn't even acknowledge you were in the Department just now. For obvious reasons."

"You said it," he responded coldly.

"Rahman has helped us throughout so he deserved that scoop. It sounds like it was going to come out very soon anyway, when he explained it. At worst, there's no reason for him not to publish. At best, it also helps the security services both sides of the Atlantic know why Bryony is such a prized asset in this whole saga. If they couldn't join the dots beforehand, then maybe they needed a little push."

The explanation appeared to fall on deaf ears, so she ploughed on. "With the injunction pending, it would all have been hushed up otherwise and the world wouldn't be helping the Agency, or whoever pulled you in, to extract Bryony from this mess. It ticks all the boxes Shay, you have to admit it. Just take a minute to think it through properly, rather than jump to your macho response." She touched his cheek as they stopped.

"No glory for you in embarrassing me then?"

All sympathy disappeared from her voice. "In case you didn't notice, the story didn't come from me and I wasn't the one shagging her. Anyway, your name still isn't in the press about it and there's no reason it should be."

He began the journey back to north London minutes later, speculating how much the authorities really knew and whether they, or the *Investigator*, were calling the tune. If not Siobhan, someone else had passed on the info. Anyway, what was Atkinson playing at, getting embroiled with Bryony? Was it coincidence? Not that he could criticise the politician's taste.

Driving past King's Cross and St Pancras stations with restorations still impressive, Radio Five Live went straight to Atkinson who was appearing live outside the Department. So this is what the journalists camped outside had been expecting. There was nothing approachable about the politician's tone today, as he spoke quickly and defiantly.

"I have just been to see the Prime Minister and felt compelled to tender my resignation. I have served my country honestly and honourably throughout and am proud of my work in shoring up the nation's defences. May I also stress that I am entirely innocent of the recent lurid accusations touted against me and shall use the opportunity from the back benches to completely and utterly clear my name of all accusations of impropriety."

Shay was just amazed Atkinson hadn't rushed Theresa and his children to Westminster for a steadfast photo in support. Though he'd surely tried.

CHAPTER THIRTY-ONE

CENTRAL LONDON

"The Prime Minister," bellowed the Speaker from his chair.

The House of Commons fell silent in anticipation. The famous green benches were packed with MPs despite, what should have been the summer recess. There were strict orders from the whips for attendance, a three line whip even, in case a no confidence vote was taken. This was decidedly not a popular instruction for those on far flung beaches. Advisers high up in the gallery, just along from the small contingent of the general public fortunate to obtain tickets for today's last-minute session, leant forward in anticipation.

The assembled Parliamentarians had two standard responses. On the Government benches, members were preparing to offer nervous support, whilst broad smiles adorned those facing them on the Opposition benches, making hay at the Government's discomfort. The latter weren't disappointed.

Angela Patterson rose tentatively to her feet. After thirty years of assiduously ascending the political ladder, she'd instinctively known how to sit back and lurk in the shadows on an unwinnable issue and likewise when to steal the limelight. This had been her hallmark throughout her rise in Scottish local politics, the Scottish Assembly, the toughly contested Edinburgh seat in the House of Commons, cabinet recognition then the prize of the top job itself. It all came down to this.

Fleetingly, her mind strayed to the now famous footage taken when she was seven at the school assembly in Aberdeen as she had received her academic prize in front of St Kilda's School.

"And I'm sure you want to achieve great things," pronounced the visiting dignitary as they'd shaken hands. She was meant to nod, receive the trophy and move on for the next recipient. Instead, turning to the microphone, Angela stared straight at her parents in the second row, announcing primarily for their benefit:

"Oh yes, I'll be the greatest Prime Minister Scotland has ever produced." Despite her tone sounding deadly serious, the audience took a collective breath before mass cheers and some laughter broke through the hall. She'd only been reminded about it in every biographical story published since. That little girl had the world in front of her.

Angela's professionalism kicked in. "The nation has faced immense pressure from its enemies over the recent period and I am proud of the extent to which my Government has managed those challenges."

A lone voice from the Opposition benches broke her flow: "Yeah by all the comfy relationships built up with Mossad." His colleagues supported with exaggerated laughter, every attempt to embarrass the government proving an additional notch.

"The country expects leadership," Angela plugged away, long used to overriding any heckles. "And that's exactly what it will get. I have just been to see His Majesty to request parliament be dissolved after this session so I now ask the nation to provide a clear mandate by means of a general election to take place on the Thursday following the August bank holiday. The country knows the strength of leadership it has received from me. Trust in the United Kingdom, trust in my government for five more years."

The Opposition mood turned instantly. Shouts were loud and clear to those in the gallery: "Resign;" and "go now." Another, unapologetically breaching the rules of conduct in the chamber with "You're a bloody disgrace, Patterson." There was uproar all round.

Rory Nicholls was the least vocal on the opposition benches, stroking his chin. A general election could go either way given the government's clear intention to fight the forthcoming battle with the Union Flag draped around it, claiming the importance of national unity at a time of crisis. There had been no reference to the scandal, no mention of her stepping down despite the media storm during the day. Just the unspoken acknowledgement that, with a wafer-thin majority, even a few defections from Patterson's party would hasten a vote of no confidence and instantly trigger a general election anyway. Clever call, seize the initiative and appear in control of events.

He rose to initiate the first skirmish of the general election in response to the announcement. Patterson had erred greatly in allowing him the final word before Parliament was dissolved. Let battle commence.

"This government has failed the people when it most needs leadership. Instead of democratic accountability, the Prime Minister's shambolic crew has hidden behind security measures more appropriate to a dictatorship. The Secretary of Homeland Security and Defence has proven nothing if not ambitious in his plotting, deceitful in his cunning and utterly ruthless in running rings round the Prime Minister. That she should give free reign to his whims in constructing the Department of his choice makes clear she is unfit to lead. That she should have to accept his resignation yesterday in such unfortunate..." his backbenchers roared, "circumstances, says everything not just about the pickle in which he found himself but also the feebleness and lack of direction of her government. Every time the security situation seemingly convalesces, it proves but a brief respite.

Mr Speaker, we welcome this general election in the name of the crusade for genuine accountability now. We welcome the electorate's ability to discriminate between a party with fear and panic at the heart of its security strategy and no ultimate success, versus one with genuine strength and direction at its core. Between a so-called leader who has lost her way, kowtowing to the whims of ministers who are meant to serve her government; and the official opposition, with the leader the country can absolutely rely on to resolve the mess caused solely by the current government."

A pause. "We welcome the people's verdict."

His advisory team had speculated long into the previous night as to the likely content of Patterson's hastily arranged speech. Fresh from Atkinson's resignation, would she go on the attack or throw in the towel? Resign, hold fast, blame Atkinson or – the least likely option according to the consensus around him – call an election. His instincts had told him otherwise and extensive preparation for the fourth outcome had proved well spent.

Only momentarily had Rory allowed himself time to guess at the conversation between Bill and Patterson yesterday. Had the man fallen on his sword immediately behind closed doors?

Politely denied the story's content and reluctantly agreed to stand down 'for the good of the Party'? That was hardly likely.

Unknown to Rory, none of those had occurred. The stand-up row between Patterson and Atkinson had been 'firework-like' according to aides and would feed Whitehall watchers in slowly released gossip over coming weeks. The pair's voices reached a crescendo ten minutes into their private meeting, with shouts, swearing – even a smashed cup echoing off the cabinet room wall – to the astonishment of those outside.

Atkinson's relatively calm announcement on the steps of his former department bore no relation to the manner of his sacking by the Prime Minister.

CHAPTER THIRTY-TWO

CENTRAL LONDON

Shay tried to following events live, albeit from the tiny television set hoisted high above holidaymakers at the airport. The unexpected call had come directly from May the evening before. It could only be important, as evidently, she'd not wanted to risk significant conversation on the phone or via any electronic communication. A ticket would await at Heathrow for the first flight out in the morning. Certainly, he'd be home by evening, she assured. All she requested was a little chat.

Was it a trap? The Government here, or certain sections at least, had seemingly taken against him. Who was to know if he'd be sent to some Guantanamo-style compound for ten years on vague charges trumped up by the Government's pals in Washington? Nothing would surprise him out there. Was Guantanamo still in existence? His mates in the army had been equally at a loss to say with any certainty, when batting the subject round in the mess recently. Everyone knew the US could play nice when it wanted to. It could also go right up to the line of legality, peer over it and jump several steps forward when it considered such tactics more appropriate.

A dose of humble pie was required firstly, leaving a voicemail for Rahman to explain where he was off to, though without providing details of who he'd be meeting, or why. A clear marker that he wanted his back watched by the journalist if the whole trip came unstuck and he didn't return promptly. Just as well Rahman hadn't answered as he was in no mood to be probed for full disclosure about May Archibald.

The flight passed without incident. Was he being watched throughout, from the point of leaving Crouch End to the arrival back in Boston? It was simplest to presume he was being monitored, the thought strangely puncturing any sense of stress.

Though if he was anyone's target, they could have struck in north London and saved the air fare.

At the same time, Rory was sitting surrounded by campaign strategists in his House of Commons office. Standing room only was available whilst a mood of chaos appeared to hold sway. This was not how he'd envisaged the battle. The presumption they'd made long ago was that Patterson would hold on, by hook or crook, for the last year of her administration. Rory silently chastised himself as he'd been so preoccupied with cementing outright control within the party that he'd taken his eye off election strategy. This rabble had better adopt a clear blueprint quickly or the opportunity would be squandered; few campaigns bounce back successfully from initial paralysis.

A knock at the door and a piece of paper was handed to a young aide who made his way through the throng to Rory. One glance and the leader's order passed authoritatively to clear the room.

"Get her in now," whispered to the aide. Despite the importance of the current meeting, the visitor may prove even more helpful.

Siobhan entered two minutes later. The aide couldn't help raising an eyebrow towards Rory as he left the room but the leader's face remained impassive. There was no chance an affair would be sinking his political career.

"So," he walked round, perching at the front of the desk as Siobhan stood uneasily just inside the door. Blocking all routes to a chair was just a power play, she reminded herself.

"Busy I guess."

Rory smiled. "Just a tad," his arm swept to the boards on the wall, filled with graphs and contact details either on printouts or scribbled on oversized paper. Dominating the wall was a massive UK constituency map displaying names of potential candidates. "Whatever you have to offer my campaign, this would be an opportune moment."

She hesitated. "The parameters have changed. That's self-evident, I supposed. Anything I provide to you now could considered a breach of the Civil Service code on impartiality during a general election. The only reason I'm able to visit you here in the Palace is because I agreed to be our departmental liaison with the opposition during the election campaign. If not for that, I'd be jumped on. But there's no one else here now, Mr Nicholls. So it appears to me as if the stakes have been raised."

Nicholls moved towards her, his eyes fleetingly cold. Had she overplayed her hand already? Fortunately it was only to reach behind and open the office door. She could sense herself exhaling.

A security woman entered clutching a handheld scanner. Siobhan had already handed over her mobile to the aide on arrival, having proceeded through the extensive security checks at St Stephen's entrance. Perhaps extra security was in place given the announcement of the election. She was clean and couldn't be caught out this time. Not even worth the risk of using the apparatus from last time.

After the check and a curt nod, the security officer left the room. Rory continued to loom in front of her though, the 'man of the people' persona still not on display.

He started. "Let's look at the evidence. I owe you nothing. There's proof of you coming to me previously and none of me attempting to entice you at any point. You've even hinted at offering me documents on an illegal basis which, of course, I politely declined.

Last time we spoke, we discussed power. That's always what it's about in a political race. Big deal if I may be a little competitive with Bill," he shrugged. "Maybe that's the way it's always been between us. And Iranian factions perhaps playing havoc on our soil whilst the security supremo engages in pillow talk with a Mossad operative? How very convenient.

I never was one for crystal balls but can't pretend the situation hasn't turned out favourably. Journalists have picked up trails and the country is awash with conspiracy rumours at present. The fact is I'll be more effective as Prime Minister than weak-willed Patterson or philandering Bill."

He looked deeply into her eyes. "I'm doing this for my country."

Siobhan ignored her instinct to laugh. Why bait him rather than keep her eye on the main goal of revealing his knowledge?

"And Stewart? Linda? Your old schoolfriends?"

"I miss them Siobhan," lowering his head. "I should add that if I win without your help, who knows how your career may fail to progress."

The mix of sweet and sour was all on show by Nicholls as he now, almost brusquely, led her to the door, clearly disabusing her of any pretence she'd been in control. What made her think she could get the better of such an experienced political manipulator? The price of staying in the lion's den was huge. For her career, for her and Tommy's future in the UK. Everything felt on the line, she sensed, as she was ushered out.

CHAPTER THIRTY-THREE

BOSTON

Shay tried not to express surprise that May awaited as his personal chauffeur, a lightly raised hand in his direction as he appeared from customs. The sweltering Boston air enclosed him immediately as they left the terminal and headed for the Chevy Camaro parked directly outside. Before he caught a glance, she'd swiftly removed the dashboard pass that allowed such a prominent parking space.

"Flight OK?"

"Err, yes I suppose."

"I'm pleased you didn't turn down our invitation. And that you didn't start any insightful conversation on the phone. Lord knows I like to talk, but there's a time and a place and that wasn't it."

"After all the loose ends left in America, I figured there wasn't much alternative. Am I right?"

May shrugged as she drove away. "It's entirely up to you, I suppose. The whole point is that we don't trust your security services, over certain matters at least. We were hardly going to inform them of any interest we may have in you, particularly after your escapade in Milan. Whatever that entailed."

Shay automatically tensed, noting there was no air con cooling the car.

"You'd know I wasn't part of any assassination squad if you had any knowledge whatsoever of events in Milan."

"Oh yes, we know that, Shay. It's a shifting situation, always, but at present the Italians are our friends behind the scenes so we're well aware you had no interest in a stunt like that. Besides," she added "if someone tried to drop a similar move at the Superbowl or World Series, the nation would tear any potential assassin limb from limb. Nothing ends a ball game before the ad break at the end, particularly if Taylor's doing half time."

"I'm honoured for the invite of course, if a little confused. Last time you made it apparent I wasn't wanted here. What's changed?"

May stayed unusually quiet. He was conscious of not giving too much, accidentally diving into areas to which she probably wasn't privy. Not least about his deductions regarding the San Siro and maintaining a slim hope that Siddique could deliver the facts to prove it. Besides, who was to say she wasn't working with someone in the UK who just wanted him fed to the wolves? The pair continued in uncomfortable silence for a while.

"All in good time, all in good time," she uttered at last.

After negotiating the airport traffic jams, three quarters of an hour later the pair arrived at the building from which, he presumed, he'd been unceremoniously removed prior to his expulsion. Once they entered the underground airport and walked to the lift, May pressed the lift button for the bottom floor, five levels below.

They entered the dull grey lift. "Either these are interrogation rooms, and I'm sure we weren't this far down last time you kindly invited me, or—" Shay let the sentence hang as they descended.

The lift doors opened as May faced him. "I'm afraid so Shay."

Their footsteps reverberated along the wooden floor of the corridor. Unlike the impressive suite of offices above, these were sparse. Arriving at a single sliding door, May repeated the iris scanner confirmation she'd employed to enter the premises from the driver's seat in the Camaro, then again to activate the lift. A quick word with the attendant inside, the first person they'd encountered in the building, who led the way along another empty route to a large metal door. The attendant stepped back. Only the hum of air con interrupted the monastic level of silence.

The only furniture in the dull lit room was the table on which the lifeless form of Bryony was set down, covered in a blue gown apart from shoulders, neck and head. Her arms were also visible.

Shay tried to suppress his anger but instinctively clenched his fists. "Tell me."

"She's not been dead long. The good news, if that's how we can term it, is that Bryony appears to have been treated OK beforehand. Physically that is, with no signs of torture, starvation or sexual assault."

They approached the corpse, with May raising the nearest of Bryony's arms. "With two exceptions. As you can see there's evidence of a little skin under her nails. We guess she lost patience with whoever was holding her and lashed out or struggled when she was taken. Of course we're running a check on those skin cells, in fact giving her a thorough DNA rundown. Nothing as yet."

"How long's it been?"

"A matter of days. We picked her up in some woods out on the road to Worcester, about 50 kilometres away. Death by lethal injection is the other giveaway on her body and some kind of barbiturate in her system along with her last meal presumably. Looks like they put her to sleep then killed her. Almost the humane way of acting this out if they felt they had to get rid of her." A pause. "I'm sorry Shay".

He struggled to take it in despite knowing the risks they were all running by being embroiled.

"I'm happy to level with you," May continued. "In return, we need help, for Bryony's sake. So, what can you tell me?"

There it was. Not hard to predict she'd use Bryony's name just before any request. He had to give her something though.

"That she may have been a Mossad agent. That she might have had an affair with one of the most senior politicians in the UK. That…"

"Shay," May's shout echoed round. "Don't give me that…bullshit. Everything you've said has been printed in your *Times* newspaper, reported on your *BBC* website. That's all junk. Give me facts I don't know."

"Okay, how's this? It's possible Atkinson's alleged involvement was fed to the media by…unreliable sources."

Her voice still strident, now pointing at his chest.

"You're talking in riddles. Do you trust those self-centred assholes you've surrounded yourself with? Wake up. They're not your friends. We can't work out who's in charge there so if you're one up on us, I suggest you tell us now. 'Cos they sure aren't helping you. At least our covert services here are all singing from the same hymn sheet and not trying to light some touch paper. This side of the Atlantic there are no rogue interests playing games with chemical threats." He managed to resist the provocation.

"Could it be a stunt for Patterson to beat down a rival?" she continued. "That still doesn't account for why the Iranians appear to be the common denominator in so many deaths, at least one of which was unmistakably meant to look accidental to the outside world. I need more, Shay."

At least she didn't appear to have a clue about the sadistic school gang. What to give her?

"Okay. In return, you keep me in the loop for everything you find. If the information isn't classified, then Harriet has the right to know it all as well. Agreed?"

"Deal."

"Bryony was tipped off. I had no idea she may have worked for Israel undercover but she was certainly instructed to leave fast. Don't ask me anymore because I just don't know. Please remember I train recruits for a living. This is not my world."

Silence, then broken by May. "You're an interesting case. Who knows what your medical records hold? Nyctophobia, huh?"

"Those are confidential. What the…?"

"Just interested, kind of fascinating in its way. I have sympathy, I really do. How did that come about? I'd like to know."

"If you must know," Shay failed to hide his displeasure. "Years ago, a night mission was being prepped. My role was to stay out of sight under a beaten old truck, all pitch black, unless the audible signal was given. The wait went on and on, eight hours or thereabouts in total. I had no idea if it was daytime or how long I'd been there by the end. It wasn't even the cramped conditions. In fact, I was fine all along, somehow stayed awake but must have been in a kind of trance with it all.

Until an explosion ripped through the air, only feet away but I was OK physically. The team got me out soon after."

"Which is why you need light?"

"Which is why I need light at all times. No sense of claustrophobia though. You could lock me in a six by three foot cupboard with no difficulty as long as I can see around." He regretted the sentence before it finished. They may just be tempted to conduct an experiment.

"It's always good to share. Look, we seem to understand each other. But you confuse me in one other aspect. It is Mason? Or O'Doherty?"

He stared back, regretting letting her in at all. "Now you're trying to fuck with me."

Was she intent on riling him or just showing she had the upper hand on info any security service could easily acquire? There was no way he'd voluntarily give up the reason and, anyway, it was none of her business. The switch to his mother's maiden name after the Olympics debacle made sense, having preoccupied his thoughts just prior to the Games anyway due to the sinking relationship with his father. Then, sealing the switch when he wanted to escape it all later. The phrase 'playing ostrich' had been mentioned by Ade at the time.

The old man had been furious he hadn't chosen to run for Ireland anyway. O'Doherty was his past and felt another lifetime ago.

CHAPTER THIRTY-FOUR

FLIGHT 528

Soon after he was whisked back to the airport, though not by May this time, the flight had taken off. Timed to perfection. The total time on the ground of three hours and twenty minutes. Before long, Shay was scanning the inflight films for the second time that day. No respite provided by the movies as a distraction technique. He'd surprised himself by shutting out the danger to Bryony more often than not during recent months. Yes, there'd been concern, but on almost on a practical, business level. He'd follow the chain, all would be safe and sound, then she'd return to her previous life. There would be some plausible, and non-violent, explanation for her disappearance.

He understood now it had all been fake suppression, and the rawness of the outcome was almost a release. Few marks, no signs of abuse. So what? At minimum, Bryony must have faced threats, absolute terror, perhaps knowing deep down the fate awaiting. Or could she cling to prayer that the ordeal, in whatever shape it manifested, would play itself out for life to continue?

The only answer was to press on with the case. There was no point deluding himself that he could waltz back on with his quiet life, in search of the odd spare hour to probe here, the occasional day there. A return to base initially was inevitable, then fathoming how exactly to blast this open.

"Chicken or fish sir?" The steward leant over, snapping Shay abruptly back to his surroundings. He didn't care. Just no hint of peanuts on the flight would be preferable.

Another thought occurred. It was unlikely there was any direct threat to him but the facts were undeniable. A mounting death toll. He, rather than the band of four, becoming the common denominator. Linda, Stewart and now Bryony. Was there any certainty he wouldn't be next? The strange idea that being killed without knowing why he was in the firing line seemed particularly vicious. Besides, security at the base was super tight. Yup, in Wales, he'd be as protected as anywhere. If not largely amongst friends, then at least amongst those he'd trust with his life.

The meal was gently placed on his tray. Lifting the tin foil corner, then realising he completely lacked any appetite. Maybe pick at it later, but for now—

No welcoming party back at Heathrow for some reason felt surprising. Surely the security services, or even the media, must have known about Bryony's body being discovered? Or would it be his responsibility to inform others? Then again, how would news leak out in the UK if no next of kin was required, even Harriet?

The simple fact was he had no idea of the protocol. Maybe he'd indirectly ticked the box of identifying the body, without the question being raised. Anyway, there must have been dental records, her DNA…after all her apartment had been thoroughly ripped apart by Archibald's team. It was Bryony, without doubt.

A text from May arrived as they landed, as if reading his thoughts. "We'll tell her." No call to Harriet needed.

That Sunday evening back at base, his mobile rang as he was completing a run after an intense work out. Desperately needing to restore his fitness once he'd returned to Wales, having returned the car to Tariq with a wad of twenties, and a fulsome apology, on the Friday. Now trying to clear his mind for the hardships to come.

It was Rahman. "There's news about Bryony. They discovered—"

"Yes, I heard. She only died recently. Cause of death not certain but she doesn't appear to have been assaulted, physically at least."

"How did you know that, Shay? Unless your trip to America—"

"It may have been connected, Rahman. Please don't ask. And as ever, I'm not the story and my name is to be kept a mile from the press. The usual rules and these ones are not to be broken by you. For once."

"I understand. I'm just speculating that you must have important friends in Washington, or wherever, to consider it worthwhile picking your brains. They only just told his widow this afternoon apparently. I'll call her now for a comment. I must say I'm surprised that you didn't tell her yourself, if you've known a couple of days."

Shay let the probing comment hang. He had nothing to justify. Agreeing to keep each other posted, Rahman gave the assurance his team were delving quickly through any connections. Little was emerging yet but, considering many of the leading protagonists were immersed in the rush for Number 10, that was hardly surprising. MPs and their aides only seemed intent on discussing the immediate struggle for Downing Street, and nothing else.

"Troublesome leg OK now, Mason?" Woodford appeared to be waiting for him specially, just beyond security, on return from the run.

"Yes sir, fully mobile again now."

"And ready for the hard slog again no doubt. Well at least putting your feet up for a week must have revitalised you. Hope you weren't too bored in London."

"No of course not. Never bored sir."

CHAPTER THIRTY-FIVE

SOUTH WALES

Election fever. The contest proved particularly hostile, with barbed personal attacks unleashed on both sides. Unnamed sources on one side portrayed Nicholls as desperate for power and untrustworthy, manipulative and deceitful. Others described Patterson as being out of her depth. 'Just a cheap pile of rotting haggis,' according to the leader column of one tabloid, a comment Nicholls repeated and, when pressed, continued to justify. 'Chucked around at the whim of the big beasts in her cabinet,' another's conclusion, this time a broadsheet, with Atkinson named specifically as the source. Referred to now in the media as "Bonking Buffalo Bill," the sex angle may have delayed his political run but the Mossad link had surely put paid to it, journalists concluded.

Days later, more revelations about Atkinson were linked to questions about Patterson's judgment in appointing him to senior roles in the first place. The deal with the Serious Fraud Office was splashed in the headlines, with all news media again enthralled. Atkinson put out another statement denying it all, resembling now a punch-drunk boxer desperately clinging to the ropes. His Westminster prospects not only beyond resuscitation, but firmly six feet under.

This was just the first week of many and prompted a call to Siobhan after the ten p.m. news.

"I don't like talking about us over the phone," her opening remark. Shay understood, the reminder to avoid direct reference to sensitive information.

Keeping to more general topics, she rebuffed his astonishment at the media frenzy, "Maybe this is the first campaign you've ever taken notice of. No interest in the greasy ladder in any line of work, let alone the vicious world of politics, were you?"

"They're always like this? Publishing allegations before they've had a chance to check them? I bet they wouldn't be so quick to chuck malicious comments about fellow journalists. Isn't there some kind of libel law?"

Siobhan's response was unexpected. She laughed before he heard her calling to her son in the background.

"Back to bed Tommy. Just read another story if you can't sleep," before answering. "There is, but all the media, particularly at election time, are adept at getting round it. Look, sit tight for now as there's little we can do at present. Besides, the press may end up looking in the right directions and actually help us."

"There is no 'us', remember. I've no idea if you're still chasing it all, but I'm off the job, in case you'd forgotten."

After the call, he switched to reality telly. Much easier to comprehend.

Four days later, wondering if the media, and Rahman in particular, held more information than they'd revealed, the focus of the election moved on suddenly. Patterson's campaign rally at Birmingham's National Exhibition Centre the day before, and Nicholls' beachfront photo opportunity on the pier in Brighton before what his team had deemed a 'key speech', were largely ignored. Shay later noticed both were highlighting security issues in their addresses, appropriately, given the importance of events that shattered the predictable election stunts.

It had started early. The Metropolitan Police had Sky News tipped off as it approached an anonymous looking block of flats in Harlesden, north west London, for the six a.m. raid. The cameras were recording from the front but embargoed for half an hour, by agreement. Later described as a 'Jihadi terrorist cell', eight police officers armed with Glocks smashed their way into a first floor flat after the obligatory warning had been shouted. Heckler & Koch MP5SF sub machine guns were trained on the front door as well, from a distance.

What happened next was soon the subject of widespread anger. The fire exit round the back was covered by officers too, but with no camera crew as witnesses. PC Liliane Scott, a mother of two, had no chance as part of the fire exit team, despite sporting extensive body armour. She'd been right next to the explosion, waiting alongside colleagues outside the adjacent flat. Their instructions had been to be out of sight from the target flat when the raid started from the front. There may have been no cameras officially, but a canny journalist, a drinking partner of the TV crew's cameraman, had been passed the tip off and recorded the scene on his mobile. Given the chaos that ensued, raid officers evidently had more to manage than ordering him to stop filming.

It later transpired that reconnaissance had been lax, rushed even. Months earlier, the suspects had apparently spotted that the flat alongside was dilapidated and empty, so decided to burrow through the crumbling wall. Maybe they'd guessed that an escape route would one day be needed.

Within minutes, the Chief Area Officer in charge was requesting, then screaming, at the official camera crew at the front not to release any footage. In response, the TV producer held his line and refused to agree. Neither were aware of the mobile recording anyway, the footage from which proved irresistible for the wider media. By lunchtime, the debacle in planning and execution of the high-profile raid resulted in the resignation of the Metropolitan Police Commissioner. The issue was firmly centre stage in the election campaign, remaining prominent for some time, despite the cell having been arrested. Connected events ran it close though.

It took little more than another four hours before the first retribution was reported. A young Muslim couple, wheeling their baby through the centre of Luton, were approached by a gang of teenage boys, reeking of cheap cider. The couple had obscene chants hurled at them, "'cop killers" included. After jostling and punches were aimed, the couple were grateful they'd escaped with bruises. Even more so that their child was unharmed.

Similar incidents were repeated around the country within days, the Muslim Council condemning the two main political parties for their failure to unreservedly condemn such attacks without also referring to terrorist attacks in the same sentence.

Hot weather was stifling and didn't help. Larger gangs in parks by day openly snorting coke on park benches, washed down with lager by the barrel load. Then followed by pub sessions spilling onto pavements as daylight stretched into evening. The police were laughed at by some sections of the media for suggesting curfews may be needed to deescalate tension, particularly when groups of Asian men decided to arm themselves. Some showed off for reporters and TV cameras, asserting it was all only in self-defence. 'Now our guardians claim they're not competent enough to protect us. Whatta cheek.' screamed one newspaper.

Simmering tension abounded until election week. Far-right parties added their voice to the mix, claiming British citizens have the right to defend themselves, with accompanying comments managing to sound vague yet sinister.

Some two hundred miles west of the worst incidents, Shay was never more grateful to concentrate on day to day duties, ever cajoling the weaker recruits, proud never to have knowingly crossed the line of bullying. The pressure cooker of the boiling cities appeared a world away. Greg was great company as ever, sensing Shay was desperate for distance from whatever had distracted him from base earlier in the year. Ribbing was unrelenting in every other way, but not over that.

Tuesday evening, two days before voting in the first August election date that pundits could remember. The pair were in the mess working their way through pasta and salad whilst reviewing the latest batch of cadets.

"Not got it, absolutely not." Greg's candid assessment of one scrawny cadet. The conversation was interrupted by buzzing, as Shay reaching for his mobile. Checking the caller ID, he raised his hand and moved outside.

"Rahman Siddique, it's been some time."

"Yup and this isn't a social call."

"How's the research gone? Surely, you've got somewhere by now?"

"Well yes and no, but let's just say we've been side-tracked somewhat and for the wrong reasons. Which is where you come in. We've been developing a very senior contact in Iran and, if his identity is revealed, it'll only end one way for him. And, Shay, confidentiality is a two way deal."

Shay considered if his phone was being monitored and concluded that was pretty unlikely, so long after being relieved of duty for the investigation.

"And?" he added hesitantly.

"The source was frighteningly precise and has proved accurate before. There's a high risk of a sarin attack in London within the next forty-eight hours apparently. Which means potential carnage and, even if casualties are minimised, it will tear the country apart given the heat that's around at the moment, politically and otherwise. I haven't taken this to my editor yet and didn't want to blow our source for the whole investigation by going to the authorities."

What the hell was he supposed to do with that?

"Thanks, so you decided to lumber me with it. That's an impossible position."

"Actually, it isn't. You obviously have a hotline to the security services. I've never probed too deep about that as it's not my business. My job at times is to ask what I need to know. I've been in this game long enough to realise that.

Use the intel quickly and covertly. If I had any more details about the attack, I'd tell you, but that's all he'd give away, maybe all he knows. Just get the word out and convince them that the threat is absolutely genuine. Without giving contacts away, me in particular."

"And if this call is monitored?"

"I'll take that risk, there isn't exactly time to play with. The only priority is them getting on top of the situation fast. I've been given no names and few pointers.

There was one other aspect though, which left me with no choice but to take this to you…the contact mentioned that you seem reliable."

Shay's confusion mounted. "What are you talking about?"

"You're evidently a celeb now in the Iranian political world. Someone out there trusts you to do the right thing. Strange how you're not considered a liability for anyone outside the UK. Please, just do it Shay."

Shay sighed, "You said few pointers?"

"They sent a picture of the guy to look out for. I'll copy the photo to WhatsApp."

As Shay waited for the incoming message, he glanced up to see sunset moving west, off to America. To think he'd been basking in the evening's rays minutes ago, sat outside with Greg, beers in hand. How come Rahman always brought trouble? Or was that unfair? After all, the tip off was loud and clear in his direction. And, judging by the photo, Zarek Behzadi must be in town, with or without his accomplice.

CHAPTER THIRTY-SIX

SOUTH WALES

Staring at his mobile, uncertain in which direction to pass the information. But the choice was stark enough. Risking Rahman's investigation being blown or passing on a message that could save lives. If Townsend wasn't his biggest fan, who exactly could he go through? Nicholls was knee deep in dishing out stories to the media, like feeding time for the piranhas. Atkinson, despite their hostile encounter, may just give him the time of day though it was unlikely. Siobhan? Did she possess sufficient clout within her own department? Probably not. He had to plump for the best of bad options.

Townsend answered quickly. Attempting to switch the narrative well away from the *Investigator* and, specifically, Rahman's role, Shay laid out the facts as he knew them. Not a great move personally to reveal how a contact of his was communicating with extremists. Townsend's raised voice in response was hardly a new occurrence and Shay had steeled himself for a barrage of questions anyway. The only aspect that mattered was convincing his former boss that he fully believed in the source. If it was good enough for Rahman, he had to trust it too.

The major had calmed by the end of the call and seemed to be taking Shay's explanation seriously enough to look into.

"Leave it with me and resist the urge to get involved at levels you aren't equipped for, Mason. You're meant to be past tense with all this anyway."

Despite the initial negative reception, Shay was still comfortable he'd utilised his quickest way into the higher ranks in Whitehall. All too quickly, the personal dimension set in though. Friends and family in and around the capital – surely, they should be warned? But how, and who, exactly? There were too many either living or working in the city – Maryanne, Ade and Julie, Siobhan just for starters, friends from the army. Each mobile call, every warning, risked a sizable leak being forwarded along the chain. Inevitably, even if the press didn't seize on it first, social media would all be abuzz with justifiable fear. There may be a requirement for the government to respond publicly. Or did threats like this, however plausible, arrive daily? Hourly?

The warning had been clear enough and he'd delivered the message for which he'd been singled out. Besides, there was no decision to make as yet, and he could spend the best part of the next day inching towards a final decision whether to alert anyone.

The response arrived early on Wednesday though, to his surprise, it was delivered in a call from Siobhan.

"Just thought you should know, the matter you took to Townsend is dealt with. In case you were tempted to warn anyone away from London. The UK is in constant contact with the Iranian Government, despite what you may read and hear in the press."

A pause. "Is that all I'm entitled to know? After clearly being the conduit for all this?"

"Okay OK. To put you in the picture, Behzadi and Hamouni had been in hiding in the Shiite enclaves in Syria, which are pretty much fully run by the Iranian Government anyway. They've been watched like hawks when they tried to leave, according to my colleagues, and were trailed to Copenhagen. The authorities in Denmark and Iran had clocked they had onward flights booked to London for later today so they've been picked up. My colleagues say they'd known about this threat anyway. At least, there were rumours, albeit completely unconfirmed, they were preparing a sarin surprise on the Piccadilly Line in the centre of town tomorrow. In effect, the Iranians were updating the terror plot instigated all those years ago in Japan's underground system. Most terror plots are copycat operations and there's seldom any originality in the terrorist rulebook.

We're lending any assistance we can, of course, and following up leads here concerning the possible whereabouts of the chemical agent. That's all I can tell you. And Shay…".

"Yes?"

"You could have brought this to me first."

After the call, a mild feeling of dissatisfaction that this was being dealt with sufficiently. An idea quickly formed, or half-formed at least, and only permeated further as Wednesday morning wore on. Woodford, fortunately, was in his office, head down, bent over paperwork.

"Sorry to bother you sir," after he'd been admitted. "It's just that I hadn't booked in to collect my licence from London so was thinking of going up tonight. There's online training anyway this week and I'd be back for Monday. I know it's late in the day but there's a reduced intake this week, so Greg's fine with them."

The reference to the licence would strike a chord with his superior. It seemed a minor formality, but all had to complete the protocol. He added that paperwork for his annual army trainer's licence had been part-submitted weeks before, but everyone involved knew it had to be signed for and collected in person from Whitehall. He could understand why all commanding officers hated the ritual too.

"No reason why not, I suppose Mason. Can it wait until next week though?"

"There's another reason, sir." Shay was unsure if his attempt to sound sheepish just came over as weak. "My polling card must be in London...apparently the local council here never received my request to move my voting address to base."

"You are meant to be organised at your level Mason." Woodford broke into a smile. "Well, I suppose so. Back for Monday sharp."

Awaking in the comfort of his own flat the next morning, he'd burnt up travel time and much of the previous evening rushing through what was supposed to comprise of ten hours' online work to complete his certificate.

Now, even the flat was baking. Glancing out of the window at the typical late August weather. Presumably it would entice a large turnout for today's election. That would be the least of his concerns though, as he washed, shaved and prepared for the day ahead, leaving the flat by seven thirty. Though not before checking the morning's breaking news story.

Italian authorities had just released the official police investigation report into the San Siro assassination, today of all days. The UK's media was presumably happy with something to report, as the splash didn't breach the 'no party politics' rule for the reporting world on an election day, after all. The narrative was anodyne at best, incompetent at worst, he noted in disbelief, browsing the online summary. Authorities were confident that a gunman, aided by an accomplice nearby, struck from the far side of the stadium. Suspects were now in custody and had a personal vendetta against the head of FIFA. Why, exactly, wasn't explained and the report's publication had, if he was piecing the story together accurately, been designed to tie in with the capture in Copenhagen. Yet the report was silent on too many crucial matters. Why had neither of the individuals in question, presumably the Iranians, been charged if they were stowed away in cells. The conclusions would fall flat on their face. Just as bad for the narrative, what if at least one was later acquitted? There was no mention of the theory that the execution was performed by someone a lot nearer the presentation party. Hadn't he made that clear to the authorities, along the line, to pass back to the reporting investigators? Why no reference at all in the official version, if only to consider and dismiss the option? He made a mental note to scour the whole document properly later.

For today, there was no road map, no grand design in place. Instinctively, he felt that others may not be taking the threat in London seriously though. Maybe it had been Siobhan's blasé tone. The strange sense also that Behzadi, if not in custody, may come for him personally. Shay had been named personally by Tehran, after all. Deliberately placing himself outside the security of the base, far away from the remoteness of the Welsh headquarters, could be described as a form of madness. Far from many he could rely on. But the pull was too great.

A short walk past the local polling station, the voting public queuing outside already. The structure, a temporary prefabricated hut hurriedly assembled on a street corner. Was there really no nearby school to utilise? It occurred that such sites would make an easy target.

He moved on towards Central London, passing queues large and small at an assortment of venues. A scruffy Triumph motorbike backfired as it passed by, prompting him to spin round. And on, the warmth of the day and lack of certainty about his and others' safety all jumbled in his mind, disordered. Then, through Islington, the screech of a taxi's brakes as he inattentively crossed the road in Upper Street. "Shay," he'd jumped out of the way. No, it was "hey," the driver shouting as he passed. All as if the portentous threat looming over the population here was singling him out, engulfing his every turn.

This was different. Completely unlike army manoeuvres and operations. Because he'd been selected and, in whatever way, targeted? Was his sharpness deserting him after the relative luxury of staying out of harm's way in Pembrokeshire? He pushed a hand through his cropped hair. All too close to home, too many he may be letting down if Townsend had made the wrong call all along.

A flash of blue right in front of him. An elderly Chinese woman, with the lead of a Pekinese strapped to her hand, stumbled. He'd knocked into her as she'd left a newsagent. Reaching out in time to catch her arm, but not sufficiently to prevent her fall. He backed away, apologising profusely. Instinctively, a tentative hand to his forehead, then to his neck's lymph glands. What was he trying to accomplish anyway? Some kind of vague protection of every voter going to the polls today? There was no logic in that, anyway. And if there was to be a target, it may not be a voting site anyway.

It didn't come as a surprise that his glands were raised. Reluctantly admitting that the threat handed to him to communicate was now out of his control, Shay sat quietly on a bench to gather his thoughts briefly, before heading back Crouch End by bus, mulling it over but awash with the sensation of futility.

His raised temperature ensured he slept through the majority of the day. By late evening, he caught the exit poll which was conclusive enough. There would be a change of government.

Waking in the early hours, Shay realised his body clock was screwed. Reaching to switch on his radio, the announcement was that Nicholls would be off to see the King. As he began to dose again, his sleep was broken by a call from Townsend. If he'd care to glance out of his window, a Daimler was on hand to bring him to Whitehall immediately. Before showering and deciding Townsend could wait, he tried Rahman's number first. There was no response. Presumably he was sleeping off election night so Shay just left a voicemail.

Yesterday had felt like engulfing paranoia, presumably heightened by the fever. Following the call from Townsend, he'd scoured his mobile for any news of an attack or, failing that, reference to any suspicious incident currently being investigated. A drunken man in his 40s had rushed towards Patterson as she arrived for her constituency count. Recently unemployed and considering the Prime Minister personally responsible, it took a few moments for the police to force the knife from his hand. In Tower Hamlets, East London, several people had been on the receiving end of acid attacks from a couple astride a motorbike. Such strikes, though few in number, had become the new normal in that area and may have been gang related.

He stretched the waiting time to forty-five minutes before emerging from the flat, the driver manifestly annoyed to be toyed with. Not surprisingly, neither was inclined to initiate a conversation.

In the car, Shay added a check for the Iranian pair, specifically. A small Reuters article referenced 'Two Iranians of interest to the security forces still held in Copenhagen as part of a significant operation.' That must be Behzadi and Hamouni, never having made it anywhere near the UK. Unless they had travelled here first or initiated local contacts intent on creating havoc? Just how precise was the forty-eight hour warning? Presumably the timekeeping of terrorists could be relied on as little as their good intentions. And those privy to only some inside knowledge would have even less idea of the timing.

Flicking off the mobile, Shay was experienced some relief that London still looked normal. Maybe he'd taken on too much of a personal burden after all? A WhatsApp photo of Stephanie appeared from Maryanne showing a gappy, shining smile. She was losing those milk teeth early. The gesture was appreciated, despite the precarious relationship with his sister. Timing was certainly ideal to further lift his spirits, also prompting a call to Orange House to check Dad was bearing up.

Did he want to chat with his father, asked the carer? Not today thanks, he'd visit soon enough. Maybe even tomorrow, he reflected, given his break from the barracks.

The black vehicle pulled up in Whitehall outside the now familiar unmarked entrance. Could it be that the loose ends of his take on the assassination were required by the Government to question the official Milanese report? Or an update on the Iranians and the charges they'd face? Although he could understand and even welcome either scenario, both seemed unlikely given the cold shoulder he'd experienced. Just a cog in the machine.

Terence Townsend arrived in reception just as Shay was clearing the X-ray machine in the lobby. The Major immediately led the way back outside the building, suggesting a "spot of sunshine" in St James' Park, but firstly requesting that Shay hand over his phone. Crossing Whitehall before walking to the top of King Charles Street opposite, Towsend slowed his pace considerably as he held forth. A lecture, not a conversation.

"You know, I've always thought of this street to be the centre of empire. The complete heart of a beating civilisation that educated the world." Townsend pointed to each side in turn, "The Foreign Office and the Treasury enveloping the sides. Both the mastery of organisation and order in managing our dominions, allied to financial control, all within a stone's throw of each other. At the end of the street," Townsend pointed at the statue, "Clive of India. Somewhat sullied of reputation by unfair critics but a true patriot who spread the word. Who exported what it meant to be English." The last word was stressed.

"I thought Clive was responsible for a string of atrocities and famine in India?"

"Ahh I can hear you're a statue demolisher at heart. The spoils of war are not to be sneezed at, Mason. Not at all. Way of the world for empire after empire, and always remember, there are only two ultimate outcomes for each protagonist in battle. Keep that in mind. The victor and the subjugated. They can try and rewrite history as much as they like, but that simple equation will always hold."

They fell into pace, Shay uncomfortable in breaking the silence. The pair crossed into the park, as they passed a harassed looking young mother, crouched low, handing small lumps of bread to two small children who squealed with delight as they haphazardly chucked the pieces across the low railings separating them from the pond. Soon after, the youngsters scuttled back to their mother to allow a group of teenage schoolchildren, sporting white vests, to run past lackadaisically.

Terence began, avoiding eye contact as they stood, and sounding unusually calm in comparison to recent exchanges.

"When we spoke the other day, it was the final proof I'd needed. That you could be relied on. You deserve no explanation but let's make clear the OSA still applies and I'll do my damnedest to see you spend the rest of your life in prison if anything comes out concerning any aspect of the operation. That's all I called you in to say, and if you have any doubt about how seriously we view this, it would be easy to switch the information around that you brought to me about a covert channel to terrorists. From the traffic incident up the road a few months ago, to your communication in recent days, it could look to the authorities as if you're in cahoots with the country's enemies.

The alternative, should we choose not to make the matter public, is for all your military postings to visit less salubrious locations. You'd be assigned from port to port, all with a high risk of accidents. Or, let's just think this through, we can make sure information is contained on your Disclosure and Barring Service record that can't be removed. In effect it would appear that you have a criminal record hanging around your neck like a noose. Maybe just insert bankruptcy evidence to your credit rating so, every time you apply for finance, a black mark will appear by your name. Who knows, your bank may request instant repayment on that lovely property in north London.

The world is our oyster, so I hope you don't take offence at my honesty. These are the cards we have on the table so walk away, there's a good boy."

He'd expected the possibility of a gentle request to back off, but not this. Shay tried to take stock.

"You paint a pretty gruesome picture, Major. I presume you'll let me know how I can avoid Dante's inferno. After all, I walked away from Whitehall last time rather than compromise my position. It's not my style to carry out work of which I don't approve, but neither do I run to the media to complain."

Townsend remained silent but sauntered to a nearby bench and extracted a bulky white DL envelope as he beckoned for Shay to sit alongside.

"You can read it if you like, but perhaps there's nothing within that you didn't expect. A change of government is such a good opportunity to put to bed projects that have reached their limit, don't you think?"

The report only ran to five typed pages and was sketchy on most details. It appeared to contain Townsend's suppositions and downplayed many of the facts Shay had uncovered. Nothing about the hunt for the video was referenced, though Shay strained to recall if Townsend had set him on that specific task in the first place. The rest was as anodyne as the Italian report summary. No conclusions about Stewart Tyler's murder were included, apart from vague wording concerning Iranian dissidents. The Kensington shooting wasn't referenced at all. Nothing of substance was uncovered relating to antics at FIFA and even events in Milan were covered far more briefly than Shay's testimony had contained, explained away as a 'frolic of his own'. Most tellingly, it was highlighted that Shay had acted unnecessarily and against orders in spreading fear across the capital, with no explanation of why the Iranians singled him out as a conduit for communication.

The report did indeed leave open the threats just outlined by the Major. Looking around, on his left taking in Horse Guards Parade, the corner of Downing Street and the Cabinet Office. Buckingham Palace was visible to his right, with flag raised to indicate the presence of the monarch. He felt dwarfed by the power of the state, just as he had previously. Justice appeared entirely out of reach. How would the Americans describe his position? A patsy, just some dumb scapegoat.

"Before I sign, you could at least let me know what purpose this all served?"

Townsend blew his nose dramatically. "Yes, well I can tell you that, I suppose. As I informed you originally, we needed a thorough investigation carried out by someone outside the confines of all this," his arm swept towards Whitehall. "And what you've produced has been of value in some ways, but we just need the official version recorded here. No make believe and unsubstantiated rumour."

The explanation wasn't very helpful.

"Just one more question if I may," Shay responded. "The fake bullet. You made a miraculous recovery for someone who'd been shot in the guts. What exactly was that about? Smoke and mirrors in a stadium of 80,000 are difficult enough to stage, but that production in Kensington was amateurish at best, with all due respect. Siobhan and I just happened to be near a window. Presumably no one apart from you two had any idea where we were going that day. Stomach wounds bleed profusely but you happened to be wearing a protective vest for a routine meeting in the heart of west London on a quiet morning. I didn't believe it then, and I certainly don't now."

The Major appeared annoyed.

"And if I tell you? Does that satisfy your inquisitive nature? I'm a war hero, or at least a survivor of a ruthless attack on my life. There's someone else who knew where we were and may just have signalled to accomplices. You, Shay." Townsend tapped the document.

"I was shot, underwent emergency surgery and have enough enemies even in my home city to require protective clothing. You both saw it all."

"Well, if that's the official line…I don't buy that for one minute but I guess it helps protect you from accusations."

Townsend shrugged, reaching into his top pocket for a pen and holding it out.

"Talking of being bought, this time I bear good news. Not that you deserve it but your bank balance is appearing substantially healthier already. The matter was reconsidered and you can keep the reward, not on my recommendation though. It's amazing what writing your name can deliver. If you can spell."

Seconds later Townsend sauntered away. Shay would mostly remember the smugness on the Major's face. The only choice had been to add his signature.

"What about my…" Shay started to call. At thirty yards, Townsend dropped the mobile on the grass as he kept moving, not turning a hair.

CHAPTER THIRTY-SEVEN

NORTH LONDON

Weighing up the options, Shay became aware he was potentially a wanted man by a host of potential aggressors. He'd sluggishly made his way to collect his trainer's authorisation nearby following the depressing encounter with his former boss. Most of the personnel in the training section were old colleagues so a quick catch up briefly revived his spirits. At least he'd fulfilled the tasks he'd set out to perform in London. His loved ones were safe and sound in the city, most significantly.

Then a quick doubletake back to the flat to collect his belongings. It would make little difference if the authorities were desperate enough to follow him round closely on CCTV, so he chose the 19 bus route from Holborn to Finsbury Park and walked the rest of the way. It was extremely unlikely every move would be tracked but, strangely infused with confidence, even staying at street level was a minor victory.

It became a particularly gratifying journey given the online check of his account, his broad grin appearing as confirmation of the full one hundred thousand payment showed up. How to spend it? Shouldn't those of his age be setting up private pensions for the proverbial rainy day? Maybe a down payment on a villa in Italy so he could visit the San Siro more regularly? The thought brought a further smile. Or just hang out there with regular runs round adjacent Lake Como? The flip side was hatred for the feeling of being bought, particularly as he'd failed Bryony.

Back at the flat Shay grabbed clothing to keep him going for a few days then, slipping out of the bedroom window at the rear, he traversed the path by neighbouring gardens until he arrived at the end of the terrace, and returned to the street. Any attempt at a disguise would probably fall flat, but he couldn't resist the addition of a beanie hat in an attempt to stay under the radar.

It remained a wonder that Ade never appeared surprised when Shay would turn up unannounced. Once, following a gruelling ten month tour of duty and little contact, Shay appeared at his friend's weekly darts night with a couple of pints in hand, Ade displaying hardly a second glance. Shay's call on approaching his workplace elicited little reaction. And again, his friend remained chilled at the entrance of the grandiose high panelled reception area of IBS' building in the heart of the city of London, along from Leadenhall Market. Yes, of course Shay could sleep on the sofa for a few days.

"As long as you don't mind being kept awake by Bradley's incessant screaming all night. He's teething now, so no one in our flat is getting any sleep. Julie's a saint."

"She always has been Ade."

"Don't I know it. Well she's working nights soon for the first time since going back, so guess I have to step up to the plate."

"Thanks mate. Later."

Shay's mobile started to sound as he strode towards Monument. Rahman responded coolly at first to the voicemail left earlier in the day asking if there were any updates on the investigation. Maybe Shay had come over as snappy and demanding in the message. After all, Rahman hardly needed prompting to secure results. He was also conscious he may take his self-loathing at taking the pay-off out on anyone in his path. Rahman's tone was reassuring though.

"Well maybe we have some kind of breakthrough. I haven't been putting my feet up, I can tell you. Can you meet in an hour? As last time?"

Sunshine appeared to bounce off the Thames as Shay spent the next hour walking along the Embankment listening to Radiohead on his earphones. Strangely, the angst-ridden lyrics provided a brief respite from his conflicting emotions. Must be a first, he reflected, the insistent drama of *OK Computer* proving a calming influence. This was probably just another holding update from Rahman anyway, he concluded by the time of the right-hand turn from the river towards Trafalgar Square, before the short walk on to Shakespeare's statue. It felt like he was walking London in a day.

The journalist arrived ten minutes late, though Shay felt no rush and had plenty of time to get to the East End. A broad smile rested on Rahman's face, accompanying his deep breaths.

"What have you got?" asked Shay.

"This time, it's opening up. Let's walk and talk."

The same route towards the Portrait Gallery. But Rahman didn't pause.

"So, Nicholls has his dream position. Who would have thought? A tonne of terror on the streets and the government gets bumped into an election it has little chance of winning. Atkinson may have held the line for them but, once he was gone, the dam broke."

"Thanks for the politics lesson. I can read."

"No, I...sorry. Noticed anything else in the media recently?"

"Arrests in Copenhagen. It could be interesting if we ever find out what exactly they're being charged with."

"Yup. And you did study the Milan report properly?"

"Study? No. It appears to be a complete whitewash according to the media summary and it's convenient the arrests in Denmark are timed to coincide with it. What does it matter if the whole thing can be blamed on a couple of Iranians who've gone rogue? That appears to be the view of the authorities all along. Their version is all out in the open now and I can't disprove a thing."

Rahman grinned. By now they were perched outside the same café as last time, ordering coffees.

"I'm having that damn burger now as well. And it's on you, after upsetting Guiseppe."

Rahman ordered. The tables around were full as the weekend approached, despite the relatively early hour, three loud elderly women weighed down with Harrods and Selfridges bags to their right, chatting away in Spanish. On their left, a smartly dressed middle aged couple sipping red wine were clearly in the midst of a heated argument.

"Well, my job is to study all the details you mere mortals miss," continued Rahman. "It could be the development we've been waiting for. The starting point, strangely, is the Appendix as to how the investigation was conducted. According to Italian law, or at least according to powers deemed legal for this investigation, the authorities were entitled to consider that all footage taken inside the stadium falls under their jurisdiction and hence they retain copyright. Knowing they would have a battle to maintain that permanently, they agreed to enforce it only until the report was published. All that footage is contained on a web link. Then, yesterday straight after publication, a small team of mine in the inquiry section at the *Investigator* began checking the footage. In fact, the election played into our hands as the rest of the office were rushing around analysing Parliamentary results, so we managed to stay under the radar. No questions asked. Anyway, we kept digging with Milan until we found what we'd suspected. Or to be precise, what you had suspected.

Ever heard of a guy called Roberto Caldarera?"

Shay shrugged, leaving the floor for Rahman to explain.

"When you set out all you remembered from Milan, I contacted Guiseppe for help. He's a good guy and has great connections regarding fraud and other investigations in Italian football."

"I'm surprised he wanted to help. I thought he hates me."

Rahman nodded.

"He does, but he'd help me. Also, you forget that being part of the team that busts this open could receive a lot of kudos. Don't look so surprised. Yes, journalists have egos too.

Anyway, I digress. Caldarera has been in Guiseppe's sights for a while and is strongly suspected of being a middleman in trying to bribe Italian players to throw matches, on behalf of the mafia. In fact, a number of players reported him to Guiseppe for precisely such approaches."

"And this Caldarera matters? Why?" Shay interjected, breaking the journalist's rapid pace. Rahman sipped his cappuccino, enjoying the explanation.

"Okay, the report covers not only the conclusion that the shooter or shooters were over on the other side of the stadium. It also discounts Stefan Persson's version or, to be precise, covers it very briefly then utterly trashes it. Makes out he was in a state of shock at the time so completely confused.

One of those interviewed for the report was Caldarera who, conveniently, happens to be the stadium's head of security. He maintains he was watching everything from the VIP area throughout at the back and was leaving his underlings to carry out administrative operations. But just in front of him was Jonah, some new pop teen sensation who apparently supports Paris."

"Unfortunately, I remember the kid."

"Anyway, Jonah's shown by the cameras three times in the stands. This is all live footage on the main TV feed so we had that anyway. On the first two occasions, Caldarera is in sight. The third time, with five minutes of the match to go, he isn't. We picked up on this, so when the bulk of the other footage came out yesterday, we checked and they'd also released official security recordings for the exits, presumably by accident.

There's no security camera in the pitch side tunnel from which the presentation party emerged, unfortunately. But guess what? Opening the fire door which leads round to the narrow staircase, five minutes from time, was Signor Caldarera himself. And who's admitted? Only a local mafia hitman, with a bulge showing in his breast pocket."

Shay didn't know where to start.

"What the—? Okay, two things. Firstly, how did you know to look for all this?"

"You didn't realise the clue you started us off with. Or rather, started Guiseppe off with. You mentioned cigar smoke in the staircase. Caldarera is frequently seen with a cigar clamped to his lips. Must have been a particularly stressful time whilst on the staircase waiting to admit an assassin, but once he'd played his part, it was safer to wait until the commotion started on the pitch than risk anyone noticing him return to the seat."

Rahman dived into his burger hurriedly.

"Okay," Shay added. "And how the heck wasn't a bullet from a matter of yards away differentiated from one supposedly fired from the other side of the stadium when it came to the investigation. Or the autopsy?"

The journalist shrugged, dabbing away ketchup by his lip.

"Presumably the shooter from the tunnel knew what was about to happen opposite and had to wait for the smoke and sound. As for the autopsy, an exploding bullet is going to rip apart anything in its way so, if the right pathologist is leant on at the appropriate time, they could be convinced to go for a convenient explanation rather than what's portrayed as a pie – or shot – in the sky theory. And anyway, the autopsy report is being withheld as confidential, supposedly for reasons of national security."

"Who—" Shay started.

"Someone with a lot of power and leverage, we're not there yet. Maybe the key to uncovering that is another angle. They could have taken Linda out at any time. Why come up with an elaborate plan that conveniently sets up a couple of Iranians who probably have no idea why they're being ordered to attend a football match? And set up a whole son et lumiere spectacular?"

Their attention switched to the adjacent table as one of the Spanish women erupted into a burst of laughter, her companions giggling at their friend's reaction. The couple on the other side shot annoyed glances at the group, the intensity of their own conversation broken.

Shay's cappuccino grew cold, as the pair tried to work out a route forward for the next half hour.

Much later in the day came the opportunity to try and switch off with Julie and Ade at their flat, five minutes from Bethnal Green tube, oversized pizzas and a few beers hitting the spot. Bradley was a handful now, Shay reflecting it must have been months since he'd seen the child. Julie's gene pool was unmistakably victorious in the boy's looks, his dark skin only slightly lighter than his mother's, with little concession to the paleness of his father's, let alone to the ginger mop.

Bradley crawled onto the sofa with energy still to burn, despite it being his bedtime, before being rescued by Julie and Ade as he prepared to launch himself back to the carpet. Shay appreciated the chance to kick back, catch up and watch junk TV with non-military friends. Fortunately, there was no opportunity for Ade to ask if they'd been any developments following those account checks he'd helped with. For the first time in days, the expectation to secure results was the last thing Shay felt inclined to chat about.

After the others had turned in, night dragged for Shay and his focus returned to the day's earlier conversations. Rahman's account of events in the San Siro had to be significant. One o'clock, two, sleep stayed at bay. It wasn't the lumpy cushions and springs threatening to poke through the battered wine-coloured sofa that were keeping him awake. By three, he'd landed on the nagging question that wasn't covered in yesterday's revelations, at least regarding Rahman's actions. Siddique had been provided with so much evidence of Nicholls conspiring to entrap others. Maybe the politician hadn't put his hand up to anything strictly illegal, but why was there no publicity regarding that aspect of grabbing the top job? Siddique would surely be asleep now, so Shay opted for the more sociable approach of messaging. Townsend had made clear Shay was definitely off the radar so probably wouldn't even bother responding to any communication now. Soon after, sleep kicked in.

A shriek of delight was accompanied by Shay being shaken awake at six thirty, as the scampering toddler darted into the room and made straight for the sofa. Shay lay as still as he could, hoping the boy would ignore him, then relieved that a strong pair of arms swiftly lifted Bradley away. There was no chance of further rest though.

Ade was already dressed for work. With Bradley squirming in his arms having stubbornly refused to be silenced with a biscuit, Ade's expression turned serious. "Let's talk. The extra info I dug up for you. Julie wouldn't approve but she's not here, is she? Anyway, you never got to the bottom of it."

"What? The account?"

"If the Tylers weren't behind it, then where were those sums coming from? Sorry mate, I know it's none of my business but I'm just intrigued. You've got me in on it. Though there are other checks possible—"

"Questionable checks?"

Ade stared back.

"You don't want to know the answer to that. But it's usually possible to find out exactly where payments emanate from, if the account operator is stupid enough to leave a footprint. Of course, the top cyberterrorists cover their tracks but you never know, you may not be dealing with such a proficient expert."

Shay had little option other than to nod and let fate take its course. At least the information that resulted would be provided directly to him and not released to gain website clicks by a journalist.

"You want to see how it's done?" asked Ade after a pause.

"Absolutely not. I'll leave you to follow the yellow brick road, thanks." Ade nodded.

"I know what you mean but sometimes we have to use all sorts of leads if we're chasing up fraud. It's standard for my line of work. I'll look in my lunch break as all the codes are kept in the office. I'm on Saturday shift today unfortunately."

"I owe you another. And for the hotel stay."

"Great, you're on babysitting duty tomorrow tonight if you're still around. Julie and I haven't been out for date night since he was born."

Ade handed Bradley over as he waved and headed for the front door. The message alert resulted in juggling his phone with the squirming toddler.

"Here," he expressed aloud, to no one in particular, as he laid Bradley on the sofa. It was Siddique's brief response to the message forwarded in the early hours.

"Sorry, I guess we've both been played. Hopefully today's splash will help make up for it. For now."

That was it? All the information Nicholls seemingly pushed Rahman's way was out there just because the *Investigator* couldn't resist chasing headlines? Even though some had been unsubstantiated in addition to patently providing Nicholls with a boost politically. There was no point calling back now. If he was directly in cahoots with the new Prime Minister then they'd be no admission, particularly via phone. Even though Rahman had listened when so many others turned their backs, then come up trumps with the Milan investigation. Ultimately, Shay couldn't fathom Siddique. Though maybe they were both pawns. at the end of the day.

Not wanting to become a burden for the couple, and finding even this glimpse of domesticity uncomfortable, Shay concluded it was definitely time to leave the flat. He'd carry out his own internet research somewhere locally for the day to stay out of the way. After all, their sofa could be needed as a stand-in bedroom for a bit longer.

Seating himself at a nearby cafe with breakfast and a double macchiato to hand, Shay started. He started by going through the *Investigator* scoop which scrutinised the official San Siro version in great detail, demolishing the formal account and prepared to name Roberto Caldarera, with the footage of him opening the door to the assassin available on a prominent link. Checking more widely, the splash on *La Gazetta dello Sport* website alleged much the same story as the translated version of the Italian website was a lifesaver. The face of the alleged mafia hitman remained pixelated though. Maybe they'd decided it was fair game to name the official raking it in at the San Siro, who presumably would be forced to watch his back for the rest of his days to ensure he kept quiet, even in prison. It was quite another to reveal the face and identity of the mafioso involved.

He finished the last of his porridge. The Italian chief of police and lead investigator had already shifted from their earlier positions, quickly giving up on their initial line that the new version of events was complete make-believe. An ever more antagonistic war of words erupted between them via the media as to whose responsibility the shoddy report really was; neither was prepared to accept the blame any time soon. When returning to the story later in the café, the *Gazetta* was openly mocking the pair, whilst bemoaning inefficiency and cover-ups all along the way.

The story, sat alongside election fallout on the UK's news websites, saw the media desperate to add their own angles in an attempt to claim at least part of the credit for the revelations. It must be great to hog the limelight like that, Shay reflected. Rahman's team would dine out on their discoveries for a long time in the media world. Presumably now it's published he'd be tied up and have no opportunity for chasing any more connections: a round of TV interviews, 'how I did it' follow ups, scoops for the Economist and Newsweek. At least Shay's name would be kept out of it.

A quick walk round the block to clear his head before heading back to the café for a whole new angle on the research. The pieces wouldn't fit though, so fingers crossed that Ade would deliver. Just as he'd collected another drink from the counter, he felt a tug on his arm and an out of breath Ade was at his side.

"You almost sent my coffee flying. What the…"

"I didn't think this could wait." They both sat. "Weekend duty usually means sitting round for something urgent to arise. Fortunately, it didn't, so I started on the research early and couldn't stop. My colleague said he'd cover for me as it's so quiet. Why didn't you ask me to check that this café is up to date with his taxes? Far more mundane." as Ade nodded towards the bespectacled boss standing bored behind the counter, unblemished cream apron bulging above his stomach.

"Shhh," Shay smiled. "How did you know I was here?"

"You've got your location switched on for your mobile. That was really high-tech stuff."

He pulled a folded print-out from his back pocket. The three double-sided pages were severely creased, evidence of Ade clearly having headed from work in a rush.

"Long trail to crack, this one. The payments weren't sent directly and, in fact, travelled via Liechtenstein, Tanzania, Chile, to name three of many. If anyone was casually looking, they'd just see legitimate payments from one account to another but, after a check of the supposed account holders along the way, all were fictitious. Eight accounts in all so a hell of a trail, but not covered up expertly enough. Good but no cigar. And in the end it all came back to one person. Here," he pointed. "Never heard of them." He leant over as Ade reached for his mobile and, a few seconds later, pointed to the screen. An immense grin spread across Shay's face.

"Oh, I most definitely have."

CHAPTER THIRTY-EIGHT

EAST LONDON

At that point, Ade's phone rang and was soon lamenting that his colleague was advising of new work that had come in for them both. He quickly left.

Shay attempted to contact Rahman again. There was no response, concluding that his supposition about the round of media interest must be true. He left another message.

The new lead would certainly be beyond him though, so someone with sufficient clout would have to reveal the name handed by Ade on a plate. An hour later, Siobhan was surprised to be met on the Department steps. She'd mentioned to Shay that, although it was unusual for her to carry out departmental work at the weekend, staff would still be completing the removal of documents deemed sensitive to the outgoing party as Nicholls had been victorious. It seemed this was no ordinary laid back weekend for many.

"Always a pleasure, I suppose. How did you know I'd emerge?" she started.

"You're a fresh air buff, guessed you needed a lunch break each day. A creature of habit."

"You're not big on compliments, are you?" she smiled.

He ignored the jibe. "I have a feeling you'll be extremely interested in what's come to light," and went through a summary of the recent Milan revelations which Siobhan had missed on the news, as well as the results of Ade's research. Her reaction wasn't as expected though, as she stopped and glanced away. Maybe just tiredness from the government turnaround, particularly given her liaison role. A tonne happening at work presumably. Whatever the reason, she didn't share his enthusiasm. She abruptly entered an Itsu. Shay started to follow her inside before she turned abruptly, now just a hair's breadth away.

"Look, maybe I've followed this through as far as I can. You don't understand. My job is on the line if I break with protocol again. I've risked prison by even hinting at a breach of confidentiality, so…no, don't stop me," she raised a hand. "I've offered the man who's now hit the highest office in the land official secrets about a political opponent. Did I deliver them? No, which is even worse in a way. I could be on his target list as someone untrustworthy around nationally sensitive information. He could have me fired."

Shay lightly touched her arm; she angrily pushed his hand away.

"Don't do that, ever." She strode to the vast open selection of food as he followed.

"What are you talking about? You didn't provide him with anything concrete. Nicholls has just secured one of the biggest landslides in decades so he's hardly going to risk his reputation as a breath of fresh air, all sweetness and light, to hunt you. It's not coming to light any time soon. If there were proof of the meetings, he'd emerge with some cock and bull story about you approaching him to attend a dinner at, I don't know, your mum's local constituency."

Her stare hardened. "My parents are still in Gothenburg, she's Irish. Why in God's name would I have—"

His voice raised in combat. "Not literally Siobhan. I don't know what he'd come up with. It obviously suits neither him nor you to make a big deal of those encounters." Then, more quietly, "Look, OK, I'll leave it. I get the message. You don't really want to bust this open at all at the moment. I'll sort it myself somehow."

Siobhan turned her back, quickly paid and hurried out with her teriyaki salad. Shay felt self-conscious in front of the staff and, with other customers staring by now, distractedly paid for his food. Ignoring the instinctive response to turn and shout, "what are you all gawping at," instead he headed back along the Strand towards Trafalgar Square, jacket draped over one arm and paper lunch bag in the other, turning down Villiers Street towards Embankment tube station. Italian, Greek and Spanish cafes were all doing take out with small queues forming outside. On the right, darkened corporate glass windows from looming structures provided the entire street with a completely unbalanced feel, as if the city's designers had collectively been on holiday when planning applications hit their department.

He'd really screwed up. Not only failing to interest Siobhan again, but she now knew information only he and Ade had been privy too. Surely, she wouldn't report straight to Townsend or her new departmental heads? Though, maybe she was right after all. It was one thing to stick his oar in when his regular life was miles away amidst the combination of freedom outdoors and the safety of the base. Quite another for someone locked into the tightest bureaucracy of them all in Whitehall, where accessing the wrong file online could bring immediate rebuke and worse.

"Hey, watch where you're going." A tourist knocked into him. Was he bearing an invisible sign saying 'pickpockets welcome'? A quick check confirmed phone and keys in his jeans were left untouched, his watch still attached to his wrist. Houdini would have struggled with that theft. Contact with the stranger would have been considered a tame shoulder barge in football or rugby, but decidedly not courteous in these genteel surroundings. The tourist, sensing he was being watched, waved an apologetic hand in the air without turning or stopping. Shay opted for a park bench in the adjacent Victoria Embankment Gardens. Reaching into the lunch bag, his hand landed on a folded A5 sheet of paper.

"Glorious May Day. Particularly in the US. Please join us at her London office via heaven."

Not so innocent a barge after all. The note would prove harmless in the hands of others but they knew Shay couldn't resist the invitation, given the gaps in his knowledge. Besides, he'd be safe in the UK, surely. Firstly, walking past Heaven, was it still considered the trendiest gay club in town? At the end a white limo awaited, the chauffeur patiently holding the back door open. They started across the river. Cruises were relatively full, but even from the bridge Shay spied cardigans, jumpers and anoraks either on or alongside the tourists aboard, in apparent distrust of a British summer.

Shay's guess at their own destination was proving correct, as they headed towards the fortress on the southern side of the Thames that was the billion-dollar American Embassy in Battersea. Seeing the building close up at first, it appeared to resemble a misshapen porcupine. On arrival, security checks were surprisingly minimal. He was soon whisked upstairs to a giant meeting room, where the May Queen was visible on a giant screen, her gaze following as he moved across the room.

"Seldom a pleasure to see you, Ms Archibald," Shay took a seat opposite across the oversized glass topped meeting table, empty save for a single item. "Can't afford the air fares for any more? Congress bitten your budget?"

"I guess there's still some gas in the tank. We thought we'd pay you a visit in this way as time is evidently of the essence. I've been straight with you and it's clear, from word we've received, that you're still chasing leads even if they're not delivering all you need."

"Go on."

May continued. "However, there's a limit to how involved we're allowed to get on UK soil and any American sticking their nose into people's business is going to alert anyone and everyone with something to hide. Your situation is different. They're all used to you rummaging around but not laying a glove on the big boys, or girls, involved. More like a gutless Tyson without the big swing, let alone Ali with no defence," she smiled.

"You do know Britain has some of the best heavyweights around at present?"

She shrugged. "The point is, I have a file to show you that fills in lots of the blanks that we came up with after Bryony was discovered." Shay faked nonchalance before gradually moving his hand to the white A4 dossier in front.

"You get an hour to read and memorise the contents, but you'll hand over your mobile and not take any notes or copies. All in return for one question that you're required to answer. For everyone's benefit. You're apparently getting close but no jackpot in sight. Are you prepared to deal?"

"How can I answer if I don't know the question?"

She leant forward, eyes unblinking, to spell out the precise terms. Not for the first time, Shay appeared to have few options, agreeing to the proposal. Tyler and his loved ones were owed that, as were Maddison and Bryony. It was as if May was reading his thoughts.

"Of course, if you want to fool yourself this is all for others, laying ghosts to rest, well that's all well and good. I don't really care why but we both understand deep down that you're following this through to sate your own ego, peace of mind, whatever you want to call it."

The screen went blank for precisely sixty minutes, the dossier's contents making clear how much progress the Americans had actually made. Without the might of US intelligence behind the operation, there was little chance of staying in the game. Not least having been awarded pariah status by the very man who'd hired him in the first place.

Maddison and the Iranian dealings. Bryony's true role – he should have known she could be trusted implicitly. Also included was an explanation of how the information had been acquired, the fact that a substantial amount came from a 'loan deal' between Danish counterterrorism and the Americans, as the two unnamed Iranians underwent a time-out in Copenhagen's American Embassy on a strictly off-the-record basis. What promises or threats were uttered, in that time, to produce revelations that blew this much open? How legal were the hacked communications? He tried to ignore that aspect, at this stage anyway. Given the FBI's involvement in chasing down FIFA's web of corruption in previous years, it hardly came as a surprise they maintained tight surveillance there too.

Not a mention of the Bard though or any conclusions regarding possible payments to the Tylers' account. That ace could stay up his sleeve, so presumably they were oblivious to Ade's revelations.

May was in place as the online conversation resumed.

"Anything you didn't know?" she enquired. He desperately wanted to sound non-committal.

"Useful enough, I guess. Thanks." She shrugged at the apparent apathy.

"Do with it what you will but ensure you come back to us with that one answer. I shouldn't need to spell out why that's important all round. There are still a number of gaps we're trying to plug but strange things appear to be happening as we speak. For the last few days, my team have been delving into under the counter payments Tyler may have been involved in. It's a long and complex road. But, lo and behold, I've been informed the encryption level has just multiplied one hundred-fold according to our experts in Langley. You wouldn't know anything about that, would you Shay? They're out of our reach at present."

Ade must have acted with great speed in adding additional encryption to hide links between the accounts. Knowing IBS had outwitted the American Government's finest would tickle him. It was only a shame there could be no ad campaign to shout it from the rooftops. Who knows? When all this was over, he could recommend Ade to May for a senior role. That is, if he and May were on speaking terms.

Working his way back to his friends' flat from south London, Shay sensed a limit to how much sitting around coffee bars could occupy the day without going insane, even if he was utilising them as office space. On the journey back, his thoughts returned to Siobhan. His company was clearly unwelcome for lunch. Maybe their relationship was programmed to self-destruct each time they got closer, just a tempestuous combination howsoever pushed together. It had all shuddered to a sudden conclusion all those years ago. Townsend's annoying little manipulative games stirring the pot between them now. Well Townsend could go to hell.

Ade chucked his bag halfway across the living room on arrival home. One for the dramatic gesture when least expected, Shay smiled. It must have been annoying to spend so much of the weekend in the office on such a blisteringly hot day, having completed the round journey twice as well. Shay expressed his gratitude. In Ade's absence, he'd been catching up with Julie over iced coffee. General chat led to more specific subject matter as Julie, as ever a good listener, helped Shay try and untangle the complexity of his feelings towards his Swedish ex. Bradley was a crawling bundle over both them and the furniture as they spoke. Julie rose on Ade's return.

"Right, got to get ready for my shift. It's only the local hospital at the moment, fortunately." Shay had forgotten her night duty was restarting. He now felt like a rude guest for hogging the conversation, realising he hadn't even asked where her next assignment would be. Julie's expertise in palliative care was in demand across the capital but she'd long preferred temporary placements, claiming it helped prevent becoming overly morbid about her job.

Julie's response elicited a smile from Shay. He excused himself and, leaving the living room while Ade reached for Bradley, put in a call to Rahman to double check. Yes, he was correct.

"Julie," he tried the wide-eyed innocent approach on his return to the living room, though knowing his chances of appearing sheepish and appealing were few and far between. "You couldn't do me a huge favour could you? In fact, the hugest since you took Ade off my hands?"

CHAPTER THIRTY-NINE

EAST LONDON

The task was doubly hard by having to convince both of the couple. Julie's absolute refusal, at first, was mitigated by Ade gradually changing his position and arriving firmly on Shay's side. Whether out of loyalty, some knowledge of his friend's torturous route just to arrive at this stage, or just the importance of following through on the results of his IT research culminating earlier in the day, Ade helped persuade her. All without Shay providing the full picture.

"The old amigos ganging up on me, is it? Alright, I'll get you in but that's as far as it goes." She stood abruptly. "Come on then, before I change my mind."

She shot out of the door heading towards her Golf as Shay grabbed his jacket, hurrying down the stairs in her wake. The air was heating rapidly.

"Keep up," Ade shouted after him, receiving an upright finger in response from Shay.

"What's this really about? No, actually Shay," she continued, "on second thoughts I really don't want to know. The number of scrapes you get into seem never ending. Beaten up in Cairo and you never found out who or why. That's strange enough."

They pulled up sharply at a red light, Julie turning towards him. "One absolute though. Promise me now you haven't placed Ade in any risk. Whatever he's been doing to help, it's all above board, isn't it?"

Shay smiled. "You're a fine one to talk. Prepared to bend work rules to help me out. You know you can always trust me."

Julie eased forward as the light turned green, pushing a wisp of curly hair away from her forehead. "That's different. I can take care of myself. And I have something of a free pass at this hospital after—" her voice trailed away as she reached towards Spotify on her phone, Sheeran's *Galway Girl* filling the space.

Ten minutes later the pair pulled into the car park by the low-rise frontage of Homerton University Hospital. Shay was unsure if the light brick used for the relatively recent construction was intended to evoke feelings of brightness and optimism during dark days for patients and visitors alike.

It was impossible to forget those worries over Julie during the pandemic though. Despite all her professional training, including the Advanced Nurse status, and presumably encountering all manner of ailments in her occupation, maybe neither Julie or Ade had fully come to terms with the events emotionally all this time later. She'd been so dedicated to her career before the virus had almost swept her away as well. For thirty-six long hours it had been touch and go, Ade's sobs over the phone at her predicament and the inability to see and touch her in this hospital whilst she – they – most needed it. The medal she was subsequently presented with by her professional body was presumably in lieu of compensation for so nearly losing her life due to the illness contracted at work.

"Just this once," exclaimed Julie as they searched for a parking space. He was grateful the journey had been brief to avoid overly dwelling on her illness. As they entered the building, she pointed away from the porters on the front desk.

"I'll go and check. You stand over there and do nothing,"

Collecting him moments later like a child at lost property in Tesco, Julie led the way along a corridor. Shay recalled how recently it was possible to find yourself lost in hospitals due to lack of adequate signage. Now, the panoply of rainbow coloured directions pointed them along further turnings, walkways and stairs until they arrived at East 3A wing. After tapping them in, Julie approached the male nurse on the ward's reception desk, still taking the lead.

"Hi Pat, all OK? I've got a friend of the patient in room seven with me. It's OK for me to check first, presumably?"

Pat, engrossed with his computer screen, ushered them along. After they approached room seven, Julie knocked then entered as Shay hung back.

"I'm sorry to disturb you. I'm Julie, you may remember me from the other day? My colleague here has stepped in urgently to assist me. I'll just go and speak to the duty doctor and be back in a mo."

Shay stepped forward as she retreated, conscious of the magnolia walls and faded charcoal patterned curtains. Presumably the design had been signed off in the nineteen nineties.

A gasp and wheezing emerged from the bed as he leant forward to catch the words. Margot Guillard looked far removed from the pristine, well-dressed high-flyer whose pictures were so abundant on the net. The recognisable light brown bob remained, but her face displayed exhaustion, whereas once her demeanour was controlled, efficient and very highly focused, even into the early stages of wheelchair use unflinchingly at Rory's side. The paleness of her lips today contrasted with the bright lipstick of old.

"You're not—" she shook her head, each word exhausting to utter, whilst pointing to her chest. That's what motor neurone disease does to you, Shay reflected. It felt almost cruel to make her speak more than necessary, as he nodded in response.

"You're right Margot, I'm afraid it's a slight exaggeration." It passed through Shay's mind that he hadn't given any thought as to how the meeting should be managed, or even consideration as to how much time he was likely to be afforded. It was too late now, definitely wise to omit any reference to Julie and hope the patient hadn't noticed her name badge if a complaint is filed.

"But there are some aspects that just don't make any sense...my career is on the line. Shay Mason."

"Why should I—" Margot rasped.

"Because there's a huge amount I do know and it will all go to the press if I can't fill in the blanks. Rahman Siddique, whom I believe you know, is a good friend of mine."

Time for a change of tack. "I'm genuinely sad to see you like this despite all the problems you've caused. To be honest...you may not be able to help atone for any of this much longer." A pause. "I know about the accounts."

Her eyes flickered, memories of the battler within. After a brief pause, Margot nodded, confirmation that an audience was granted as Shay pulled up a plastic chair alongside her bed, wires and equipment taking up a large proportion of the other side.

Margot turned away, reaching clumsily for an overbed table containing an oversized keyboard. Helping her position the equipment, Shay adjusted the small monitor alongside. He prayed there wouldn't be any interruptions from genuine staff, Julie included any time soon. This would be a one-shot opportunity.

"Where do you want to start?" the typed response. "It was all my planning, my intentions. No one else involved."

"Okay, to save you the effort, I'll tell you my theory and you can confirm or deny. Maybe expand if I'm wide of the mark. Is that all right? And no, I'm not recording our conversation."

She nodded gently before typing, "Good, my voice isn't all it's cracked up to be."

Shay smiled and dived in. "This was a chance to kill many birds at the same time. You knew you were getting worse so I'd guess this was all put into action around six months ago? A year in the planning maybe?

The Government could go in one of two directions. Either gain in strength or collapse. It was clear Patterson's leadership was under fire from Atkinson and you could bring the whole pile crashing down just by raising the stakes. As if your current position wasn't sufficient enough to get hold of the information you needed, your previous job didn't do any harm. In the Foreign Office you were Deputy Head of Liaison with other Whitehall departments, so you really had the contacts presumably."

Silence from Margot, taking that as agreement.

"You just had to join the dots and start up the juggernaut. You knew about the school friendships and contacts – maybe Nicholls had mentioned the little gang of four who all became stars in their fields. He seemed particularly proud of Stewart and the Nobel Prize, maybe because that award involved genuine discovery far more than self-promotion. But it wasn't difficult for you to dig around and confirm Stewart Tyler was sinking into debt, paying big money to bad people to access illegal opioids. As he was desperate, that must have come with a hell of a premium blackmail charge to keep his reputation clean. He'd have been terrified of losing his prestigious job and career.

Presumably you thought approaching Tyler with the offer of substantial payment would be too good to turn down? Even it was to be in exchange for passing chemical information for the Iranians. You were the one enticing him to the House of Commons for meetings to try and persuade him by whatever means. He booked in under the name of a female MP so guess it had to be a woman answering the phone as he arrived at security. It wouldn't have been difficult to request the use of an office for a few hours from one of the aspiring MPs at that time." Margot still didn't respond, Shay unsure if she was deep in thought or just finding the accusations too tiring to answer.

"And look who happened to be on the Middle Eastern desk in the Foreign Office all those years ago, knee deep in hostage negotiations with Iranian splinter groups at the time? Your experience from that period must have been invaluable, and presumably those contacts proved particularly useful more recently with Barjam on the rocks. Those payments were fed to Tyler by you, as now uncovered by IT experts and despite your attempts to cover up the trail." In lieu of a response, Shay nodded.

"A very different response from another of the schoolfriends. Maddison was fully prepared to act as go-between with the Iranians, assisted by sympathetic Egyptian authorities at times and particularly when FIFA visited Cairo. Maddison had diplomatic immunity so could pass communications in any direction, as well as arranging drops. Money was flowing in from Tehran by then, presumably helping Maddison pay for both her legitimate campaign for the top spot at FIFA, as well as bribes to shell out along the way. That money was also used to help you fund Tyler. But he wouldn't touch the account and the threats didn't work, did they?"

She moved her fingers slowly, "stubborn bastard" soon appearing on her typed screen.

"So, you needed an alternative option. The other route in was via Bryony Simmons at Bircham. You discovered her family connection to Tyler, believing she was privy to the same level of information about chemical formulae and, more importantly, the process of developing lethal gas. Despite Tyler's protestations, you presumed Bircham must be aware of his research and were possibly even part-funding it.

Was it easy to convince her to play ball?"

Wording appeared. "Became Jewish when engaged to Israeli years ago." She paused before adding "stupid peacenik, went soft when he died."

Shay couldn't complain about the outcome of the conversation to date, as each allegation seemed to be accepted. This was no time to give in to his anger regarding the danger in which she'd placed Bryony.

"You must have convinced her it was all for a good cause, trying to improve relations between Iran and Israel. Breaking the impasse of intransigent leaders on both sides – who could resist? Eventually, either she worked out she wasn't innocently sharing confidential information for the good of humanity or, like Tyler, was pushed too far. And she was later snatched by Iranian extremists in the US. Just as she was about to confide in me," and couldn't resist adding "I know she was."

Measured typing, as if twisting the knife. "Poor boy. Love let you down?" Shay tried not to flinch. Sentimentality was clearly scorned by Margot, despite being laid so low with only weeks remaining on this earth, by the look of her. A heart of stone, seemingly.

Shay continued. "Whether she actually passed on any information…was she even privy to that level of sensitive material in her business field?"

Guillard's typing seemed faster now. "She tried. Couldn't deliver though. Should never have brought her in."

"It was all going horribly wrong by then."

No response. Continuing, the heat of the room eliciting sweat on Sway's brow. "Stewart was getting increasingly erratic, paranoid maybe, at his lack of control over events. Maybe he was about to expose all the rackets lined up against him, even if it would spell the end of his career. So, who cracked first?"

Rapid typing, "Iranians lost patience, couldn't risk it all coming out. Silencing him was meant to be an accident but CARELESS."

"Well, the Iranians used dissidents who were completely unreliable, that much was clear. Members of the God squad whom Tehran's authorities presumed would stay at arm's length with deniability if needed, the flip side being that they couldn't be trusted to follow orders. Nice touch in trying to set up the peanut scam which may just have diverted attention. Given the problems with flying these days, even the airline may have tried to shut down any autopsy leak if it genuinely thought a simple little snack was responsible." The keyboard tapped again. "Tehran ordered a covert hit only." A slight splutter from Guillard who jerkily motioned for water. Reaching for the glass on the table, he lifted the straw to her mouth. A few sips sufficient, as she leant back on the pillow.

"But these guys weren't to be pushed around. In fact, the chance to spread chaos in the west was too much to resist. They broke ranks with Tehran?" A slight nod in return. "Hamouni couldn't resist a sarin scare right here in London and maybe really did intend to cause damage. Iran was terrified it would be exposed. This was all much too public for them." This time a sneer obvious on Guillard's face.

Standing, strolling towards the window. Someone was trying to park a BMW, and badly, in an already packed car park. The driver was inching around looking for a space, starting to annoy other vehicle users behind. "What started as a nice trail of backhanders and a useful side-line in information to boost your pension pot…"

For once, Guillard's rasping voice rang out, rather than a typed response. "For my children."

"Well that's fine then. As long as you're trying to provide for your offspring then it doesn't matter who gets hurt." She couldn't maintain eye contact.

"And so the whole lot had to be closed down by Iran. You were losing face and couldn't deliver for them, despite the success of making the Government here look incompetent and out of touch. Maddison was a very public assassination. Maybe she'd become too greedy or had to confess that they'd never be a major football tournament held in Tehran during her leadership after all, especially given the rumours about her funding for the top job. The Iranian leadership must have been furious, felt they'd been conned out of big money. After that, the London debacle, then Hamouni and Behzadi were enticed to Milan. How was that done?"

After a moment, typing started. "Told they'd meet a contact with further instructions in the stadium. They wouldn't take out Maddison. Too public for them."

"Okay," continued Shay, "instead they were set up for the hit at the San Siro. Better still, maybe Tehran counted on the pair trying to fight their way of the ground if they were cornered. Being gunned down in a timely hail of bullets would have suited you all perfectly. Let's just say I heard on the grapevine that 'livid' doesn't start to describe their reaction at being set up. You may have missed the real account of events being published by the *Investigator* recently."

She reached for the keyboard. "Read the news still, not dead yet."

A memory came to mind. What was Siddique's reference to having been misled along the way?

"Atkinson and Bryony. They weren't involved, were they? One by one you and the Iranians were wiping out all the trails you'd started, all of which were causing havoc but not providing them with either assistance for their chemical operations or international prestige. We uncovered a warning in Hebrew telling Bryony to get out. The chances of that being the only warning sent to her is exceedingly unlikely, so I'd guess a whole trail of breadcrumbs were sent. And they were all bullshit, presumably intended to rile the Iranians who'd kidnapped her into assuming she was a Mossad agent. Her fate was sealed."

A shrug from Margot. Annoyed shouts and car horns sounded from the car park as drivers behind the BMW must have run out of patience. He glanced outside. A ten mile an hour speed limit sign was prominently displayed, but this joker was sauntering around at a crawl.

"Iran may have been trying to row back fast, but our government was snookered into panic measures that brought them down."

More coughing from Margot and Shay paused briefly before assisting with the straw. His mind had to stay on the goal – to uncover the facts rather than act as judge and jury.

"Enough," she typed slowly, appearing resigned, her energy spent. "Rory knows nothing about this."

Shaking his head, Shay felt the heat in his cheeks. The temptation to shout, shake this bundle of amorality was increasing, but for no benefit. It was more important to work out what to do with the goldmine of information. Although Margot hadn't provided much in the way of new material, and couldn't in her state, she'd confirmed the plot and the main participants, which was worth everything. And for someone steeped in the dark arts that sometimes dominated political communications, she hadn't half given away the golden nugget.

A light snore was audible as Margot's eyes closed. Time for Shay to make his way out of the room and back along the corridors towards the front of the hospital. Firstly, a cold can from the bright cafeteria alongside reception was required in response to the hospital's unnecessary heating. God knows he needed it. But there was something not fitting that he couldn't put his finger on. Having taken the drink to the counter and reached for his phone in payment, the atmosphere of calmness was ended by an almighty crash outside at the intensity of thunder overhead. The window by the serving desk afforded a clear view of the car park. The idiot driver had smashed into the parked car in front, with the alarm from the latter shrieking at great volume. Some folk could clearly afford cars they had no idea how to drive.

At that moment, Shay sensed the colour drain from his cheeks. What if Zarek Behzadi and Abdul Hamouni weren't the pair arrested? And even if they were, patently others must have worked with them. Neither could have been in America when Bryony went missing. If their cell were still out in the cold due to the series of events that suited others, sensing betrayal…

The can was sent sprawling as his hand left the counter. By the time shouts followed from the irate cashier, he was through the corridor doors, sprinting past the wards he'd sauntered along only minutes ago. The accident outside was purely diverting attention. Bursting through the final door, it was apparent that Margot Guillard wouldn't be taking another breath. They'd got to her. Glancing through the window, Shay viewed two figures scurrying away from the hospital grounds and round the corner, then out of sight. For now, at least, out of reach.

CHAPTER FORTY

CENTRAL LONDON

The next hours passed in a blur. Fear of being out of his depth, utterly unmoored, hadn't bobbed to the surface for years, even at the point of most pressure situations in his career. The best chance was to disappear quickly, so as to avoid questioning and hope the authorities didn't catch up with him. Maybe Townsend had enough clout to intervene once word got round the security forces that he could be at the centre of another shitstorm that was not of his making. No one high up would want him wrapped up in this, surely.

Margot's machine hadn't even been switched off. Presumably a pillow over the face for a few seconds was enough to carry her away, so there may be no immediate uncovering of murder. Possibly no autopsy either.

As if the nearer he approached to understanding it all, the lower his spirits. A trek into London straight after, arriving at the Kensington address with no advance notice, admitted without the drama of entry he'd encountered last time. The Iranians had made it look like an accident but presumably wouldn't have hesitated to shoot or stab their way past him to silence Margot if he'd dared intervene. One thing to encounter danger overseas and quite another to face cold blooded murder in a London hospital.

They sat side by side on the sofa for the best part of an hour, mostly in silence, punctuated only by Shay relaying the basic facts of the hospital visit and his suspicions of foul play, less so the preceding conversation details confirmed by Margot. He'd be at a loss to explain why.

Their voices remained at a whisper just in case. It was challenging to process the lack of control, metamorphosing into a stooge pulled from pillar to post at the bidding of others.

The lounge door opened gingerly. A mop of curly hair appeared first, with giant earphones adorning the boy's head as if in an attempt to shelter his looks from the outside world. Presumably the youngster had fallen asleep listening to something in his room.

"Tommy, this is Shay, an old friend of mine. Come and say hello." Siobhan had quickly risen, already at the door leading him in. The boy clearly had no interest in the stranger, responding only with a question as to whether tea was ready.

"Tea? Yes of course. Sit down and talk while I bring it in."

Neither were in much mood for chat, though after they'd all eaten – Siobhan had made clear the meal would stretch – Tommy visibly relaxed as Shay joined alongside on the boy's Xbox. The conversation started to flow, tentatively at first – video games, Doctor Who, and another seemingly old-fashioned birthday present the boy had received and tried to master without success. At Tommy's urging, his mum accepted Shay's offer to help out the following weekend.

Shay was flat out on the sofa an hour later. The next day, tracing back through the capital, he collected his bag left at Julie and Ade's before returning initially to Crouch End, then on to Wales for duty.

The fallout at the hospital had escalated in the days after Margot's death, as Julie was interviewed extensively about Shay's presence, with foul play clearly now suspected. She hadn't caught the names and positions of those interviewing, unsure if they were regular police. Certainly non-uniform, but they didn't read her any rights, so presumably she wasn't suspected of culpability.

Ade had relayed all this in a conversation with Shay days later. After much cajoling, Ade had eventually agreed to another quick check for his friend. Was it possible to hack Townsend's laptop from a distance? The answer was apparently not, with no evidence of it even being linked to the Department's mainframe or back-up systems. This was hardly a surprise for Shay, given there was no evidence from the start of an official tie up between Townsend and the Department, or indeed with any official government agency. There was literally nothing to hack into.

True to his word, Shay arrived at one p.m. on the dot for Tommy the following Saturday. Siobhan greeted him warmly.

"He's just getting ready. Thanks so much for this, you really didn't need to. And you've brought your old one. You big kid." He looked down at his battered old skateboard with pride.

"I found it buried under a pile of clothes at the back of my wardrobe," he lied. "Wasn't even sure I still had it." Had he ever confided to her it was the last present from his mother? Even if never used again, he couldn't imagine parting with it.

Siobhan seemed less sure of herself as they chatted in the hall. "Before you go, there's something I should tell you, after all the time we've spent together recently and our past. I've decided the UK doesn't hold much for me anymore. I've achieved so much here and built up a good career but it's time to move on. My parents aren't getting any younger and need help with shopping, even pottering around and…I just want to be there for them." She rubbed his back as if offering a pep talk to her son.

Shay was caught off guard by his sense of disappointment. "How long?"

"We're off in a week. The sooner the better for all of us."

"Ready Shay," a fresh-faced look of enthusiasm as Tommy came round the corner. Like a desperately needed release, the youngster's inquisitiveness and sheer exuberance was refreshing during the tube journey heading south, crossing the river at Waterloo. The contrast to the hopeless cynicism he'd encountered from Margot Guillard, even in what proved her final minutes, was immense. Then, sauntering from the station towards the Thames and along, Shay remembering he'd once known that final part of the route blindfolded. Maybe most kids were out of London for the holidays as, certainly, the skatepark alongside the South Bank, nestled under the giant edifices of theatres, concert halls and restaurants, was pretty empty for a Saturday afternoon. Only a handful of teenagers were occupying the space. It hadn't changed much in the years since last visiting – low cement ceilings almost inducing claustrophobia at first, layer upon layer of seemingly random graffiti in bright, clashing hues, oblivious adults passing by the river promenade to attend more sedentary events.

A young teenage girl, sporting bright pink hair and black painted nails, was working her way through basic routines – bomb drops, kick turns, caveman – all well-known to Shay.

Tommy appeared mesmerised. Shay stepped back discretely as, impressively, the boy overcame his shyness and approached, asking if she could teach him. At first her face appeared impassive, chewing gum more exaggeratedly, then a simple "here" and a wave over.

Shay left to find a coffee. On his return twenty minutes later, there was no sign of Tommy or the girl. Panic set in as he rushed round, asking surrounding teenagers if they'd seen them, getting increasingly desperate. At last, one pointed outside and, sitting on a bench, the girl was explaining in a matter of fact tone how to attain the best leverage and reach the ideal height. A teacher in the making. Shay felt the surge of relief.

Two hours later saw the start of their return to Kensington. From humid, baking sunshine as they left Waterloo, Shay and Tommy were caught out by a severe shower on the walk back from High Street Kensington tube, leaving both drenched. They broke into a run, which soon became competitive for Tommy. The boy laughed as they reached the mansion block.

Immediately on opening the front door, Siobhan pointed her son towards the bathroom. "I'll get you a towel too in a minute," calling back to Shay.

Looking around, the hall table was mostly bare. A couple of unopened bills, their passports and the flight tickets for the following Saturday evening. She was gathering the paperwork early. Musing later, had it been nosiness or just to pass the time? The items just sitting there, tempting. Maybe the outing had almost gone too well, Shay considering he was really bonding with the boy. Before checking dates, the idea was already crystallising in his head. Surely, Siobhan couldn't be so callous? After all, it wasn't impossible he'd just spent an afternoon in the company of his own son.

Tommy's date of birth resonated as he flicked through the passport before catching sight of the rest. Siobhan's voice started before she was in sight.

"He's in the bath, soaked through. He had a fantastic—" she stopped in full flow seeing him staring at the passport.

"We should go next door," her tone suddenly serious, handing Shay a bright orange towel as he moved towards the living room.

"No, not there," she added, "the landing outside – in case we can't keep our voices down," as they stepped through the front door.

"I can see the question in your face," she continued. "He's not your son. You know I would have…"

Shay interjected. "I know he's not mine from his date of birth. Also, from his name. Were you going to tell me ever? Given what I've been through, I deserve that much respect at least."

"Thomas Andersson," whispered Siobhan, not meeting his eye.

"No, Siobhan," his voice rising despite himself. "Thomas St John Andersson. Who the hell calls their child that, if they're half Swedish and half Irish? William Atkinson is clearly his dad, and you never thought it important to mention it?"

He noted her mouth opening and closing, no sound emerging. For a while they sat in silence on the adjacent stairs.

"Is that why we split up? Because of him?" Shay started, then sharply pulling back as she reached for his hand.

"He was a backbencher then, quite senior on the Defence committee. We got close over time. It just happened, there was no intention to hurt you. But as soon as it started it wasn't fair to string you along."

"That's why we ended?"

"There's no point raking over it all these years later, now we've both moved on."

He stared at her. "Look, right now I really don't care how good or bad a boyfriend I was then. But the least you could do is explain his involvement in all this."

She left for the flat, returning with two glasses of wine before starting.

"There was no question of Bill leaving his wife, though he was really excited about having a child because they couldn't have kids. He helped set us up here and we thought of it as our family nest," waving towards the flat. "A lifestyle I could never have given Tommy otherwise. I didn't ask for it and Bill insisted he wanted to spend money on people he loved.

All was fine for quite a while. We'd meet whenever possible as his career really took off, so it wasn't always easy. The word 'mistress' with all its connotations was always just around the corner, though certainly not how we thought of our relationship. But what if the media found out? How would his wife react?

"Siobhan Andersson, a kept woman. Not what I'd ever expect," Shay's voice was etched with disappointment.

She raised her eyebrows. "There are all types of relationships. And I was hardly going to pull the plug on Tommy's expensive schooling and tell him why I couldn't afford it anymore. I've had a great career here so we both brought an income to the table. Sorry if your expectations don't hit reality, but it's none of your business. My life and my choice. And now I'm buying a place in Gothenburg. This is the time to make the move, so Tommy can really get to know his grandparents."

The fact Atkinson was some kind of political ogre he despised? The standard of living he'd never have provided for her? Having flesh and blood you could truly love as your own? Shay couldn't untangle which felt sharper.

His mobile tone broke the intensity. Siddique.

"Thought I'd catch up. Not a bad time to speak, is it?" The journalist ploughed on, not waiting for the answer. "I really owe you one after the scoops you've put my way."

There was no point keeping anything from Siobhan now. He'd uncovered the relationship with Atkinson and she'd be leaving the country soon. Like it or not, she'd soon be past tense for his life in London. "Rahman, there are loose ends to tie up; a number of them actually. You're right, you do owe me." He looked up. "As do you, Siobhan. We'll call you back."

After explaining his plan, Siobhan's suggestion of approaching an elderly neighbour to ask if her friend could use the phone, claiming their mobile batteries were both dead, proved successful. Rahman picked up straight away.

"Right, a trip to God's own country for a pub night tomorrow is called for," was decidedly delivered by Shay as a command, not a question.

CHAPTER FORTY-ONE

YORKSHIRE

The Yorkshire Dales were a four and a half hour drive away, mostly along the roadwork-laden M1, and provided ample opportunity for the three to finalise plans. Shay had made it abundantly clear she should help finish what they'd started, fully aware she'd be reluctant to turn him down after their conversation.

It hadn't been difficult for her to access Yorkshire regimental data, including the predecessors of the Yorkshires, by logging on to the Department's database from home. She'd quickly obtained Townsend's home address. Shay's research was undertaken from Ade and Julie's flat that morning, his early arrival not greeted warmly by parents praying for no early start from their youngster. The doorbell had woken the youngster.

He'd established there was only one pub within miles of Townsend's home hosting tonight's quiz. *The Old Duke* was indeed in Grassington, that had to be it. Tommy had been dropped off at a friend's house at the start of the journey north, Siobhan having rented a car at lunchtime. Shay presumed her operational vehicle had also been recalled long ago by Townsend.

Arriving late in the afternoon in the Dales and parking out of sight from Townsend's home, Shay had only been mildly surprised that Rahman had agreed to the plan in the first place. Maybe in comparison to most of his investigative digging, this was child's play and it was best not to question what methods the journalist usually employed. Rahman was now heading down the country lane towards the cottage like an eager puppy.

Siobhan's presence felt uncomfortable without the journalist to mediate, Shay not able to shake off the sense of being slighted. She was needed for this, but conversation between the pair remained decidedly stilted. It all seemed so redundant after realising he was excluded from such a crucial chunk of her life. He tried to remind himself she was only a girlfriend from the dim and distant past. Within half an hour Rahman returned, not a moment too soon.

"It worked a treat. When I said we were collecting for Yorkshire troops to attend the Invictus Games, he couldn't have been more generous. I'd dug out items from the office such as charity collection ID. The story worked – my dad was in the Yorkshire Volunteers years ago. I wasn't sure where he'd served and he now has Alzheimer's. Townsend plainly didn't recognise me, unless he's the best actor in town.

Anyway, he bought it. Trundled away to search for his wallet, having left his keys within sight by the front door. Unfortunately, he came back all too soon before I could take a mould. I didn't get to use my replica key set after all. Shame, I like that toy."

Siobhan asked first, "But you said it went well?"

"Don't rush a journalist regaling you his adventures. I asked to use his downstairs toilet. There's no window lock so you could easily jemmy your way in. It's all in the reconnaissance. But you'd know that in your line of work."

An hour later, Townsend set off for the five mile drive in his Subaru, arriving at his usual parking spot near, but not outside, the pub. Rahman had arrived prior to Townsend and, without being asked, had joined a quiz team he suspected were in need of extra help. The three had toyed with the idea of Rahman waiting outside but his competitive streak had come to the fore, the challenge of turning a desperate team into potential winners was too tempting an opportunity. Siobhan waited patiently outside, ensuring she stayed out of Townsend's eyeline. She could just make him out through the window lifting a first pint off the counter.

After dropping the others, Shay had returned to Townsend's remote cottage, parking well away until receiving Siobhan's message that the Major was happily ensconced in the pub. He approached the property on foot for the last quarter of a mile. If it all went wrong and Townsend rushed home for any reason, he should be able to hear and see the vehicle from some distance away, providing time to hide or clear out. An unexpected car in the driveway was not so easy to explain, if the circumstances arose.

It only took seconds to jemmy the window open and climb through five feet up, having stood on adjacent branches to lever himself through the gap. He would have torn a strip off his recruits for failing such a flexibility challenge.

The building was in darkness with no signs of an alarm, Shay thankful that Rahman had also reported back there was no telltale box by the front door or ceiling monitors visible. Not risking the main lights, Shay relied on his mobile's torch, quickly making his way into the living room. As soon as he'd entered, a faint scratching was audible followed by a high pitched screech. Shay jumped, dropping his phone, and had to scramble around on all fours for it. The intrusive noise seemed to encircle the room. An alarm? Guard dogs? This was utterly disorientating.

Returning to his feet with phone in hand, Shay soon trained the light on a five foot cage along one wall, containing two auburn mongooses baring their teeth in alarm at being disturbed. He stepped back, clutching the mobile ever tighter. Who keeps pets like that? Shaking his head and returning to the task in hand, he noticed the laptop charging on a table.

Now, sat in front of the machine, was the golden opportunity. Shay delved into his pocket for the device borrowed from Ade that morning. The visit to their flat had been ostensibly just to apologise again to Julie and promise two nights of babysitting as token compensation. Wary of asking Ade for further help, apart from laptop use to look up local Yorkshire quiz locations, he'd remembered a late night conversation a year earlier when the subject had turned to computer hacking, and specifically the tools required to do the job. Ade had boasted that virtually any home pc or laptop could be accessed via a device the size of a memory stick that he kept in a drawer in the living room. Soon brandishing it at the time, Ade had accessed Shay's laptop and emails within seconds as an example, returning the device to the same place.

He'd used the opportunity to temporarily liberate it when Ade made coffee. It would be returned soon, all being well.

Shay recalled that no key had been needed by Ade in the demonstration, so he tried plugging it in and hoped. There was no response. A quick internet search on his mobile indicated that the devices were already outmoded, and even the most rudimentary protection software could cope with it. Definitely not in the plan. Shay thought through his limited knowledge of software encryption to avoid making that humiliating call for help to his friend. Embarrassingly, he'd also have to admit temporary possession of the stick.

The start screen glowed invitingly across the room. There seemed no option as he tentatively made the call to Ade, keeping detail and location to the minimum, though aware his friend could easily track his whereabouts. Despite Ade expressing his reservations, after only a few minutes imparting the relevant codes, he was in. Downloads were attempted for as many files as possible in quick succession, with no time to check all were fully saved. He endeavoured, at the same time, to ignore the off-putting shrieks from the animals. Honestly, the weirdest of hobbies.

After, relief to discover the backdoor leading from the kitchen wasn't locked, which was far preferable to climbing back out of the window. It wasn't the physical obstacle that concerned him, but rather not being able to fully secure the window behind him. This way, there'd be no trace of his ever having visited the house, if he were lucky.

The best laid plans. Just as he set foot outside, having spotted a path leading round to the drive, lights were ablaze accompanied by the wail of a piercing siren. What was it with Townsend and ear-splitting noise? Freezing instantly, as if caught in the spotlight, Shay quickly donned a balaclava in the hope of avoiding recognition as he sprinted off the property.

Inside *The Old Duke*, the quiz's first round had just been completed. With the focus on politics and current affairs, Rahman was in his element answering all the questions immediately, impressing his teammates at first, then unmistakably causing annoyance. Out of the corner of his eye, he noted Townsend's countenance alter as he reached for his mobile then ambled towards the door, muttering a few words to his deserted teammates.

Siobhan had set to work outside. At first, she'd been confused about the location of Townsend's car, as it certainly wasn't outside the pub. Why park so far down the road? As if reading her mind, a text came in from Rahman. Townsend was on to his third pint already and, according to a teammate, the Major had been stopped for drink driving six months earlier and was loathe to park outside the tavern. This was particularly the case as a competitive quiz rival had been the arresting officer.

Wheezing to reach his four wheeler, Townsend noted at once that the body of the vehicle didn't feel right. Not the suspension, surely? There was no point starting the engine. Quickly exiting, he soon discovered the rear left tyre fully deflated. Fifty away in the undergrowth, Siobhan smiled as she sensed the weight of the helpful penknife folded deep in her pocket. Far more time for Shay to escape.

Soon the three were heading back to London with, hopefully, their mission accomplished. Siobhan drove, as the others occupied the back seats, all the easier to start sifting through the contents now uploaded to Rahman's laptop. At first glance they'd hit the jackpot. How could Townsend be so naïve as to keep this material so easily accessible? Pure arrogance, Shay presumed. Copious amounts of information appeared to explain the whole mission from scratch.

The pair smiled, catching sight of each other with raised eyebrows. Shay was instantly reminded of that demob feeling, the flight home from tours abroad. Siobhan had concentration etched on her face as they wound their way back to the motorway.

It proved awkward sharing the device, despite increasing the font size, so after a while Rahman took over the machine and started skim reading aloud. He nodded along to some of his own comments.

"Looks like Townsend's mission was set up solely by Atkinson. That makes sense, given he had Whitehall clout at the time. Likewise, it explains why it kept covertly running after Atkinson resigned, but while his Party still held the reins of power. After that, Nicholls' lot would have been all over it like a shot. Especially considering at the heart of this appears to be some kind of crazy rivalry between the pair.

Here, take a look at this. It's about you."

Shay took the laptop and started scanning down. "I was recruited after Atkinson had been keeping tabs on me for ages and 'admired my resolve' whilst working at what was the Ministry all that time ago. Who the hell uses language like that in the twenty-first century?" looking up quizzically.

"He considered I'd go to any lengths if a cause appeared genuine and fair. But had the advantage of not being steeped in the current intelligence community so wouldn't alert anyone internally." Shay glanced away momentarily, fearing what was coming next. Townsend seemed transfixed in some kind of amateur psychological profiling.

"Here we go, having been referred to Atkinson by..." he looked up at the driver's mirror, "you, Siobhan. What was this, part of your pillow talk? So honoured I got a mention."

There was no response. Maybe it was best she didn't return his gaze given the challenging trail to the M1, light rain beginning to fall. A nod from Shay in her direction. "This one and Atkinson, thick as thieves."

"That's not fair," an almost whispered comment from the front, the car quickening slightly.

Shay continued. "There's more about us. The combination of working together wasn't only to complement skills but also...we'd never fully trust each other given our personal history. Andersson successful in bringing school links to Mason's attention." He looked up, as if the driver's mirror would prompt recollection of how or when exactly they'd come across the connections. When rummaging through Tyler's possessions possibly? It was pretty irrelevant now. Somehow, she could have hyped up its importance if they hadn't latched on otherwise. He was momentarily stunned.

Rahman grabbed the laptop back, eager to digest more.

"Here's another section about the mission's aim. Just one word, Bard. Is this what it's all about Shay? I don't even know what that refers to." His voice hardening, "Have you been levelling with me? There's no description of what a Bard could be."

Shay took a deep breath. "Okay, it's off the record regarding Harriet's involvement," before setting out what they'd discovered on the tape. Rahman's eyes narrowed, clearly annoyed at being left out of the secret. He resumed scanning the text.

"Yup, the whole bloody scam from Townsend and Atkinson was ultimately to find out if it still existed. Presumably Atkinson had to be sure before he made his move for the top of the ladder. The authorities under his command even ransacked the Tylers' home specifically looking for it, apparently. It also says here that Townsend didn't have to push too hard on what you knew about the Bard trail, as Siobhan was willing to report everything back. Ultimately, they concluded there was no tape out there anymore."

"So," Shay interjected, "all those with some modicum of power – Maddison, Atkinson and Nicholls – were hardly going to spill the beans. Which just left Tyler as a potential loose cannon. Presumably they thought his death suspicious enough to be sure someone was chasing that tape. He hadn't even been planning to go to Egypt. Remember, there were no travel documents on him at all when searching his belongings. That touch was added by Townsend to point towards Linda. Or for muggins to, anyway," his eyes focused again on the driver. "What the hell were you playing at?"

Within seconds the vehicle slowed and pulled into a siding, headlights focusing on hedgerow, the dashboard and laptop casting the only light within.

She turned; her eyes bloodshot.

"Really, it's not as it seems. Yes, Bill thought he could count on me." Shay turned away. "He also knew that I was good, really good at what I could offer an investigation like this. And if he considered you were the perfect foil for me then I could live with that. Let's not play games here Shay. I presume you were offered as much of a tidy sum to run with the whole thing as I was. Not money to be sneezed at and more in the bank for Tommy's future." She shook her head as she added, "there was no way I was going to turn that down."

"Government money, not private money," Rahman responded indignantly.

She snapped back. "That's for you to deal with if you like. Look, this is less of a big deal than it seems. I have an important role in the Department and it really isn't unusual to be called into subcommittees and other offshoots to carry out assignments. When Townsend recruited me, I was just doing my job, nothing more. I was still on the inside and trusted by Bill. That mattered for Tommy, if not for myself. Besides, weren't we both told this all involved a breach of confidential information that could endanger the country? In his separate briefing to me, Townsend never spelt out what the Bard was. Just that we had to have it."

"And was Atkinson behind the little surprise I encountered in Cairo?" Shay intervened. "Beyond your little soft porn exhibition?"

"Not as far as I know. He's not a monster. You originally thought Kruger was behind the attack. From what I can work out you were right, he was. But probably at Linda's bidding. You may find this surprising, but you tend to annoy people at times, Shay."

"Okay. The bigger question. You never asked about the tape after a while, seemed to go quiet about it. We never even had the conversation of whether it existed." The thought hit him. The tape…where was it now? Had Harriet kept or destroyed it? Which was safer for both him and Harriet? Maybe it was better he couldn't be sure of its whereabouts.

She looked away, then returning his stare before replying. "Because by then I'd worked out Townsend's little power trip was nothing to do with protecting national security and everything to do with political rivalry."

The largely barren countryside around was plain eerie, the only sounds on the deserted road being the rain now lashing down and wind sweeping in from the moors, the combination starting to pummel the windscreen.

Shay leant forward, his head inches from Siobhan's. She held her nerve.

"Are you threatening me?"

"For god's sake. I'm only hearing half your involvement with Townsend here."

"Oh, so this is big swinging dick time?" she raised her eyebrows in annoyance.

"Okay, so maybe you can explain that little incident outside your flat when Townsend and I came round? Tommy happened to be on a school trip and we had a convenient view from an upstairs window where we could watch the performance play out." No response. "Townsend's supposed shooting. We couldn't see a trace of blood on the ground afterwards and he patently was not suffering from the effect of a shooting in my subsequent meetings with him. Conveniently, he was bundled straight into the chauffeur-driven car as if in rescue. All a charade, wasn't it?"

A shrug in response this time. "They tipped me off that Townsend would appear to be on the receiving end of some kind of attack to underline the seriousness of the operation. I had my doubts it would fool you when it all played out, but just had to play along."

"You don't think it occurred to me that you'd keep Tommy a million miles away from that flat if there was any chance of it being targeted? Yet you seemed happy enough to keep living there."

Shay slumped back on his seat. "Just prior to the election, when the more responsible elements in Tehran relayed their concerns about a terror attack to you, Rahman, Townsend hardly cared about the info I brought him. Iranian threats weren't in his remit and he only half-heartedly passed them on, if at all. After the scare in Parliament Square all those months ago, I was hardly going to turn my back on the risk. My name was singled out as the unfortunate conduit throughout.

Siobhan, after all this time together, you couldn't even tell me the truth…"

"I was trying to do my job. That's all I ever did here. That's all I ever—" her voice rising, the mirror betraying eyes welling up.

Their vehicle lurched forwards suddenly, the pair in the back pushed back. Fleetingly he recalled a theme park years before, a ride that shot from zero to 70 miles an hour in a matter of seconds. That had been much more fun.

"Siobhan, stop," he was shouting now.

"All this is…fucked. I could face decades in prison. You don't realise how easy it is to point the finger at scapegoats within Whitehall."

The small mercy was that, at least, she hadn't switched the headlights off. The vehicle hurtled round a bend at around fifty miles an hour. Diving forward he tried to grab the wheel; the angle of the attempt lurched the vehicle to the left, almost heading towards a tree. Slamming into the back seat again as she forcefully shoved him off. This wouldn't work. The vehicle must be at sixty, now seventy, veering erratically on the tight country roads. A pair of headlights appeared and a horn blared before the oncoming truck was suddenly passing alongside. She hadn't made up her mind, thank god. There was no chance of physically stopping her. Shay had a single opportunity.

"Tommy, think of Tommy. He needs you."

There was a very slight slowdown before the speed dropped dramatically and they pulled to a stop on a verge. All remained stunned for a few seconds, Siobhan shaking in the front, staring into the distance then opening her car door and leaning out to be sick.

Each of the rear passengers exhaled.

"I wondered when you were going to take control of the situation. Soldier boy," Rahman whispered to him, patting his leg and reaching for the exit.

Shay took the wheel when they resumed, sensing all would appreciate a cautious journey southbound. Despite the blustery conditions, they ended up as the only vehicle sticking strictly to the seventy mile an hour rule on the motorway. Rahman remained in the back with Siobhan alongside, the former devouring the rest of the laptop's stolen contents. At one point, an hour outside London, Rahman looked up almost mournfully at the driving mirror. Shay noted the glance but firmly came down on resisting further questions for now. They didn't stop again before the capital.

The pair guided Siobhan into the Kensington flat. Appearing drained, utterly defeated, she barely had the energy to remove her shoes before she slumped on top of her bed.

Shay followed Rahman out of the bedroom. "I'll stay with her tonight. She needs someone here."

Rahman nodded, then paused at the front door. "There was something else you should know about in Townsend's files, although he only had a passing interest in the international storm that was brewing. Bryony was certainly held by that Iranian faction in America. But she wasn't killed by them though. It was a rescue mission gone wrong. American special forces fired the fatal shot and she died instantly according to the report. I'm sorry Shay."

287

There had been too much to take in for one evening. It was now early Monday, Shay setting his phone for five a.m. to start the trek back to base.

Three a.m. blinked on the alarm clock next to the bed as she stirred in the half-light, facing away, a twitch from her. Was she awake? Her arm reached round and patted the bed once. Gently leaving the chair and lying behind, he reached round, holding her until sleep enveloped them both.

PART FOUR

CHAPTER FORTY-TWO

STANSTED AIRPORT

Had she thought of him? Shay's mind wondered to Siobhan packing up during the week. The spacious Kensington apartment would soon be devoid of evidence that she and Tommy had ever lived there.

Two aspects were clear enough though. He'd miss the simplicity of his time with Tommy, the board park trip that had included a barrage of questions as to what his mother was like all those years ago.

"Did she have a boyfriend?" No way he'd face up to that one. "No idea, maybe she fell in love. Who knows?" The bullet successfully dodged.

A second certainty. Whether out of embarrassment at the whole spectacle last Sunday night, knowing they were all a jolt of the steering wheel from death, she'd made it abundantly clear she had no wish to discuss the events once his alarm had gone off. Taking the hint, he'd left quickly the following morning.

The flight tickets stated it would be Saturday, six p.m., at Stansted. Fortunately, his schedule included only a weekday training programme, so there was no problem travelling to see them off.

Rahman had been immense in uncovering the trail to date. Even now, Shay felt guilt at having retained some aspects from the journalist. But it was necessary. He still needed time and space to mull over the sequence of events alone, some pieces clear as daylight, others just out of reach.

His mind pictured numerous TV quizzes with frustrating jingles, counting down for the contestants to provide their answer. Time was running out for face to face answers from her so it was a no-brainer to set off early in the hope of intercepting them. Siobhan's near obsession for arriving long in advance of a flight had to be factored into the timing as well. In place three and a half hours before the flight, Shay had ascertained which desks would be open for their check-in. A change of plans? It was certainly a possibility. An hour later, still no sign of the pair. Then, into view as they turned the corner and headed towards the desk, only a suitcase and couple of lighter bags in tow. Presumably all those possessions in the flat would be transported separately. Or left behind as a distant memory of another life.

Tommy saw him first and rushed forward in excitement.

"Mum, Shay's come to see us off." His mother's grimace stood in stark contrast, Siobhan patently trying not to cause a scene in front of those queuing.

"Hi Tommy, I wanted to wish you both all the best for your new, exciting life in Sweden. And I also hoped for a chat with your mother. Is that OK?" She remained tight-lipped until checking in the bags, glancing around as if desperate for any way out of granting Shay an audience.

"You're both so early for the plane. There's lots of time, isn't there?" he tried.

Her shrug, as they headed towards the nearby coffee shop, appeared to acknowledge there was little option. She set Tommy up with his book and a hot chocolate at a nearby table in the sparsely filled premises, before taking a seat opposite Shay as they nursed their coffees.

"This had better be quick, we don't have long." No apology for endangering all their lives on Sunday. For some reason, he'd expected that as her opening gambit. If that's how she wanted to play it. The acidic tone entered his voice.

"Okay, you can kill yourself if you like but your son needs you every day of his childhood. God knows Atkinson doesn't appear to have been a real father to him. You could have taken your backseat passengers to kingdom come too. And…why?

He paused. "Townsend's insights didn't uncover everything did they? The full facts now. Please."

"I told you..."

"What you said about Atkinson, Townsend's mission, may have been accurate. Also, being my minder, or however you considered the role. But you kind of omitted a pretty important factor in your account. You referred to Bill as past tense in your life but mentioned he thought he could count on you. Here's what I reckon and correct me if I'm wrong.

You may have accepted being Atkinson's girlfriend, or mistress, or whatever, but I checked with Rahman. The *Investigator* published details of the supposed relationship between Bill and Bryony, so they must have considered they'd uncovered sufficient evidence. But that was all baloney. As Rahman has since told me when rather shamefaced, they were fed doctored information by Nicholls' office. And you didn't help, exactly. You were the one to give the OK to publish all this...rubbish about Bryony. Not caring what the consequences would be for anyone. Maybe it was lucky for you that rumours about an affair with a British MP were the least of Bryony's worries at the time. And I don't think it was high up on the Iranians' radar, do you? However, publishing that she was Mossad was probably a death sentence.

You must feel great, Siobhan."

Remaining tight-lipped, she stared at the steaming drink as if it would miraculously provide her with an alibi.

"I tried to cause the least harm. Even managed to convince Townsend that having a light on in a confined space was your idea of hell and that you'd be putty in their hands. I mentioned you suffered from claustrophobia rather than nyctophobia."

"I can't believe you want a medal. For not contributing to me being tortured? You're something else," shaking his head. "Which leads on to a couple of other things. Atkinson never cheated on you with Bryony. But Rahman did give me the heads up on an affair Bill was having last year with his PA, which was rumoured in the media but without sufficient facts for anyone to publish. They would have been sued to high heaven."

On a roll now, he may as well place all his cards on the table.

"My guess is that you found out. You were prepared to be the love of his life sacrificed for the good of his career, if you wanted to justify it to yourself. But you weren't prepared to accept being just another lay; an occasional few hours between departmental meetings when he was bored. That wasn't the Siobhan I got to know and doubt it was ever what you'd accept.

So, you decided to extract revenge. You'd stayed in contact with Margot since her interdepartmental liaison work and now she was working for the Opposition. Maybe she was a consoling friend every time Bill went back to his wife? Or played the long game and was waiting to break the whole story, with a hint or more of blackmail? Who knows? Either way, the lucky ticket had fallen into her hands. You were inside the MoD and hated Atkinson so much you were prepared to hurt him within touching distance of his goal; accessing high level Governmental confidential files about his past business dealings, the SFO payment even. You discovered where the bodies were buried. For all I know, it may have been you in the house with him when it was raided. An awkward position for him as he wasn't allowed to destroy those files until he climbed high enough to acquire security tsar status, or however it was termed. But ripe for someone prepared to sacrifice everything to bring him down. You'd survive without his money and the grace and favour flat. But there was no way you'd accept being humiliated. Information was fed to Margot about whatever wanted, having no idea it was all intended to endanger the country and bring Nicholls to power. Or maybe you didn't care by then."

Silence for thirty seconds was awkward for both. They turned to look at Tommy, engrossed in his book, oblivious to their stares.

"Of course I would have cared. I was just so unsure where I stood," she responded calmly. "I seem to have lived my life in the opposite direction as most people. With you, I was so careful and measured and, well, everything was so deliberate. With Bill it was different, maybe the recklessness was addictive at first. Then all that mattered was building a happy childhood for Tommy.

Yes, Bill started to lose interest in his second family. Margot didn't put any pressure on me or, if she did, I chose not to notice. All she obtained from me was Bill's shady deal after the diamonds fiasco, a few bits about Tyler and confirmation of current approachable contacts in certain Middle East countries.

Which, incidentally, was shared between Defence and the Foreign Office anyway. She pretended the aim was to establish friendly ties with countries, should her boss be elected.

I'm not a traitor."

"I know Siobhan, I know you're not. But it all started to get horrific."

Nodding mournfully, she was in full flow. "One shitstorm after another. It was soon apparent events weren't for the good of the country. Or for some gentle one-upmanship. People were dying, Shay. Tyler, Bryony went AWOL, Linda. I'd been stupid. A little low-level reconnaissance, Margot had said. Suddenly, I was in too deep. Margot was ill; she was just desperate to get her boss into power as her last act."

He interjected, "And then it clicked. What you'd said in the car on Sunday night, at your lowest ebb, about facing decades in prison – 'it's easy to find scapegoats'. Margot would, in effect, have sacrificed her reputation posthumously if this ever came to light and Nicholls could say he wasn't involved in this sordid business, that he still has clean hands. Even acting the sheriff by sending you inside for passing on highly confidential Government information about the Iranians, Barjam, Tyler's high level research even, any of it. Trials about breaches of official secrets are held in camera, away from the public gaze. Your worry, when you met up with Nicholls both times, was that you'd already handed over a treasure trove to Guillard in your vendetta against Atkinson. Nicholls could be heading for power. At the same time, she was both playing you and acting as your shield."

Only "I tried," in response.

"I know you did. The wording of your encounter with Nicholls on the Embankment. Did you have to gamble that McMahon wasn't involved in anything underhand?"

"There was no reason to think he would be. It was Margot's brainchild so by then I just had to know if Nicholls was involved too. This was a serious mess and it was terrifying to think he'd get into power having orchestrated all that."

"But he didn't," said Shay. "I've gone over the recording of your meeting with Nicholls and he never took the bait. All he referred to was pretty much public knowledge by then anyway, or info he'd picked up from friendly media pals. Rahman wasn't his only contact in that world, in fact far from it. There was no admission of anything illegal. Nicholls just went through the aspects we already know and suggested that your ex – your political ex, shall we say – was somehow the chief conductor. You told me about the later encounter with Nicholls in his office at the Commons, but again I presume no joy. That was your last throw of the dice."

If Shay was awaiting confirmation, it didn't arrive. "After that, we were all on the ropes. My name was even thrown out there as a distraction."

She nodded. "I wondered about that. Presumably they just wanted to cast suspicion on you in their little game. Guillard was well aware who you were and was toying with you, presumably having handed your name to the Iranians with directions as to when and where it should be raised.

Shay tried to contain the temptation to raise his voice. "Well that's just great, Siobhan. How's does that look for me? Did I get a moment's thought?"

"Margot was always manipulative, I guess," her voice barely audible. "I felt so stupid for letting all that personal stuff get the better of me so had to check how far this went.

Well, congratulations. Your Prime Minister doesn't have dirty hands."

The pair hadn't noticed Tommy, smear of hot chocolate adorning his upper lip, alongside them.

"Can we go now Mum? When's our flight?" How much had he heard? Shay relaxed. Overhearing was hardly a risk to their future safety. In fact, it was OK to relax completely now. Or at least soon.

He had no idea how to say goodbye at first. A few minutes later, the hug for his ex at the entrance to security was genuine and tight. Maybe he was going soft. He could only wish Siobhan well in her desire for a fresh start in Sweden, away from all this madness. Perhaps she'd never even belonged here.

With a slight tear in his eye, Shay knew this was too much to untangle at present in its rawness.

Returning sombrely to the airport's train station for London, he hesitated, lost in thought as he approached the single oversized barrier to the platform, the only entrance point not under repair. Had his reassurance helped? There was no room for malice, It had to be worthwhile if she benefitted from peace of mind; able to cast aside, for a short time, her risk of imprisonment.

"When you're ready," a man of Asian descent with wife, three children and as many luggage trolleys behind snapped him back to his surroundings.

"Sorry," he muttered, reaching for his mobile to tap in. "Sorry."

A run round Finsbury Park that afternoon utterly failed to clear his head. A group in their early twenties was playing rounders; were there American students lodging in the area? His mind pictured Bryony, smiling in the morning, her head propped on an arm watching him from the Boston bed. Her last morning of freedom.

A young mother trying, in vain, to teach a boy of about five to ride an oversized bike, a picture of pride and joy on her face as he sped faster before wobbling and falling. A father attempting, unsuccessfully, to interest his children with a bright yellow kite that could only clear the ground a few feet before instantly crash landing; not a good plan for a windless early September day. Divorced? It would take far more to regain their interest. Energetic teenagers on an adjacent gentle slope engaged in a raucous game of football with shirts as posts.

It was all there but couldn't fill the emptiness. Returning to the flat, he quickly texted Rahman to request a number. Two encounters left, though realistically if he could line up even one that would constitute a miracle. The calls were made in quick succession, to London then abroad. He'd particularly delight in spoiling any weekend plans May might have harboured.

If they happen, Shay decided, they're on my terms. No more running to the beck and call of so-called superiors. It was all about to end anyway. Back to the fresh Welsh air. Who cares if it's bracing, autumnal weather all too soon? The landscape demanding no allegiance; no Machiavellian intrigue. In the capital, not knowing who was pulling the strings and where you fit into their selfish plans. Always a lowly foot soldier, that much was clear enough.

Early to bed, for what would be an extremely early start.

EPILOGUE

Sunday morning birdsong wasn't even underway as the alarm kicked in at 3.30. Yesterday's run had been far too brief and unrewarding and, anyway, soon he'd have to return to peak fitness for the elites who were scheduled in a few weeks. Absolutely no corners to cut as their trainer. A quick set of squat thrusts and push ups to shake off the cobwebs, before he was off, passing little traffic and fewer pedestrians as his route took him down Holloway Road, then on through Clerkenwell.

Unsure of these parts of London now. Was there even a meat market in existence at Smithfield these days? Recalling the bizarre sight of carcasses delivered from there for sale to consumers in London and the home counties, particularly the restaurant trade. Certainly unable to deal with the smell this early in the morning anyway. Steering clear, once reaching the Thames, he turned right along the Embankment at Blackfriars until stopping less than a mile along, slowing to a walk then approaching the memorial.

Now this area was familiar. Encountering the giant modernist stone structure up close always had an effect, appearing from a distance like a misshapen roughhewn bullet with a perfect circle at its centre. On one side of the edifice, "Iraq," on the other, "Afghanistan". It took until 2017 to unveil the monument, even though it commemorated all those who fell and suffered in the campaigns since 1990. Shay had always considered the object's form to be suitably opaque and therefore utterly appropriate for the whole sequence of mad events, whether justified or just politically expedient. He continued to stare from ten yards away.

The footsteps approaching were gentle. He didn't turn, waiting to be joined alongside. In yesterday's call, McMahon had calmly taken down details of the request to meet in person, politely placed him on hold then confirmed the appointment, all within a two minute conversation.

"All of this appears pretty appropriate given the contempt that your boss has for the population," Shay started.

The response was delivered in a soft Ulster brogue. "Your call yesterday intrigued. Something about a question for the Prime Minister as to his association with Margot. Not a particularly enticing topic, I would have expected, yet the PM instructed me to meet. After all, the whole world knows Margot was his dedicated press supremo for more years than I care to remember. She was brilliant and we all miss her."

"The question wasn't about her job title," responded Shay. "More to the point, what she was prepared to carry out to push him into number ten. You know, a number of people have been through the wringer, reputations hit hard and even lives lost. And all for someone who orchestrated havoc."

His companion sounded less accommodating now. Noticeably well trained by Margot to meet fire with fire.

"At last, we have an honest government." A pause. "Look, where you fit in, I don't know and I don't care. Any hint of corruption or skulduggery on the PM's part is utter rubbish. The grapevine has always held Margot to account for certain excesses, but he played no part. Mr Nicholls just wouldn't do that. Besides, by the end, the drugs she took for her illness were probably throwing her into utter confusion. Really."

Shay interjected. "When my name was thrown into the mix by the Iranians just before election day, Guillard was hardly conscious at that stage. Of course she wasn't giving orders then. It must have been Nicholls."

"What you think and what you say are completely different aspects. We only care about the latter. And, by the way, you may be interested in an attempted break out by the Iranians being held in Copenhagen. Unfortunately, both were killed in the effort."

"How regrettable for you. I'm sure you're heartbroken."

"Indeed Lieutenant Mason. Indeed."

Turning to McMahon at last, Shay took in the giant of a man who somehow also portrayed a convincing demeanour. Maybe the aide genuinely believed the message; maybe it was even true. There was no way Shay could admit any contact with Margot just before her death and hopefully his presence at the hospital hadn't been identified by the authorities. If they only found out now, the security forces could jump on him like a tonne of bricks and concoct more lies about him. He'd experienced enough for a lifetime.

No, this encounter was worth a try but it hadn't worked. It was time, again, to take stock.

With a slight bow of the head, McMahon turned and strolled back to the Embankment. Shay's gaze moved from the memorial towards the main road. Presumably the black Jaguar XJ Sentinel had sat there throughout. As McMahon opened the front passenger door, the window lowered slightly by the seat behind. A fleeting grin from those boyish looks that he'd started to loathe were distinctly aimed in his direction. As quickly, the window closed as the vehicle moved at regal pace towards Downing Street.

Margot was a PR expert according to Rahman. The best. The only message she'd uttered twice during their conversation, her last will and testament in a way, was that Nicholls hadn't been aware of any of this. What was that line memorised for his school play once? The lady doth protest too much, methinks.

5.15 a.m.. The monument, situated directly outside New Scotland Yard, was certainly no place to linger at this time. Cameras would be trained on him all round. He grimaced at the idea yet another cell would be reserved for him, so chose to run up through Piccadilly Circus and try to catch a light breakfast before continuing. Should he be under government surveillance, it was actually all the better. In fact it would be fantastic if word of his next appointment makes it back to Nicholls, so the bastard sweats. The Bard could remain, if not on the politician's conscience, at least as a permanent worry of his career unravelling.

A sprinkling of club dwellers that he'd passed on the route into central London was now partially replaced by early bird workers, mostly weekend cleaners emerging from buses. Also, the odd sports car returning from a night's partying. Experiencing a combination of finality and mental exhaustion but knowing soon, very soon, he could lay off the trail, telling himself there was no more to do. No doors to prise open, secrets to uncover. Weariness that he couldn't save so many he cared about in various ways, Siobhan's absence from the city felt like another added weight.

The first section of the run was relaxed, virtually laid back, before he stopped midway, the bleary-eyed café owner confused at the alertness of the day's first customer. Then on, faster, angrier as he turned into Regent Street, past the sleeping facades of Hamleys, Nike. Oxford Circus loomed as he turned towards the Georgian mansions of Portland Place, the gleaming façade of the *BBC* all but deserted. A small, utterly silent demonstration for animal rights outside an offshoot of the Chinese Embassy. Admiring their dedication, given the time of day. Faster still after crossing Marylebone Road and into Regents Park then left round the outer circle.

As he neared, male and female officers with machine guns at the side of the road, alongside an unmarked grey van presumably jam packed with sensors, trackers and more personnel, stared as he ran past on the pavement opposite in the park's ring road. Approaching the destination now, the ornate iron gates appeared to bow before him as they parted. Clearly his second call yesterday had proved successful. He presumed US security still had the final say in the area as to how their ambassador's residence was policed. Recalling a comment from a senior Whitehall official years ago, that if any disaster befell Winfield House and the Brits had cocked up, the shit really would hit the fan. No, the Americans definitely ruled the roost here.

The driveway, once through the gates and passing the security hut, seemed empty. The building was akin to a palace, he observed, taking in the grandeur of the dark brick edifice surrounding a lighter portico from the south, a series of perfectly spaced oversized windows at two levels. It all served to reassure Shay that his choice of venue was perfect. How had May explained his presence to the ambassador? Maybe she'd just commanded.

With no sign of life outside, the front door opened as he approached revealing an official in a double-breasted suit who silently led him to an adjacent reception room near the front door. Presumably it was designed for quick meetings and guests not invited to hang around.

A pair of dark green two-seater Chesterfield sofas were positioned opposite each other, five feet apart, with bird-filled William Morris wallpaper awash with blues and greens on the walls. May stood behind the furthest sofa and pointed to the other. He ignored the request and remained standing, May launching in regardless.

"Your call yesterday was rather out of the blue. Suggesting, no demanding, a meeting here today. You do know I have other work, other meetings? There was a White House security conference planned for today. My apologies did not go down well so this had better be good. And, by the way, cool business meeting attire."

Taking a deep breath, he tried to formulate the right wording. You bastards knew how Bryony died and, more than that, were responsible. An American bullet. A cock up, but were you ever going to let me know? Not a chance.

This was not the time to let rip though, not least as it wouldn't do any good. If he screamed from the rooftops, undoubtedly any investigation that resulted would conclude May's team had acted perfectly. Complete angels, all of them. He vehemently wished she'd lose her job over the White House snub. The Americans had acted like spoilt brats whilst Nicholls or his acolytes had put Bryony in increased danger. And ramped up the pressure on Siobhan to the point of nearly leaving her son growing up without a mother. But, ultimately, the prospect of handing such leverage to a foreign government was abhorrent.

"Very kind of you to come over for a quick visit. We had a deal and I presume you wanted to know the outcome in person. When we last 'met' in the US Embassy, you asked me for one conclusion from my…investigation. Whether Nicholls was behind it all with full knowledge, and even in control of those spiralling events. The answer is no, May. He definitely wasn't in the loop."

May nodded, trying to appear apathetic. "I expect we shan't meet again. But if we can ever be of service—"

This time, there was no chance of resisting temptation as Shay marched up to within inches of her, controlling his voice. "Just like you protected Bryony." The stark memory of her body spread out on the slab returned instantly.

The longest, sternest pause from Archibald. "What are you trying to say, Shay? You're on American soil. Anything could happen."

"Moot point May. You want to try smuggling out a UK citizen seen by Scotland Yard eagerly running into the ambassador's front door, with gates opening in welcome? A member of the military at that. Certainly an interesting call," and with that he turned to leave.

The pitch of her voice rose as she called after him. "The Iranians would have cut her to ribbons if we hadn't tried to intervene. Islamic extremists weren't her greatest fans."

Already he had the door open, hurrying towards the residence's entrance. Never seeing that woman again would be all too soon. Shay broke into a jog towards the exit gate, presuming it would open. May was just another user.

The gates began to part. He paused after they drew together smoothly behind him. Suddenly a huge lungful of air poured in, briefly bring him to his knees. It was over. Still early, but the noise of distant traffic around the park pulled him gradually back to his surrounds. As if all energy had drained out though.

Nearby were a host of stations, Baker Street included, but he remained desperate for the calm of Regents Park first. After taking the underground north, he'd stroll through Finsbury Park. That would do it. The capital could keep its debilitating bustle for those who wanted it. Pack up at home then head back to Wales. Was it even worth keeping the London flat?

He broke into a slow jog, into the inner circle and alongside the open air theatre which seemed to patiently await the afternoon's audience. Further on, the brickwork and ivy of Regent College was alongside. Shay knew Marylebone Road was near. A few of those protesters with animal rights banners from Portland Place were just ahead on York Bridge, the small crossing out of the park. One, an elderly woman, had a black and white border collie alongside, eliciting a memory of the miserable events from decades ago that had started this devastating chain.

As he passed them, his phone signalled an incoming message. It was from Townsend, with a stream of invective making clear he knew who'd broken into his house and why. Shay pressed delete and, for the first time in what seemed an exceptionally long spell, felt solely in the present.

Printed in Great Britain
by Amazon